A RIFT IN THE HOUSE OF BRUIN

The Hiraeth Chronicles
Vol. I

T.S. Kinley

A Rift in the House of Bruin
The Hiraeth Chronicles Volume I
by T. S. Kinley

Copyright © 2025 by T. S. Kinley
ISBN 978-1-964877-07-5

First Paperback edition July 2025
Book design by T.S. Kinley
Editing by Samantha Swart
Cover design by Eye Candy Grafix
WWW.TSKinleyBooks.com

To the warriors who have faced the darkest storms,
whose scars tell stories of survival, not surrender.
This tale is for you:
for the strength behind your softness,
the hope stitched into every breath,
and the love that endures even when the body falters.
May you find magic in your healing,
and romance in the life you've fought to reclaim.

AUTHOR'S NOTE

The content in this book contains sexually explicit depictions. Please be aware of the following possible trigger warnings and read at your own discretion. Lewd NSFW depictions of sexual acts, attempted rape, drug use, graphic violence, gore, hanging, abduction, assault, hostage situations, mind control, anxiety, depression, suicidal ideation, cancer, death.

VAELRYTH

BRUIN LANDS

ATHERFALL

CALDREIM RIVER

LYACON LANDS

HIRAETH

STEGGR LANDS

DUNHARROW

WHISPERHOLD

THORNWYN
FOREST

REPERE LANDS

"It is not death that a man should fear, but he should fear never beginning to live" - Marcus Aurelius

PROLOGUE
-ARTOS KING OF THE SECOND REALM-
RULER OF THE HOUSE OF BRUIN

Artos King of the Second Realm, Ruler of the House of Bruin

"That's preposterous," I snapped at the young scribe. "You're simply mistaken."

Enda's translation echoed in my mind. *The king's reign will shatter in his tragic demise.* When the royal scribe had called for a private audience with me, I'd assumed she had made progress deciphering the prophecy. But this? This was lunacy.

"Your Highness, respectfully, I know I'm relatively young, but I have dedicated my entire life to this. I was trained by your highest-ranking scribes to ensure the realm had a new generation capable of translating the ancient tomes." Enda pushed up the navy-blue sleeves of her robe, exposing what I already knew was emblazoned on her forearms. The coveted marks of a Hiraethian scribe were only awarded once an apprentice had transcended to the highest levels. "I've devoted my life to transcribing the Divine word." She looked up at me, a pained look in her icy blue eyes. "I cannot change the words simply to appease the throne. Although alarming, the text is clear."

Enda spoke with gentle conviction. Her delicate fingers trembled as she traced the symbols within the ancient tome. She repeated the translation once again. "'The raptor shall feast where the bruin once roared.'"

I fought the growing unease in my throat and swallowed hard. The musty vanilla scent of the scriptorium—once comforting—now invaded my senses like a thick, bile-inducing fog.

Enda ignored my obvious displeasure and continued with the offending prophecy. "'The king's reign will shatter in his tragic demise. For the ring forged in righteousness shall crack, and the tyrant's reign shall become rule.'"

The cold stone walls of the alcove felt suffocating as the reality of the situation closed in around me. Tragic demise? What was she implying? I stood up from the table, anxiously pacing.

The ring forged in righteousness.

Spinning the Bloodstone Sigil around my little finger, I contemplated the weight of her words. The ring was deceptively light despite the power it carried. Inside, it pulsed with the lifeblood of Hiraeth's great houses, bound by oath and sacrifice. A relic of unity, worn only by the reigning king, its magic was meant to shield, to strengthen, to command. Now it felt like a curse foretelling my demise.

My beautiful queen's belly was beginning to swell with our first litter. Danya and I had struggled to conceive, and without an heir to the throne, my line was vulnerable. Herold, the standing lord from the House of Rapere, was the appointed steward. If this ridiculousness got out... I shuddered at the thought. I pulled in a cleansing breath, reasoning with my trepidation, and centered myself.

Enda was wrong. She had to be.

"I was able to translate a substantial portion of the text. Shall I continue?" she asked, pausing—the color draining from her face.

I'd held on to the possibility that the Divine had offered a way out of this dark premonition, but the stark look on Enda's face quickly diminished any hope I had left. I allowed my eyes to focus on the endless rows of books and scrolls lining the walls outside the alcove. A room once bustling with scribes was now cold and quiet. Countless years of history and prophecy were housed within its confines. Not once had we faced such a dire future.

"I'm sorry. Yes, please—continue."

Enda's voice trembled. "'The waters, once pure, shall run black with betrayal. The harvest will wither and decay in fields once bountiful. For the land itself shall rise against the hand that bears the ring.'"

"I think I've heard enough."

"My Lord, there is one more thing. The prophecy mentions a human. I haven't completely figured out the context, but the word is littered throughout the text."

"A human?" I questioned, shaking my head at the absurdity of her words. "Do any of your supposed translations end with me keeping the crown?"

She remained silent, her lips pressed together in a thin line—and it was all the answer I needed. I forced a nervous chuckle, trying to lighten the darkness washing over our meeting. "I have always respected your knowledge of the old language, Enda. You're one of the last living Hiraethians who can decipher the old text within the Book of Astrium. But your translation is simply incorrect."

"It is clear, My Lord. The prophecy states you will fall from your position of power in Hiraeth."

"You are wrong," I said, pulling the tome toward me, scanning the ancient text that looked like random scratches on the page. "These glyphs could mean any number of things." I pushed the dusty book back toward her and lowered my tone. "Try again."

"My Lord"—she bowed her head—"I mean no disrespect. The prophecy is what it is. My translations are accurate. We must begin planning for the inevitable."

"You will try again," I pleaded, "or I'll have no choice but to take action."

She looked up at me from the table, her chin held high. "My Lord, I... I—" she paused. "My position as royal scribe is to translate the prophecy. I hold that responsibility in the highest regard. I will not sully my name with a lie. I stand by my translations."

"You understand that if this information were to get out to the people, my life—my legacy—would be in danger. Lord Herold would see this as an opportunity to usurp the kingdom for his own personal gain. If your translations are correct, he will single-handedly destroy all of Hiraeth."

"Yes, My Lord." She hung her head in defeat. "I understand the weight of the situation."

"Then I have no other options before me. The prophecy must remain secret." I bowed my head to Enda. "Thank you for your selfless sacrifice and service to the realm."

Enda bravely looked me in the eyes, tears silently falling down her cheeks. "I accept my fate. It's been my honor to serve you, My Lord." She bowed before me, returning the Book of Astrium to my hands. I tapped my pocket, anxiously feeling for the skeleton key. The book must be returned to its home—locked away from prying eyes.

Before she could sway my decision, I turned my back to her, leaving the alcove and the young scribe behind me. Being king required you to think of the greater good. Compassion and humanity could often lead you astray. I had to make a choice that protected my people. A choice to save the realm.

Unfortunately for Enda, her time in this incarnation was about to come to an end.

Closing the heavy door of the scriptorium behind me, I

stopped to inform the guard of my decision. Enda's death was to be quick and painless.

"Make sure she is buried in a place of honor. This meeting never happened."

It was time to plan Herold's assassination.

PART

ONE

CHAPTER I
FAIRYTALES WERE REAL
-MICHAELA-

Black ink splattered on the enchanted parchment. The patter of droplets echoed like the ticking of a clock, impatient for words that wouldn't come. A dark stain spread across the page while the quill remained motionless in my hand. I couldn't construct a convincing letter if my life depended on it and there was a real chance it did. I'd been attempting to write to my sister for days, and the blank scroll mocked me.

My arrival in Aetherfall—the capital city carved into the mountains of Hiraeth—had been anything but normal. I should have been looking forward to the mundane task of writing to Gwen. Congratulating her on her recent nuptials. Basking in her happiness now that she'd reached her happily ever after. But instead, it was the one thing I wanted to avoid the most.

A smile tugged at the corner of my lips as a vision of her flashed in my memory. I could easily imagine the impatient scowl etched into her features at this very moment. But the smile faded quickly.

My sister had risked everything to make sure I made it this far. I wouldn't let her put her life on the line for me again. Not when she had so much to lose. I had to make this work without her. A simple letter to reassure her I'd arrived safely—that was all I needed. Then she could live her life in blissful ignorance.

But as I sat alone in this godforsaken castle, in an extravagant bedroom clearly reserved for royalty—not an inconsequential human girl—words eluded me. I wanted to paint her a pretty picture. Confirm that we'd made the right choice sending me here. But the idea of lying to her made my skin crawl.

I couldn't tell her that Artos, Lord of the House of Bruin and King of all Hiraeth, was dead. Or that the realm was in such upheaval, that even the princes seemed worried. I couldn't tell her that the moment I arrived, something changed inside me—and it terrified me. No, that would only send her spiraling into unnecessary panic. I didn't want her gallivanting around the cosmos trying to save me all over again. Silence was the better choice. At least, that was the excuse I clung to. Deep down, I knew it was just another lie.

A sudden pop and crack of tinder in the enormous fireplace had me nearly jumping out of my skin.

"What have you gotten yourself into, Mic?" I sighed, pinching the bridge of my nose and rolling my shoulders to ease the tension that had been building all day. But it did nothing to dispel the lingering nausea roiling in my gut. The hiss of the fire reminded me of whispered voices—bits and pieces of spoken word on the edge of comprehension.

Even alone, the castle seemed to watch me.

Either I was losing my mind or the universe was trying its damnedest to warn me of something. I couldn't shake the sickening feeling. The homespun shawl wrapped tight around my shoulders failed to ward off the shiver creeping up my spine.

For days I'd been brushing it off as nerves. But my anxiety was taking on a life of its own. A darkness settled in the pit of my stomach and refused to be quelled. And the fact that I didn't belong here wasn't helping.

I'd realized it the moment I followed six beast princes through what looked like an ordinary mirror and ended up at Mathenholm Castle—the seat of power in Hiraeth. A realm I hadn't known existed six months ago.

I'd become a real-life Alice in Wonderland, falling through the looking glass. And just like Alice, I found Hiraeth wasn't the Wonderland I'd been hoping for. Now, in my twenty-one years of existence, I knew three things to be true: fairytales were real, Neverland existed, and magic wove everything together.

From the moment I'd left the comforts of London and realized the universe was much larger than I'd imagined, the life I thought I knew had gone all topsy-turvy. I was only along for the ride.

The unannounced return of the princes had set off a firestorm across the entire kingdom. News that they'd returned with a human on their arm only fanned the flames. Whispers drifted through the stone halls like smoke, curling with words I wasn't meant to hear. In the tangle of gossip and speculation, one name kept surfacing: Johan, steward of the throne of Hiraeth. I hadn't seen his face, but I didn't need to. The message was clear—he was furious they'd brought me here.

What unsettled me most was how carefully the princes kept him away from me. Not a single introduction. Not a passing encounter. Just silence, and closed doors. I didn't know if he was trying to shield me from Johan's wrath, or hide me from his judgment. Maybe he regretted bringing me at all. The thought sank its teeth into my chest and refused to let go. I dropped the quill onto the gilded vanity. My inability to focus only worsened as I stared at the empty page.

I caught sight of myself in the mirror. The girl looking back wasn't someone I was used to seeing. My face had filled out with a healthy blush, and thick, chocolate hair hung in tangles over my shoulder. It had been so long since I'd seen myself with a full head of hair and rose-colored cheeks that this new reflection still shocked me.

If I looked closely, I could barely make out the familiar dark circles returning under my eyes. My cheekbones were a bit too pronounced. Subtle to the unfamiliar eye, but the mask of death hadn't left me completely—it was just harder to see now.

If I wanted to keep up this pretense, I would need a healer soon. That was the whole reason the princes had lured me here.

A sudden creak and groan from the bedroom door snapped me out of my thoughts. I jumped to my feet, rushing to the bed and hastily tucked the unfinished letter beneath a pillow, knocking over the ink well in the process. There was nothing on the parchment save for a few ink splatters, but I didn't know who I could trust here. My half of the paired scrolls—the Loquentes Cartis—was the only thing of value I owned. And their innate magic seemed like a tempting prize for anyone looking for an opportunity. It was my lifeline back to Gwen in Neverland. I couldn't afford to lose it.

"Fuck! Shit!" I muttered under my breath, righting myself and stepping in front of the spilled ink. I tucked my hair behind my ear and flattened my woolen dress, trying to appear inconspicuous.

A petite, redheaded girl bustled into the room with an armful of crimson silks, stopping in her tracks when she saw me.

"Is everything... alright, My Lady?" she asked, a flash of intrigue in her grey eyes.

"Yep... umm... yes. Perfect. As you can see, I'm perfectly perfect. Thank you."

"Are you *sure?*" she asked, and I knew I wasn't fooling anyone.

"Yep. Nothing to worry about here."

"Shame," she said, shaking her head as she moved deeper into the room, placing the silks in a heap on the bed. "The kitchen maids are desperate for a bit of gossip about the princes' new pet."

"Sorry to be such a disappointment. Maybe "pets" aren't all that interesting."

"I mean no offense, My Lady. But it's not every day The Seven break the rules and bring home a stray human. It's all anyone can talk about. But not to worry—the night's still young. Plenty of time for you to tell me everything."

"Rules? The Seven? I'm not sure I follow."

She faltered for the first time, dropping her gaze to her fidgeting hands. "Well, I guess technically it's The Six now, what with everything that happened with Prince Lu—I mean, well... the princes of Hiraeth have always been called The Seven. Old habits die hard."

"Prince Lucius, you mean?" I asked. My heart squeezed at the mention of the seventh son of Artos, who'd sent me away with his brothers while he remained in Neverland. The exiled prince was the very reason I'd taken a chance and left my sister behind. His dark curls and tortured eyes had clouded my better judgment.

She frantically waved a finger over her lips, her eyes

darting around the room. "Shh! The lost prince cannot be named here. His banishment from Hiraeth means the court considers him dead. Mentioning his name will only bring attention you do not want."

"It's that bad? Can you tell me what happened? Umm—I don't think I got your name?"

"Oh, curse the damn fates! Mirabelle, where's your manners? One look at her and decorum's gone out the window."

I watched her bewildered as she seemingly scolded herself aloud. A hand popped over her mouth and a deep flush colored her cheeks, accentuating a smattering of freckles.

"What I meant to say was," she cleared her throat and dipped into an uncoordinated curtsy. "Begging your pardon, My Lady. My name's Mirabelle. I've been assigned as your lady's maid."

"I'm Michaela Darling Carlisle," I replied, offering my hand. She blinked at me in confusion. I glanced down and realized my hand was stained with ink. Shoving it into the folds of my dress, I felt my own cheeks flush. Even a simple conversation with a servant girl proved impossible without appearing strange, dooming any hope I had of blending in with the nobility. "It's a pleasure to meet you, Mirabelle. Now, what can you tell me about Lu—"

Her hand clamped over my mouth. "For your own good, please don't mention his name. If you make it through tonight, I'm sure we'll be seeing more of each other. Then

I'll tell you the story of the lost prince of Hiraeth. The *real* story."

My heart raced at her words. "If you make it through tonight." I brushed it off, pretending her veiled warning was nothing more than a poor turn of phrase. "I appreciate the gesture, but I have no need for a lady's maid. You can tell the princes that—"

"It wasn't the princes who sent me, My Lady. It was Lady Fallon. She insisted I get you ready for tonight's feast. Mourning for the House of Bruin is over. The lords of all the Houses will be in attendance for the Crownspire."

Alarm simmered into full-blown panic. Lady Fallon— the imperious princess of Hiraeth—was the eldest sibling of the princes and matriarch of the House of Bruin. We'd had formal introductions the day we arrived. If looks could kill, she'd be a very accomplished assassin. Before my name had even left Nico's lips, she'd waved me off and delivered the news of their father's death to her eldest brother. I'd become the most inconvenient houseguest from that moment on.

Several days had passed, and I'd been mostly ignored. Only Nico and Luca had tried to check on me. Though I'd yearned to comfort them, I'd placated them with reassurances, sending them off to mourn with their family.

Why had Fallon taken an interest in me now? I'd convinced myself she'd all but forgotten I existed. "I appreciate the offer, but—"

"If you're about to dismiss me," she interrupted, "let me

stop you right there. I mean no disrespect, but I'm here at Lady Fallon's behest."

"Yes, I understand, but I don't need a lady's maid. I'm not feeling like myself tonight, so I'll save everyone the hassle and have dinner in my room."

"No, you're not understanding me. Tonight is no ordinary feast. Tonight is the Crownspire—it marks the transfer of power from the steward to the rightful king. Lady Fallon has insisted on your presence. To put it plainly, I serve her, not you. You'd be doing us both a favor if you allow me to dress you, do something nice with your hair, and teach you what's expected of an honored guest in our realm. Lady Fallon will be damned if some human girl disgraces the House of Bruin during a time like this."

"Are you telling me I don't have a choice?"

She huffed a relieved sigh. "I knew Cook was wrong. You do have a brain under all that pretty hair. Now, let's see what we're working with." She ripped the shawl from my shoulders and looked me over. "Umm... let's get started. We'll need all the time we have. You talk, I'll work."

She spun me around and sat me back down in front of the mirror. An ink-smudged reflection greeted me. No wonder she'd questioned me—I was a complete mess.

"Er... excuse me, My Lady. I think I'll need some help if we're to have you ready in time." Mirabelle crossed to the window and flung open the shutters, hands on her hips as she stared out at the fading light. "Well, come on now, don't be shy," she scolded, seemingly to no one. The flutter of wings was the only warning before a flurry of birds swarmed through the open window.

"What in the bloody hell?" I mumbled, crouching lower in my chair. Tiny birds circled the high ceiling once before settling on every available surface.

"Now, I was thinking of weaving her locks back from the crown and leaving a cascade of curls over one shoulder. Maybe a few pieces to frame her face," Mirabelle said, deftly arranging strands of hair as she talked.

"I think that sounds—"

"Yes, yes, I knew you'd all agree." She ignored me entirely, responding instead to the chatter of the surrounding birds. "Rook, you hold this strand while I start on the other side." She gestured to a small purple finch perched on the mirror, who instantly took flight. Tiny wings fluttered around my head as he picked up pieces of hair with clawed feet.

"Oh. Okay. The birds are going to help. Nothing unusual about that at all," I murmured to myself. Apparently, all manner of logic was out the window here.

I sat still as Mirabelle and her flock of helpers cleaned the ink from my face and applied rouge to my cheeks and lips to match the dress laid out on the bed.

"Such a beauty," she cooed as she pulled the corset laces unbearably tight. The stays dug into my skin from breast to hip, cinching my waist before flaring out at the hips. The heavy crimson skirts spilled in voluminous waves, each pleat giving subtle contrast in varying shades of red. "Once everyone sees you looking the picture of health, the rumors will die down."

"Rumors? There are rumors about me?"

"You're the first human to set foot in Hiraeth in centuries, and you think people aren't going to talk? But don't mind your head about it. The only excitement we servants get is castle gossip—it's harmless, really. There's talk that you've got... the Tribulation," she whispered the last part into my ear as though someone might be listening. "Some think that's what sparked the new illness plaguing the peasants in Dunharrow. But they're just looking for someone to blame for all this death and hardship, rather than risk saying what's really causing it."

I tensed. My arms instinctively rose to shield my exposed décolletage, as if she could see the sickness burning in my blood. "Then what is causing it?" I asked, trying to deflect.

Mirabelle froze mid-tug, and the birds fell silent. I glanced over my shoulder in time to see the color drain from her face.

"I may have been too bold, My Lady."

"No, please continue. You did say you were here to educate me on Hiraeth."

She leaned in close. "Between you and me," she whispered, "not everyone in this court is an ally of The Seven. The Bruin princes have been away for far too long. Males lose their crowns when they're off conquering the cosmos."

The chill returned despite the roaring fire and the

pleasant company. Mirabelle had been a welcome distraction, but the unease was back with a vengeance. "Are you saying the princes aren't safe here?"

She hurried to tie off my laces and ushered me back to the chair, fidgeting with my hair as though nothing had happened. "All I'm saying is keep your head. You seem like a smart enough girl. Just be mindful—these are dangerous times. And it's still not clear whether The Seven can fix that."

I turned to face her after she slid the final pin into my hair. "Tell me more," I pleaded, grasping her hands. "Something feels wrong here. What do you know?"

"I've said too much already."

"Please, Mirabelle."

She drew in a breath, about to speak when the groan of ancient hinges interrupted us. My bedroom door opened again, followed by the rhythmic clicking of heels across the slate floor.

CHAPTER II
RED IS MOST CERTAINLY YOUR COLOR
-MICHAELA-

My pulse quickened into a frenzied pace when Lady Fallon stepped into the candlelight. Her flawless, pale skin stood out in contrast to the shadows, like a specter stepping out from the darkened corners. She exuded an air of confidence that was palpable the moment she entered the room.

I stood from the vanity as Mirabelle fell into a deep curtsy beside me. The petite lady's maid and her entourage of birds had gone silent. I froze—like a fawn in the jaws of the enemy—panic plucking any pleasantries from my throat.

She appraised me with sharp, fathomless eyes. It only took a moment before my hands began to fidget and my entire psyche squirmed under her silent scrutiny.

"This is the best you could do?" she asked, her tone

dripping with disapproval. The beaded silver dress she wore glinted in the firelight. The satin garment clung to her slight frame as she walked around me.

"Please forgive me, My Lady. She was in a terrible state when I arrived. If I had a bit more time, I could—"

"It'll have to do. All the time in the cosmos wouldn't wipe the human smell from her. You could dress her in the latest fashions and cover her body in Hiraethian runes and our enemies would scent her from a mile away."

"I don't have to go tonight. Apparently, that was your decision," I blurted.

Her dark eyes widened for a beat before a smug smirk lifted her lips. "Leave us."

As soon as the words had been spoken, a flutter of wings filled the room.

"Not so fast, Rook. Get some clothes on. The missives are ready and must be delivered to the houses immediately."

In the blink of an eye, the tiny finch morphed into a gangly young male, cupping himself as he bowed to Lady Fallon. "Yes, My Lady," he said, and quickly ducked out into the hall.

Mirabelle grasped my hands, drawing my attention back from the naked male that had been a bird only moments before. "Good luck tonight, My Lady. Hope to see you in the morning. Remember what I said." She gave me an empathetic look before the air around her shimmered. A slight percussion, like the pop of a balloon, made me blink. When I opened my eyes, she was gone—replaced by the

24

fluttering wings of a tawny little sparrow. A heap of clothing was all that remained of the young female.

"What in the bloody hell…" my words trailed off as Mirabelle flitted out the window, leaving me alone with Lady Fallon.

Fallon's long, delicate finger twirled absently in her cropped, ebony hair. She reached into a jeweled clutch hanging from her wrist and pulled out what appeared to be a cigarette. A mask of boredom settled on her face as she pulled it to her lips and lit it on the sconce set into the wall. Smoke curled from her scarlet lips, smelling faintly of cloves and some other rich herb I couldn't place. She was stunning to look at, like a 1920s socialite who'd just walked out of a Gatsby party.

"Loyal help is hard to come by. She's a good one. One you can trust," she said.

"Can I trust you?"

"Asks the human girl who's bewitched my incredibly rich and powerful brothers."

"I didn't bewitch anyone. I only need a…" I paused before telling her I was here to find a healer, unsure how much of my story I should reveal. She was ultimately a stranger. I had to look out for myself. I wasn't aware of how much her brothers had told her about me. The less I shared, the better. At least it would keep me from being caught in a lie. "I only need to attend to a few things and I'll be on my way. Besides, Lucius is my friend. He vouched for me."

She visibly flinched at the mention of her exiled brother.

She brought the cigarette to her lips again, this time with trembling fingers, taking a deep drag.

"You've seen Lu—umm, the lost prince?" she asked, her gaze drifting off in feigned disinterest.

"Yes."

"So he's good, then?"

"A little broken and rough around the edges, but he's good. I owe him my life."

She tapped the cigarette against her lip, letting out an amused laugh that didn't fit the mood of our conversation. Her eyes glazed over, as though she wasn't entirely present in the moment.

"Well then, let's get on with it," she said, snapping out of it, all trace of emotion wiped from her face in a heartbeat. The only lingering sign was a glassy sheen to her dark brown eyes. "I've come to collect you. There's a family meeting. We have a few things to discuss before the Crownspire."

"Family meeting? Attending the festivities is one thing, but I don't think it's right for me to sit in on a family meeting. I'm only a guest here."

"Only a guest? If only it were that simple." She walked to the window, snubbing out her cigarette on the heavy wooden shutter, then tossed out the remnants. "Nothing is simple anymore, girl. But I get the feeling you knew that already."

"I don't know what any of this has to do with me. Maybe it's better if I just go home." As the words slipped

26

out, I realized there was nothing to return home to. Going back to London was a death sentence.

"Spare me the 'woe is me' routine. You'll not find an ounce of empathy from me. Fate has made you a part of this, whether you're a willing participant or not. You'll come to this family meeting. You'll hear what needs to be said, and then you'll play your part. End of story."

"Apparently, guest is synonymous with prisoner here."

"Coercion, yes. But you'd rue the day you became my prisoner. So I suggest you get moving."

I FOLLOWED Fallon out of the visitor's wing. In the days since I arrived, I'd been cooped up in my assigned room and hadn't ventured far. The pair of heavily armed guards who stood watch at the end of the cavernous hallway had been a convincing deterrent. With Fallon in the lead, we breezed past without so much as a sideways glance.

The nagging concern over tonight's festivities was momentarily forgotten as the grandeur of Mathenholm Castle filled me with wonder. Hallways split in every direction, and there seemed to be no end to the sprawling castle. Frescos of males and beasts covered the soaring ceilings overhead.

A grand hall led into a breathtaking solarium crowned by a domed glass ceiling. The evening's newly born stars flickered down on the lush garden as twilight set in. Inlaid into the floor was a massive mosaic of a bear, warm ochre and amber glass flecked with gold gave the illusion that sunlight was dancing across its body.

The solarium itself was arranged like a compass, with four towering archways marking the cardinal points. Each bore a distinct house name carved into the stone above in its own unique style. To the east stood the House of Steggr, mirrored by the House of Lycaon to the west. The House of Rapere loomed to the south, and finally, the largest of the four—the House of Bruin—stood like a sentinel in the north.

Fallon directed me to the arched wooden doors set at the back of the enormous room. Their sheer size appeared better suited for giants. As we approached, I couldn't help but feel the weight of the place, as though each house held secrets heavy enough to crush bone. She moved without hesitation, never missing a step as the doors groaned, opening of their own volition. The elegantly carved "House of Bruin" welcomed us as we passed beneath it. A knot of tension squirmed in my gut, leaving me nauseous as the doors closed behind us—warning me that each step brought me closer to a fate I couldn't run from.

Fallon led me through a maze of hallways, remaining annoyingly silent as we delved deeper into the estate. It did nothing to placate my anxious mind. My overactive imagination fed me an array of possible scenarios—none of which ended well for me.

She finally paused at another set of doors, her hands resting on the polished knobs for a beat, seeming to collect herself before pushing through. We entered a large sitting room. At one end, an intricate stone fireplace cast a soft glow across the elegant furnishings. Shelves packed with books lined the back walls. A round mahogany table stood at the center. Eight leather-clad chairs sat empty around it, each bearing words in a language I'd never seen before.

Only three of the princes were present, clustered near the fireplace, deep in conversation and completely oblivious to our arrival. My eyes landed on Nico. The eldest—and largest—of the brothers, he possessed a presence that commanded all the attention in the room. In the short time I'd known him, he'd worn plain, functional clothing, needing no adornment to amplify his already striking features. But now, he looked every bit the king he was destined to be.

He had swept his long brown hair back and secured it away from his bearded face. A thick fur mantle enhanced his already broad shoulders, and a black doublet with gleaming gold buttons clung to his massive frame. A heavy leather belt rested at his hips, holding a myriad of jeweled daggers. Polished black leather vambraces adorned his forearms, adding a touch of menace to his regal appearance.

Fallon cleared her throat, unceremoniously. Nico and his brothers—Luca and Hunter—turned to face us, all three locking eyes on me.

"All right, boys. Pick your chins off the floor and get your wits about you. We have business to attend to before this fiasco of an evening begins. Where are the others?" Fallon asked.

The brothers reanimated, shifting positions and straightening their jackets, all three dressed in finery that marked them unmistakably as nobility.

Luca stepped forward and dipped into a practiced bow, his blonde-streaked hair spilling over one shoulder. "Allow me to be the first to say how absolutely stunning you are." He rose, warm honey eyes meeting mine. "If you'll allow me?" He reached for my hand with tattooed fingers—a striking contrast to the dark green of his jacket. He pulled it toward him, his warm smile faltering just long enough to place a kiss on my knuckles.

I stood frozen. The touch of his hand, the playful gleam in his eyes, and that damn charming smile sent a flush of heat coursing through me. I managed a mumbled, "Thank you," that infuriated me. I'd never let men get to me like that before. A momentary weakness I'd have to move past quickly if I wanted to survive in this place.

"You're monopolizing the lady's time, my brother," Nico's gruff voice cut in, breaking the spell. "Michaela, I'm so glad you could join us."

"Thank you for inviting me. I hope I'm not intruding. I know this is a difficult time for—"

"Let me look at you." He interrupted, taking my hand from Luca's. He whisked me away from the others and spun me around in front of the fire. "Perfection. Hiraeth suits you. Red is most certainly your color—like a dahlia in full bloom." He leaned in close, brushing a loose curl from my neck before whispering in my ear, "And you smell positively divine."

The warmth of his breath on my neck set me on fire. If I hadn't been blushing before, my face was surely the same shade of scarlet as my dress.

"This is exactly what I've been talking about, Nico," Fallon snapped. "This girl is yet another thing on a long list of distractions. You've had your time to play. Now you need to focus on this family."

Nico let out a low growl. "I've always put the interests of our house first and foremost."

"Devoting all those years in Neverland was in whose best interest? Spare me. You were running from your responsibilities."

"I was expanding our kingdom abroad. The beasts now have a foothold in Neverland and a loyal ally."

"Neverland is weak. Pirates and pixies are no match for what we're up against."

"Might I remind you, sister," Luca interjected, "we were also keeping an eye on Lucius. He may be a rebellious little shit who ruined our plans when he got himself exiled, but he's still our brother."

Fallon blanched and took an unsteady step back at the mention of Lucius. The room fell into a tense silence.

I felt like an intruder, eavesdropping on a deeply private conversation. But my curiosity was piqued. I considered

Lucius a friend, but I knew next to nothing about him—or any of the princes, for that matter.

Hunter stepped toward his sister, an empathetic look softening his rugged features. He'd lingered back in the shadows as the others talked, but Fallon's reaction lured him out. He brushed his dirty blonde hair back, before resting his hands gently on her shoulders.

"We should've come back sooner. We should've sent word before we brought a human…" His gaze flicked to me. "Before we brought Michaela back home. We fucked up. And I'm sorry."

Fallon looked at him for a brief moment before shrugging off his touch and pushing his bearded chin away. Composure returned like armor snapping into place.

"You all stoked the ember, and now we have a full-blown fire on our hands," she said, ignoring his apology. "Do you know the kind of cover I've had to run for you since you broke our laws? The nobles are using her arrival to spread rumors about the sickness that's broken out among the peasants. Without Nico's decree protecting her, they would've sacrificed her already."

Now it was my turn to blanch. Was that why the guards were stationed outside the visitors' wing? Not to keep me in —but to keep out those who wanted me dead?

"What are you all talking about?" I asked, unable to stay silent. I was sick of them speaking as if I weren't standing in the room. So many questions demanded answers.

"It's nothing, Mic. An outdated law my father passed a

long time ago," Nico said, trying to brush it off. "It's time we buried it for good. My father was a great king, but he had his flaws. He was a purist. He thought it best to keep our realm separate from others—especially the non-magic ones like yours."

"I didn't come here to cause trouble. Take me back to the portal. I'll go to Neverland. Back to my sister. I'm sure I can find help there."

"Absolutely not!" Nico and Luca said in unison.

"We have the best healers here," Nico added. "You must stay so we can get you the help you need."

I leaned into him, lowering my voice so only he could hear. "I've already outlived my time. Every day past that is a gift. I'm sure there's a healer in Neverland. Or I'll keep using the faerie dust until it stops working. I don't deserve anything more than that. It's not worth tearing your kingdom apart."

Oddly, I felt at peace as I laid it out. Death had been calling my name for years, and yet I'd found a way to cheat it over and over again. Someday, my luck would run out. There had always been something freeing about knowing you were dying. It simplified things. It was almost a mercy, compared to the uncertainty now stretching out before me.

Nico held my gaze, his warm eyes searching mine before he spoke—slow and deliberate.

"We made the right choice bringing you here. I will get you healed if it's the last—"

His words were cut off as the doors burst open.

CHAPTER III
YOU'RE IMAGINING THINGS
-MICHAELA-

J ase, Finn, and Gunner strolled into the room with drinks in hand, their laughter echoing off the stone walls. Jase said something to Finn I couldn't quite catch, but it had him nearly doubling over, his grin wide and unguarded.

"Where have you all been?" Fallon yelled over their continued amusement. "Of all the days for you to be fucking around. I told you to be on time!"

"Relax, sister," Jase said, a half-cocked smile on a face far too handsome for his own good. "I told you not to worry. It's not good for your health." He was the perfect male counterpart to his fiery sister—his black locks and sharp tongue matching hers. The only thing disrupting his dark features were pale blue eyes that danced with mischief.

"Since you asked so kindly, I'll tell you. We've been out mingling with the nobles. Getting a feel from every house and offering some favors to ensure we have the support we need. We've actually been doing the work to keep our line in power, instead of destroying it from within," he added, eyes locking on me in an unspoken accusation. He wasn't even trying to hide his hostility.

"Jase, you're young, but I never thought you were that naïve. There's a web of alliances that's been years in the making. You can't flit back into court and unwind everything with your charm and a stiff drink. They plan to take the crown from us," Fallon scolded, stepping up to him. Her petite frame looked almost comical as she challenged her brother.

"You're imagining things. Why don't—"

"She's right!" I interrupted.

"Oh? Do you know something, Mic?" Nico asked, taking an interest in the sibling rivalry. All eyes in the room shifted to me, and I instantly regretted speaking up.

"Mirabelle… I mean, the maid. She told me we couldn't trust everyone. That you'd lost your kingdom while you were away." I stumbled through the sorry excuse for evidence, hoping to corroborate Fallon's claims.

A heavy silence settled over the room. The pop and crack of the fire sounded annoyingly loud as I fidgeted, waiting for someone to speak.

"The maid?" Jase laughed. "You've been in Hiraeth a few days and you think we should condemn the entire kingdom based on the loose tongue of a gossiping lady's maid?" He kept laughing while the other princes joined in —everyone except Nico and Luca.

"I can't believe I'm saying this, but you should listen to the girl," Fallon said. "You don't know what I've seen since Father died."

"You don't need to worry anymore, Fallon. The males have returned. You can go back to planning your parties, fucking your way through the married nobles, and getting high on brimshade," Jase said.

A loud crack made me jump as her hand connected with his face. "How dare you! I held this place together while you were off gallivanting around the cosmos. I'm not some hapless female. I know what I'm talking about." Her lip trembled as she fought back emotion.

"Have you looked around, Fallon? The realm is falling apart under your watch. You should have sent for us the moment Father died instead of pretending you could run the house alone. You let Johan get too comfortable in the stewardship. You're not cut out for this. You're too fragile."

"That's enough, Jase," Nico commanded. "But he's right about one thing—there's nothing to worry about. Everything will go as planned with the Crownspire. Johan will return the Bloodstone Sigil to me."

"And what if he doesn't?" Fallon asked.

"He has no choice. The ring will reject him. I am the rightful king," Nico asserted.

"Are you so sure?" Fallon challenged. "He's worn it all this time without any of the signs."

"He never should have been allowed to place it on his finger to begin with," Finn chided. "Now the ring has granted him all of our father's secrets."

"You weren't fucking here," Fallon hissed through clenched teeth.

"The ring gave him enough power to manage the stewardship, nothing more. He's not the chosen king, and no one will stand behind him—not while the realm is in such upheaval. The poor are poorer, the fields are failing, jails are full of debtors and thieves, disease is rampant in Dunharrow. The houses once supported our father. Rest assured, they'll support my rightful ascension. Besides, we are unstoppable now that Hiraeth has restored our gifts."

A shiver ran down my spine. I knew the princes were shifters. I'd seen them transform into bears with my own eyes. But now it seemed their return home had unlocked even more powers—powers I knew nothing about. I'd thought I imagined it when I crossed the veil into Hiraeth, a strange feeling like something inside me had shifted. Had the realm itself altered *me* somehow?

I'd always known I wasn't normal. A terminal cancer diagnosis at fifteen proved that to be true. Even that had changed when I finally learned the truth. What our realm called cancer was something else entirely—a dangerous manifestation of magic in a body too weak to contain it. A trial I hadn't yet survived. One I still didn't understand. The fae called it Tribulation, as if giving it a name wrapped in prophecy and purpose could make it easier to bear. But I could never bring myself to call it that. To me, it would always be cancer—a word sharp with memory. A worthy opponent I'd spent my life fighting. The power thrumming through me wasn't a gift. It was a curse waiting to devour me from the inside out.

Hiraeth must have sensed it. Or maybe it had only amplified what was already there. The nausea. The tightening in my chest. The voices in my head. The cold sweat down my spine. It all coalesced into a suffocating sense of dread, like death himself was breathing down my neck and whispering sweet nothings into my ear.

Now, standing among these brothers I barely knew— who claimed they wanted to help me—I couldn't shake the feeling I'd wandered into something far more dangerous than I realized. I might be the unwitting prey that followed the predators right into their den. If I survived the night, I'd need to find answers. I refused to be vulnerable any longer.

"Everyone needs to be on their best behavior tonight," Nico continued. "Plan to be here first thing in the morning. We begin the hard work of getting this realm back on track."

"What are you going to tell them about her?" Finn spoke from the back of the room, his massive figure lounging against the fireplace. He was second in line behind Nico and clearly didn't want me at this family meeting. His hawkish eyes had tracked every move I'd made from across the room. "And for the record, I'm not in favor of her coming tonight. It brings too much tension to an already fucked situation," he added, pushing off the mantle.

"Her presence at the Crownspire is not up for debate," Nico said.

"Yeah, I didn't think so. Just like her supposed role in the prophecy. You've shut down all conversations about that, too."

"Now is not the time, Finn. All you need to know is that I have the best scribes working on it. We'll sort through it once this transfer of power business is behind us."

What in the bloody hell was going on? This meeting only served to shine a light on the fact that I knew absolutely nothing. Powers and prophecies, back stabbing nobles and family skeletons? How had I gotten myself so entangled in this madness?

"We can tell them she's his concubine," Jase cut in. "A strange fetish for our new king. The staff will be talking for months."

Finn waved him off. "Nice try, Jase. That might not go over so well with his betrothed. Nyla Taryn won't tolerate that kind of hit to her reputation. Her family would make trouble for us over something like that."

The news hit me like a blow to the chest. Nico was already spoken for. I barely knew him, and yet I felt a deep, inexplicable sadness. Like missing a chance I hadn't known I wanted. It was completely irrational. He was a goddamned king-to-be. Don't be stupid, Mic. This isn't London. The idea that I could start any kind of relationship here was absurd. But it stung nonetheless.

"You'll draw attention. There's no avoiding it," Nico said to me. "Just be polite. Don't offer more than pleasantries." It sounded too simple, but I nodded at his instructions. "Fallon, I want you to watch her tonight. Keep the vultures away. She'll be easy prey on her own."

"You can't be serious," Fallon shot back.

"Brother," Gunner interrupted, "the festivities have already begun. Need I remind you it's bad form to be late to your own coronation. We should make our entrance soon, before we truly lose their favor." He was the exact replica of his twin brother, Hunter, save for his shaved head.

"Something isn't right," Fallon insisted. "We need a plan for when it all falls apart. Please. Listen to me. My intuition isn't wrong this time."

"We've been down this road before," Jase said. "We can't trust your powers. Not after the last time."

"Let's quit fucking around and put it to a vote," Gunner said. "All who believe tonight will go smoothly and end with our dear brother on the throne before daybreak, say aye!"

All of them said "aye," except Fallon.

"You know what that means, sis. We voted. You're overruled. Now, are you ready to go, Your Highness?" Gunner mocked, bowing to Nico.

"Fuck this family," Fallon muttered, pulling another cigarette from her clutch.

Jase chuckled on his way to the door. "Now that's the

sister I know. Keep smoking that brimshade and leave the ruling to us."

The rest offered their goodbyes as they filed out.

"Gunner," Fallon called. "Promise me you'll bring your weapons tonight."

He looked at her curiously, his green eyes softening. "Sure, if it'll make you happy. Might ruffle the older nobles, but what's life without a little chaos?" His gaze shifted to me, and I jumped when he caught me staring. "You should have something too." He bent low, pulled a small dagger from his boot, and handed it to me. "Here. This is an eidris. A hidden blade. Do you know how to use one?"

"The pointy end's for stabbing," I deadpanned.

He laughed, and I couldn't help but smile. "Yeah, you'll do alright. It's not meant for combat—just enough to throw off an attacker to get a head start."

"I guess it's a good thing I'm fast."

"A very good thing," he said, eyes full of mirth. "When this is over, maybe I'll teach you a few tricks."

"If we make it through the night, I think I'd like that," I said, unable to keep the flirtation out of my voice.

When he placed the sleek blade in my hand, a sense of impending doom bubbled up from the darkness that had taken up residence in my core. It was an instant reaction that I couldn't shake.

"Don't worry, beautiful. It'll all be fine. I'll find you in the morning."

As he walked away, my heart pounded, aching with

worry that nothing would be the same after tonight. Blood roared in my ears and the whispers that had haunted me since arriving grew louder. It sounded like the walls were hissing "death" in my ear. I was surely losing my mind.

"The look on your face matches how I feel," Fallon said, yanking me from the spiral I'd been falling down, effectively cutting off the whispers. "Mark my words. This won't end well tonight. And my obstinate brothers can't see reason. Let's hope the price for their ignorance isn't too high."

"Is there anything we can do?"

"There's nothing you can do. If I hadn't fucked things up with Lucius, he'd be here. He'd be on my side. We would've fixed all this if I hadn't gotten him sent away." Her face fell into her hands, trembling in the firelight. "But it's too late. Time to get what I deserve. No use prolonging it anymore. Let's go, girl. May the Divine have mercy on you."

"I need to go back to my room first. Just for a moment. There's something I need to take care of before we go."

CHAPTER IV
DON'T SHOW THEM YOUR FEAR
-MICHAELA-

My Dearest Sweetie,

My quill hesitated over the parchment yet again. The festivities had already begun, and my absence wouldn't be tolerated for long. My window of opportunity was shrinking by the second. I had to finish this letter. It was time to scrap the original plan to reassure Gwen that everything was going smoothly in Hiraeth. After hearing Fallon's concern ignored, I'd made up my mind—I needed to convince Gwen to send Lucius home. And I had to do it without raising alarm. The last thing I wanted was for her to come charging into Hiraeth, fanning the flames already licking at our heels.

I think I have read and reread your letter a thousand times. You would have laughed if you heard the squeal that came out of me when I read the news. It is bitter sweet though. I should have been there. We should have walked arm and arm down that aisle. I should have been there to give you away. You know I would have made each and every one of them grovel before I gave my blessing. Because you deserve a happy life. You've earned your happily ever after, so you better damn well be enjoying every minute of it.

My eyes welled with tears as I imagined Gwen on her wedding day. She must've been a vision of beauty. Her "boys," as she always called them, had brought forth a light into her darkness in a way I'd never seen before. No one deserved that kind of happiness more than she did. I'd never allowed myself to dream of her wedding—not when the cancer had all but stolen any hope of reaching life's milestones. I wasn't supposed to survive another year. It was simply easier to avoid dreaming of the things I was destined to miss. But once we discovered the possibility of a cure lay just beyond the veil of our world, everything changed. My life, my reality, my entire outlook took a sharp turn overnight.

I want you to know how proud I am of you. After everything that happened, you never gave up. You've always been true to yourself, and you never lost sight of what's most important... love. I knew you'd find your way. Your light shines through, even down the darkest of paths. Never forget that, and make sure those boys remember just how perfect you are! I love you to the moon and back, sweetie.

I could stand to learn a thing or two from Gwen's resilience. She never gave up. No matter the consequences. And now, it was time for me to shine a light on my own shadowed path—channel her courage and find a way. If I was going to be here in Hiraeth, I was going to do my part to protect it. The realm, my health... my future depended on it.

I wish this letter could be nothing more than catching up and simple rejoicing, but I need your help. I know I was supposed to write the moment I got here, but things haven't exactly gone according to plan. The situation in Hiraeth is dire. While the princes were trying to establish a foothold in Neverland, their own kingdom was falling through their fingertips. Everything has been compromised. Not to mention that it didn't help their cause when the princes waltzed back into the realm with a human girl on their arm. My presence has taken a tense situation and poured fuel on the fire. I can't go into detail because I have no idea who we can trust, and I wouldn't want these scrolls to fall into the wrong hands.

I hate to ask for your help, just when you're finally getting to the good part, but I need you to convince Lucius to come home. I know he's not the easiest to get along with. And I swear I can hear you cursing to yourself all the way from here, but I need you to work your charm and get him to return. He'll say no. He'll tell you he can't come back— that it's forbidden. But there is no other way. The kingdom and his brothers depend on it. He's more a part of this than he realizes.

Just remember, I need Lucius to come here. Not you! Are you listening? I don't want you to come here. Stay in Neverland with your husbands. I will return once everything has settled here and we'll have a proper celebration. I promise I'll be fine. Your life is just beginning! Go and live it... It's an awfully big adventure.

Love Always,
Mic

I stared at the scroll. It was done. The words were written. The request made. Now I could only wait. I closed my eyes and prayed Gwen would receive it quickly. Time flowed differently between realms, and I still didn't fully understand how it all worked. While Gwen had been away in Neverland, for her it was only a few days. In my reality back in London, she had been gone for months. A day here in Hiraeth could stretch into weeks or even longer in Neverland. I hoped the letter reached her in time to make a difference. That I had made the right decision and that the princes wouldn't see my meddling as betrayal.

A loud knock stopped my heart in its tracks and pulled me from my worrisome thoughts. I tried in vain to hide the scroll as the door opened, and an irritated Finn stepped inside.

"What's the point of knocking if you aren't going to wait for an answer?" I snapped, shoving the Loquentes Cartis under my pillow. "Am I not allowed a modicum of privacy?"

Like all his brothers, Finn was painfully attractive. He wasn't quite as tall as Nico or Luca, but he still towered over me. All the princes were intimidatingly large. Tall and muscular. A nod to the feral bear looming inside each of them. His long wavy brown hair was neatly tied back at his nape. Hints of highlights caught in the dim light like spun gold.

"Fallon sent me to escort you to the feast. Apparently, I've been reduced to your governess for the evening." His words were filled with disdain as he dismissed my question. "They're waiting for us in the great hall."

I glared at him. "My governess?" I repeated. "I don't need a glorified babysitter to walk me across a bloody courtyard."

He arched a brow, clearly unimpressed. "That remains to be seen."

"Are you sure I even need to be there? Fallon said—"

"Fallon has a tendency to speak out of turn," he cut in. "I personally think this is a mistake, but Nico wants you there. So, you will be there."

"I don't want to cause a scene. Sounds like you already have enough to deal with."

Finn huffed under his breath. "You've caused a commotion alright."

I glared at him, silently scolding his blunt remark. The last thing I wanted was to be put on display for everyone to gossip about. "See? That's my point. This whole Crownspire… thing is a monumental occasion, right? Why would Nico want me there if I'm only going to be a distraction?"

"The Crownspire is indeed monumental, and that is why my brother wants you there. A distraction might be exactly what we need. Discussion over. It's time to go."

CHAPTER IV

. . .

THE GREAT HALL was alive with music and dancing. Finn and I made our entrance without drawing much attention—just a few glances from prying eyes. Nothing like the overly dramatic scene I had envisioned. I let my shoulders drop as I relaxed.

Large dining tables adorned with linens, flowers, and elaborate candle-scapes lined the perimeter of the room. Giant iron chandeliers hung from the stone ceiling, casting a flickering glow over the enchanting ambiance. The heavenly aroma of savory spices filled the air—a promise of the delectable feast being prepared for the evening's festivities.

I took a moment to reflect on how far I had come. I'd been on the brink of death only a few weeks ago. And now, I was living in a real-life fairytale—a life I'd never dreamed of living. Despite the dark premonitions lingering over the evening, in this place, I couldn't help but bask in the promise of time... the possibility of a future. A smile spread across my face, and I squeezed Finn's arm, seeking proof this wasn't just a dream.

The table at the end of the hall was raised on a dais. A large, ornate seat sat at the center, with three chairs flanking each side—seven seats of honor. Nico sat in the chair just right of center, a large drinking horn in his hand. Luca sat beside him, the two engaged in heavy conversation. To Nico's left was a large, greasy-looking male. Dark curls hung heavy over his forehead, and his beard—speckled with grey —gave away his age. He loomed over the room with a scowl on his face, mindlessly sipping from his cup as he watched the festivities in silence.

"Go, find Fallon, and stay out of trouble." Finn dismissed me with a flick of his hand.

"But… I…" The words stumbled from my mouth. "You're going to leave me alone?" My skin prickled with sweat. So much for being relaxed. I couldn't help feeling like he was leaving me to the wolves—easy prey for the court gossips.

"You'll be fine, Mic. Don't speak to anyone. Remember, pleasantries only." He raised his brow, waiting for my acknowledgment. "Fallon's around here somewhere. I have things to attend to."

And just like that, I found myself alone. Gone was my moment of hope and optimism—quickly snuffed out by fear and trepidation. *You've got this, Mic. Chin up. Don't show them your fear. Animals can smell that shit, right?* I giggled to myself. *Are shifters animals?* I still had so much to learn.

I started to make my way around the room, pacing myself while casually scanning the crowd for Fallon. I nodded at passersby in a silent hello—calm, cool, and collected. No one tried to engage in small talk. They either stared from afar or returned my nod with a smug smile before moving on. I was clearly a subject of interest—something new, something worthy of conversation. I pretended not to notice, keeping my chin high and a smile on my face.

Behind the dining tables were several hallways leading in and out of the chamber. I decided to shift gears and make my way along the outer perimeter rather than aimlessly wandering the center of the room. If I were Fallon—and expecting the worst—I'd want to be near an exit. If she wasn't there, I could always work my way back into the chaos in the middle.

There appeared to be two hallways extending from each side of the room, with several doors and openings along their endless lengths. Mathenholm was massive. I wondered if I'd ever get a feel for its layout.

I made my way down the entire right side of the hall with no luck. Where was she? Nico had clearly instructed her to remain with me. And yet, being forced to be my babysitter for the evening clearly didn't sit well with her. Maybe she was avoiding me on purpose?

The left side of the room was identical to the right. Two more endless hallways—and still no sign of Fallon. I turned and began making my way back.

Keep your wits, Mic. She's here somewhere. You'll find her. She's probably dancing in the heart of the crowd. Remember to smile.

"Ooh," I gasped. I'd walked straight into a paunchy male. "Forgive me," I blurted, flushing with embarrassment. "I... I..." My heart stopped. The room around me closed in.

He needed no introduction.

I immediately recognized him as the greasy male seated beside Nico on the dais. I had bumped into the damn steward. An uneasy feeling settled in the back of my throat.

"My Lady," he greeted, steadying me on my feet.

"Lord Steward, I beg your pardon. Please forgive me—I wasn't paying attention."

"It appears my reputation precedes me." He raked his eyes up and down my body. "You're the human girl I've been hearing about."

"It's an honor to meet you." I dropped into a curtsey, trying my best to play the part.

"Please,"—he reached for my hand—"the honor's all mine. Join me."

Linking our arms, he silently ushered me down a nearby hallway and swiftly tucked us into a private alcove. My heart pounded. Why was he isolating us? How was I going to get out of this one?

"You've caused quite a stir amongst the houses. And yet, I still don't have your name?"

"Your Lordship, I meant no disrespect. I'm Michaela Darling Carlisle." I extended my hand, expecting a formal handshake. Instead, he pulled it close and pressed an inappropriately long kiss to the back of it.

"A fitting name for a beautiful girl. Johan Vellere, Ruler of the House of Rapere. Steward to the throne of Hiraeth." He bowed his head. "Please, call me Johan."

"Johan," I said, clearing my throat, trying to come up

with an excuse to rejoin the festivities. "I should be getting back to the—"

"Nonsense. They haven't even started serving yet."

Fuck. Damn you, Finn, for leaving me alone.

"Besides, I'm enjoying our time away from all the commotion." He took a step closer, forcing me back against the stone wall. His grey, lifeless eyes drilled into me. "Tell me, Michaela, what brings a human woman to Hiraeth?"

He was close enough that I could smell the mead on his breath. I couldn't tell if he was threatening me or coming on to me. I pressed myself back against the stone wall, praying a hidden door would magically open and I'd be free of the situation.

"I'm in need of a healer." The words were out of my mouth before I could think of a better answer. So much for simple pleasantries. My nerves were getting the best of me. How could I let that slip?

"A healer?" His gaze swept over me again, lingering too long at my décolleté. "You look like the picture of health to me."

I froze.

Johan braced one hand against the wall, blocking my only exit. I silently begged one of the beasts who insisted I attend tonight's festivities to come looking for me. Where was Fallon?

The corner of his mouth curled up while his eyes fixated on my neck. Without hesitation, he leaned in—his nose skimming my skin as he inhaled deeply. "There's a layer of sweet death perfuming your intoxicating vanilla scent."

Did he just… sniff me?

Was that supposed to be a compliment?

I remembered Gunner's eidris. It was strapped to my thigh. Of all the places I could have hidden it, why had I chosen my thigh? Why did they always show that in the movies? It wasn't exactly easy access.

"Michaela?" Fallon's voice echoed down the hall.

Finally!

"Fallon!" I called out. Breathing a sigh of relief when Johan quickly pulled away.

"Sounds like your keepers are looking for you. Such a shame—we were just getting to know each other."

I dropped into a curtsey. "Another time, Your Lordship. I must be going."

Fallon was just outside the alcove, hurrying toward me. "I've been looking everywhere for you." She grabbed my hand and spun us around, marching us back toward the main hall.

"Finn left and told me to find you. I… I bumped into—"

"Fucking Johan. I know."

"You knew? Why did you leave me with him for so long?" I stared at her, confused and furious. "Wait, were you watching me?"

"I have better things to do than waste my time watching you. I felt something."

I stopped her. "What do you mean, you *felt* something?"

Fallon sighed. "Intuition. It's my... gift."

I stared at her, wide-eyed. "You have powers too?"

"Ugh, we don't have time for this. Michaela, did he touch you?"

How was I going to explain what transpired? "He, um... he sniffed me. Then he proceeded to tell me I smelled like death. Not exactly a charmer."

"He said you smell like death?"

"I believe it was "a layer of sweet death" perfuming my scent." Such an odd thing to say to someone.

"Fucking vultures. Don't ever let that vile Rapere get you alone again. Do you hear me? He's a fucking scavenger by nature."

It was all starting to come together. Vellere. House of Rapere. All bird references. The "sweet death." Johan was a vulture shifter.

I immediately felt unclean.

Fallon laughed. "That look on your face says it all. You figured it out—he's a vulture."

"Why doesn't anyone tell me these things?"

"Here's a little tip for you. Whatever you do, don't watch him eat." Her face scrunched with disgust.

I raised my brows. "Why? Does he peck at it?"

"Haha, that would be hysterical. You'll see. Speaking of eating, we've got to get seated. They're about to serve the meal. If Nico's right, everything will go as planned.

Otherwise… remember to stay calm, no matter what happens."

THE CROWNSPIRE FEAST WAS MASSIVE. I had never seen anything like it. Course after course was served with meticulous care. All of the cuisine was completely foreign to me, each plate more delicious than the last. Just when I thought I couldn't eat another bite, the most beautiful, glistening desserts were placed before us.

Fallon and I were seated at a table of honor to the right of the dais. We were out of earshot but had a clear view of everything. She had been right about Johan's eating habits. He ripped and tore at his food with his mouth in the most uncivilized way. Not quite pecking per se, but close enough that, if you knew his true form, you could see the vulture in his movements. I wondered if that was why his face appeared so greasy.

"When does the transfer of power happen?" I asked Fallon.

"It should be anytime now. Once the royal family has had their fill, Johan should summon the court musicians to start the ceremony." Fallon began to fidget with her dress, watching her brothers intently.

"Everything seems to be going smoothly." I hoped Nico had been right, and Fallon's concern was only petty gossip. There had been no indication that things were out of the ordinary. But who was I to assume I'd notice if something were amiss? I had never seen a Hiraethian transfer of power before. I had no idea what to expect.

"You think so? Was your little escapade with Johan part of the plan?"

"Well, no. Not exactly."

"Nothing about this evening is smooth." Fallon's gaze swept the room. "They're taking too long. I don't like it."

CHAPTER V
THE CROWNSPIRE
-MICHAELA-

The percussion of drums vibrated in my core. The court musicians had begun, and the crowd quieted. Hollow, rhythmic strikes reverberated off the vast stone walls, echoing like distant thunder.

The throng of people parted, revealing Johan and Nico at the center of the great hall. Adolescent males stood around them in a semicircle, each bearing a banner with emblems etched in black and crimson, rippling in a wind that didn't exist.

"They represent the noble Houses of Hiraeth," Fallon whispered in my ear, answering the question that had only just formed in my mind. "The shifter bloodlines that have ruled these lands for generations. The falcon for the House of Rapere. The buck for the House of Steggr. The wolf for the House of Lycaon, and of course, the bear for the House of Bruin. These alliances have held since the dawn of our existence—until tonight."

"Is there a chance you could be wrong?" I whispered as a heavy silence fell.

Before she could answer, Johan began to speak. "Welcome, my fellow Hiraethians! I can only speak for myself when I say, I am so pleased that all of you are here to bear witness to a new chapter in our history. It's time for Hiraeth to turn the page and begin anew. What a glorious night indeed! Now comrades, join me... TO THE THRONE ROOM!" he bellowed, and wild cheers erupted. Fallon's cold fingers clamped down on my arm as the drums resumed, horns joining the raw, guttural music as the banner bearers led the march out of the hall.

I was fully immersed in the spectacle. It was a relief not to be the center of attention anymore, but I couldn't shake the feeling someone was still watching me. I scanned the crowd until my eyes locked with Gunner's. While the rest of the princes marched solemnly behind Nico, he was staring at me. When he realized he'd been caught, his lips tugged into a half-cocked smile. He raised a hand in salute, as though signaling the real game was about to begin. A polished bow rested over his shoulder, a quiver of arrows strapped at his side. He'd kept his promise to Fallon.

The warmth of his attention and his playful demeanor somehow eased my nerves, as if he were telling me everything would be alright. I wanted to believe him.

My eyes darted around the crowd, feeling exposed, wondering if anyone had noticed our exchange—but all eyes were on Nico. As the procession passed, the crowd closed in behind them. The press of bodies was overwhelming, but Fallon's cold grip held me in place against the flow.

"Shouldn't we follow?" I whispered.

"Not yet. I need space to see what's coming."

When the crowd thinned, Fallon pulled me forward, leading us into the adjacent throne room. Unlike the communal ambiance of the great hall, this place was built for ceremonies. Rows of soldiers in polished armor lined an elongated chamber designed to fit hundreds. Immensely tall ceilings arched overhead, and lancet windows stretched from floor to ceiling. The full moon was perfectly framed within the intricate lattice of a rose window looming above a tiered dais, where a large throne sat at the center. As we approached, I realized it was a morbid composition of interlocking bones from various animals.

"The throne is made from the remains of the original leaders of the founding houses. The magic of our ancestors flows through the seat of power in Hiraeth," Fallon said, once again reading my thoughts before I could voice them.

"And who is he?" I asked, pointing to a cloaked figure behind a stone altar.

"He's the sage. Our holy man. He'll oversee the transfer of power." Fur-lined robes hung heavily from his thin frame, casting his face into shadow.

"Do you trust him?" I asked.

"With my life. But it's not him I'm worried about." Fallon pulled at my hand, dragging me into a dark alcove carved into the eastern wall. Deep shadows played across the arched recess, cast by flickering candlelight arranged around a small altar. Intricate iron lattice scrolled over thick glass, entombing a book within the wall.

"May the Divine forgive me," Fallon whispered, pulling a skeleton key from her clutch. A subtle click, and the lattice popped open, revealing solid glass beneath. She fished into her clutch again, replacing the key with a tiny silver pistol. I jumped as she slammed the butt of the gun against the glass. A spiderweb of cracks raced across the surface. Two more blows, and the case shattered in a splintering crash, leaving a plain, leather-bound book exposed in a sea of glittering shards.

"What are you doing?" I hissed as she pulled it from the debris.

"Here. Hold on to this for me. Tuck it into your dress." She shoved it into my hands.

"Seriously? What are we doing, Fallon?" I tried to stare her down, desperate for answers. Ignoring me, she turned, blowing out the candles at the altar, cloaking everything in darkness before I could even see a title.

"Fallon... what is this?" I asked as she turned her back, peeking out at the crowd from our hiding spot.

"What?"

"The book? What is it?"

"It's nothing. Just keep it hidden and forget about it. It won't help us now. Watch!" she commanded, ending the conversation. I wedged the book into the stays of my corset, silently cursing the fact that I was blindly going along with whatever outlandish plan she was concocting.

The sage raised his arms, the feathers woven into his cuffs rustling like wings. His deep, rasping voice grated through the murmur of the crowd.

"By the bones of the land and the breath of the sky, by the blood that binds beast to spirit, we gather beneath the eye of the Divine. Tonight, the mantle of the realm passes from one hand to another. From the steward, whose shoulders bore the weight of the crown-less years, to the king, chosen by blood." He turned to Nico, who dropped to his knees. "Nico of the Bruin," he intoned, holding a gnarled hand over his bowed head. "The ring is not only a source of power, but it represents the bond that links spirit and beast, land and ruler. With the Bloodstone Sigil, do you swear to protect these lands, to honor its people, and to wield this power with wisdom and courage, as the Divine decrees?"

"I swear it." Nico's voice carried over the crowd, and I felt a knot of tension begin to loosen. Maybe I'd been too quick to judge. I'd stupidly let Fallon play on my emotions. Not only would I have to write Gwen immediately and insist she tell Lu my letter had been a false alarm, but now I'd have to explain to the princes why I'd helped steal an obviously important artifact. The book dug into my skin, a painful reminder of my poor decisions.

"What are you doing, sister?" Fallon and I both jumped at the graveled whisper behind us.

"Gunner!" Fallon slapped his shoulder, scowling. "You know why I'm here. I wasn't about to stand with our house. We all may be cursed, but I'm not about to give them an easy target."

"You're being ridiculous. Look, the ceremony's going as planned. Nico's given the oath. All that's left is for the sage to stop rambling and initiate the transfer of the ring."

"I'm being ridiculous?" She gestured to a small golden orb at his belt. "I asked you to bring a weapon, not a solric. That thing will blow us all to the afterlife, not just our enemies."

"One can never be too prepared. Besides, you owe me. I know that you're wrong, but I brought a weapon anyway. Or did you miss the bow on my back?"

"Once Nico is king, then you can tell me I'm wrong. Until then, I'm staying put." Fallon turned, focusing back on the ceremony.

"Maybe you shouldn't have worn such a flashy dress if you wanted to hide in the shadows. You're like a beacon, refracting light like a distress call."

"Fuck off, Gunner. No one asked you. Go back to being a lapdog for our brother."

I had to stifle a laugh, which became nearly impossible when Gunner chuckled.

"Johan of the Rapere, your watch has ended. You have been a shield in the storm, a light in the shadowed wood. Do you relinquish the Bloodstone Sigil and with it, the burden of rule?"

The room held its breath. This was the moment Fallon had been so afraid of. I, too waited with bated breath while the entire realm teetered on a precipice.

Johan twisted the ring on his greasy finger. The silence was deafening.

"It has been the honor of my life to be one of many to serve Hiraeth," he began, his voice echoing off the walls. "Our realm has seen many great rulers come and go. From the dawn of our kingdom, the Divine granted Hiraeth with the gift of sight. Prophecy was given to the chosen few so that we, the people, would know the Divine's will."

"Curse the damn fates! We don't need a history lesson. Get on with it, Johan," Gunner muttered, his stance shifting. He was getting nervous.

"The House of Bruin has led for centuries—a glorious and storied dynasty. But I am ashamed to admit that the Divine's word has been lost to us. Lost because some kings refused to share it. Evil kings, who twisted prophecy to their favor. Now that I bear the Sigil, it's revealed all of the secrets the kings before me kept. King Artos was the worst of them all!"

The crowd gasped, chaotic chatter erupting.

"Fucking bastard," Gunner hissed, reaching for his bow.

Nico stepped forward, fists clenched, restraint etched deep in his scowl. "Johan, you're skirting a fine line."

"My father, Herold, was one of Artos's closest friends. That didn't stop him from murdering him in cold blood."

"That's a lie and you know it!" Nico growled.

Johan ignored him, turning back to the crowd. "My father was killed for the unfortunate crime of being born to the wrong house at the wrong time. Artos murdered him because the Divine foretold the House of Rapere would rule. I've seen the old texts. I've been translating the Book of Astrium. The proof is overwhelming. Many of you already know this to be true. We cannot allow his line to ascend the throne!"

The room dissolved into a frenzy.

"They are tainted!"

"The sins of the father shall fall to the sons!"

"Eradicate the entire line!"

Gunner stepped in front of us, arrow knocked, as the chaos escalated.

"Do you believe me now?" Fallon shouted.

"Not a great time for 'I told you so'!" Gunner barked.

Johan's voice boomed again. "We cannot allow the Sigil to pass to the Bruin line. We must root out the evil and usher in a new era. The House of Rapere shall restore our rightful destiny. And we'll begin at its core!"

He stepped behind the sage, drawing his ceremonial dagger and slit the holy man's throat.

As if on cue, the guards lining the throne room sprang into action, surrounding the nobles of Bruin House.

"Take them alive if you can," Johan ordered. "The realm deserves to see them hung for the crimes of their house."

They reached Finn first, four of them dragging the unarmed prince to the floor.

"Get her out of here!" Gunner shouted at Fallon.

"But Gunner—"

"I don't have time for your fucking mouth. Just do it!" He turned to me, emotion blazing in his eyes. "Now's the time to prove how fast you really are. No matter what happens, I'll find you at the end."

He reached for me, a calloused thumb barely brushing my cheek. Before I could register the touch, it was gone. The whispering hiss of the arrow leaving his bow, followed by the sickening thud as it hit its mark, was the last thing I heard before he vanished into the throng.

I stood frozen, watching the carnage unfold. Candlelight glinted off a sea of silver armor as guards poured into the throne room. Panicked screams of fleeing nobles echoed in my ears. Only a stark few from Bruin House stood with the princes, their ceremonial swords drawn in what looked like a losing battle. It was death's symphony. The clashing of steel on steel. The agonized cries. The wet thud of bodies hitting stone. I should have been overwhelmed. Nothing in my sheltered life had prepared me for this. But in the midst of so much death, the anxiety that had plagued me since my arrival transformed into a strange calm in the pit of my belly.

Fallon stood beside me, trembling, but made no move to follow Gunner's orders and flee.

"Should we go?" I asked, touching her arm gently. She stayed silent. "Fallon!" I shook her harder, trying to break through her stupor.

"I can't. If I leave now, they all die."

"You don't know that. If we stay here, there's a real chance *you* will die."

"True. But it would be a fate I deserve. Return to the House of Bruin. Find the king's chambers. The mirror is there. Go back to Neverland and tell my brother what happened."

"I'm not leaving you."

"That's your choice. I won't stop you. But remember— it's a decision you'll have to live... or die with."

"Don't worry about me. Death and I are well acquainted."

Fallon raised the silver pistol still clutched in her hand and began firing as she moved into the fray. I pulled the eidris and followed, cursing the excessive amount of unnecessary fabric of my skirts. I was an enormous target. The crimson color of the dress now felt ironic. Still, I couldn't bring myself to run. The princes had saved me once. Now it was my turn to return the favor or die trying.

Johan watched from the stolen throne as Nico engaged in a lethal dance before the dais. His ceremonial blade, wholly inadequate against the guards' weaponry, was clutched in his hand. The once-opulent weapon, with its jeweled hilt, now dripped with blood. His fur mantle hung torn and limp around his shoulders. Strands of hair had pulled loose from their tie, adding to the feral look on his face.

Luca and Gunner still pushed back the surge of guards at the center of the hall. Hunter and Finn weren't so fortunate. They were on their knees, straining against their captors with shackled hands. Jase stood quietly, also in chains, but looking resigned. There was no resistance in him at all. Unlike his brothers, he'd calmly accepted there was no escape—which seemed at odds with the smug bastard I'd seen only hours earlier.

It looked like we were out of time. Fallon and I had been largely overlooked in the chaos until a hulking guard spotted us and shifted his trajectory. I tried to warn her, but she was locked in a trance, her pistol occupied elsewhere.

Fuck, fuck, fuck.

The male barreled toward us, and my mind cycled through every scenario. In each one, his broadsword cut me down before my blade could ever graze his skin. The odds were dead set against me. But at least it was better than dying of cancer, withering away in my bed while my own magic ate me alive.

A half-cocked smile curled my lips as I welcomed my fate. But the utter malice plastered on the guard's face faltered—along with his steps. His jaw slackened, his pupils blew wide, and his eyes went vacant. His body collapsed face-first at my feet, an axe protruding from his back.

My chest heaved, adrenaline burning like cinders in my bones. How was I still alive?

My gaze followed his path, and my heart leapt into my throat when I saw a familiar face. Lucius. His amber eyes locked on mine, a mix of rage and relief warring on his handsome face. Gwen had come through. The exiled prince of Hiraeth had come for me.

"Lucius?" Fallon's voice came out in a whisper as she stumbled toward him. "Lucius!" She screamed his name. The raw emotion in her voice echoed off the walls as she sank to her knees. The fighting paused at her outburst, and Johan's sinister chuckle filled the silence.

"So the murderous whelp returns! The Divine has smiled upon me today. You've saved me the trouble of hunting down the last of your bloodline."

"Murderous? No more than you, Johan. And if you think I'll make it easy for you, then you're further gone than I thought."

"Two down, four to go. It's been great fun, but it's getting rather dull. Guards, stop toying with your prey. I want them dead or in chains before dawn."

Johan rose from the throne, armed guards surrounding him as he strode out of the room. The great doors slammed behind him, locking us in.

"Loni, I need you to pull it together," Lucius said, lifting Fallon to her feet before turning to me. "We've gotta go,

Dove," he said, grabbing my arm and steering me toward the dais.

"How? He's locked us in."

"My father had tunnels built. We just have to reach the altar—there are hidden passages underneath."

"What about the others?"

Sorrow flickered in his eyes as he looked at his brothers still fighting for their lives. "I'll do what I can. But I have to get you out. They'd want me to save you first and avenge them later."

My heart sank, and tears blurred my vision. "Why don't you all shift? Nico mentioned powers. He said the odds would be in your favor."

"The throne room is spelled. No shifting, no powers, unless you're king. And Nico isn't king yet. I'm sorry, Dove. We don't have other options."

He abruptly shoved Fallon and me to the floor as a new wave of guards surged toward us. I clung to Fallon, her face streaked with tears and makeup. "I'm sorry. I'm so sorry," she kept moaning over and over.

I pulled the pistol from her rigid hand. I couldn't just sit on the floor and do nothing while they tried to kill Lucius. I'd never fired a gun in my life, but it didn't stop me from pulling the trigger. The guard was dead before he hit the floor. I felt his soul leave his body and wondered if everyone felt that when they took a life. But there was no remorse. I'd evened the odds for Lucius, and he finished off the rest in quick order.

"Nico—we're running out of time. Open the tunnel!" Lucius shouted, pulling us up again as we raced toward the altar.

"Not that easy!" Nico barked from across the room. He'd gained the high ground, holding off the horde of soldiers from the steps of the dais.

"Go! I'll cover you!" Gunner called, nocking another arrow. Nico hesitated, uncertainty flashing across his face.

"Do it now. I'll hold them off."

He charged through the soldiers. His sheer size gave him the edge. Arrows began to fly, sailing a mere breadth from Nico before finding their mark, but he kept moving.

He reached the altar moments before we did, swiping a gash across his arm, coating his fingers in blood. With it, he drew a glyph on the altar. The floor rumbled. Stone grated against stone, and a section opened, revealing a spiral staircase that descended into darkness.

Lucius pushed Fallon down the stairs first, then reached for me. But I was staring at the chaos behind us. Finn, Jase, and Hunter were gone. Luca had reached the altar. Gunner was still surrounded, still battling more guards than he could ever fight off on his own.

"Lucius, we can't leave him!" I tried to break his grip, desperate to help.

But he lifted me, strong arms slinging me over his shoulder.

"I'm sorry, Dove. I hope one day you'll forgive me."

"No! Stop! Put me down!" I screamed. Gunner turned

toward my voice, panic darkened his eyes as a broadsword pierced through his chest.

"No! Please… no!" Tears poured down my cheeks as he dropped to his knees, lips parting in a soft exhale. The tension in his face eased. As the guards closed in, he pulled the small golden ball from his belt. With a steady hand, he kissed his bloodied fingers and held my gaze.

"Fuck! Everyone, get down!" Nico roared.

Lucius carried me down the stairwell as the entire room exploded in a deafening blast—and everything went black.

CHAPTER VI
MY INTENTION
-MICHAELA-

Maybe I was dead... but surely death couldn't be this uncomfortable. My body ached all over. An acrid stench filled my nostrils and clawed at my lungs, while a noxious grit coated my throat and threatened to choke me. My ears rang with a relentless whine that consumed every corner of my mind, drowning everything else out. No, I was definitely alive—pain was a key characteristic of the living.

It took a moment to get my bearings as the world came crashing back. I felt the ground beneath me, rough and unyielding. Darkness clung to me like a heavy veil, and when I forced my eyes open, it remained.

"Mic? Mic, are you—" Lucius' raw voice was cut short by a coughing fit. He sounded distant, like he was calling to me from the bottom of a well, but I couldn't be certain of his proximity with the ringing in my ears.

A nearby scratch and a spark flared in the darkness. A small match illuminated Fallon's face. Dust and debris swirled in the air around her. A fine white coating covered her skin, caked streaks marking where her tears had fallen. She got to her feet, grabbed a dormant torch inlaid into the tunnel wall, lighting it quickly. The flame cast a glow on those of us who'd made it out. Nico, Luca, and Lucius were only a few feet away, slowly rising. Each of them was covered in soot, the trails of blood on their battered bodies standing out in stark contrast.

"Mic, are you alright?" Lucius finished. He stepped toward me, offering his hand.

"I'm fine." My tone didn't convey the same message, but I couldn't bring myself to placate him any more than that. I wasn't fine. Gunner was dead. Finn, Hunter, and Jase—they could be dead, too. The last thing I wanted was to be coddled. I scrambled to my feet, ignoring his proffered hand.

I saw his jaw working as he wrung his wrists, but he said nothing. I wasn't trying to be rude. If it weren't for Lucius, I'd be dead. But I needed time to process this on my own. Not dying meant I had to face everything we'd just lost.

"We need to get out of here before Johan and the rest realize not all of us died in that blast," Luca said.

Nico took the torch from Fallon. "This way. We'll follow

the tunnels to the eastern side of the castle. We can make our escape from there."

We followed behind Nico in silence. I let my mind go numb. Time became irrelevant as we walked through the dark maze beneath Mathenholm Castle. Nothing mattered. I simply put one foot in front of the other. The monotony was a mercy. I felt Lucius hovering nearby, but I couldn't even find comfort in that. I was in shock. And I wasn't sure I ever wanted to come out of it.

I was no stranger to grief. I'd lost my parents when I was eighteen, not long after the doctors gave me a terminal cancer diagnosis. I had a slew of fucked-up coping mechanisms to choose from. The stage when your brain checks out because it can't accept what's happened—that's my favorite. The fact I *had* a favorite phase of grief told me I'd had more than my fair share. And with that came the knowledge that it wouldn't last long.

The king's tunnels dumped us into the wilderness, just beyond the castle ramparts. The full moon was still high overhead. My life had completely upended in a single night —and it wasn't even over yet. I gripped my bare arms as a cold breeze raised goosebumps across my skin. Tucked away in the confines of the castle, the sunny days seemed warm and inviting, when in reality, it was more like a crisp autumn night in London. I steeled myself against the cold, willing my teeth not to chatter. I'd be damned if my shivering drew any more masculine attention.

"Where are you going?" Luca asked as Nico led us to

the thick, coniferous forest surrounding the castle. "Bruin Castle is this way." He gestured northward, and our group pulled to a nervous halt.

"Think, Luca. We can't return to our lands. That'll be the first place Johan looks. We head to Whisperhold. The Caldreim River is only a mile east. We have to reach the water if we want even the slightest chance of escape."

Lucius and Luca both nodded in agreement, while Fallon and I remained silent. There were only two options: follow the princes blindly, as I had since the beginning—or throw myself at the mercy of that vulture, Johan. I chose to keep my blinders in place, at least for now.

We walked single file into the forest, close behind Nico. I didn't know how he knew the way. The moonlight barely pierced the dense canopy. He'd snuffed out our torch as soon as we left the tunnels, letting the darkness cloak us from our enemies.

I HEARD the rush of water creep into the silence of the night long before we arrived. I let out a sigh of relief when we broke through the trees. We'd made it to the river—our only chance at salvation. The surface shimmered like liquid silver in the moonlight as it meandered through the forest.

"Come on, Mic. I'll carry you." Lucius offered his hand.

"Carry me? I don't need you to carry me. I can walk."

"We have to walk in the water. It's the only way to mask our scent. Johan will send trackers as soon as he realizes we escaped. You won't be able to make it through in that dress."

I stared at the rippling surface, and suddenly it didn't look so beautiful.

"Or I can carry you, if you prefer my company over his," Luca offered, elbowing Lucius aside.

"Or I," Nico added, sounding hopeful.

The last thing I wanted was to be carried like a child.

I reached into my skirts, pulling out the eidris Gunner had given me. My heart squeezed at the sight of it. Without hesitation, I began hacking at the dress. I slashed through the fine silk with wild abandon, hot tears spilling from my cheeks.

"I didn't like this stupid fucking dress anyway," I muttered through gritted teeth.

No one said a word or tried to stop me. I couldn't hold back the anger or the heartache. I knew it was irrational. It didn't make sense. I'd only just met Gunner. I'd survived losing my parents—the two most important people in my life. His death shouldn't have broken me like this, and yet it did. A part of me had died in that room with him. Gunner had offered the promise of something more. And once again, I'd been cheated out of another choice. The Reaper had been denied my soul, and now it delighted in destroying it instead.

When I finished, the once-beautiful gown now had a ragged hemline that hung to my knees.

"All right, gentlemen. Shall we?" I stepped into the river,

feeling a bit lighter, both mentally and physically. I hissed as the frigid water swirled around my ankles, but I welcomed the cold.

Nico followed behind, cradling Fallon in his arms. She'd been a ghost of herself since the Crownspire. Luca and Lucius flanked me. I knew they were waiting for me to make a misstep and fall, but to their credit, they let me find my footing on my own.

"I know you're not thrilled with me right now," Lucius said. "But at least take my shirt. I can hear your teeth chattering."

"How's my sister?" I asked, deflecting.

He sighed but indulged me. "She's good. Probably sore as hell after marrying five husbands."

"Eww! I didn't need to hear that, Lu!" I smacked his shoulder.

"Five husbands, you say," Luca added. "That's nothing. Seven would be a better number—one for each day of the week." He cleared his throat, and the cheeky smile faltered. "Then again, maybe seven isn't the lucky number we thought it was."

Lu reached out, laying a hand on Luca's back. "Gunner saved all of our asses back there. He died an honorable death. He wouldn't have settled for anything less."

Luca looked at me, brows drawn together as he studied my face. "I think *she* would've made him want to live a very long life."

We made camp at dawn—if you could call it that. I'd

nearly collapsed when we reached a towering wayward pine. If I hadn't been so exhausted, I would've marveled at its massive size. Something I would have believed only existed within the pages of a fairytale. Its boughs, heavy with needles, hung low to the ground, creating a hidden sanctuary beneath.

Nico refused to let us build a fire. Apparently, it was too risky. Luca and Lu had split off to lay decoy trails in case Johan's trackers caught up with us. Fallon curled into a ball under Nico's oversized jacket and drifted to sleep without a word.

I found a quiet space beneath the tree and started gathering needles to soften the unforgiving ground. My body was stiff with cold. And even though I'd relented and taken Luca's jacket, I still shivered. I was pushing myself too hard. The cancer was a growing weight in my chest, a queasy churning in my stomach. My body was shutting down, and I didn't know how much longer I could keep up this pace without help from a healer. I did my best to hide the pain, but I could feel Nico appraising me as he huddled in his own corner.

"Mic…" he started, my name lingering between us as he picked his words. Could he already tell I was fading? "I need to tell you how sorry I am. When I brought you to Hiraeth, I meant to protect you. Instead, I've done the opposite."

"This isn't your fault, Nico."

"You're too kind. You should be telling me how much of

a disappointment I am. I was arrogant. I ignored the signs. I made some really terrible decisions back there."

"But you got us out alive."

"Not all of us." His face fell, and I saw the weight of Gunner's death settle on his shoulders.

"I should be the one apologizing… for Gunner." My voice cracked as I said his name.

"I'll carry that burden the rest of my life. My arrogance and selfishness are what got him killed. I saw only what I wanted to see. I should've listened to you, to Fallon."

"You couldn't have known this would happen."

"I think you're far too good for someone like me, Michaela. But I promise I'll fix this. My father—paranoid as he was—built a safe house: Whisperhold. It's hidden deep in Thornwyn Forest. Only blood family knows of it. I'll get you there, find a healer, and send you back to your sister and the protection of the Lost Boys."

"Nico, you need to stop worrying about me. Your kingdom is literally falling apart. Focus on your family."

Luca and Lucius ducked under the boughs, interrupting our conversation. The three of them together made our little sanctuary feel cramped.

Nico leaned closer, lowering his voice. "I think several of us would like to make you part of this family." He smiled, turning to his brothers to talk quietly.

What did that mean? I was too tired, too cold, too sore to think straight. I tucked the comment away for later—after some sleep, I'd think clearly again. I curled into the pine needles, wrapped in Luca's jacket, and let the scent of cloves and aged whiskey lull me into a fitful sleep.

I was caught somewhere between sleep and waking. Whispered voices hissed in my ear, but I couldn't make out the words. Panic and despair rose like a tide. I felt like I was falling—sinking through layers of darkness.

"Don't be afraid. I told you I'd find you at the end." Gunner's voice rang clear in my mind. Everything stilled. A calming warmth spread through me, and I drifted—finally—into the peaceful oblivion my body craved.

When I woke, that peace lingered. I instinctively curled toward the warmth beside me. But memory returned quickly, dragging reality with it. My eyes fluttered open and found a transparent apparition of a bear lying beside me.

I shrank back, swallowing a scream. Before I could fully register what I was seeing, the faint blue specter shimmered and vanished. Light streamed through the branches, illuminating the empty space where it had lain.

Had I imagined it?

Was I dreaming?

My mind was beginning to play tricks on me again.

CHAPTER VII
DEATH WARMED OVER
-MICHAELA-

I took a deep breath, convincing myself it had all been a dream. A deranged, grief-induced dream. A sharp stab of pain shot through my chest, dragging all my discomfort to the forefront of my mind. My entire body was stiff, every joint ached as I tried to straighten myself and find some semblance of comfort.

My corset laces were still tightly bound. I'd been too tired to loosen them last night. I reached down to adjust the dress and found the solid outline of the book Fallon had handed me. With a quick tug, I freed it from its hiding place, finally able to pull in a full breath without the damn thing digging into my ribs.

I'd completely forgotten about it. After everything that happened, it no longer seemed important. But Fallon had insisted I take it, going so far as to steal it from behind lock and key. There had to be a reason.

The warmth of the leather binding radiated into my hands. It was rather unimpressive for a relic worthy of a glass case and hidden altar. I traced the foreign words embossed into the smooth grain, flipping it open as speculation ran wild. Alongside the unfamiliar writings were vivid drawings of males and beasts. The simple cover gave no hint of the beauty hidden within.

I stopped at the last image and froze. It was a female astride a bear, flanked by six others. She looked exactly like me.

"Couldn't sleep?" Luca's voice startled me, and the book fell from my hands. I quickly shoved it beneath my tattered skirts, unsure if I was even meant to have seen it.

"Oh... I am... I was..." I raised my gaze and my jaw dropped. He was completely naked, dripping water, and carrying several fish.

"Any chance you're partial to raw fish?" he asked.

I completely forgot myself, throwing etiquette out the window as I stared.

He was magnificent. Water slid down his perfectly sculpted body—sharp lines carved down his hips, while bold tattoos curled over his chest, creeping up his neck and down his arms. I'd seen naked men before—in magazines and movies—but never like this. Never this close.

His manhood was a thing of beauty. It hung heavy and

thick between his thighs, demanding admiration with its perfection.

"Mic?"

"Umm… what did you say?" I mumbled, forcing my gaze away.

"Raw fish?"

"Right… fish. You didn't happen to bring any wasabi with you?" I asked, trying to break the tension growing between us.

He raised an eyebrow and set the gutted fish on a flat rock. I tried to keep my eyes from wandering to his ass, but I'm not sure any warm-blooded woman could have averted her gaze.

"I don't think we have any of that in Hiraeth, but you're in luck. I'm feeling generous today." He shook his body, spraying me with a fine mist.

"Forgive me if I'm not feeling the generosity," I said, wiping a droplet from my cheek.

I should've asked him to put on clothes to spare my virtue or something, but I couldn't bring myself to say anything.

"Watch." Luca arranged the fish on a flat rock before touching two fingers to the stone. Within moments, smoke curled from the fillets, the sizzle of cooking fish filling the quiet space.

"How did…" I trailed off, the aroma reminding me how long it had been since I'd eaten.

"My gift. I can channel a flux of energy into anything—or radiate it from my body."

"Where were you last night when we were freezing?" I snarked. I knew I was being a brat. He didn't owe me anything, but his excessively exuberant attitude brought it out of me.

"Well, it took a miracle to get you to take my coat, so I wasn't about to push my luck," he said with a laugh. "But honestly, I would have, only it takes time to recharge. The spells around the throne room drained me. I can only rebuild when I'm in contact with the land. The magic comes from Hiraeth itself."

"Speaking of clothes," Lucius muttered as he rolled over, "you can stop giving Mic a show. She's a fucking lady, asshole." He chucked a shirt at Luca before getting up. Both Nico and Fallon pulled themselves from their beds and joined us.

"Are you feeling alright, Mic?" Nico asked, skipping pleasantries.

"I'm fine."

"You look... a little under the weather." It was a polite way of saying I looked like shit. I could only imagine what he saw. I probably looked like I'd lost ten pounds overnight. The aching joints, the feverish skin, the dizziness had returned with a vengeance. They were all things I was used to dealing with. Without a healer or faerie dust to keep it in check, the cancer—technically, my magic—was wreaking havoc on my body.

"I said I'm alright." I didn't bother to hide the snap in my voice. I was done talking about it.

"Luca, do you still have your drinking horn?" Fallon asked, changing the subject and saving me from further questions. She'd been nearly catatonic last night, and yet she seemed calm and collected this morning, even if her short hair stuck out wildly in all directions. "I'll get some water and herbs for tea," she said, stepping out into the deep orange light of sunset.

I ATE in silence while the brothers discussed our next steps. Nico made it a point to consult with Fallon at every decision. The time for mourning Gunner had been shelved —survival was first and foremost. We'd travel at night to avoid detection from Johan's trackers, staying close to the river. We'd reach Whisperhold in a few days—if we were lucky.

Panic clawed at me. I'd been running on adrenaline and willpower alone. I wasn't sure how I'd be able to keep up with the days of hard travel ahead. I needed a healer. I should've brought faerie dust with me from Neverland to tide me over—an oversight I deeply regretted. Did pixies exist in Hiraeth too? I'd have to ask Fallon later.

As the knot of tension grew, my stomach turned. I lurched to my feet, scrambling out from under the pine. I made it a few paces before emptying the contents of my stomach into the bushes. The entire meal went to waste.

Not only was my body failing now I had nothing to fuel me. Fuck! I staggered to the river, splashed my face with the frigid water, and rinsed my mouth.

"Enough with the act. Let me heal you already," Lucius said. The setting sun cast his face in a warm glow.

"I don't want your pity, Lu." I tried to rise on shaky legs —it took everything I had.

"It's not pity. You can barely stand, you can't keep food down, you look like you're wasting away before my eyes. And you're too damn stubborn to let me help."

Lucius had healed me before. That's the whole reason I'd ended up here. It felt like a lifetime ago when Gwen and I set out on a journey to save my life, beginning with our ill-fated trip to Neverland. I'd given up hope, but Gwen had it in spades. It had burned so brightly within her it couldn't be shuttered. I'd followed along and dared to dream. But now, I'd caused so many terrible things just trying to survive, I wasn't sure healing was worth it.

"It's not simply 'helping.' We don't know what happens when you give your power to me. You could lose years every time you 'help'."

"And I'd give them gladly if it saved even one day of yours."

I stared at him and my heart stuttered. Why did he care so much? We were friends—sure. We'd only recently met. What was he hoping to get out of this?

Maybe I didn't understand men. I'd written them off when I thought I only had months left. I'd resigned myself to dying a virgin and save it for the love of my *next* life—because after this one, I was guaranteed something epic, right?

"Listen, I know you hate me because of Gunner, and I'm sorry," he said.

"I don't hate you. You saved my life in that throne room. I wasn't thinking clearly."

The tension in his face fell, replaced with a tenderness he rarely showed. Did you open the gift I gave you before you left?"

My mind reeled with the sharp turn in conversation. Lucius had given me a gift before I left Neverland. I'd toyed with opening it during those days of solitude after arriving in Hiraeth. But I wanted to hold on to that moment for as long as I could.

"No. I'd been meaning to, but unfortunately, it's back in my room at Mathenholm."

He sighed and hung his head.

"I'm sorry. I should have opened it."

"You don't have to apologize. It was yours to open when you were ready. I just… I hoped…"

Guilt coiled tight in my stomach. "Can you tell me what it is?"

"Nothing really. Something that was special to me." He hesitated. "Something I hoped would matter to you too. Eventually."

"Now you have to tell me."

"It's not important right now," he said, but we both

knew that wasn't true. "It's just a token. It would've explained a lot. But maybe it's for the best that you didn't open it."

"Why didn't you tell me when you gave it to me?"

His jaw flexed. "Because I needed to know you'd open it for the right reason."

"And what reason is that?"

A smile tugged at his lips, but it didn't reach his eyes. "Because you missed me."

Whatever that gift was, it wasn't simply a trinket. It was a truth he wasn't ready to say—or maybe one I wasn't ready to hear.

"Lucius, I…" The words failed me. There was nothing more to say and we both knew it.

"Why don't you stop being so obstinate and let me heal you?" He shifted the conversation again. I wasn't sure if I was grateful or not.

"Fine. But you have to promise me one thing."

"Anything." His eyes lit up.

"You can only heal me a little. Last time, you looked like death warmed over for days. We need you strong in case Johan's trackers catch up to us."

"I looked like death warmed over?" He raised a brow and scratched his chin. "If you could see yourself now, you'd accept my help—no conditions attached."

"Are you saying I *look* like death?"

"I didn't say it. I'm just saying you shouldn't be putting limitations on my help."

"Promise—or no deal."

"I could hold you down and heal you against your will. And there'd be nothing you could do to stop me." He stepped closer. I took an awkward step back. He didn't hide the feral look in his eyes, and I wasn't sure if I was afraid or excited.

"You'd never do that. Not to me." I called his bluff. But I couldn't help wondering what it would be like to be dominated by him.

He let out a low growl. "Fine. We have a deal. Now get over here."

I crossed the space between us and reached for him. I watched as a faint blue light spilled from his palms, pooling around mine and curling up my arms. I sensed his foreign power as it washed over me. The feeling was strange and yet familiar, as if my own magic recognized his.

My eyes fluttered shut. A soft moan escaped my lips. The euphoria was strangely intimate, and it ended far too quickly.

When he withdrew his magic, it was almost painful. I opened my eyes. Lucius was so close—his lips a breadth from mine. My whole body burned for something more.

"Michaela, I…"

His arms had somehow found their way around my waist. Being held was something I didn't realize I needed. There were no words to explain what was transpiring between us. I pressed my lips to his without any thought of the consequences.

He kissed me back, crushing me to his chest with a restrained need, harsh and soft in a way that had me melting in his arms. His tongue flicked my lips, a question of more, and I opened for him. I explored his tongue with my own, relishing in the feel of him. Nothing in my short life had ever felt this good.

But I'd gone too far. I'd taken too much from him, more than I deserved. I wouldn't let the possibilities of a future sink its claws into me only to be ripped out later. I pulled back, stepping out of his arms. My body felt strong again, but my mind still whirled with his kiss.

"I'm sorry, Lu. Thank you for the help. Now… can we forget that last part ever happened?"

CHAPTER VIII
NOTHING MORE THAN A BURDEN
-MICHAELA-

W e traveled for days, each mile feeling longer than the last. The energy I'd received from Lu became more and more depleted as we continued. Each time he healed me, Lucius paid a price. He tried to brush it off, but he couldn't hide the obvious drain it caused him. I wouldn't be the cause of his demise. I tried my best to hide my growing weakness, but I was lagging further behind the group with each step.

"Can we rest for a minute?" I asked through labored breaths.

Nico circled back, his eyes scanning my feeble frame. "Are you okay?" he asked, his face unable to hide the concern.

"Yeah… I just need a moment… to catch my breath."

"You're growing weaker by the minute." Before I could argue, Nico gently scooped me up, effortlessly cradling me in his arms.

"I don't need you to carry me. I just need a minute."

"I'm carrying you the rest of the way. End of discussion."

I never was one to accept help freely, especially when it came to my health. But the Bruins were good at not taking no for an answer.

The warmth radiating from Nico's body comforted the piercing chill aching in my bones. I nuzzled into his chest, noting his rich earthy scent.

I couldn't help but think we looked like the cover of a romance novel. A ripped, absurdly handsome man carrying his frail damsel in distress. Her tightly corseted gown billowing in the wind. Except my gown was shredded, my prince charming had a betrothed, and I was nothing more than a burden.

The cancer was gaining strength, pulling at me with its vicious claws, whispering its promise of eternal rest. This time felt different. It was taking me down fast, and it had me questioning everything. Maybe I was destined to die young? Until recently, I never questioned my cards. I simply accepted my fate. What if I was wrong to hold on to my newfound hope? To think that my painful life had purpose and what I was forced to endure wasn't for naught. What if my purpose was to help Gwen get back to Neverland? Maybe I didn't get a knight in shining armor so that my little sister could have many? My time in this existence was running out. I was fighting a losing battle.

"She doesn't look good, Nico." Lu walked up beside us, placing his hand on my knee. "She's cold. We need to life-bind, now." He pulled the heavy fur from his shoulders, tucking it in around my legs.

"We can't. Not yet." Nico seemed unfazed, his tone stoic as he forged ahead.

Lu stepped in front of his brother and growled, stopping Nico dead in his tracks.

"Lucius, I won't tolerate your attitude. We're almost to Whisperhold. Once we arrive, restoring Michaela is priority number one. Now step aside."

"What's life-binding?" I asked.

"Life-binding is the technical term for how we've been healing you. And we need to do it now," Lucius explained.

"Lu, I'm fine. Really, I'm just exceptionally tired. It's been a rough few days." I tried to reassure him, but he could see through my facade.

"She doesn't have time to wait. We need to stop—"

"Lucius!" Fallon snarled, interrupting him. She'd stopped walking and stared coldly at her brother. "We both know stopping to life-bind puts all of us at risk. I shouldn't have to remind you that Johan's trackers, and likely the commoners are searching for us. We cannot stop now. I will not sacrifice another brother. Take a breath, put your focus on arriving at Whisperhold in one piece, and I promise you we'll all do our best to help Michaela."

I heard Lucius sigh loudly and mutter something under his breath.

How bad did I look?

I'd never seen Lu posture to his brothers like that before. "You should put me down. If he realizes I can walk on my own, maybe he won't be so worried. I don't want to be any trouble."

"Don't worry about Lucius." Nico pulled me in tighter against his body. "You're no trouble. Rest your eyes, little bird. I promise, I won't let anything happen to you. We'll be at the safe house before dawn."

Clearly, I wasn't going to convince him. I pulled in a deep breath, enveloping myself in his delicious scent, and allowed the gentle rocking of his gait and the far-off songs of the owls lull me into sleep.

"Fuck." Nico's whispered frustration ushered me back to consciousness.

"We don't have time for this shit," Lucius fumed.

"Let's not jump to conclusions. It's probably just someone who stumbled upon the vacant dwelling and took advantage." Luca's words hit me like a truck. What was going on?

Off in the distance, silhouetted by the breaking dawn,

was a large log cabin. Smoke billowed out from the chimney and a faint flickering glow emanated from inside the windows.

"Michaela," Nico looked down at me. "I'm gonna need you to stay here with Fallon."

"Wait, I thought… what about the safe house?" I asked, trying my best to remain calm.

"We've arrived at Whisperhold. However, I'm not so sure how safe it is anymore." Nico gently set me on the ground. "Are you okay to stand, or should we sit you down?"

"I'm good." I smiled a moment before my knees buckled under me. Nico quickly reached for me, buffering my fall. "I guess I'm not as good as I thought. Maybe sitting is best."

He ushered me to the ground, sitting me up against a small tree. "I'm going to take Luca and Lucius to investigate what's going on. You stay here with Fallon. She'll keep you safe. Once we figure out who or what is at the house, we'll deal with it and come back for you both. Hang in there a bit longer, little bird." Nico repositioned Lu's heavy fur, draping it across my bare legs. "Fallon"—he turned to look at his sister, "I trust you to keep her safe and warm."

She pulled the cigarette from her lips, exhaling a large plume of smoke as she sighed, "I've got her. Go find out who the fuck is in our house. I'm over this shit."

"Lu, wait!" I blurted. Something was tugging at my mind. I had to say goodbye. "Please, before you go…"

"What is it, Dove?" He squatted down next to me, pulling his fur up closer to my chin.

"I feel silly saying it, but… Please be careful."

"Don't waste your energy worrying about me. I'll be fine, and soon we'll have you feeling better than ever. I promise." He leaned in, placing a gentle kiss on my forehead before joining his brothers.

"I've never seen Lucius so smitten with a female. What exactly happened in Neverland?" Fallon sat next to me, tucking her own legs under the fur beside mine. "Fuck the Divine. You're freezing! Give me your hands."

Fallon's hands felt like little heaters gripping my icy fingers. I leaned into her side, tucking my head into the crook of her neck, siphoning her warmth. "I don't know what to say." The words came slow, zapping what little energy I had left. "Lu has been doting on me… from the moment he saw me."

Fallon nervously looked over her shoulder, distracted from our conversation. "I'm sorry. I thought I heard something. Must have been a small animal foraging nearby." She turned her attention back to me. "It's not only Lucius, you know. Nico and Luca dote on you, too."

A cold, hard blade bit against my neck. A grating female voice hissed in my ear. "Identify yourselves. Now."

So this is how it ends. Please, God, the Divine, whoever's in charge here—let my death be quick and painless.

We couldn't see our attackers, but from the corner of my eye I could tell Fallon was in the same position. They had us both pinned between their blades and the tree.

"Or what?" Fallon gritted out. "We don't owe you an explanation. We have every right to be here as you."

"You're dressed awfully fancy for a camping trip," a male voice retorted.

"The weak one smells like rotting flesh," the female spat.

"Does she have the sickness?" the male asked.

"She certainly doesn't look good. Her skin is blue—or is it grey?" the female added to her growing list of compliments.

Was my color really that bad?

"Let us go now, and I'll make sure your lives are spared," Fallon sneered.

The male chuckled. "You'll make sure *we're* spared? Darling, I think you have it backwards. You're the ones who should be begging for your lives."

"Yeah." The female tightened her grip. I sucked in a breath as the blade bit deeper into my skin. "Looks like I'd be doing you a favor. If she's as sick as she looks. She'll be dying a horrific death soon anyway."

"If you so much as sever a single hair on her head, my brothers will see to it you're disposed of in the most horrendous way."

"Your brothers are being dealt with as we speak. They're probably dead already. Answer the question. Who are you?"

Fallon laughed. "You underestimate my brothers. Let us go now." She was losing patience. I could hear it in her voice. We were in no position to fight off these outlaws. I could barely speak, let alone defend myself.

"I'm going to ask you one last time, then I won't be so kind. Who are you?"

Fallon lifted her chin higher, giving the male full access to her neck in a defiant move. "I am Fallon, First Daughter of Artos, Princess of the Second Realm."

Immediately, the blade fell away from my neck. I sighed with relief, reaching up to find a small trickle of blood. It was a risky move, outing our identity while we were on the lam. What if they were Johan's trackers? Fallon had to be the most self-assured, reckless person I'd ever met.

"My Lady, forgive me. One can never be too cautious out here in Thornwyn." The male stepped out from behind the tree. He was well dressed, but caked in a layer of grime. His dark hair was mussed and slick with oil. He clearly hadn't bathed in several days. He bowed before us. "Artos was a great ruler. The realm hasn't been the same since his death. The name's Levi Brackenbark of the Raven's Hand. How may I be of service?"

The female was equally filthy, dressed in pants and a tunic. Her red curls were wild with frizz and leaves. "Fiona Briggs, humbly at your service, My Lady."

"That's more like it." Fallon stood, tucking the fur tight around me. "Call off the others before they do something they'll regret."

Fiona promptly took off towards the cabin without a word. I only hoped it wasn't too late.

"Levi, I need you to carry my friend back to the cabin. Can you do that?"

106

"Yes, My Lady. It would be my honor."

"Treat her with the utmost care… as though your life depends on it." Fallon smiled. "Because it does."

"Is she sick with—"

"What she's sick with is none of your concern."

Levi squatted by my side and gently scooped me into his arms. He smelled as bad as he looked. Though to be fair, they did say I smelled like death, I guess we were both a bit fragrant.

"Nice to meet you, Levi." I struggled to get the words out. They were barely a whisper. "My name is Michaela. Please, don't fear me." The surging adrenaline began to subside and take with it all the strength I had left. I could no longer hold my head up and it lolled against his chest. "I'm not contagious."

I felt him breathe a sigh of relief as the tension in his arms softened and he headed toward the cabin.

"Mic! Why is there blood on her neck? Give her to me now!" Lu's voice jolted me awake. I must've drifted off.

"You're not bringing a sick one in here, are you?" a foreign voice called from behind me.

"Cole," Levi warned. I felt him shake his head no in a silent plea to stop.

"Fuck the Divine, she's on death's doorstep." Another strange voice added to the melee. "You can't bring her in here."

"You will shut your fucking mouth before I shut it for you," Luca snapped. "This isn't your home. We don't owe you hospitality. One more word and I'll dispose of you all."

"Sir," Levi addressed Lucius. "She's losing color quickly." He passed me gently into Lu's arms, and he rushed me into the cabin.

"I've got you, Dove. We're gonna make you better now. Hang on a few more minutes. Luca! We need you too. She's severely depleted."

My mind was too tired for thoughts. Every limb felt as though it was a dead weight dragging me down. Begging me to rest. My body wanted nothing more than to sleep. My eyes continued to close, despite the effort to keep them open.

Lu laid me on the bed, ripped off his shirt. The mattress dipped with his weight as he climbed in beside me. He pressed my hand to his heart. Nico joined on the other side, mimicking his brother. Luca climbed in at the foot of the bed, pulling off my shoes and placing my feet against his warm chest.

Energy poured into my broken body, casting the room in a soft blue glow. I'd been through this before—but never with all three of them at once. The soothing energy shifted into an intense pulsing. Rhythmic whooshing filled my ears. Brilliant flashes of the forest flooded my mind's eye. Tufts of fur in vibrant copper, russet, and chestnut so real I swear I could feel it brushing through my fingertips. Then the room tilted, catapulting me into a haze of heat and shadow. Too vivid to be a dream. Too strange to be real.

. . .

I woke, exhaustion still clouding my mind. The room was quiet save for the crackling warmth of a fire burning nearby. Richly colored logs made up the walls, wrapping the room in their cozy, rustic arms. I rolled to my side and watched in awe as Luca sat on the floor in front of the hearth. His bare back, decorated with sprawling tattoos, flexed in the most alluring way as he wound his hair into a topknot. I'd been awake all of a few minutes, and already my stomach was filled with flitting butterflies.

Luca heaved a heavy sigh before turning back to find me staring sleepily at him. "Mic," he said softly, rushing to my side. "There you are. I've missed those beautiful brown eyes." He reached for my face, tucking my hair behind my ear. "How are you feeling?"

I yawned, stretching my sore limbs. "I'm sleepy, but feeling..." I paused, trying to find the words to describe it. "Whole."

He smiled, caressing my face. "Can I get you something to eat? You've been out for a whole day."

"Do we have anything other than fish?"

Luca chuckled. "How about some berries?"

"That sounds lovely, thank you."

He spun around, calling out to the others as he walked out of the room. "Guys! She's awake!"

I had but a minute to myself before Lu and Nico came barreling into the room.

"Michaela?"

"Dove!"

"Good morning? I think?"

"It doesn't matter. You've been asleep for quite a while." Lu helped sit me up, stuffing large pillows behind my back.

"How are you feeling, little bird? You gave us all quite a scare." Nico took a seat on the edge of the bed.

"I'm still tired, but..." I looked down at my hands, flexing the stiff joints. My color was back to its normal pasty, pale pink. No signs of blue or grey anywhere. "I'm feeling like myself again. Thank you all for saving me."

"My lady requested berries." Luca returned with a large bowl of bright yellow-orange berries and placed it in my lap.

"Slowly," Lu cautioned. "Your body's been through a lot."

I popped one in my mouth and was treated to a delightfully refreshing burst of sweet, tangy flavor. "Mmm, these are delicious."

"Salmonberries," Luca blurted, a smile plastered to his face. "They're my favorite."

"If you're done gushing about the salmonberries, I'd like to say hello." Fallon peeked her head over Luca's shoulder. "How are you feeling, Michaela?"

"Better," I mumbled between berries. "Are we alone?" I asked, vaguely recalling the unwanted guests we found upon arrival.

"Levi and the others are in the living room," Fallon huffed. "Nico's refused to send them away."

"They could prove to be useful allies," Nico chided.

"Or they could be playing us to get in good with Johan," Lucius grumbled. "If you ask me, they're as sly as snakes in the grass."

"Fallon, could you please shut the door?" I swallowed hard, forcing down the rising anxiety at the back of my throat. "I have something to share with the family."

Her brows drew together, and her head tilted slightly. "Sure. Is everything okay?"

The room fell silent. Every Bruin had their eyes glued to me. Lucius grabbed my hand. "What is it, Dove?"

"While I was unconscious, I had the most vivid dream." I shook my head, trying to clear the unease taking hold of my thoughts. They were going to think I was delusional. "I dreamt of Hunter. Only it was as though he was really there. I could feel him with me. Not like I knew he was there —I could actually feel his presence. He's imprisoned back at Mathenholm. He told me to give you all a message."

The room remained silent as the Bruins waited with bated breath.

"He said, 'You should leave Hiraeth now, before it's too late. Take our girl back to Neverland and live out the lives you've been destined to have. Do it for us.'"

CHAPTER IX
GIFTS
-LUCIUS-

She looked like a lost fawn sitting there in my father's oversized bed. Those beautiful brown eyes were wide with expectation, still haunted by her dream of Hunter. She was eager for answers—but all I could think about was how close we'd come to losing her.

At least the dark mark of death had vanished from beneath her eyes. A soft blush now colored her cheeks, and her scent had returned to normal—the warm shades of vanilla free of the sickly reek of death. I rolled my shoulders, trying to ease the ache that pulsed deep in my bones. Life-binding was never meant to be used so close to the edge. Fuck Nico and his cautious approach. He should've had this handled. Now I was taking matters into my own hands, and unlike my brothers, I wasn't held to the same standard. Perks of being the family fuck-up.

She shifted slightly, and the gauzy linen nightgown slipped from her shoulder. Her brow furrowed as she fingered the fabric. "Who changed me?" she asked softly, cheeks darkening to a deep scarlet.

"Don't worry, Mic. It was me," Fallon said quickly, and Michaela's shoulders sagged as the tension melted from her brow. "If you'll excuse me—I need a moment to... I'll be right back." Fallon stood from the bed and made a hasty exit. Hunter's message had shaken her, and I knew exactly where she was headed: straight for a brimshade fix.

Silence fell over the room. None of us knew where to begin. There was so much she didn't know—and she looked far too fragile to carry all of it at once.

"Will you all stop staring at me and tell me what's going on?" she snapped.

"It's your dream," Nico said gently. "I don't believe it was a normal dream."

"Try to rest, Mic. We can talk later," I cut in before he could start down a rabbit hole of Hiraethian gifts. She didn't need a damn history lesson right now—she needed sleep.

"No! Tell me now. I'm tired of being kept in the dark. I deserve to know what you've gotten me into." Her voice was firm, and I winced. She wasn't wrong. My brothers should've told her everything the moment they arrived in Hiraeth. But instead, they'd wasted time bowing to nobles once they realized our father was dead. May that bastard rot in the afterlife. He might've been a great king, but he was a shit father.

"You remember when I told you about my gift?" Luca said, sliding to the edge of the bed and taking her hand like a damn puppy dog vying for any opportunity to get in Mic's good graces. I was still pissed at his whole naked routine—fucking show off. "How I can wield the energy around me?"

She nodded.

"Well, Hunter's a dream walker. He can enter dreams—manipulate them."

"Does that mean he's alive?" Her eyes lit up with hope.

"I think it's a good sign," Nico said. "Usually, he can't project that far. I'm sure Johan has him bound and dosed with wolfsbane, but maybe with you… there's some kind of connection we don't fully understand."

"Wolfsbane?" she echoed.

"You've got a similar species of plant in your realm. Toxic to our kind. It weakens our gifts, blocks us from shifting. The crown uses it on prisoners to keep them in line. I'm sure Johan's not taking any chances—not with how powerful those three are."

I tried not to roll my eyes. I was thrilled that Hunter was alive—truly I was. But there was a darker part of me, something primal, that wanted Michaela for myself. The concern in her voice every time she said his name made my blood boil.

I'd seen the image in the Book of Astrium. There was

no denying that Michaela was depicted in the prophecy with seven bears. But she was only astride one. Who would she choose? The ancient text was written in the lost language. The last scribe who could translate the ancient tongue had died years ago, with no successor. Everything now was speculation. And if it came down to brother against brother for her hand, I wasn't above playing dirty.

"Do you think he'll visit me again? Can I send a message to him? Let him know we're coming for them," she rattled off in quick succession.

"Hold on a minute, Mic," Nico said, raising a hand. "I'm sure he'll visit you again. But right now, there's no feasible way to break them out of Mathenholm. We'd need an army to get them out. We have to be strategic—look at this from all angles before we move."

"We can't leave them there! What about Levi and the others? The Raven's Hand—they seemed loyal to the crown. Maybe they could help."

Nico's expression softened. "They might claim loyalty to the Bruin name, but they answer to no one but themselves. They're outlaws, Mic. Smugglers, thieves, blades-for-hire. The kind of people who rob a lord's carriage one day and feed a starving village the next. You never know which version you're going to get. We can't trust them. Not yet."

She raked her fingers through her thick, dark hair, a wild strand falling loose across her face. I barely managed to hide the smile tugging at my mouth. She was adorable when she was pissed.

"Mic," I started, hoping I could reason with her, "you were at death's door yesterday. We have to get you stable before we even think about storming the castle. There are thousands of soldiers within the crown's army who want nothing more than to see us hanging from a short noose."

"Really, Lu?" Nico chastised. The fucker had picked up her damn nickname for me.

"She wants honesty. There's no way to get them out of there. No. Possible. Way. I'm not going to lie to her."

The room fell into awkward silence, with all the animosity directed my way. The once comforting warmth of Whisperhold's wooden timbers suddenly felt suffocating.

"It's not what I wanted to hear," Mic said softly, "but I appreciate your honesty, Lucius. Can you please continue to be honest with me? All of you?"

"Whatever you want to know, just ask," Nico promised, his voice like a warm blanket, peaceful and calm. I felt the tension drain from my body and realized he was using his gift on us. I wanted to be pissed at him for swaying my mind into submission, but he was too strong to resist.

"Tell me about your gifts," Mic insisted. She was still defiant, but the crease in her brow had softened, and I knew she was feeling the influence of Nico's magic.

"For starters," I said, "Nico can reshape your thoughts, emotions, perceptions—make you feel whatever he wants. Like right now. I bet you were angry that he's kept so much from you, and suddenly it all melted away just like that." I snapped my fingers for effect. "Replaced by a sense of peace and optimism."

Her eyes widened. "Are you serious? Nico, are you manipulating me right now?" He was going to have to pour it on thick if he was going to weasel his way out of this one. He had the good sense to look ashamed.

"I'm sorry, Mic. It's a habit. I didn't mean to offend you. My intentions were pure. I don't like seeing you worry so much," Nico admitted.

"What other powers have you been using against me?" she snapped. "Did I even come here of my own free will?"

"None of them had access to their gifts in Neverland," I cut in before Nico could fumble his way through a response.

"And you? What's your secret power? The art of being a complete asshole to everyone around you?" she shot back.

I deserved that. No one had ever accused me of being a bastion of politeness, but still, her words stung more than I liked.

"I don't have a gift," I growled, refusing to lie but hating the taste of inadequacy on my tongue.

"At least not that we know of yet," Nico added quickly, trying to sound supportive.

"I'm the only one who doesn't," I muttered. "At least you can rest easy knowing that even if I wanted to, I can't influence you against your will."

"And what about the others?" she asked.

"Finn can hear your thoughts and feel your emotions. Jase can project spectral shadows that do his bidding. And

Gunner—well I guess that doesn't matter now…" Nico trailed off.

"Tell me anyway."

"He was a marksman," Luca said. "Perfect aim. No matter the weapon, no matter the distance, he never missed. The ultimate warrior."

The mood shifted quickly. Nico was clearly holding his gift in check for Michaela's sake, and grief threaded through the silence.

The door burst open. Fallon strode in without looking at any of us, making a beeline for Mic. Her expression was unreadable, mask firmly back in place and a purpose in her step. Two females from the Raven's Hand followed behind, each carrying buckets of steaming water.

"The tub is in the adjoining washroom," Fallon instructed them before pushing Luca aside and reclaiming her perch at the edge of Mic's bed. "It's about time you got some color in your cheeks. Death isn't a good look on you."

She had officially let Mic in. A bond was forming between them, something quiet but strong. "I've arranged for you to have a bath. The pump is down, so these ladies agreed to help. I'll get Luca to make it hot enough to melt the last few days right off you. You'll be good as new."

"Thank you, Fallon. That's exactly what I need right now."

"Yes, well, it seems like a much better option than… whatever interrogation was going on in here," she said, shooting all of us an exasperated look.

"I could use a human moment to collect myself," Mic admitted. "But this conversation isn't over. I know you're still keeping things from me."

"You heard the lady," Fallon said briskly. "Now is not the time for a heart-to-heart. Get out! All of you."

We hesitated.

"Out! Out! Out!" she barked when we didn't move fast enough. I'd forgotten how bossy my sister could be.

We filed out and I paused in the doorway, casting one longing look back at Mic. I hated leaving her. She looked so damn fragile, but I had to force myself to give her some space. After she had time to process, I'd find a moment to talk, just the two of us. Maybe then, I could stop screwing everything up.

"Lucius?" Fallon's voice caught me just outside the door. She closed it behind her and stepped into the hall, catching me before I could disappear. "I know there hasn't been time." She paused for a moment before throwing herself at me, wrapping me in a smothering embrace. "I'm so sorry," she whispered against my shoulder.

"You've got nothing to apologize for."

She pulled back and held me at arm's length. "Yes, I do. You should have never been exiled. I could've handled myself, but you and your damn gallantry had to take the punishment meant for me. Father would've been lenient with me."

"You're delusional if you think he'd ever overlook the fact that you murdered your newly wedded husband. The

Raperes would never have let that stand. You killed the heir to their house in cold blood."

Images of that night flashed in my mind—Fallon's piercing scream, the blood-soaked sheets, the plume of brimshade smoke curling from her lips as she stood over her husband's corpse with a serene smile.

"It wasn't cold blood," she said hotly. "My blood was boiling when I drove that blade through his heart. What he did to me… he deserved so much worse than what I gave him."

"I'm not judging you, Loni. If I'd known, I would've killed him myself. But I wasn't about to let Father give you over to his soldiers in some sick form of punishment. I couldn't live with that. Taking the blame only got me exiled. For you, it would've been far worse."

"You should've told our brothers the truth when they followed you to Neverland. It's not right that they think so poorly of you."

"It's not my secret to tell. It never has been. Besides—" I shrugged. "I don't give a shit what they think."

She looked up at me with glassy eyes, her chin trembling. "I'm the oldest. I'm supposed to look out for you. Not the other way around. I'll never forgive myself for that."

"I forgive you," I said simply. The tears came then, slipping down her cheeks. "In a strange way, you saved me. Exile got me out of the life Father had chained me to. And if I hadn't left, I never would've met Mic. I guess… I have you to thank for that."

Fallon wiped her face and grabbed my chin, tilting my head down so she could stare me in the eyes. "What are you doing?" she asked.

"What do you mean? I'm having a heart-to-heart with my sister," I said deadpan, trying to throw her off from the questions I knew she was about to ask.

"No," she said, eyes narrowing. "I mean, what are you doing with this girl? You really are smitten, aren't you? Is it because of the prophecy?"

I broke her stare. I was still trying to wrap my head around my feelings for Mic. The last thing I wanted was to talk about it. "We don't know what the prophecy says. All we have is a picture. The way I feel about her has nothing to do with it."

"But she can share power with the three of you. That's unheard of. There've only ever been paired fateds. And she's human. That shouldn't be possible."

"I know. Trust me—I've mulled it over a hundred times. But it happened. She shared power with all of us in Neverland. Maybe… maybe the rules don't apply to her."

"Keep telling yourself that," Fallon muttered. "Maybe one day, you'll believe it."

CHAPTER IX

I SQUINTED against the brilliance of the sun after days of traveling in the dark. The forest beyond Whisperhold slowly came into focus—ancient trees cloaked in vivid greens, splashes of wildflowers stubbornly clinging to the last breaths of summer, and the heady sweetness of ripe berries lingering in the air. For a moment, I stood still, overwhelmed by the realization that I had lived to see another sunrise in Hiraeth—something I never thought I'd see again. The warmth of the sun on my skin was a gentle, wordless reminder: I was home.

My father's hidden cabin, humble and weathered, could never rival the grandeur of Mathenholm, but its simplicity offered a solace the gilded halls never could. Here, in the moss-draped embrace of the forest, I felt a belonging no castle could grant.

I'd left Fallon in the hallway. She had the good sense to know when I'd said all I wanted about Mic. I needed more time to figure out why the thought of her drove me mad. Why I couldn't get that fucking kiss out of my head. She'd asked me to forget it ever happened—like there was any chance in hell I could forget that.

My cock had been uncomfortably hard most of the day, just thinking about how she molded herself against me, how soft her lips were, how intoxicatingly sweet her scent was. I'd smelled her desire—and the animal in me wanted to pin her down and rut with her on the forest floor. Shit. I couldn't keep going down this line of thinking. Not when she'd shut me down so completely.

I spotted Luca and Nico in the clearing by the creek. A few males had gathered around them. The more people who saw us, the more vulnerable we became. Any of these peasants could rat us out to the new monarchy.

The tall one they called Sawyer stood back, taking it all in with cunning eyes and his arms crossed over his broad chest. His silver-blond hair made him look older than his years. He was the one to watch. They hadn't said it outright, but I knew a leader when I saw one.

"The price on your head is substantial. They're offering more laurric than I could earn in two lifetimes," a gaunt, older male in tattered clothes rattled off as I approached.

"There are reports of crown soldiers pouring into Dunharrow. They won't stop until they find you," Levi confirmed. "It may take more than your family name to keep your secrets when that much is on the line."

Nico stroked his beard, listening carefully to Levi's warning. "I can't tell you how to make that kind of decision. I understand—coin like that could change your lives. My only request is that you think carefully. Do you trust Johan? You know the kind of lecherous scavenger he is. Would he simply give you all those riches and let you waltz into court with the other nobles? Or would he kill you the moment you gave him our whereabouts? It'd be a lot easier to slit your throat than allow you to live. A constant reminder of his mistakes."

The men murmured among themselves, shifting uneasily. Nico had painted them a bleak picture.

"The entire realm has fallen on dark times since the vulture took over," Sawyer finally spoke. "Once fertile land has stopped producing crops. Taxes keep rising, stealing what little we have to feed the gluttony of the noble houses. Sickness is burning through Dunharrow like wildfire. That's why so many are fleeing the city. It's not safe anymore. We can't go on living like this."

"I understand what—"

"You understand nothing!" Sawyer snapped. "You're a spoiled cub, masquerading as a king. When we needed you most, you were off drinking and spreading your seed across the cosmos. Your privilege made you too weak to lead."

The others rallied behind him, standing defiant before us. I could feel the tide shifting against us.

"Maybe now's the time to use your skills," Luca whispered to Nico.

"You think I want to manipulate these people after Mic called me out?" Nico muttered. "If I'm going to win them over, it'll be because I earned it."

"Spoiled cubs? That's all you see when you look at us?" I spoke up, unable to contain my anger. They looked to one another for confirmation, nodding, mumbling their agreement. "You know nothing—other than the lies the noble houses have fed you for years. Yes, we were born of royal blood. But we've spilled that blood in defense of Hiraeth. I stood side by side with the crowned Queen of Neverland—against the bastard prince."

A wave of chatter rippled through the group. The myth

of the bastard prince had spread far and wide across Hiraeth. The very mention of his name still sparked fear into those who knew the stories.

"We fought back against his dark armies. We were in his grasp—and still, we defeated him. When the other realms abandoned Neverland, the Hiraethian princes were there. We fought and won in a war of the realms. We are battle-hardened soldiers. The things we've seen would give you nightmares for the rest of your life. Now tell me—what have *you* done for this realm?"

Silence followed. Hostile stares faded into awe and wary admiration.

"I understand your hesitation," Nico said quickly, seizing the moment. "I'll prove myself to you. Prove I'm worthy to lead. Just give me a chance."

"And how do you propose to do that?" Sawyer asked.

"How any real Hiraethian settles things," Nico said. "We let our beasts sort it out. Me against your best male."

"What are the terms?" Sawyer stroked his beard as his eyes filled with mirth.

"If I lose, Whisperhold is yours. I'll even surrender myself—no resistance, no fight. But only if you let my family go."

His damn honor would be the death of him.

"And if you win?"

"If I win, you lead me to your camp. Introduce me to the leaders of the Raven's Hand. Let me share my side of the story. If they don't like what I have to offer, we part ways."

Sawyer stepped back as the group huddled around him, whispering among themselves.

"This is stupid," I muttered. "We should finish off any loose ends and keep our heads down. We can't trust them."

But it was a waste of breath. I could see it in Nico's eyes —his mind was made up.

"I thought Neverland had changed you," he said. "You're going to have to learn to trust someone, or we'll never save her."

He patted my shoulder just as Sawyer stepped forward again.

"We accept the terms," he said, spitting into his palm and offering it to Nico.

There were few who could rival Nico's size. Sawyer was one of them. He stood at least an inch taller, with shoulders broad enough for two grown males. Nico didn't flinch. He stepped forward and shook his hand with a firm grip.

"Who do you name as your champion?" Nico asked.

"It's you and me, cub king," Sawyer said with a smirk.

Nico's jaw clenched at the insult, but he nodded and turned to prepare for the fight. "If things go sideways, take Mic and Fallon north to Vaelryth," he told me, tugging his hair back into a knot as he pulled off his tunic. "There's a portal in the ruins we visited as kids."

"Here's a thought—don't lose," Luca muttered, taking Nico's clothes before gripping his shoulder.

Nico shrugged him off, refusing the energy boost Luca tried to give him.

His honor was going to get us all killed.

Sawyer handed a worn leather chest plate and a belt heavy with weapons to Levi. The armor was clearly too small for his frame—and far too expensive for a man living in the slums of Dunharrow.

Either his family had fallen from grace at some point, or he was a damn good thief. Either way, he wasn't someone to be messed with.

The two of them stood ready in the clearing, the sun bleeding through the ancient canopy and highlighting the patch of green. Nico raised the small blade in his hand and ran it over the veska on his chest—the small scar we all bore. The place where we drew the blood offering to release our beasts from their corporeal bonds.

The air shifted around me, hitting like the soundless blast of a solric as Nico shifted. A massive bear now stood where my brother had been. He shook his molten copper coat, raw muscle rippling in the sun as he settled into his new form.

My skin crawled with the urge to join him, the veska on my palm ached. My own beast keened for release. But this had to be a fair fight. If any of us got involved, everything Nico was trying to accomplish would fall into chaos.

Sawyer sized him up briefly before drawing his own knife across the veska scar on his forearm. Another wave of energy crashed through me as Sawyer's beast tore free. I stared in stunned disbelief as a giant white bear shook its enormous head.

"A spirit bruin," Luca breathed. "I didn't know they still existed."

I'd heard of spirit beasts—a high gift given by the Divine. They were rare and said to possess special powers. Legend claimed they could weave the veil of the cosmos to their need and walk between the spirit realm and the physical world. I'd never seen one before in my life. Some even considered them a myth.

"Fuck. What the hell has Nico gotten us into? Start thinking of our best escape route," I muttered to him.

Sawyer's every movement was fluid, each step calculated, like he carried something otherworldly on his sloped shoulders. His pale blue eyes regarded Nico with an unsettling calm, a stillness that seemed to seep into the surrounding forest.

I leaned against a tree at the edge of the clearing, arms crossed tight over my chest, trying to appear indifferent. But I wasn't fooling anyone—least of all myself.

Nico broke the silence with a piercing roar before he charged. Black taloned claws tore into the rich soil as he barreled toward Sawyer. Their bodies collided with a thud, like falling trees, echoing through the glade. Nico went on the offense, his hooked claws drawing first blood. Crimson standing out in stark contrast against white fur. It was a glancing blow, and Sawyer shifted with preternatural grace.

Nico was relentless, vicious teeth snapping, trying to

seize the upper hand. Each strike was a contest of primal strength, but it wasn't clear if this was a battle he could win. Sawyer's sheer size alone gave him the advantage, and Nico couldn't avoid his brutal counterattack. Blood spilled from his wounds, leaving dark, matted patches on his copper coat. He moved with precision, but there was tension in his movements I hadn't seen before.

Sawyer was relentless, every swipe of his claws was a brutal reminder of how high the stakes were. Each impact vibrated through the ground, and I swallowed hard, trying to keep the bile from rising in my throat. The onlookers cheered, their excitement grating on my nerves. Idiots. They had no idea what was really at risk. To them, this was entertainment. To us, it was survival.

Luca circled the perimeter, scanning the males to ensure Nico had a fair fight. A solid clap on the shoulder was all it took to render one useless. All of their energy drained away in a heartbeat. His magic was impressive, but it made him a piss-poor sparring partner.

I sensed her presence before she stepped beside me. Her scent hit like a wave, ripping my attention from the fight. My breath hitched, and for a moment, all I could do was stare. Her eyes burned with determination as they locked onto mine.

"What's going on, Lu?"

"Mic—" Her name tumbled out of my mouth like an admission of guilt. "I didn't expect you to... are you..." I stammered. My brain scrambled for a coherent thought. Damn it, pull yourself together.

Her gaze flicked past me to the brawling bears. "You didn't answer my question. What's happening?"

"It's…" I glanced over my shoulder, watching Nico and Sawyer collide again, their snarls ripping through the clearing. "It's nothing. Nico's got it handled. They're just sorting things out." I shifted to block her view, hoping to distract her. "I thought you were still bathing?"

She crossed her arms. "The cabin was shaking like it was about to collapse. Seeing as we're being hunted, I thought I'd make sure you weren't all dead."

Guilt prickled at the back of my neck. "Shit, Mic. I'm sorry. We didn't think—"

"No, you didn't," she snapped. "None of you have given much thought to my feelings at all, have you?"

Her words hit like a blow, and I stiffened, unsure how to respond. Before I could find the right words, she sighed, her expression softening.

"But that's beside the point. Are you sure Nico has it handled?"

I hesitated, glancing back at the fight. Sawyer landed a brutal blow, and Nico stumbled—his coat saturated with blood. My throat tightened. "He's the best fighter I know," I said, though my voice lacked conviction. "He won't lose."

"Why are they fighting?"

My jaw clenched. How much should I tell her? She

deserved the truth—but how could I explain this without making her worry?

"Nico's proving himself," I muttered, the words bitter in my mouth.

Her brow furrowed. "Proving himself? This is about pride? Are males in every realm this predictable?"

"It's not just that," I said, voice low. "The Raven's Hand wants to turn us over to the crown. Johan's put a price on our heads. Nico's making sure that doesn't happen."

The color drained from her face. "The crown," she whispered. "So we're back to running for our lives?"

Before I could answer, a roar ripped through the air— raw and primal. Michaela flinched, and instinct took over. I grabbed her arm and pulled her back just as Sawyer's massive paw swiped too close for comfort. We hit the ground hard, and I wrapped myself around her, shielding her as dust and debris filled the air.

"Mic, are you alright?" I asked, voice tight. My hands trembled as I held her shoulders, searching her face for any sign of injury.

"I'm fine," she said breathlessly. Her wide eyes met mine, and for a moment, the world stilled.

Guttural sounds rumbled behind us. I scrambled to get Mic back to her feet. I knew what was coming. The bond we all shared with her was harder to ignore when our beasts took over. Sawyer had crossed a line. Nico would never let it stand.

The vibrations grew until a roar exploded from Nico like

rolling thunder. He charged Sawyer with renewed fury. The bears reared up, colliding mid-air. Nico's jaws locked around Sawyer's neck, shaking his head and slamming him to the forest floor like a rag doll.

The ground shuddered, the land itself crying out beneath the weight of the vicious blow.

The white bear lay vanquished on the ground, making no attempt to fight. Nico pinned him down, standing victorious over his opponent. He let out another thunderous roar, reverberating over the crowd—settling the score once and for all.

"Is he… dead?" she whispered, shooting a wary glance at the silent crowd, who stood in shocked awe.

"No, he's just showing reverence. He'll be fine," I said, keeping her tucked against my side in case these vagabonds lacked a sense of honor.

Nico stepped back, blood dripping from his muzzle. His copper bear ambled out of the clearing, the remaining males parting to let him pass. He returned a heartbeat later, a tangled mess of leaves, crimson flowers, and their dirt-caked roots clutched in his jaws. His eyes found Michaela, and my chest tightened. He moved toward her, each step deliberate. My body tensed, but I stayed locked in place— torn between the instinct to protect her and the knowledge that this moment wasn't mine to interfere with.

Nico lowered his massive head and placed the tangle of flowers at her feet. Crimson dahlias caught the light, their vibrant hue mirroring the blood-stained ground.

My heart sank.

I knew the significance of the gesture. It wasn't simply an offering. It was a claim.

Before I could process it, Nico shifted back. Bruised and battered, he knelt before Michaela, his devotion written in every line of his body.

I looked away, fists clenched at my sides. This wasn't a battle I could win.

"Nico, are you alright?" Michaela's voice was soft and full of concern. She knelt beside him, her hands fluttering over his injuries. I forced myself to stay back, watching as she tore a strip of fabric from her dress to tend his wounds.

"I'm fine," he said, voice rough but steady. His dark eyes flicked to me briefly before returning to Michaela. "I'm sorry you had to see that."

Sawyer's voice interrupted. "Son of Artos," he called, his tone surprisingly light despite his injuries. "I almost had you."

Nico chuckled, rising to his feet, shaking Sawyer's hand. "You're stronger than I expected."

Sawyer smirked, wiping blood from his face. "The spirits were worried I was about to join them. If I'd known your fated was here, I might've been more cautious."

My stomach dropped. Fated.

The word hung heavy in the air, and Michaela stiffened. She opened her mouth to speak, but Nico cut her off.

"It was a fair fight, Sawyer. You're the one who kept the fact that you're a spirit shifter a secret. I didn't know any still existed." A smooth transition—one he clearly didn't want to explain in front of her now. How could he? None of us really knew how we fit into the tangled mess of bonds that tied us to this beautiful human girl.

"We're more common in trying times. Maybe it's the Divine's way of evening the odds," Sawyer said, saying nothing further on the subject.

"Let me get cleaned up, and we'll make plans for you to fulfill your part of the bargain."

Sawyer's grin widened as he swept into a dramatic bow. "Let me start by introducing you to the leader of the Raven's Hand." His voice rang out like a performer on stage. "Sawyer Briarhart, humble captain of the most notorious band of outlaws this side of the Caldreim River. At your service, My Lord."

A flicker of intrigue crossed Nico's face before he schooled his expression into a mask of mild indifference, tilting his head as if he'd expected nothing less. A practiced smile curved his mouth.

"Well then, lead on, Captain Briarhart. We leave in the morning. Lucius," he called, turning to me. "You'll stay behind and keep an eye on Mic while we're gone."

"I'm coming with you," she announced, like it was already decided.

Nico stared at her, a faint smile tugging at his lips. I wondered if he would go back on his word and use his powers to sway her mind. Anger began to stir in my chest. I wouldn't let him crush her free will with a flex of power.

"Alright, Mic. If you're up for it, you can come," he finally agreed and she let out a breath, a look of triumph lighting her face.

"Fair enough. We leave at dawn," Sawyer proclaimed, settling the matter.

As everyone began preparing to leave, I stayed close to Michaela, my protective instincts on high alert. I couldn't voice everything I felt, but one thing was certain: no matter what happened, I'd do everything in my power to keep her safe.

Even if it meant watching her slip further out of my reach.

CHAPTER X
THE RAVEN'S HAND
-MICHAELA-

Our traveling party consisted of three Hiraethian princes, four members of an outlawed band, and one human girl. Needless to say, I felt a bit out of place. We'd left Fallon behind to watch over Whisperhold with a few members of the Raven's Hand, and I was desperately missing her company.

We traveled all day, moving deeper into the heart of Thornwyn Forest. The dense wood, which had once felt like a sanctuary, no longer felt inviting. The pines towered overhead, leaving us in a perpetual twilight, while shadows lurked in every corner. It made my skin crawl and anxiety pool in my stomach. The gnawing trepidation had become my ever-present companion, worming its way through my veins until everything seemed like a potential threat. I couldn't imagine why anyone would choose to set up camp in these woods.

Sawyer let out a whooping call that reverberated through the trees, which was quickly answered in kind. A resounding announcement of our arrival. "Welcome to our home," he said as we crested a small knoll.

Situated in a wooded dell was a sprawling encampment. Without Sawyer, I would have walked right past this place without a second glance. The shelters were simple, thatched with pine boughs and hidden under a thick carpet of fallen leaves—perfectly camouflaged against the wooded backdrop. I'd expected a bustling settlement, something like the Lost Boys' camp in Neverland, but this place appeared abandoned. A greeting bellowed down from a male on a high platform nestled in the trees.

"It's not much, but it's ours. Come, my friends, let me make introductions," Sawyer said, clapping Nico on the back.

As they spoke, people emerged from the shelters. I'd expected rogue males—outlaws and vagabonds—but this was a community. Females stood beside elders while dirty-faced children peeked out from behind their skirts with wide, curious eyes. Warm glances and wary looks greeted our arrival.

"Comrades!" Sawyer's voice boomed in the clearing, quieting the whispers. "We've brought news. The Divine has chosen for our paths to cross with the prodigal sons of Artos. Please join me in welcoming Lucius, Luca, and Nico to our humble home." A hush fell over the crowd, stunned looks plastered on their faces. "Now, before anyone gets their feathers ruffled, I ask that you listen to the stories they have to tell with an open mind. Let us settle in, show these lads some hospitality, and we'll meet at the communal fire for the evening meal."

They gave the four of us our own shelter. I was mortified when they moved others out to make room for us, but Nico stopped me when I tried to turn it down. "I know you're trying to be polite, but turning down hospitality would be a mark of shame for our hosts," he explained. So I smiled and thanked them profusely.

A sweet elderly female named Maeve was the only one brave enough to approach us, though I couldn't tell if the choice had been hers or not. She said little, bowing politely, but her deep-set eyes were curious, watching my every move. Smile lines framed her face, but her lips remained pressed in a firm line, as if she were holding back a flood of questions for the human girl in their midst. I couldn't shake the feeling that I was little more than a circus sideshow to these people. She dropped off a skein of water, a few hand-carved cups, and bedrolls before shuffling back to a waiting gaggle of nosy females who failed miserably at appearing inconspicuous.

Dusk settled in fast. What little light remained was quickly swallowed, like a Divine hand pulling a blanket of night across the sky. The brothers stayed close as we took up a place of honor by the fire. None of them voiced any concerns, but I could sense their unease—the stiffness in their posture, the knowing glances that passed between them.

The snap and pop of the fire was a welcome distraction from the otherworldly sounds moaning through the trees. I could've sworn I heard voices calling to me.

"Do you hear that?" I whispered to Luca, who had taken the seat beside me.

"I don't know. What am I supposed to be hearing?" he asked, leaning in conspiratorially.

I paused, waiting for it to call to me again. A soft hiss spilled over the leaves, a beautifully haunting siren's song in a strange language I couldn't understand. "There! Did you hear that?"

"Is the wind making you nervous?" he asked, raising an eyebrow.

"Apparently the wind in Hiraeth can talk," I mumbled, and he let out a soft chuckle.

"That may actually be true. They say this forest is haunted."

"Really? I don't know if I should believe you or if you're trying to make a fool of me."

"Aw, Mic, I would never do such a thing," he said, gripping my shoulder and pulling me in closer. "Lucius," he called, leaning across me to speak to his brother on my other side. "What do they say about these woods?"

"That they're full of pompous assholes," Lu grumbled, chucking a stick at him.

"He's talking about the Lady of the Wood," Sawyer cut in, his deep, resonant voice laced with warning. "Legend has it there's a witch who lives in this forest. Her dark magic runs wild through the trees, waiting to devour any living creature that wanders here. That's why we made camp in Thornwyn. The myths help keep the king's army away."

"So the legends are false, then?" I asked, needing reassurance that I wasn't losing my mind.

"I can't say for sure. None of us have fallen victim to the Lady of the Wood, but there are things I've seen that I can't explain. Levi here swears he saw her walking through the trees—but he's also a glutton for attention."

"I heard that, Sawyer, you bastard. I saw her! Prettiest witch you've ever seen," Levi shot back.

"Now we know you're lying," Sawyer said with a chuckle. The crowd relaxed, laughter easing the tension.

The females began serving the evening meal. Soup that was little more than broth with a few meager vegetables. Yet to these people, it was a feast. I watched in silence as they smiled and laughed over so little, and a hollow ache grew in my chest. How were these people going to help us save Jase, Finn, and Hunter when they could barely feed themselves? Nico said we needed an army. But all I saw were hollow faces and weary bodies barely clinging to survival. Even if we could trust them, they didn't look like warriors. And yet they were the only hope we had.

"Help yourselves to the ale. Food may be scarce, but the crown always ensures we have enough drink to warm our hollow bellies," Levi said, pouring the pungent liquid into outstretched cups.

"Seems like the grain could be more useful as a food source," Nico suggested.

"Nah. They killed the will of the people. The alcohol keeps them numb. There's no fight left in us... so we drink," Sawyer said before taking a hearty swig.

Once everyone was served and cups were overflowing, Nico began his story. He was a gifted storyteller, captivating the group, and I found myself spellbound—seeing my own experiences through an entirely new perspective.

"I am not my father—I know this," he said in conclusion. "I do not wear his crown, and I have not yet earned the honor of your allegiance. But I know this to be true: the Bloodstone Sigil now rests on the finger of a traitor. A male whose only ambition is to oppress his people for his own benefit. He would see you divided and broken. I am young, yes. Unproven in your eyes. But I am also unshaken. I do not stand before you as a spoiled prince seeking glory, but as a son, seeking to honor his father and reclaim what has been stolen. I don't expect you to make a decision now. All I ask is that—for the sake of my father—please consider what I've said tonight, and envision what kind of Hiraeth you want to see tomorrow."

Silence settled over the fire.

"Have you seen the Book of Astrium?" Sawyer asked, seemingly out of nowhere.

"I have," Nico answered solemnly.

"Is there some prophecy you're hiding from us?"

"I've seen the book, but the prophecies remain a mystery. There are no scribes who can translate the text. That's common knowledge."

"I have to assume that you know something we don't. Or else why throw your lot in with the lowest of society? How are we supposed to fight this war—because that is what you're asking. Levi over here, they took his farm when he couldn't pay the taxes. Maeve's fated died in the brig for stealing a loaf of bread. Fiona lost her husband and daughter to the illness. The nobles haven't lifted a finger to stop the plague. It's Dunharrow's dirty little secret. And every one of us has a story like that," Sawyer said. My heart broke for these people, for all the suffering they'd endured. And from the darkness clouding Nico's eyes, I knew he felt it too. "And by your own words, Johan wears the Bloodstone Sigil. If he's not the divinely chosen king, how is that possible? How do you plan to overthrow him when he controls all four houses?"

"The Bloodstone Sigil is a tool. There is more to being king than donning a piece of jewelry. Have faith, Sawyer. I'll prove I'm the rightful bearer of the ring."

"You're asking a lot, cub king."

"If you choose not to fight beside me, let me ask you this —what do you have left to live for?"

I TURNED OVER AGAIN, for what felt like the hundredth time. The bedroll felt tight and constricting, as if the blankets were conspiring to suffocate me. My thoughts swirled in a dark current of consciousness that I couldn't escape.

The night had ended without the Raven's Hand officially joining our cause, though Nico seemed optimistic. I'd returned to our shelter with Lucius and Luca, while Nico had taken the first watch with Sawyer. I'd tried to settle in, anticipating a peaceful reprieve from the weight of my life— but I couldn't stop thinking about everything Sawyer had said. What was a fated? What was the Book of Astrium? Was that the mysterious book I still had hidden at the bottom of my pack?

The questions burned in my mind, and I had no answers. Conveniently, there'd been no time to ask the princes. I suffered in silence, my wandering mind wholly unsatisfied. Lu slept soundly only a few paces away, his soft, rhythmic snores were getting under my skin.

I froze when I heard Luca stir. He quietly got up and poured himself a cup of water. The warm light cast from dying embers caught on the sharp planes of his bare chest, highlighting the tattoos that canvassed his skin. He was a work of art. The image of him naked was burned into my memory, one I'd tucked away and revisited an embarrassing number of times. Now, I ached to trace the lines that scrolled over his chest and up his neck.

Maybe this was the moment I'd been waiting for. Luca had never tried to hide his affections, and there had been very few private moments between us. This was a gift I needed to take advantage of. He was the most forthcoming of the brothers. If I could sweeten him up—play into his flirtatious nature—maybe he would finally answer the questions that stretched like unmapped constellations in my mind.

"Luca," I whispered quickly, before I could think better of it. "Are you awake?"

"No, Mic. I am sound asleep," he said with a chuckle. I was grateful for the veil of night to hide the flush rising in my cheeks. Once, conversations with men had come easy. But romance? That was foreign, awkward—uncharted territory I'd never dared explore. Everything I knew about love came from the sappy movies Gwen and I used to binge.

"What I meant to say is... if you're awake, would you be interested in some company and possibly sharing a bit of warmth with your favorite human?"

Before I'd even finished speaking, he was collecting his bedroll and laying it beside mine.

"Whatever you wish," he said as he slipped under the blankets and wrapped his arm around me. "You know, this works better skin to skin."

I smiled in relief, relaxing into his presence. Being with him was easy. I was the one putting up roadblocks where there didn't need to be any. I decided then and there to let my guard down—to indulge his shameless flirting and see where it might lead.

I wiggled out of my bedroll and into his, settling my back against his bare chest. My own insecurities kept me from meeting his eyes. "Is this better?" I asked.

"You tell me," he said. The warmth of his body radiated over me, his power channeling heat into our shared space. I melted into him, his body cocooning mine, and a soft moan escaped as I snuggled closer.

"I can be your designated warmer from here on out," he offered, his scorching fingers tracing lazy patterns along my arms.

"That sounds awfully official."

"Absolutely. I'll dutifully sleep beside you every night and make sure you're never cold. It's a very important position. And if you moan like that every night," he added, nuzzling the back of my neck, "I'll know I'm doing a good job."

"Like a real-life teddy bear."

"Teddy? Who's Teddy?" he asked, pausing his ministrations. It took me a moment to remember—we came from completely different worlds.

"Never mind. It's just a human thing," I deflected. How do you explain a beloved plush bear to someone who could actually shift into one? It sounded absurd in my head.

"I don't know what or who a teddy bear is, but I'll be your Luca bear." As he said it, I felt the telltale tingling of his magic mixing with mine. A soft blue light glowed beneath the blankets as he began to life-bind with me.

"You don't have to do that, Luca. I'm feeling fine, really." I tried to shift away, but his strong arms locked me in place.

"I know I don't have to. But I want to. I know when you're hurting, and I can't stand it anymore."

"Why? Why are you all so determined to help me? Is it because I'm a fated?" The question tumbled out before I could stop it. I couldn't waste my chance to bring it up.

He tensed. Silence lingered, fragile and loaded. I wanted him to tell me so desperately I half-hoped my will alone could force the answer out of him.

My heart fell as the seconds ticked by. When I'd convinced myself he wouldn't answer, he broke the silence. "What do you know about fateds, Mic?"

"I know Sawyer referred to me as one after he fought Nico. What does it mean?"

"Sawyer never should've said that. It's a beast thing," he said simply, and I knew he was trying to brush me off.

I wouldn't let it go. I steeled myself and turned in the bedroll to face him. His honey-colored eyes looked dull in the dark, shadowed by things that had nothing to do with the lighting. "Don't do that to me, Luca. Not you."

"Oh, so it's fine for you to shut me out—say it's a 'human thing'—but I'm supposed to explain every nuance of my world?" he whispered, a sharpness in his tone. "I never thought of you as a hypocrite."

"That's not fair," I said, trying to shove him away and failing miserably. "A teddy bear is just... it's something trivial. A child's toy in my realm—a stuffed likeness of a bear that kids cuddle at night or share tea parties with."

"Really? You snuggled with a likeness of me as a child?" he asked, a smile tugging at his lips.

"Don't change the subject. You can't keep hiding things from me. Do you really think so little of me that you can't even share your world with me?"

"Honestly, Mic, I'm not sure how to explain it. I don't even know if the term 'fated' applies to a human. You should've asked Nico. He's better with words."

"I'm asking you," I pleaded. He tried to turn away, but I cupped his jaw and brought his gaze back to mine. "Please."

He huffed and placed his hand over mine, holding it there as his eyes closed.

"A fated is... something better shown than explained," he murmured, and when his eyes reopened, they burned with something I hadn't seen before. "Have you ever been drawn to something so completely?" he asked, brushing a lock of hair from my face, tucking it behind my ear. His fingers left a scalding line along my jaw. His thumb grazed my lip, rubbing over the sensitive skin, setting off a firestorm. "Have you ever felt a bond you couldn't explain?" His voice wrapped around me, unraveling logic with every syllable. My thoughts scattered under the weight of his stare. "Have you ever wanted something so badly you'd kill for it?"

He leaned in, and I swore I might die if I didn't have more. When his lips finally touched mine, it was electric. My soul felt radiant. I knew that I was exactly where I was supposed to be.

His kiss was soft, a question lingering on his lips. I leaned into it, giving him my unspoken answer. He responded in kind, deepening the kiss. His tongue found mine, both of us exploring with equal hunger. One hand tangled in my hair, the other roamed across my body, worshiping my curves and palming my breast. His thumb grazed my nipple and I felt it in my core. I'd never been touched like that before—my body bloomed to life, hungry for more.

"No! Mic!" Lucius called into the darkness, voice thick with emotion. We froze. Panic overtook me, smothering every ounce of pleasure from my body. I braced for Lucius to call me a whore, to say I disgusted him. But instead, only a stream of incomprehensible mumbles followed as he rolled over in his sleep.

"He's only dreaming," Luca whispered. I let out a shaky breath. The moment was gone. The passion snuffed out. Darkness returned to Luca's gaze. "You should try to get some rest, Mic. You need to keep your strength."

Neither of us were ready to face Lucius's reaction. Still, a hot wave of guilt settled in my chest. What had I done? Had I manipulated Luca into making some egregious mistake?

My sister had five husbands—but that wasn't the norm.

And how could something like that ever work between brothers?

"Luca, I—"

"You don't have to say anything. Nothing's changed. I'll still stay and keep you warm." He kissed my forehead gently, and rolled onto his back, resting a tattooed arm over his eyes.

That was it. The conversation was over. And now I was more confused than ever.

CHAPTER XI
SPIRIT BEAR
-MICHAELA-

I 'd expected my wounded pride to banish any hope of rest—the sting of it sharp enough to keep me awake for the rest of the night. But as I lay beside Luca, his steady presence and the warmth radiating between us lulled me into a fitful sleep.

Hunter tore into my dreams again. But this time, it was different. Images cycled through my mind like flashes of lightning: a dark cell, his beaten and battered body, the glint of light off bloodied steel. His green eyes, shrouded in pain, met mine a moment before his screams reverberated in my head, trapped there within the dream.

I bolted upright, my heart pounding. The nightmare Hunter had shared with me left a lingering sickness in my stomach. I knew what I'd seen was real, and I could do nothing to help him. Yet again, I was proving to be useless to those I cared about. I rubbed at my eyes, trying to banish the dream and my futile tears. I realized I was alone in the shelter and was thankful for the moment of privacy.

A shiver ran down my spine. I heard the screams again, but this time, it wasn't in my dreams. The high-pitched trill pierced the quiet of the dawn. I scrambled to my feet, stumbling through the makeshift door and into camp. People had begun to gather, and I breathed a small sigh of relief when I saw Nico striding toward me.

"Is everything alright, Mic?"

"Yeah, I'm fine. I heard screaming and I—"

A female came barreling into the camp, barefoot and disheveled. "Help me! Please! I need Sawyer!" she cried as she stumbled and fell to her knees. The females of the Raven's Hand rushed to her, all of them speaking at once. They helped her to her feet, she clung to their clothes, a wild, desperate look in her tear-streaked eyes.

"I need him! I need him now! He has to come!" she wailed.

"Luella, it's alright. I'm here. What's happened?" Sawyer arrived, gently taking the hysterical female into his arms, holding her by the shoulders to meet her gaze.

"It's Mica. He's got the sickness." A collective groan rippled through the crowd. "I went to the healer first, but he refuses to see him anymore. I'm losing him, Sawyer. I don't know what to do." She burst into heavy sobs, her whole body shaking. "Please," she choked out. "You have to be there to reconnect his spirit, in case…" Another sob swallowed her words, and Sawyer pulled her closer, her body sagging against him.

"Let me gather some things and we'll follow you back to Dunharrow," Sawyer said, handing her off to the others in the camp.

Nico grabbed his arm. "What's going on?"

"Her boy is dying."

"Can you tell me more about this sickness? My sources at Mathenholm couldn't provide many details."

"Of course not. They're too busy pretending it's not happening," Sawyer scowled. "When the fever sets in, it erodes the bond to our beast. Once the connection is severed…"

"They die," Nico finished grimly, the color draining from his face.

Sawyer nodded. "I have to go back with her."

"If there's nothing that can be done for the boy, why risk it? It isn't safe with the Hiraethian army scouring the cities."

"My power lets me skirt the line between the living and the spirit realms. When the boy dies, I'll have a small window to reconnect his spirit with his beast, or they'll wander aimlessly for eternity, searching for one another. The only way to reach eternal rest is if a spirit shifter reunites them." He shook off Nico's grip and stalked off. "I don't have time to explain things you should already know."

"I'm coming with you. I need to see it for myself. Maybe we could be of some help," Nico called after him.

Sawyer stopped in his tracks, turning to scrutinize Nico as if he could measure his worth with a single look. "It's at your own peril, cub king. But maybe it's exactly what you need to see."

Lucius and Luca arrived just as Sawyer departed. "Grab your bags, brothers. We're headed to Dunharrow," Nico said, ducking into our shelter.

"Dunharrow? Are you serious—or are you partial to suicide these days?" Lucius asked. "And what about Mic? I don't trust any of them enough to leave her here."

"No, she's coming with us," Nico said and my thoughts faltered, derailed entirely by the weight of his words. The carefully rehearsed argument I'd crafted dissolved on my tongue. I'd come ready to fight for my place beside them, but it seemed the battle had already been won.

"I don't care if you want to throw your own life away, but I draw the line when it comes to her. You're being reckless," Lucius said, crossing his arms over his chest.

"She isn't a child. She knows her own mind, and if she wants to come with us, then she comes. None of us can control when the Divine calls us back. Even if she remains here, there's no guarantee she'll be safe. And like it or not, Lucius, her fate is inextricably tangled with ours. Wherever we go, she goes."

Nico's words silenced any further protest from Lu, their truth painting a bleak picture. His shoulders sagged with the reluctant realization that there were no safe places left for us in this realm.

"That is, only if you want to come, Mic. You're no stranger to grief. Maybe you could be a comfort to them?"

"Umm… yes. Yes, of course I want to go. Thank you, Nico." My voice caught as I spoke. For the first time, I felt useful—not an obligation to be looked after.

"The woman mentioned a healer," Nico continued. "This might be our chance to find someone who can help you. I don't know how long you have until your body fails, and I can't sit back and watch that happen again."

I KNEW we were close when the stench hit us. Extending an unpleasant welcome that reached us before the city gates even came into view. A pungent mix of waste and unwashed bodies hung thick in the air like a suffocating fog. I adjusted the shawl hiding my hair to cover my nose in a futile attempt to block out the smell.

Dunharrow sat in a dry valley. Once, it might've been lush and green, but now it was a graveyard of stunted trees and dried brush. Cobbled streets were littered with garbage, pushed into corners and accompanied by hordes of flies. Drab buildings in varying states of disrepair lined the streets. Faded paint peeled from warped wood. Shops and homes stood like ghosts of their former glory. Busy patrons filled the streets, their heads bowed, somber expressions fixed on their faces. Amid the filth, vagrants mumbled incoherently, clutching bottles and begging for handouts.

Sawyer led our party deeper into the trenches of the town. I tried to remain vigilant, watching him for cues, but my gaze kept wandering, appalled by the squalor surrounding us. He stopped abruptly and held up a fist, signaling us to halt. With a quick flick of his head, he darted into a narrow alleyway, and we followed close behind.

Nico's hand closed firmly around mine, anchoring me to his side as we sprinted for cover. The world blurred past until the shadows swallowed us, and he spun me into his arms, pulling me tightly against his chest—a silent promise of protection in the dark.

The streets became unusually quiet for a heartbeat. People scattered like rats before a storm. The heavy tread of marching soldiers echoed off the walls. A detachment of the crown's army passed by our hiding place, their armor clinking softly. We pressed ourselves against the wall and held our breath until the last soldier disappeared.

"Hurry, please. My place is just down the street," Luella whispered, frantic to get back to her son. She led us to a dilapidated building and down a long hallway. Several scantily clad females stood in open doorways.

"Looking for a good time?" they cooed as we passed. This was no place for a mother and child, but just as that thought entered my mind, two scruffy children slipped out of an apartment and disappeared down the street, no parents in sight.

Luella brought us into a cramped room at the end of the hall. The smell hit me first. It was different from the reek of the streets—stale and cloying, a blend of sour sweat and moldy bread. I inhaled through my mouth, but the taste still coated my tongue. It felt like the walls had absorbed the boy's illness, amplifying its presence.

He lay in the corner on a sagging mattress. A colorful patchwork quilt was tucked beneath his chin, a bright splash in an otherwise muted space. Though his body trembled with chills, his cheeks were flushed, and beads of sweat dotted his brow. Moans slipped past his chapped lips, though his eyes remained closed. He couldn't have been older than eight or nine. My heart sank, knowing there was nothing I could do.

A female sat on the edge of the bed, soaking a rag in a chipped basin and swabbing his forehead.

"This is my sister, Laurel. And this"—Luella rushed to the child's side—"this is Mica."

Laurel rose to greet us, offering a tired but warm smile. "My place is across the hall. I can take some of you over there to rest. We don't have much food, but—"

"No need," Sawyer interrupted. "We brought our own. We're here to help, not to be a burden. Let me take a look at him." He strode to the bed, placing one hand on Mica's forehead and the other over his chest. "How long has he been getting headaches when he shifts?"

"It's hard to say. They were so mild. His weren't as bad as the others, he—"

"How long?" Sawyer demanded and Luella jumped.

"It'll be three full moon cycles in two days," she answered, her whole body sagging with the admission.

Sawyer sighed, then turned to Nico. "We'll settle in and wait. It won't be long now."

"It begins with headaches after every shift. No one has lived past three moon phases once those start. We'll know it's time when he bleeds from his eyes, ears, and nose—a final offering to his beast. And then he'll be gone. I'd say within the day. Will you wait with me, or return to Thornwyn?"

"She mentioned a healer. Do you know where I can find him? I have things of value. I could barter for the boy's treatment," Nico offered.

"There is a healer. A damn good one, too. But there are some things even his magic can't fix. There is no cure for this. It's a death sentence."

WE SAT in silence through the night. Death had taken up residence in the room—I could feel it in my bones. Mica's mother never left his side, doing whatever she could to ease his suffering. At dawn, she began to falter, her eyes heavy with exhaustion.

I stood and stretched my stiff joints. Nico's gaze tracked my every movement as I pulled out my bedroll. I laid it beside the bed and knelt beside Luella, gently resting my hand on her shoulder.

"Why don't you get a bit of sleep? I've set something up beside Mica. I'll sit with him and wake you if anything changes."

"Only an hour. That's all I need. Not a minute more," she mumbled, too tired to argue.

I settled beside the boy, studying his face, wondering if this was what I looked like each time death came for me. The mattress dipped, and I looked up to see Nico sitting across from me.

He offered a soft smile that didn't quite reach his eyes, but I saw the intention behind it, and I was grateful for his presence.

I grabbed the water basin and gingerly wiped the boy's brow, careful not to touch his skin. For some irrational reason, I was afraid to touch him. I'd cheated death too many times and I feared that touching him might siphon off what little time he had left. Like I was some kind of leech, draining life from those around me. Tears welled in my eyes, and for a moment, I wished I could trade places with him.

"Mic, are you alright?" Nico asked quietly.

"No, actually. I don't think I am." I let my head fall forward, hiding my tears behind a curtain of hair. "None of this is fair. I should be the one in that bed, and yet somehow I'm still here. Why doesn't he get a second chance? How can your Divine be so cruel?"

"I try to remind myself in times like these that the Divine has a greater plan and that we're not meant to know all the details. Life would lose its meaning if we did."

"I feel so helpless. When I knew I was dying, my sister fought so fiercely. Even after I gave up, she held onto hope with everything she had. I wish I had that kind of passion so I could give it to this boy." The words felt like grit in my throat, coated in grief as I spoke them. I knew I'd regret being so raw in front of him, this king-to-be, but it felt cathartic.

"We all have a purpose. Sometimes it's small. Sometimes it's fleeting. But I know his mother would tell you his life had meaning. And I know there's a reason you're still here, Mic." He brushed a tear from my cheek, gently tucking my hair behind my ear.

"The only purpose I've served is being a burden to the people I care about. Poor Michaela—always needing to be saved. Sometimes I wish you'd all give up and let me die already," I whispered, laying bare the darkest corners of myself.

"When I wake up in the morning, it's your smile I think of. It reminds me this harsh world can still be soft, and kind, and beautiful. It's your words that lift my spirit, your courage that gives me strength, your selflessness that makes me want to be more." He sighed, turning my chin toward him, his chestnut eyes meeting mine. "You awaken something in me—a desire to rise above my flaws. To become someone worthy of standing by your side."

My heart stuttered to a stop. The crushing despair and the fetid room melted away, leaving only him and me. His words made me feel whole, stirring a light within me that had no right to bloom amid such darkness.

"Nico. That was… I…" The silence lingered between us. The things I wanted to say wouldn't form into the right words and so they sat, unspoken, heavy on my tongue.

The floorboards creaked beside us, and I jumped.

"His eyes are the softest shade of brown," Luella's voice broke the spell between us and the cruel world came crashing back down around us. The boy still lay in the bed, fighting for each breath, and guilt over our stolen moment washed over me like a wave. "They're the same shade as yours," she added, motioning to Nico. "I'd give anything to look into his eyes one more time, to hear him tell me he loves me. But I don't think the Divine is listening to my prayers anymore."

I tried to think of something—anything—that might sound remotely comforting, but everything that came to mind felt wrong, and the silence lingered.

A weak moan escaped the boy's lips. I reached for him, forgetting my fear, and stroked his cheek. He settled under my touch, the furrow in his brow softening. His face tilted into my palm, and then, fluttering lashes gave way to wide, brown eyes.

"Mica?" Luella breathed, in stunned disbelief. I recoiled as though his clammy skin had burned me, stumbling backward from the bed. What was happening?

"Mom—"

"Oh my Divine! Laurel! Come quick—it's a miracle!" she shouted.

"Mom, listen to me!" Mica insisted, sitting up and grabbing her shoulders. "I have to go."

"Go? Go where? The Divine just healed you," she said, as the room filled with onlookers.

No, Mom. It's not a cure—it's a goodbye. We've been given a gift."

"I don't understand," she whispered, the hope already draining from her eyes.

"I get the chance to tell you I love you. I'm supposed to tell you not to worry. That I know where I'm going, and I'm gonna be okay." Luella trembled as he spoke, silent tears spilling down her cheeks as she struggled to stay strong for him.

"I love you too. But I can't bear to lose you," she pleaded.

"Yes ya can. The Divine tells me so. You're gonna be okay, too."

The two embraced in a moment so heartbreakingly beautiful, I could feel tears spilling down my cheeks.

Mica looked past his mother's shoulder, his warm brown eyes locking onto mine.

"I have a message for you," he said, and a chill burrow down into my bones. What message could he possibly have for me? I'd never seen this child before.

He pulled away from Luella and stood on the bed. A radiant light emanated from him, momentarily blinding me. When the colors of the room returned, I focused on his eyes—no longer the soft brown, but a swirling, milky white.

"The words are buried, a tongue long turned to dust," he said in an ethereal voice. My throat went dry. "But one still draws breath who can speak them. Not all who bleed are broken. Look for the flame that chose silence over glory. When the shield breaks from within, he will speak. The true wound has yet to be struck. While you reach for what was taken, the veil is surely woven. If you fail to see it, you will lose them all."

I nodded slowly, unable to speak. I had no idea what the words meant, but I could feel an otherworldly presence in the room. This message had come from some higher power. Before I could contemplate what had transpired, Mica collapsed back into the bed. The milky cast to his eyes disappeared, shifting back to brown.

"Goodbye, Mom," he whispered in his own innocent voice. His lids fell shut, and crimson tears slid down his cheeks. Blood trickled from his nose and ears. Sawyer stepped beside me, his expression wary. I could feel him assessing me, seeing me differently now.

A few last rattled breaths escaped the boy, and when it finally fell silent, his family began to wail.

I stood frozen, horror spreading through me as a faint blue apparition of the boy materialized beside the bed. Staring past his mother, his eyes locked on Sawyer and me. I glanced around the room. Nico, Luca, and Lucius were all staring at the dead boy laying in the bed. But Sawyer stared at the apparition, stepping toward him.

Another figure appeared, this one of a young wolf, padding forward to join the boy. My jaw dropped in shocked awe as the boy and the wolf reunited. Mica fell to his knees, wrapping his arms around the beast, who lapped at his face with a joy that transcended death. Together, they faded away.

"It's done," Sawyer said. "You can rest easy, Luella. He's passed over to the eternal resting grounds."

After allowing Luella some time with her son, I helped the females clean the boy's body and prepare him for burial. Nico and the others stood in quiet counsel with Sawyer. I didn't hear a word they said. I was still in shock, struggling to process what in the bloody hell I'd just witnessed.

"Dove," Lucius said softly as he came up beside me. "Sawyer knows of a healer. Levi agreed to take us there. Nico and Luca are going to meet with a few leaders of the Raven's Hand scattered across the city and regroup with us at Whisperhold. Do you think you're up for the trip?"

CHAPTER XII
FORMER IS YOUR KEY WORD
-MICHAELA-

We followed Levi blindly into Thornwyn Forest. I tried desperately to focus on the positive. I was on my way to see a healer—but I couldn't shake the weight of the day's events pressing down on my mind.

I was no stranger to sadness, but this was different. There was a new layer now, something that defied logic. Why was I seeing spirits? Gunner, I could make sense of—but Mica? I had no connection to that child. And his message had left more questions than answers. "The words are buried, a tongue long turned to dust." What did that even mean? "Look for the flame that chose silence over glory." He spoke in riddles, and I had no clue what he was trying to tell me.

I should've been focused on healing. My quest for a cure

was finally within reach. Levi had informed us that Maxfield —or 'Medicine Max' as the townspeople called him— preferred to remain a recluse, living deep within the woods. He'd retired from his time serving the throne and, much to his chagrin, had become something of a local legend. He was our best chance at finding the cure I so desperately needed.

After what felt like several hours of walking, a large glade seemed to appear out of nowhere. Nestled among the tall grass was an unbelievably charming little cottage. The quintessential fairytale abode. Rudimentary fencing lined the property, old and crumbling, offering no real protection. The wattle-and-daub structure had a thatched roof cloaked in moss. Ivy crept along its corners, and drying herbs dangled from the eaves, gently swaying in the breeze. Barrels of rainwater stood beside woven baskets of harvested goods, ensuring its habitants were well stocked.

"This is where you'll find Medicine Max," Levi said, stepping through the broken fence. "He's the best we can offer here in Thornwyn. Mind you, he can be a bit ornery."

A stone walkway led us to a dark wooden door crowned with an impressive rack of stag horns. Levi knocked loudly.

"Go away! No one's home!" a dry, raspy voice shouted from within.

"You just answered us, you old bastard. Open the door —it's Levi."

Unintelligible grumbling came from behind the wooden

slab as several locks slid free from inside. The door slowly creaked open, revealing a weathered old male. Deep wrinkles mapped the lines of his face, emphasizing sunken cheeks. His thick white beard complimented his hauntingly light grey eyes, giving him a wizard-like appearance. He wore tattered linen robes and looked like he hadn't bathed in weeks—not exactly a trait I sought in a healer, but I didn't have many options left.

"What do you want? I'm busy."

"Are you Medicine Max?" I asked sheepishly.

"I don't practice medicine anymore. Now, if you don't mind, I'm busy." He tried to shut the door, but Lucius shoved his foot into the frame, stopping it in its tracks.

"Are you not a former healer to the throne?" Lucius questioned, pushing the door open wider.

"Former is your key word. The king I served is long dead. I'm retired, and I intend to stay that way. Now kindly remove your foot."

My options were diminishing quickly, and my heart pounded with growing dread. How long could I hold out without a healer? The last few weeks had made it painfully clear—I wouldn't last without intervention. "Please," I blurted before taking a breath and regaining my composure. "I need your help."

"Without your assistance, she'll die," Lucius said bluntly, but the old male showed no sympathy.

"Humans don't belong in Hiraeth anyway. She's better off dead."

A low growl rumbled from Lucius's throat. "One more comment like that, and *you'll* be the one needing a healer."

"Now, now, friends, let's not be hasty," Levi said, stepping in. "Maxfield, Michaela's a worthy case. Do it as a favor to the Raven's Hand."

"We can reward you greatly for your service," Lucius added.

The old male sighed. "For fuck's sake. Come in."

Levi stepped aside, letting Lucius and me through the doorway. "I'll head back to camp. You two are in good hands." He leaned in and whispered into my ear, "Give him a chance. I promise—he's really a big softie."

The inside of the cottage was as charming and cluttered as its exterior. A single bed, mussed from the night's sleep, sat across from the fireplace. Rows of bound herbs dried above the mantle in the warm glow of the fire. A small washing basin overflowed with dirty dishes. A table with two chairs and a wall full of shelves packed with bottled concoctions made up the rest of the space. I was relieved not to find a makeshift surgical suite hidden in a corner. My mind had been bracing for something far worse in the hands of an otherworldly healer. Not that healthcare back home had been much better. The pain and suffering inflicted on me in the name of 'healing,' was nothing short of nightmarish.

"I haven't got all day. What seems to be the problem? Is she sick with the illness? I've told them all before—I can't cure malediction."

"She's going through the Tribulation," Lucius said, skipping pleasantries entirely.

"Sit." Maxfield pointed to a chair, his interest clearly piqued. Gently, he tilted my head down and drew a deep breath, smelling the top of my head. "Mm-hmm." He lifted my chin with icy hands, pulled down my lower eyelids, and stared into my eyes, silent and focused. His hot breath smelled stale. "Stick out your tongue."

It was the most ridiculous examination of my life. He asked nothing about my history, showed no interest in my symptoms. It felt like a child playing doctor.

"She looks fine to me."

"Respectfully, Medicine Max," Lucius said, the condescension heavy in his voice. "We've been life-binding to keep her alive. Faerie dust offered some relief, but she burns through it rapidly. She's doing well *now*, but it's becoming less effective."

"Life-binding, you say…" Maxfield scratched his brow, glancing between us. "Interesting, only—"

"Yes," Lucius interrupted, cutting off whatever the old male was about to say. "She needs a more permanent solution to help her transition into her magic safely."

"The cancer—I mean, the Tribulation—has been coming on stronger. Even life-binding doesn't last the way it used to." I said as Lucius reached for my hand. Though my focus was on Maxfield, I could feel Lu staring at me. His concern was palpable.

"Tribulation can't be cured. It's not an illness."

My heart sank. Everything I had been offered a taste of —a future, romantic love, a family of my own—was ripped away in a single breath. And I believed him. I'd heard it my entire life: *your* cancer is terminal. Why would Hiraeth be any different?

"You call yourself a healer?" Lucius snapped. "Dove, he doesn't know what he's talking about. Iver Pennington assured us she could be healed."

"Never heard of him." Maxfield turned his back on us, busying himself with his wall of jars. "If he can cure Tribulation, then why aren't you seeking his help, instead of bothering me?"

"Iver died in service to the House of Bruin. He was the royal healer," I informed him. Maxfield's lips parted slightly at the mention of the Bruin name, and for a brief moment, his brow furrowed. It was so subtle that if I hadn't been staring at him, I would have missed it. "He was a kind, gentle soul. Unlike some others I've met."

I hadn't thought of the old healer in some time. Not because our time together in Neverland didn't matter, but because remembering him hurt more than I liked to admit. He was the first person who'd given me a real reason to believe a cure might exist—the first to look at me and see more than a lost cause. And for that, he paid with his life. He hadn't been a warrior, just a kind soul who happened to find himself between Tiger Lily and her obsession with ending the Darling bloodline. He chose to protect me anyway. And she chose to kill him for it.

"Shame. He also lied to you," Maxfield said bluntly.

"Iver had no reason to lie." I was quickly losing patience. If Maxfield couldn't help me, then we were wasting precious time. "Lucius, maybe we should go."

"If a cure is what you're looking for, then I can be of no help. True remission from the Tribulation must be earned. I can, however, offer you sprite ash."

"What's sprite ash?" Lu asked cautiously.

"Just a little something. Stronger than your run-of-the-mill faerie dust."

"Last time I checked, sprites didn't produce dust." Lu's head tilted, his brows pinching together. "Are you sure you're not trying to sell us snake oil?"

"I never said sprite dust. Sprite *ash* is what's left when you use a mortar and pestle on the remains of deceased sprites."

Lu's face contorted with disgust. "I wish I never asked. Thank you for clearing that up. I think."

"Wait—you're killing sprites? For medicine?" I asked, horrified. I may have been desperate to find something, anything, to extend my time here with the Bruins—but killing innocent fae and desecrating their remains? I had to draw the line somewhere. My life wasn't worth sacrificing another.

"No one said anything about killing sprites. What kind of monster do you take me for? Sprites live very short lives. Their remains are ethically sourced. By offering their empty vessels, they inherently become everlasting."

"So their bodies are willingly donated?" I asked for clarity.

"Yes. I told you—I'm not a monster. Do you want the medicine or not?"

"Will it help?"

"It'll definitely help. You can expect it to act similarly to faerie dust, only its effects are more potent and last longer. The true cure will come from honing your growing magic." Maxfield held up a jar, revealing a silvery-blue dust.

"But I don't have any magical abilities. How am I supposed to hone my skills?"

"You have magic, Michaela, or you wouldn't be going through the Tribulation. Your Divine trial is to figure out what that magic entails—and learn to harness it instead of letting it burn like wildfire, consuming your vessel."

"You're an alchemist. You understand magic. Could you help me make sense of my abilities?"

Maxfield sighed. "I am but a healer. And a retired one, at that. I have no time for teaching."

"Sounds to me like you've got all the time in the world," Lucius sneered. "I can reward you handsomely. How much for the jar and your tutelage?"

"The jar?" Maxfield laughed. "No, no. All you'll need is a small vial. A little smear will do the trick. As for my tutelage—some things aren't for sale."

Lucius huffed, unable to hide the irritation on his face. "Let me formally introduce myself: Lucius, Seventh Son of Artos, rightful Prince of the Second Realm."

Maxfield gave an exaggerated bow. "Forgive my casualness, My Lord. Your father was a great leader."

Something flickered across Lu's face. It vanished in a blink, but not before I noticed the tightening of his jaw. A cold glint dulled the warmth in his eyes. He didn't respond to the compliment. Didn't even acknowledge it. Instead, he pivoted sharply, his tone clipped.

"Let me ask you again. How much?"

Maxfield, unbothered by the sudden shift, shrugged. "Life-binding, you say?"

"It's the only reason she's still with us."

Maxfield sighed. "For a son of Artos, I'll make an exception. Let's say... five hundred laurric?"

Lucius nodded once. "Deal."

THE AFTERNOON SUN filtered through the forest canopy, casting twinkling shadows across the leaf-littered ground. We had a long walk back to the cabin ahead of us.

"Should I try the sprite ash now?" I asked Lu as we passed the outskirts of Maxfield's glade.

"Do you need it?" He raised a brow. "How are you feeling?"

"No, I'm good—I don't need it. But I'd rather know now what I'm getting into than wait until I'm desperate for help." I didn't want to put all my faith into a remedy that might not work.

"Actually... now that you mention it, I like the idea of you trying it while we're still fairly close to Maxfield's. You know, in case something goes wrong."

"Bloody hell, Lu! I hadn't even thought about possible side effects. That settles it." I glanced around for a place to sit, settling on a moss-covered rock. "Do you think it needs to go somewhere specific?" I asked, rolling the vial between my fingers.

"He said, 'a little smear will do the trick.' I'm guessing you use it like faerie dust."

I popped open the vial, pressed a fingertip to the opening, and tilted it. A sparkling silver-blue powder clung to my skin. "It's pretty," I said, then hesitated before smearing it across my cheekbones like an ethereal highlighter. Except... it wasn't makeup. It was the remains of a small creature. I tried to remind myself that the sprites had offered their remains in hopes of eternal life—but the idea still gave me the ick. I decided it was best not to think about it.

Almost instantly, my head spun. Colors became more vibrant. The sounds of the forest sharpened. Energy surged through me, and a giddiness bloomed—like the warm buzz of one too many drinks. My limbs, and my...other parts were tingling. I began giggling uncontrollably.

"This is getting interesting," Lu said, biting his lip to hide a smile.

"I wonder if it can make you fly—like faerie dust?" I focused for a moment, centering on all the things I had to be happy for.

Nothing happened. My feet remained firmly planted on the ground. I guess sprite ash wasn't *exactly* like faerie dust. "Well, I'm not flying, but... I feel amazing! Lu, I haven't felt this good—ever. I feel like I could run a marathon."

"I'm not sure what that means, but seeing you full of life is intoxicating. There's a light in your eyes I've never seen before."

I felt childlike—simple and uncomplicated. Most of my life had been filled with fear and trepidation. Hospitals and doctors, needles and chemo. But before the cancer, before the dreaded terminal diagnosis, I'd been filled with hope and innocence. Aspirations for the future, dreams of becoming the fairytale princess from Gram's stories.

It was all back. The fire, the clarity, the weight of who I was. The real Michaela—raw and unadulterated.

And not only did I have the attention of my very own prince charming—I had caught the eye of several.

I decided right here and now: I wouldn't waste this moment.

I stood and tapped Lu on the knee. "Tag, you're it!"

Then I ran, not a care in the world.

"Wait—what?" Lu stammered, confusion flickering across his face as he scrambled to his feet. A heartbeat later, realization hit, and a mischievous grin spread over his lips. "Oh, it's on. You better run fast, Dove!"

I could hear his heavy footsteps gaining behind me. I ducked behind a wide tree, trying to still my breath.

"You think you're clever?" Lu called out. He was close. I could hear the leaves crunching under his boots. "You can't hide from me."

I screamed as his head popped around the trunk. He was fast—but I wasn't ready to give up the chase.

I bolted, narrowly escaping his grasp. Laughter erupted from deep in my belly as I weaved through the trees. I couldn't remember the last time I'd had so much fun.

Lu was right behind me. He reached for my shoulders, catching me off guard and spinning me around—only to trip on a root, knocking us both to the ground with a thud.

He landed on top of me, his face mere centimeters from my own. "I'm so sorry—are you okay?" he asked, nervously brushing the hair from my face, inspecting me for injuries.

"I'm fine," I giggled, breathless. "Better, now that you've caught me." Before I could second-guess it, I lifted my head and kissed him. The heady scent of his musk, mixed with the dried leaves of the forest floor, roused my carnal desires.

He kissed me back—hard. Warmth spread through me as I parted my lips, letting his tongue slide into my mouth. It was tender yet possessive, and it ignited sparks within me. I slid my hands into his hair, gripping his head to mine, eliciting a low growl deep within his chest. I didn't want it to end. His lips were soft, yet firm, his tongue gentle, yet demanding.

Lu's hands roamed my body with a desperate need.

Palming my breast through my dress, drawing a soft moan from my lips. My body was alive with nervous energy and I wanted more.

"I need to touch you," he groaned, pulling at the edges of my clothing. His rough hands explored the delicate curve of my waist, sending a shiver down my spine.

Wetness pooled between my legs, and I shamelessly ground against him seeking friction. I could feel his own excitement pressed firmly against my thigh. As though he could read my mind, Lu began to explore further down my waist, gliding over my dress and finding that sweet spot between my legs.

I couldn't believe this was really happening. I'd all but forgotten we were lying on the forest floor. Butterflies bloomed in my belly, and I fought my body's urge to tremble. I spread my legs, giving him silent consent to continue.

Lu gently stroked my core, stoking the fire blazing within. "No one has ever made me feel this way," I confessed through panted breaths.

Lu stopped abruptly, pulling in a large breath. "This can't happen here. In the middle of Thornwyn Forest, on the ground. Michaela, I'm... I'm so sorry." He quickly sat up, brushing the dead leaves from his clothes.

Embarrassment consumed me. Did I do something wrong? I had never been with a man before. While my friends were out messing around with boys and going to clubs, I was either in the hospital or recovering at home.

Chemo chic wasn't exactly a desirable look. My dating history was non existent. Maybe I wasn't any good at it?

"Lu… Was I—?"

"Michaela." He reached for my chin, gently turning my face to him. "I want nothing more than to take you right here, right now. But you deserve better than a quick rut in the dirt. I won't defile your virtue."

"Is it that obvious?" I asked, dreading his answer.

"I'm not sure I understand what you mean?"

"My virtue. You mean my virginity, right? My inexperience?" I rubbed my hand down my face, trying to wipe the embarrassment away.

His gaze softened. "I didn't realize you were a virgin. Please, forgive my forwardness. I never would have—You did nothing wrong. In fact, you did everything right." He glanced down to his obvious erection, adjusting himself. "I'm glad I stopped. Michaela, your first time should be special. Not a lust-fueled quickie. You are everything I could ever desire in a woman. When that time comes, it'll be perfect, simply because it's with you."

"You really want that… with me?"

"There's nothing I want more."

I couldn't help the smile spreading across my face with his confession.

"I've wanted you since the first moment I saw you— through your window. The night I brought your sister back from Neverland."

"But I was on my deathbed?" My face scrunched up. I

was literally on hospice when Gwen came home. "Lu, that's weird."

"It only seems weird because you don't understand how being fated works."

"You're right. I don't."

He took a deep breath. "Do you feel an unexplainable pull… no that's not the right way to describe it." He reached for my hand. "When we life-bind, do you feel a connection?"

"I feel the transfer of power, yes."

"It goes deeper than that. I don't know exactly how to explain it other than just saying it. Michaela, life-binding is only possible with… fated mates."

There was that word again. I had asked Luca to explain it to me once and that only led to more confusion and a lusty encounter. "Fated mates?"

"Yes. You and I are—"

"Fated mates," I said the words out loud again, not sure I grasped exactly what he was saying.

"Nico, Luca, Finn, Jase, Hunter… all of us are inexplicably connected to you."

"…Gunner?"

"Yes. Gunner, too." Lu's head dropped at the mention of his lost brother. "We're all fated… to you."

The idea of fated mates was a common theme in the fairytales Gram told us as children. I always assumed it was a romanticized notion. A way for us to hold on to hope that there was one true love destined for you somewhere out in the world. But if what Lucius was telling me was true, I was fated to not one, but seven.

Suddenly, it all made sense. The little flirtations, their need to protect me. My overwhelming attraction to all of them. "So... what exactly does that mean here in Hiraeth? Are we all together? Like, in some strange prearranged relationship?"

"That's not quite how it works. Though, I'd be lying if I said I didn't want you as mine." He looked down at our joined hands, then took a breath. "Even if it means I have to share you with my brothers."

"Share me?" It sounded weird saying it out loud. The idea of being shared by the six of them had me overwhelmed. Gwen had married five—and it didn't seem strange at all when I saw them together. They made it work.

"If my brothers feel for you the way I do..." He took another deep breath, rubbing the back of his neck. "It wouldn't be right to deny them that truth. Please know Michaela, you are in control here. I cannot speak for my brothers. But if you want me, I am yours. I belong to no other."

"Why didn't you tell me sooner?"

"I tried, Dove. So many times, I tried. What we are experiencing—it's complicated. I still have a lot of questions myself."

"Thank you for being honest."

"I'm sorry. I should have told you sooner." He reached

for an errand strand of hair, tucking it behind my ear. "You deserve nothing but the truth."

There was a tenderness in his eyes I hadn't noticed before. A longing for understanding and forgiveness. A vulnerability that softened something deep inside me. I wanted him in ways I couldn't comprehend and he was offering himself to me here, now.

Time had never been promised to me. Was I wasting it hung up on the variables? What if this was it? My only chance for a happily ever after? So what if my *ever after* wasn't long. It wouldn't change the undeniable pull I felt to each and every one of them. What was I waiting for? I'd be a fool to deny myself a chance at happiness simply because my time might be cut short. This *was* it! I simply had to accept him.

"If you are mine," I said softly, "then I am yours."

Lu's smile lit up his whole face. "Nothing makes me happier than to hear those words." He gently gripped my chin and pulled me in for a gentle kiss. "Let's get back to Whisperhold. I have something I want to share with you." A cunning smirk spread across his face.

"I've never had a boyfriend before," I admitted as he helped me up.

"Well," he said, brushing the leaves from my dress, "now you've got something better. You have a mate."

CHAPTER XIII
MY BODY MY SOUL
-MICHAELA-

Whisperhold was quiet. Nico and Luca hadn't yet returned. The sun had begun to set, blanketing the sky in a soft pink glow. Fallon was in the kitchen busying herself with the night's meal.

"Hey! Just you and Lucius? Everything go okay with the Raven's Hand?" she asked, a brimshade cigarette burning between her lips.

"Dove, why don't you tell her about Maxfield. I have something I need to take care of. I'll be right back." Lu kissed me on the cheek before leaving me with his sister.

"Nice to see you too, Lucius," Fallon called out after her brother.

"We've had… a particularly heavy day." I wasn't sure how much I should tell Fallon. Too much had happened since I'd last seen her—things I hadn't even begun to untangle. "Levi brought us to a healer. Maxfield. He's apparently retired from serving the throne."

"Maxfield? I don't remember that name."

"He said the king he served had long since passed."

"Gods, how old was he?" Fallon's lips curled into a frown, trying to calculate Maxfield's age.

I chuckled. "He looked... mature. A bit rough around the edges, but he offered me help. I'm going to work with him personally to learn how to harness my magic. In the meantime, he gave me something called sprite ash to keep the Tribulation in check."

"Sprite ash? I've never heard of it."

I pulled the vial out and offered it to Fallon. "He said it's similar to faerie dust. Don't ask how it's made." I scrunched up my face. "It seems to be quite powerful. Honestly, I've never felt better."

"Finally, some good news." Fallon held the vial up to the light. "It's quite pretty."

"I know, right!"

"Michaela," Lu interrupted, reaching for my hand. "If you'll join me."

"Uh, okay. Fallon, we'll fill you in on the rest later."

"But what about the Raven's Hand? Lucius, where are your brothers?"

"Later," was all Lu said as he dragged me back toward the king's room, ignoring his sister's questions. Fallon shook her head and went back to preparing the night's meal.

Standing in front of the door, Lu placed his hand on the knob. "Close your eyes."

I cocked my head to the side. "Okay." Blindly, I let him lead me into the room. I could hear the crackling fireplace warming the space. The butterflies from earlier in the forest were back and swarming in my belly. Lu's thumb caressed the back of my hand as I stood anxiously awaiting his surprise.

"Go ahead, open your eyes."

The room was filled with flickering candles, casting a romantic glow over the space. The bedding had been turned down for the evening, beckoning me into its warm embrace. He was trying to romance me, and it was working.

"Aww, Lu, this looks beautiful."

Pulling me in front of him to face the fire, Lucius wrapped his arms around my waist, nuzzling into the back of my neck.

"I thought maybe"—he kissed that soft spot below my ear—"we could further explore what we started in the woods?" Lu's lips continued to roam my neck.

My nerves were fighting with my libido. Before I could stop myself, I giggled awkwardly, failing miserably to mask my nervousness. I wanted this, but I had no idea what I was doing.

"Lu, I..." I hesitated, spinning around to face him. I'd been waiting for this moment, and here I was, fucking it up.

"Do you still want this?" he asked.

"Yes!" I said, a little too excited. "I mean yes, I do. But I'd be lying to you if I said I wasn't nervous."

"And that is why we are going to take our time."

He tilted my chin toward him and claimed my lips in a gentle kiss, his tongue stealing a taste before pulling away.

"There's no need to be nervous, Dove." Lu tugged at my belt, releasing the buckle and letting it drop to the floor with a thud. "I'm going to take care of you."

I couldn't believe this was really happening. He pulled off his shirt in one fluid motion. My God, his chest was chiseled perfection—artfully adorned with large, sprawling tattoos. I'd always been attracted to Lu, but I'd never allowed myself to really look at his body. At least not in a lascivious way. My eyes trailed down his abs, lingering on the V dipping below his pants.

His belt was next to go, joining mine on the floor. Lu reached for my trembling hand, placing it on his pounding heart.

"This beats for you. My body, my soul... my beast, is yours."

Slowly tracing my fingers over the hard planes of his body, I explored his muscular frame. Musky, vanilla heat radiated off his skin, intoxicating my senses.

Lu turned me around. Tugging at my laces, row by row he untied the corseting, allowing my dress to slip from my shoulders.

I gripped the fabric to my breasts as I turned back around, afraid to bare myself to his gaze. Lucius was a perfect specimen. I was a skinny, sickly girl with virtually no curves. My breasts were small. What if he didn't like my body?

Lu placed his hand on mine. "May I?"

I nodded, unable to say the words, and allowed him to slip the dress to my waist, where he paused for a moment before pushing it over my hips and to the floor.

His eyes were glued to my naked body. I fidgeted under his gaze, unsure what to do with my arms. At my sides? Covering myself? Heat crept up my neck as I shifted my weight, wishing for anything to hide behind—until his jaw went slack.

"You're more beautiful than I could have ever imagined."

I let out a breath I didn't know I was holding and smiled. He thought I was beautiful.

Feeling brave, I reached for his pants, fumbling with the ties. He was patient with me, allowing me to find my way. Slowly, I pulled the waist loose and dropped them to the floor.

Lu's erection was massive.

"Is this okay?" he asked, checking in.

"Yes," I said, biting my lip with anticipation.

Seeing his naked physique had me wet with desire. But I'd be lying if I said his size didn't give me pause. Was a human man built like this? Would it fit? Was it going to hurt? My mind was reeling with the unknown.

"You can touch me, if you want."

I reached for his manhood, gingerly exploring the shaft. I'd never touched a penis before. It was harder than I expected and covered in a labyrinth of veins. Lu groaned, placing his hand over mine, squeezing, guiding my movements. His breath hitched, and the tip of his cock became slick.

"I'm so hard for you," he said.

The sounds he was making had me eager for more. Knowing I was the one making him feel this way empowered me, dampening the underlying fear of what was next.

Lu pulled me to him, bending down to meet me in a kiss, our bodies pressed against each other. I slid my hands up his muscled back and opened my mouth to allow his tongue inside. I relaxed into the feeling and let him lead me.

Lu's hands slid down my waist, cupping my ass before he scooped me up in his arms, carrying me to the bed.

Gently, he laid me down, climbing in beside me.

"I'm going to touch you now."

I nodded before speaking the words. "Yes."

Lu's caress was soft. I closed my eyes and focused on the sensation. His warm hands felt like fire, the flames kissing my skin. Slowly, he traced along my neck, finding my collarbone, trailing between my breasts before circling them with his fingertips. Chills spread down my spine and goosebumps broke out along my skin. My nipples ached for him, and I arched my back, chasing his touch.

Each breath against my neck was a tether, anchoring me

to the moment as his hands traveled further down my belly, stopping at the curve of my hip. His mouth descended upon my breast, pulling my nipple into his teeth and caressing it with his tongue. I sighed with pleasure as he moved to the other side, distracting me from his wandering hand.

Fingertips slid down my thighs, gently parting my legs. Wetness dripped from my now throbbing core. I wanted to feel him touch me... there. I spread my legs wider, giving him more access.

"Feeling a little eager, are we?" Lu teased, coming up for a kiss and halting the assault on my thighs.

"My body's aching to be touched," I gasped between kisses. I felt like I was going to combust. "Please, don't deny me any longer."

Lu's fingers found me slick with need. Growling with approval, a devious smile spread across his face. "You're so wet for me." Tenderly, he stroked me, circling my swollen clit. My breathing was becoming erratic, my body and mind were consumed with pleasure. Lu explored my opening, gently pressing a finger inside.

"Ohhh," I gasped at the foreign sensation.

"That's my girl." His words guided me through as he added a second finger, gently stretching me. "I want you ready for me."

Tension built rapidly, and I found myself grinding against his hand.

"Not yet, Dove," he said, pulling his fingers from my

body. "I want to taste you." Before I could protest, his fingers were in his mouth and he was purring. "Divine."

Lu descended down my torso, spreading my legs before his face. "So pretty, all wet for me." His tongue was on me, bathing my most private parts, and I was far from ashamed. It felt amazing—and I wanted more. I reached for his hair, pressing his head to my core, and he growled with approval. His fingers were back, this time in harmony with his tongue. The tension coiled, reaching its breaking point as my breaths became moans, and I fell over the edge. Pleasure overpowered me and my legs clamped around his head. My body was no longer my own. My core pulsed from inside while Lu continued to consume me, gripping my legs tight until the sensations subsided.

"I could do that all day," Lu confessed as he climbed up my now-relaxed body. Reaching between us, he pressed his hardness against my center. "We're gonna go slow, okay?"

"Okay."

"Try to relax."

I took a deep breath and exhaled as Lu slowly pushed against my opening. I could feel the delightful stretch as, inch by inch, he entered me, claiming my virginity. It was intense—a delicious pressure that filled me completely, leaving me feeling whole. Like a missing piece had finally found its home.

"Michaela," Lu groaned. "Are you okay?"

I nodded, unable to form words.

"You feel amazing." He slowly rocked into my body, and that delicious tension began to build once again.

Together, we created a symphony of moans, both of us lost in the rhythmic pleasure building between us.

Lu's thrusts intensified, each one driving deeper, while our cries grew louder and more animalistic. I didn't want it to end, but the tension grew tighter with every move. I lifted my hips to meet his, finding a new sensation—so intense that I fell over the edge again, this time taking Lu with me into the depths of ecstasy. He collapsed on top of me, sweaty and out of breath.

"Lu, that—I have no words," I giggled in the post-coitus high. "Um, wow."

"I knew we would be amazing."

Wait, what? I clearly heard Lu's words, yet he remained silent. How?

"Am I hearing things, or did you just say something?" I responded silently, simply thinking the words.

Lu turned his head, his eyes wide with shock. "How did you do that?"

"Me? You did it first."

"I have no idea what just happened. I mean, I expected our connection to grow, but I certainly didn't expect this."

"Is this a fated thing?"

"I don't know. But I meant what I said. We are amazing together."

"I'd say," I chuckled, not knowing what to think about our newfound ability. "When can we do it again?"

Lu laughed. "We have the rest of our lives to do it. And if I have my way, we will—again, and again, and again."

I smiled at the thought of spending what time we had left making love to Lu. The two of us making up for lost time. "Can you hear all of my thoughts?"

"Doesn't seem like it. Why, what are you thinking?"

"I was thinking I want to stay here in bed. I'm not ready to go back out there. I want to just lay here in your arms."

"How are you feeling? Is the sprite ash still working?"

"I feel wonderful," I smiled at the realization that, for the first time, the cancer had been completely gone from my thoughts. I couldn't remember a time when my illness hadn't plagued my every move. "The buzz wore off back in the woods, but I'm feeling stable."

"That makes me happy." Lu kissed my forehead. "I should probably get us something to eat. Check to see if the others have returned."

"Oh God," I gasped, hiding my face in Lu's embrace. "Do you think they'll know?"

Lu chuckled. "Would it upset you if they did?"

"No, I just… I don't know. I don't want to upset anyone."

"Dove," Lu tilted my chin to face him, "I assure you, aside from being jealous of me, no one will be upset with you. Remember what I told you in the woods? We are all fated, inexplicably connected. This doesn't change that."

I was still a little unsure of the logistics of the situation. Nico and Luca had expressed interest. Hell, Luca had shared a very intimate moment with me only a few nights ago. But what about Finn and Hunter? Jase had never really been happy that I came back to Hiraeth. I wasn't sure that simply being fated automatically meant they were all going to want me—at least not in that way. What if it meant we were all fated to work together, to fix Hiraeth?

"I'll be back with something delicious. Keep the bed warm for me. We'll indulge here as long as we can." Lu kissed me quickly before throwing on his pants. "I promise I'll be quick." He slipped out the door, leaving me with my thoughts. *"I miss you already."*

CHAPTER XIV
RELATIONSHIPS AND REVOLUTIONS
-MICHAELA-

The dappled light of day lured me from the best sleep I could ever remember having. With a contented groan, I stretched, feeling a soreness in places I'd never felt before, and everything from the prior night came rushing back to me. I reached for Lucius in the oversized bed, but his spot beside me was cold. I sat up, pulling the sheets with me to cover myself, only to find I was alone in the room.

Resting on his pillow was a folded piece of parchment and a single red dahlia. I snatched it up with greedy fingers, eager to devour every word he'd written. I paused with it in my hands, a cloud of doubt dashing my excitement. What if this was a nicely worded farewell rather than a love letter?

Stop it, Mic! I refused to let myself always settle on the

worst-case scenario. I took a deep breath and opened the letter.

> Good morning, Dove,
> I'm sorry I didn't wake you, but you were sleeping so peacefully that I couldn't bring myself to disturb you. I hope you're feeling well today. Although I must admit, a part of me wishes that you're pleasantly sore, so you'll be reminded of me.
> Please excuse my absence. I woke with the dawn feeling transformed. I am a different man than I was only yesterday, and the urge to welcome a new day was overwhelming. But don't worry about me—I'll be back shortly, because I am quite literally incapable of being away from you for too long.
> I hope this dahlia will make up for my absence. They are the last flowers to bloom before winter, steadfast until the end. In my realm, dahlias represent kindness, inner strength, beauty, and commitment—all of the things that you represent to me. Know that you'll be on my mind until I see you again.
> Love always,
> Lucius

I clutched the letter to my chest, his words melting me into a puddle of emotions. There was a side of him that no one else saw—a side he'd always kept just for me. I knew in that moment he was truly mine, no matter what happened when I stepped outside this room.

I grabbed the dahlia, admiring the deep crimson petals as I pulled it to my nose. The faint floral scent transported me to a sunlit glade, alive with warmth and possibilities. Lu's enthusiasm was contagious, urging me to get up and start this new, confusing chapter in my life.

I dressed quickly, slipping on the homespun skirts, admiring the deep burgundy color. Gunner's eidris was strapped to my thigh—a habit I'd formed since we'd been on the run. I took extra time to arrange my hair. I hadn't put much effort into my appearance lately, but today felt special. I pulled the front pieces away from my face and secured them at the nape of my neck, tucking the dahlia into my hair as a finishing touch.

My courage began to wane as I entered the main living quarters of the cabin. Fallon was busy serving Nico and Luca, who sat at the long dining table, engrossed in discussion. Lucius had assured me there would be no ill will between us, but I wasn't so sure.

"There you are, Mic. You ready for some breakfast?" Fallon asked, spotting me lingering at the edge of the hallway. I was a goddamned coward.

"Sure, sure… that would be great. Have you seen Lucius this morning?" I asked, as Luca and Nico turned to greet me with achingly handsome smiles.

"Oh, he left early this morning. He seemed unusually

chipper for Lucius," Fallon said, and I could see the mirth in her eyes as she smiled at me. She knew. "Come on over here. You can't eat from all the way over there." I could hear the challenge in her voice. This was her way of pushing me out of the gate, so to speak.

With a huff, I made my way to the table, sitting as far away from Nico and Luca as I could manage. The moment I sat down, my scent hit them. I could see it on their faces—both of them tensed, straightening in their chairs. All conversation ended abruptly. The line in Nico's brow deepened, and Luca's jaw ticked. You could've heard a pin drop in that moment.

"Suns out today," I said awkwardly in a poor attempt at small talk. Anything to fill the demoralizing silence.

"Lucius? Really?" Luca said. There was a grit to his voice, but he didn't sound malicious.

"Well, Lucius and I… we've been friends for a while and…" I stammered, words failing me completely.

"She doesn't owe us an explanation," Nico said. "Lucius has made no attempt to hide his feelings for Michaela. I'm genuinely happy for him. But with that being said—"

"Game on," Luca growled, finishing Nico's sentence.

Lucius strolled into the room. His hair looked windblown, an uncharacteristic smile set into his flushed face, as if he'd been running wild in the woods.

"Morning, brothers. Fallon… Dove, you look lovely this morning," he said sweetly, a complete contrast to his typical demeanor.

"Well played. Well played," Luca said as he got up from his chair and shook Lu's hand. This wasn't what I was expecting at all, and I felt my cheeks flush the same color as the dahlia in my hair.

"Does this mean that you two are an item now?" Fallon asked.

"I am whatever Mic wants me to be," Lu answered as he came to stand behind me.

Luca's brow raised. "Mic, I always knew you were amazing, but what you've done with my asshole of a brother... you're a goddess."

I giggled, feeling a wash of relief that things seemed relatively normal. "Lu and I are still figuring out what all this means. Relationships and revolutions don't typically go hand in hand, but—"

"That's the best time to start a relationship," Nico interrupted. "When you don't know how much time you have left, you should go after what you want with a blind passion. Don't let anyone or anything deter you."

Nico got up from the table, a sobering look on his face. "Lucius, come find me in the study once you've tended to Mic. There's news from the leaders in Dunharrow. We've got a rendezvous with the Raven's Hand later."

Lucius sat with me while I ate breakfast before heading off to meet with Nico. Everyone seemed busy. Fallon had gone to "run errands." I'd offered to go with her, but she made some excuse why it was best she go alone. I think she was in search of more brimshade. She'd smoked her last cigarette this morning, and she seemed on edge.

Luca had gone hunting, which left me with time on my hands. I hadn't had a moment alone since we'd left Mathenholm, and I wasn't sure I was prepared to face everything that had happened. Maybe this was the universe's way of forcing me to digest my feelings for these brothers and figure out what the fuck I was going to do now that my heart had gotten tangled in this fated mess.

I made my way back to the room in search of paper and a quill. If I could write it down, then maybe I could make sense of it all. Before I reached the door, Nico stepped out of an adjacent room and into the shadowed hallway with me.

"I thought you were meeting with Lucius?" I asked casually, before I could make out the look on his face. His jaw was set in a hard line and his brow furrowed, a darkness cast over his eyes. He took purposeful strides toward me, and I backed away from him instinctively. I hit the door, the handle digging into the small of my back as Nico cornered me with his muscled arms.

"Is everything alright?" I asked, fighting to keep the edge of fear from my voice. Nico would never hurt me.

"It should have been me," he said, breaking my stare. His gaze roamed over my lips and neck. "I was raised to be logical. To analyze every aspect. It's a trait of a good king—or so I've been led to believe. I never should have hesitated when it came to you."

His face was so close to mine I felt like I couldn't breathe.

"Hesitate? You're destined to take the throne. Your life's already been planned out for you. You have a betrothed, for God's sake. I don't fit into your world, Nico. I never expected you to drop everything because your Divine has placed some mythical expectations upon us."

"It's not a myth," he growled, pounding a fist into the door behind me. "Don't you feel it? Or am I the only one of us in agony?"

"Yes. I feel it. But I want you to choose to be with me—not because the meddling of some deity forced you into it."

"Now that Lucius has told you about being fated, there's no taking it back. How can I prove to you how I feel? You'll always second-guess me."

"If you truly want this—"

"I want it more than I want my next breath."

"Then you'll have to work for it. Just because we have the title of 'fated' doesn't mean you get to skip all the good parts. I'm quite fond of the idea of falling in love with you."

Nico growled again, pressing his body into mine. "Challenge accepted, little bird. But just so you know, I'm done waiting on the sidelines. I know what I want, and you'll find that I'm not easily deterred."

"I was hoping you weren't," I whispered, trying to be bold even though butterflies swarmed at my core.

His lips slammed on mine—fierce and consuming. A heady rush washed over me and I kissed him back. I wanted no regrets in whatever life I had left, and in that moment, I couldn't deny that I wanted him. I wanted him to lift me up and bring me into the bedroom. To explore this newfound passion and see how he could make my body sing.

His hands wrapped into my hair, pulling tight and pinning me in place while he explored my mouth. I hitched my leg around him, trying to pull him closer even though our bodies were already molded together. But as I yearned for more, he ended it—pulling away from me, leaving my scorched body behind.

"The lady has asked to be wooed. Not ravaged in a dark hallway," he said, taking another step away from me, leaving altogether too much space between us.

"I don't remember saying that ravaging was off the table."

Nico laughed, and the sound filled me. It was those small glimpses of joy in these dark moments that made it all worth it. "After I meet with Lucius, I'll be taking him and Luca with me on a raid. You'll be safe here with Fallon until we get back."

The joy faded just like that, and our reality came crashing back. "A raid?"

Nico sighed, his gaze shifting to the ceiling. "It's necessary. We'll never be safe here if I can't take out Johan. We need weapons so I can build an army, and I need an army so I can protect you. Johan has an order of iron coming in from the northern territories. The plan is to relieve him of that shipment and use it for our own."

"A few days in the woods and you're already becoming a thief. I'd say there's some truth to the dark magic in this forest," I said, joking. But Nico only offered me a sad smile.

"Don't think too poorly of me. Every move I make now has good intentions, I promise."

"I don't doubt it one bit. Make sure all of you come back to me safely."

CHAPTER XV
DAYDREAMS
-MICHAELA-

I stayed close to the cabin, wandering just far enough to find the perfect spot to clear my head. Sun-warmed stones stood cradled into a bend of the river. It was an idyllic place, with tall, proud pines skirting the riverbanks. The perfect spot to sort out the complete mess I'd made of my life.

I pulled the piece of parchment and quill from my pack, along with the tiny vial of sprite ash. The jar of glittering dust felt cool and smooth between my fingers, and I contemplated taking another dose. I didn't need it. My health was stable. But I was holding a release in my hands. The ash would take away my racing thoughts and give me a moment of peace. Even if it was fabricated, the thought was extremely enticing.

I dropped the vial back in my pack, refusing to take the easy way out, and settled on writing a letter to my sister. I needed a sympathetic ear—someone to give me advice. A role Gwen had filled my entire life. My half of the Loquentes Cartis had been left behind when we fled Mathenholm Castle, so there was no possible way to get a letter to her in Neverland. But the realms between us wouldn't prevent me from pouring my heart out to her— even if she'd never hear my words.

I situated myself against a boulder, using my pack as a desk, cleared my mind, and began to write.

> Dearest Sweetie,
>
> I don't know why I am writing this. Maybe it's because if I don't, I might break. Even though you will never see these words, I need to feel you here with me. You think dying of a terminal disease would be enough. Now I'm embroiled in a rebellion, there's a price on my head, I'm seeing ghosts, I'm no closer to a cure, and to top it all off, I've got some kind of fated bond to all ~~seven~~ six of the beast princes.
>
> I'm not sure I can face all of this on my own. I'm not strong like you. You've always had a hope for the future that I could never understand. Maybe because mine was stolen by death himself, a long time ago. Now, eternal rest

seems like the easy way out rather than facing it all.

I wish you were here with me. To tell me that no matter what, it'll all work out. Because even though I'm surrounded by these princes— who claim that, by some miracle of destiny, we're fated to be together—I feel so uncertain.

Before, it was foolish to fantasize about love. But now that there's a chance, I think I may be too afraid to take it. The way I feel when I'm with them... it's like being entranced by a flame. It's beautiful and warm. But if I get too close, will I be burned in the end?

If I'm meant to die young, loving them now will only make it harder to accept. I'm getting ahead of myself, because none of it is real. Their affections are nothing but a trick of the Divine. A notion of love forced upon them, and it could break on a celestial whim. I'll never know if they truly love me—

"I don't believe that's the case at all." A familiar voice intruded into my thoughts, and I jumped.

"Lucius? Is that you?" I whispered, looking around my little sanctuary, but there was no noise save for the rushing water of the river.

A hearty chuckle echoed in my head. *"Try again. I'll give you a hint—I'm far more handsome than my brother."*

My mind reeled. It had already been disconcerting when Lu had spoken in my mind, and now there was another one of them in my head?

"Who is this?" I called out, clutching the letter I'd just written to my chest in a ridiculous attempt to conceal the words from my mental intruder.

"I thought you were smarter than that, Michaela. What would your governess think?"

"Finn?"

"The one and only. No need to hide that letter of yours. I already know what you're thinking. And you're wrong."

Fuck. That was Finn's power. He could read my thoughts. But how the hell was he in my head? Was I going mad? Had the cancer finally addled my mind? That seemed to make the most sense. I'd seen Gunner's ghost, and now I was hearing voices from Finn—who could very well be dead.

I should have opted for the sprite ash.

"You're not going crazy. And I'm not dead!"

"Stop that! Has anyone ever told you it's rude to read other people's thoughts?" I chided, feeling more vulnerable than ever knowing my mind could betray me.

"Most people never know I'm there. But with you, it's a two-way connection. And since I convinced one of the guards to delay our daily dose of wolfsbane, I couldn't help myself. Beats staring blankly at this cell wall."

"I don't know how you're in my head but… thank God you're alive." A wave of relief washed over me.

"And here I was thinking you didn't care. Now, be a good girl and close your eyes. I want to show you something."

I hesitated, still questioning my sanity.

"Don't be a brat. Do as I ask."

I rolled my eyes, letting my annoyance burn hot so Finn got the point, before doing as he asked. When I closed my eyes, it was as though I had blinked and everything changed. One minute I was at the river's edge—and now, I was back home in London.

My bedroom looked exactly as it had when I was a child. Before I'd gotten sick and they'd moved in all the medical equipment. I'd thought of it often. This had been the place of so many happy memories. A time before the world tried its best to break me.

I reached out in awe, touching the cream-colored wallpaper and tracing the small pink flowers I'd loved so much. Light filtered in through the frilly curtains. And there, standing next to my four-poster bed, were Finn and Hunter.

"How is this possible?" I asked, turning around and inhaling the comforting scent of my mother's perfume, still lingering in the air.

"I've seen this place in your thoughts before. I ventured that it might be a good place for us to talk. Hunter created the visual. I provided the memory." He picked up my teddy bear, still nestled among the pillows on my bed, and raised an eyebrow at me.

"Am I dreaming?" I asked hesitantly, waiting for the visions of Hunter and Finn to confirm that I was, indeed, mad. But there was no hint this was a dream. I'd been wide awake only moments before.

"Do you like it?" Hunter asked with a hopeful look.

That was all I needed to give in to the delusion. I was desperate to feel at home again.

"Hunter, it's beautiful." I closed the distance between us, wrapping my arms around him. He stood stoic for a moment, stunned by my forwardness—but in a heartbeat, his arms wrapped around me, locking me to him. Clinging to me as though I were his only lifeline.

"The builder gets all the credit when it was the artist who made the masterpiece," Finn remarked, tossing my teddy back on the bed.

I reluctantly pulled away from Hunter and turned to Finn. "I thought you already knew what I was feeling?"

"It's always nice to feel appreciated. And I know exactly how much this place means to you," he said, holding my stare with inquisitive hazel eyes.

"How often have you been eavesdropping on my thoughts?" I almost didn't want to know the answer. My cheeks flushed with preemptive embarrassment.

"Whenever the wolfsbane begins to wear off. Your mind's been a sanctuary. I much prefer it to this cell."

I wanted to be angry with him for the violation of my privacy, but how could I, with an answer like that?

Hesitantly, I reached for his hand, taking it gently in mine, feeling more reserved around him than I did with Hunter.

"I'm so sorry. Nico and the others, they told me there was no way to free you from the dungeons," I admitted, ashamed that I hadn't pushed harder to come after them.

"Don't feel bad, beautiful. Nico's right. Without an army, there is no getting us out of here," he assured me, squeezing my hand. "That's why I've been visiting your thoughts when I can. I don't know how much time we have left. It might be the only way I get to know you."

"Don't think like that. They've kept you alive this long. And Nico is working on a plan. We'll get you all out..." I trailed off. "Where is Jase?" I asked, realizing that Hunter had only pulled me and Finn into the dream.

They shared a look.

"We don't know," Hunter answered. "Finn is in the cell beside me, so I can pull him into dreams. But Jase... wherever he is, he's too far for me to reach."

"Do you... do you think he's dead?" I swallowed the lump in my throat and sat down on my bed.

"You tell me," Finn said.

"What do you mean? We've gotten no word if any of you were dead or alive."

"You would have felt it if he no longer walked this realm. The same emptiness you felt when Gunner died. The longer you're in Hiraeth, the stronger our connection grows."

"Is that the reason you can reach me when we're so far from the castle?"

"With you, everything is different. There's an unbreakable connection. It doesn't matter how far you are —we can still reach you," Hunter explained.

"Is that some special perk of being fated?" I asked, the edge of sarcasm coming out a bit too strong.

"You scoff at the idea of being fated, like it's just some meddling gods pulling strings, but it's more than that," Finn said, running his hands through his thick hair as he paced my small room, looking annoyingly handsome in his irritation.

"You say that, and yet you barely acknowledged me from the moment we met. I distinctly remember you pushing against Nico's decision to bring me here."

Finn tensed, pausing his pacing as he shot me a sideways glance. "We may be living in a nightmare, but I've learned a lot. It just so happens that the scribes' quarters are directly above the dungeon. Apparently, Johan values them only slightly more than prisoners. They've been doing research— not *only* about prophecies, but fateds too. I've been eavesdropping on their thoughts. He has them studying fated bonds. How they are created. How they can be destroyed. Life-binding, ancient blood rites, and the like."

Finn resumed pacing, stopping to pick up a jewelry box with a ballerina on the top before continuing. "It's not meddling, as you so callously called it. They're more important than you realize. Everything is woven into the fabric of fate. Each of us a string, adding to both the light and the dark. A masterpiece of life. Some are bound together to ensure that balance remains. It is rare for strings to be tied to one another the way ours are. Being fated is more than love. Our threads are now equal parts of the same soul."

My heart was racing as he spoke, enraptured by his words. I wanted so badly to believe the beautiful picture he was painting for me, but my relationship with these beasts only seemed to grow more complicated. Shouldn't we simply click into place, recognizing our kindred bonds, and live happily ever after?

"And you believe the scribes that are loyal to Johan?" I asked, trying to play devil's advocate.

"They are *equally* as captive as we are. They'd be killed if they refused him. Besides, I can hear every thought—I'd know if they were lying."

"You hear every thought? Does that mean you've heard all of my thoughts?" I asked, almost afraid I would die of embarrassment if he had.

"If you're referring to what happened between you and Lucius, the answer is—unfortunately—yes."

I chucked my teddy at his head. "That was supposed to be private!"

"What are you two talking about?" Hunter asked, his brows drawn together as he looked between Finn and me.

"The fact that Lucius has carnal knowledge of our fated," he said matter-of-factly, and I momentarily considered throwing my eidris at him, until I remembered this was only a dream.

"Lucius? Really?" Hunter rubbed his chin as he looked at me. "I know we all dreamed of being the first, but I always assumed it would be Nico, or maybe even Luca... but the runt?"

"He's always been true to me. Genuine in his feelings from the very start. While the rest of you fought with your own reservations over this fated shit. I have no regrets," I said, lifting my chin.

"Reservations?" Finn shot back. "That's a little unfair, when you were literally writing down your own reservations just now. Do we not deserve the same grace?" There was an edge to his voice as he stalked toward me, invading my personal space.

"I'm sorry... you're right. But in my defense, you've all had plenty of time to tell me. Even now you're keeping secrets from me, and it feels like betrayal."

Finn leaned in, forcing me backward on the bed while he planted two fists on either side of my legs. I tried to pull away from him, but the bed creaked as Hunter crawled up behind me—the two of them sandwiching me in. My heart was in my throat, pounding away at an erratic rhythm. My mind struggled to remember this was only a dream.

Hunter pulled my hair to one side, and I shivered as cool air rushed across my neck.

Finn was so close I could feel his breath on my lips as he spoke. "Maybe it's to protect you. To keep you in blissful ignorance, so you can go one more day without knowing things that might make you wish you'd never set foot in Hiraeth."

The air between us was charged. My mind clung to Finn's words, imagining invisible threads pulling taut—bringing us together.

"Finn, we have to wrap this up. Guards are coming," Hunter said, grit in his voice. He sucked in a deep breath at my neck before pulling away.

Finn grumbled, leaning forward until his forehead met mine. "Tell my brothers that Johan is planning something. *He will* cut out the heart of this little revolution if Nico doesn't act fast. The vulture plans to make the populous bleed until they happily give you over. Nico needs to enact his plans now... or consider that all is lost in Hiraeth, and seek safe haven in Neverland."

CHAPTER XVI
THERE WILL BE BLOOD
-MICHAELA-

Nico, Luca, and Lucius had left at sunset to meet with the Raven's Hand, promising they'd return in the morning. I'd had the brilliant idea to turn in early, hoping Hunter and Finn might visit me again. If nothing else, I'd take the coward's way of passing the time until I knew they were safe.

But God, the Divine, or whoever was in charge—had other plans. I tossed and turned as if shifting positions might banish the gnawing thoughts crowding my mind. The more I craved sleep, the farther it slipped from reach.

When dawn's light finally began to break through the darkness, I gave up. I found Fallon sitting on the steps outside, a cigarette resting between her elegant fingers, staring into the shadowed forest beyond.

"Sleep well?" she asked, not even bothering to look up at me.

"Like shit," I grumbled, taking a seat beside her. My joints ached, and my thoughts drifted to the sprite ash. Maybe I should dose myself before the boys returned so they wouldn't worry.

"In that case, we can both be miserable together," she said, offering me her cigarette. The rich scent I now recognized as brimshade wafted up in scrolled columns of smoke. Apparently, her errands had proven fruitful.

I hesitated for a moment, but decided *what the fuck*. Maybe it was comparable to the medical-grade marijuana I'd been prescribed back home.

I took a drag. The ember flared cherry red in the dark, and the smoke went down smooth, leaving a subtle tingle in my lungs as I exhaled. The effects were immediate. The tension in my shoulders melted away, and the knot of anxiety in my chest began to ease.

"Now I understand the appeal," I said, handing it back. "Finn and Hunter visited me yesterday," I added after a beat, needing to share it with someone. The admission hung in the air while Fallon remained silent, pulling in a deep drag.

I wasn't sure if she even heard me, or the mention of them had become too painful. But then she asked, "Are they alright?"

"They seemed okay. But it felt like… a goodbye. They told me Johan is planning something."

She turned toward me, her eyes glassy under the weight of her emotions. "Did they tell you what it was?"

"No. Just that we should leave Hiraeth altogether."

"Do me a favor, Mic. Don't tell my brothers."

"Okay… but why?"

"It'll only sow seeds of doubt. Johan will always be planning something. They need to focus—not worry about contingency plans. That will only get them killed."

"What's your gut say? Think we can win?"

"That depends on how you measure success," she said. "If you mean, did they relieve the fake king of his iron and his coin tonight—then yes, they were successful. But they've poked the bear, so to speak. Johan won't take this lightly. They've won this battle, but the war is only just beginning."

I didn't ask her to elaborate. I wasn't sure I wanted to know more.

"They'll be back within the hour," she said. "We should prepare something for them to eat. Today, the planning begins."

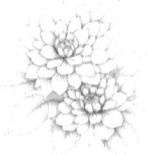

"You should've seen his face, Mic," Luca laughed, his breakfast sitting mostly untouched as he recounted the night's events. "Red as his coat. He was all, '*You'll* pay for this! Johan will hang your bodies from the walls of

Mathenholm.'" He pounded his fist on the table as he continued to laugh.

"You should've let me kill him," Lucius grumbled.

"No, no—it was perfect." Luca shot Nico a grin. "Thank you for not melting his mind into submission. I really needed a good laugh."

"We needed him alive," Nico replied. "We need witnesses to spread the word. When people hear we're taking a stand, they'll join us. And it sends a message to Johan: we're not backing down."

"It's already working," Fallon added. "The Raven's Hand will bring new alliances today—I can feel it. They'll be here soon."

"So when do I get to join in on all the fun?" I asked. Lucius visibly stiffened.

"Yes, Mic! You're such a badass. I can totally picture you in tight leather armor," Luca said, looking me over as though he could already envision it.

"Dove, I don't think—" Lucius started.

"Lucius, don't you dare tell me it's not a good idea. I want to help," I pleaded before shifting my attention to Nico. We all knew he had the final say.

He held my stare for a moment, then nodded. "If the lady's willing to train until she can hold her own, I see no reason why she can't come along."

Lucius narrowed his eyes at me. I knew he was already crafting a litany of rules I'd have to abide by in order to go.

"Don't you all need to rest before the Raven's Hand

arrive?" I said, throwing a salmonberry at his head before he could plead his case any further.

Luca leaned toward me, grinning. "Why? Are you offering to go to bed with me? As you've just pointed out, I can go all night."

"There will be no sleeping—or anything else you're trying to get away with!" Lu growled.

"One of us might be able to make an exception for the lady if she requires a bed mate. ," Nico said smoothly, his brow raised in challenge. "As next in line to the throne, I'm officially laying claim to that honor."

Lucius looked like he was about to draw a dagger on both of them.

Before I could die of further embarrassment, Sawyer and Levi entered the room. A handful of males and females I didn't recognize filtered in behind them.

"Are you ready for the meeting, my friend?" Sawyer asked, motioning to Nico. "I've got some people eager to meet you."

"Yes, we're all here." Nico stood from his chair and stepped to me, pressing a kiss to the top of my head. "You're welcome to join us—or you can enjoy your breakfast."

"I'd like to come," I said, grabbing a few salmonberries from the table before rising to join him.

Nico shot me a half cocked smile. "I guess we'll see about that later," he said, his voice dripping with innuendo as he took my hand.

. . .

THE KING'S STUDY, which Luca had dubbed the war room—
was enormous. Nico offered me a seat between Lucius and
Luca at the circular table in the center. Maps, scrolls, and
open books littered the surface. The rest of the group filed
in, taking up all available space.

Fallon had been right. Word of our rebellion was
spreading.

Nico stood stoic, scanning the crowd until all of them
fell silent. "Thank you for coming," he said, his voice gritty.
"I wish our meeting came under better circumstances. Johan
sits on a stolen throne—a vulture feasting on dying land. No
more."

A murmur of agreement rippled through the room.

Sawyer stepped forward. "We're with you or we
wouldn't be here. But how do we strike at him?
Mathenholm is a fortress. It's crawling with soldiers. We're
ghosts in these woods, but ghosts don't storm castles."

Nico leaned forward, fists planted on the table. "Maybe
that's exactly what we should be—ghosts. He won't expect
us to be so bold. We'll haunt him in his own halls."

"And the Bloodstone Sigil?" Levi asked. "You still
haven't told us how you'll get the ring off his traitorous
finger."

Nico glanced down at the map beneath his hands,
choosing his words. "I'm working on it."

"His power grows every day that ring stays on his
finger," Levi warned.

"Or… the Sigil will reject him," Nico replied. "We don't

have enough intel to prove otherwise. For now, we must act swiftly. We'll focus on one thing at a time. But I promise you this—if I have to sever his hand from his body to get my father's ring back, I will."

"I'm not sure, but I'll ask him," a large male boomed, using his weight to push through the crowd. Silver threaded through his auburn curls, which tumbled around his head like a wild mane. A thick beard framed his ruddy face, barely hiding the crooked grin beneath. He straightened himself as he stood before Nico, adjusting a rusted breastplate that hung over tattered robes.

"This is Amos," Sawyer said. "The sage I told you about."

Nico nodded at him. "What's your question?"

Amos uncorked his flask with his teeth, took a long swig, then asked, "Will ya fight by our sides, or tuck tail and run at the first sign of blood? Because the Divine tells me..." he grinned, "there will be blood."

"The Divine tells you this?" Nico asked, arching a brow.

"Aye. Now answer the damn question," Amos said, grinning even wider.

"What did you say?" Lucius seethed at the stranger, his hand resting on his sword.

"It's okay, Lucius." Nico lifted his hands to calm the tension in the room. "And the answer is no—I will not run. I'm prepared to fight, even if it means forfeiting my life."

Amos fidgeted with the myriad of small bones hanging from his belt as he glanced up at the ceiling. I jumped when he doubled over in a full-bellied laugh. After the initial shock, his glee was contagious, and I sealed my lips to hold in the chuckle bubbling up.

"The Divine does not favor you, my friend. I do apologize," he said once he'd composed himself, wiping tears from his eyes.

"You're mad, old timer," Lucius grumbled as he stepped closer to me.

"You say I'm mad—perhaps. But madness is simply seeing what others ignore. Like her." He pointed a meaty hand at me. "Sitting so quietly when she's a favorite. You should listen to everything she has to say."

I squirmed in my chair, feeling all eyes land on me. I shot a worried glance at Nico, hoping he wouldn't start asking my opinion on war tactics. I was far out of my league here.

"Yes, Michaela is an important part of this council. We're all thankful to have you—and the Divine—here with us," Nico said, shooting Lu a withering look. "Maybe you could put in a request for blessings on our plan."

"Let's hear it, then!" Amos cheered, lifting his flask and taking a swig. He pulled the nearest chair up and settled his large frame, giving himself a front-row seat across from Nico.

"We'll start by cutting off supply lines. Aetherfall requires vast amounts of goods to be brought in daily in order to function. Once the court is cut off from the spoils of your labor, Mathenholm will fall into disarray. We'll reroute food and supplies back into Dunharrow and the lesser cities and towns. Levi, I want you to head this up. You'll need to distribute everything discreetly—we can't have the crown's army catching wind of it."

"The Divine says, 'Eat well, fight hard, and die laughing.' Who am I to argue?" Amos chuckled, nodding his head in agreement. "Between you and me…" he whispered, "I'm adding, 'drink deep' to that list as well."

"Glad you agree, Amos. But that's not all." Nico continued, "We'll also target payments going to the sovereign cities. Johan is paying the nobles to send soldiers. We need to cut off his supply of hired thugs. And to that end, we'll start building our own militia. I'm appointing my brothers, Luca and Lucius, as my generals."

"We'll begin training here," Luca added, rising from his chair to address the group. "Small battalions will rotate through. My brother and I will prepare them for covert missions. Like ghosts in the night, we'll take out Johan's most loyal supporters one by one until they regret choosing his side."

Lucius joined his brothers, pulling a lump of glittering iron ore from his pocket and setting it on the table. "Sawyer has helped negotiate a deal with the ironworkers in Dunharrow. They've agreed to start forging blades, spearpoints, and arrowheads. Weapons training is crucial if we're going to beat hardened soldiers."

"Sawyer, I want you to be the voice of this movement," Nico said, pointing to the hulking male. "And you, Amos—

our people have lost their faith. For too long, they've been beaten down. Now, they have nothing left to live for. Without purpose, there's no passion to fight. I need to give them a reason to live again. Can you help me with that?"

"Ah, faith and steel. Two things that'll never fail you," Amos said, grinning. "I'm most humbled to provide my services—so long as I get the chance to kill those deceiving bastards."

"That's a promise I can keep. You'll have more than enough chances to spill traitorous blood."

"And what of the illness?" Fiona asked. "Nineteen died this morning. New cases are reported daily. We can't fight the crown if we're dropping dead from a silent killer."

Lucius moved through the crowd and opened the door as the room fell silent. "Have you brought our friend, Fallon?" he called.

There was a scuffle in the hallway, followed by muffled protests.

"Unhand me at once! This isn't the behavior of a lady. I have no less than six poisons that would drop you dead!" a raspy voice snapped.

Fallon shoved a disheveled Maxfield into the study.

"Save it, Medicine Max. It'll take more than empty threats to kill me," Fallon said, rolling her eyes.

Maxfield smoothed his already tattered robes and adjusted his slouch hat over a head of wild hair. All eyes turned to him.

"Maxfield. Welcome," Lucius said.

"It's not a welcome when you're dragged out of your home against your will," he grumbled.

Lu tsked and crowded into his space. "We had a deal. Now tell these fine people what you told me about the malediction."

Maxfield's eyes widened as he scanned the room, realizing everyone was eagerly focused on him. "I... I've said it before. It's not an illness," he began, straightening his hunched posture. "If it were, it would only affect the physical body. Our trusted remedies would ease the symptoms, and some would be some strong enough to survive. This is a curse." He punctuated the word with a sharp jab of his gnarled finger.

The room erupted, voices clashing all at once—directing their ire at the healer.

"It's true!" Maxfield shouted over the noise. "Sickness affects the physical. Malediction affects the spiritual!"

"Now, now!" Nico boomed, silencing the crowd. "Let him speak. We're all looking for a way to end this plague."

"It's a malediction because it destroys the bond to our beasts. That bond is a spiritual connection. Nothing in nature could sever that. The only hope of ending this is to break the curse behind it."

"And how do we do that?" I asked, leaning forward. I knew what it was like to live with something inside you, slowly stripping away pieces of who you were. If there was even a whisper of a way to stop it, I was ready to help any way I could.

"I'm a healer. Don't you think if I knew the answer, I'd have ended this already?" Maxfield snapped. "It'd be nice not to have people at my doorstep every damn day, desperate for a cure I don't have. I need some peace."

"Have there ever been curses like this before?" I asked.

"Curses, yes. But like this one... never," he said.

"There might be some accounts in ancient texts," Sawyer offered. "Clues on how to break it. But we might be hard pressed to gain access to the archives."

"I think I know a way," Lu suggested. "Someone in Vaelryth might be inclined to help, with the right leverage."

"Good, then it's settled," Nico said. "Maxfield, share everything you know. Lucius, you'll—"

A scream echoed down the hall, followed by the crash of dishes. The room itself seemed to darken. Shadows stretched along the walls as the study door burst open.

A male stumbled in, dried blood matted in his jet-black hair. But when those pale blue eyes met mine, my heart stuttered to a stop.

CHAPTER XVII
WHY ARE YOU DOING THIS
-MICHAELA-

"Jase," his name fell from my lips in a soft exhale. I couldn't believe my eyes.

"Brother?" Nico broke the silence that had fallen upon the room.

Jase nodded, his head bowed in respect. "Nico."

Sawyer shifted his gaze around the room, as though mapping out an exit plan. "I take it you know this male?"

"Sawyer, this is our brother—Jase. He was taken captive the night of the Crownspire," Nico said.

"It's really you," Fallon whispered, afraid to startle the specter impersonating her brother. She jumped up, rushing him and embraced him in a vice-like hug.

Lu watched in disbelief, his brow furrowed and his jaw slack. "How… how are you here?"

"It's nice to see you too," Jase snarked back at Lu's question. The tension in the room grew thicker by the second.

"No, really, how are you here? The cells in Mathenholm are inescapable." Luca's eyes narrowed.

"Did Johan release you? Where are Hunter and Finn?" Nico questioned.

"What a lovely welcome from my family." Jase reached up, rubbing at the back of his neck. "I assume Hunter and Finn are still at Mathenholm? Does it really matter how I escaped?"

Why was everyone so concerned about how he got here? He was here—safely away from Johan. What else mattered?

I made my way to his side. His handsome face was swollen and mottled with bruises. A large, oozing laceration over his right eye left caked trails of dried blood along his cheek. The celebratory attire he wore the night of the Crownspire was filthy, tattered, and dappled with macabre stains. Seeing him like this made my heart ache. His brothers were clearly taken aback by his return, and their interrogation only added to my sympathies. Were they not happy he was safe? I felt compelled to pull him aside and nurse his wounds.

"Jase, since no one else has said it," I side eyed Nico, "welcome home. Please, let me help you settle in." I spoke to him as though he were a fear-stricken animal on the verge of bolting. Offering my hand, I silently pleaded for his acceptance.

"Go with Michaela and get yourself cleaned up. We'll finish things here," Nico dismissed him.

Fallon jumped into action, heading straight for the kitchen. "We'll heat some water. You need a proper bath."

Jase scowled at his family's commanding tone. "I don't need her help. But I see what's going on here. I'd rather not speak in front of all these..." He looked around the room. "Who are these peasants anyway?"

The room remained awkwardly silent. Everyone's eyes were on the new Bruin. I didn't understand the response to his return. One less of our group was trapped in harm's way. And Jase added one more able body to our ranks. Those months my sister had been missing in Neverland... I would've given my life to have her home safely. I didn't care where she had been or what had happened. I was just happy to have her back. He didn't deserve this interrogation—at least not the moment he arrived.

"I'll fill you in later," Nico said and I could tell by his tone that he was losing patience.

Refusing to take my hand, Jase reluctantly followed me back into the king's room. "I'm sure we can find you something clean—"

Before I could finish my sentence, he began to strip—pulling off his shirt and revealing another large, dark purple bruise over the right side of his ribcage. He was no stranger to torture. The word *traitor* had been carved into his chest, a punishment for meddling in Neverland's affairs. The corded, shiny scars were still clearly legible. I tried not to imagine the horrors he'd endured at the hands of Johan.

Fallon showed herself in, walking straight to the washroom with buckets in tow. "Give me a minute. I'll be back with more," she said, quickly heading back out of the room.

"The tub is—"

"I know where the tub is, Michaela."

"Sorry, of course you would know. Would you like some privacy?"

A delicate knock at the door interrupted our awkward exchange. Fallon was back with more buckets.

"My Divine," she cursed under her breath. "You look like shit. What did they do to you?"

"Don't act like you care now," he chided. "Make yourself useful and give me one of your brimshade cigarettes. I could use some pain relief."

Fallon reached into her pocket, pulled out a cigarette, and handed it to him. She looked at me for assurance, as if leaving me alone with her brother was cause for concern. "Are you sure you're okay?"

"We're fine. You can finish up with the others." I reassured her.

The click of the door closing behind her ushered in an awkward silence. Maybe I shouldn't have sent her away so quickly?

Jase wasted no time lighting the brimshade, sighing with relief as he exhaled a large plume of pale grey smoke.

"I'm sorry about your brothers. I imagine that was not the way you envisioned your return."

"They are what they are. Sovereignty requires a certain level of suspicion. But no, it didn't go how I imagined."

"May I help... clean your wounds?"

He huffed. "Would that make you feel useful, little human?"

"I sincerely want to help. You've clearly been through something horrific. Allow me to bring you some modicum of comfort."

He didn't answer but turned and walked to the washroom, dropping his pants in the entryway. "Are you coming to help, or was the offer all talk?"

I swallowed my inhibitions and followed him. Before I abandoned all decorum, I turned my back on him while he poured the warm water into the tub and sat down.

"What's the matter, Mic? Never seen a naked male before?"

"I just—I... Uhh."

He laughed and took a long drag from the brimshade. "You won't be much help from over there."

"It's called being polite," I said, turning around. If he wanted an audience, who was I to deny him? "But clearly, you're not shy."

I didn't know where to start. I'd never bathed anyone but myself—especially not someone I felt an otherworldly attraction to. I grabbed the small sponge floating in the tub and started to wash his well-muscled back. A sizable tattoo of a snarling bear head sat in the center of his frame. Thick smoke swirled up from behind the large figure and trailed across his shoulder blades, curling up over his broad back.

He sighed, relaxing into the bath. His shoulders dropped and rounded forward.

"Your tattoo is beautiful. Does the smoke represent your power?"

"How about you mind your business." His response was abrupt, taking me by surprise.

"I was simply making small talk. I wasn't trying to pry." I was beginning to second-guess my desire to help him. Jase had never agreed with me coming to Hiraeth. From the very beginning, he'd questioned Lu's decision to help me with the Tribulation.

"You gonna help wash my front too?" he quipped, shifting the conversation.

"I think you're fully capable of washing yourself," I shot back, resisting the urge to jab his bruised ribs. "Let me see your face."

He turned to look at me, a sarcastic smile plastered across his rugged features.

"This cut above your eye is covered in filth. On second thought, so is your hair. Let's start there."

"Sorry, Johan didn't offer proper bathing facilities to his prisoners," he mocked.

"I wasn't reprimanding you," I clarified, filling the bucket.

Closing his eyes, Jase tilted back his head, allowing me to

wet his blood-caked hair. I could almost hear a faint purr rumbling from his chest as I massaged his scalp. There were no visible wounds on his head—just dried blood from the gash above his eye. I continued to wash his hair in silence, giving him a moment of peaceful pleasure. After a final rinse, I turned his face back toward me.

"This is probably going to sting," I warned, gently dabbing at the swollen cut.

He winced at my touch. "Why are you doing this?"

I paused, staring into his icy blue eyes. "That's a great question. I'm beginning to wonder that myself." He put on an impeccable facade, but if you took a moment to really look, deep within his gaze was tremendous pain. I was all too familiar with masking for the sake of my loved ones. I could see right through it.

I hesitated, debating whether to pour my heart out to him. To tell him that my soul demanded I take care of him. That I knew that we were all connected, whether we liked it or not. "Because even though I shouldn't... I care."

He stared at me, silent. And for a moment, I swore I saw a smile start to claim the corner of his mouth.

"Lu told me."

"Told you what?"

"That we're all—fated."

He laughed, his defenses snapping back into place. "Did he?" He told you we are *all* fated?"

"He said—"

"I don't care what he said. Did he explain that none of

us know what that even means? That no human has ever been fated to a Hiraethian? Not once in the history of our realm has it *ever* been documented."

"Well, no." I continued cleaning up his face, avoiding his gaze. Lu definitely hadn't mentioned any of those things. "He didn't say—"

"Did he tell you that there has *never* been a case of fated mates involving more than two souls?"

"I don't know what any of it means," I admitted. "But I feel something I can't explain." I was losing my nerve. Jase had made some good points, and I was beginning to question everything. "Do you not feel a connection?"

He scoffed. "I find you attractive, sure. That doesn't mean we're fated. Lots of females get my dick hard. What makes you think you're special?"

My heart sank. "I guess to you, I'm not," I said it matter-of-factly, mimicking his nonchalant remark. I wouldn't let him know he had landed a blow.

"Just because your likeness is in the Book of Ast—" He paused and took a deep breath. "Look, I'm not saying there isn't *something* going on here. But fated *mates*. It's simply not possible. We're not even the same species. It's not natural."

"You know what, you're probably right." His words made a cruel kind of sense. We definitely were not the same species. That alone would certainly make things difficult. What if I got pregnant? Would I birth a bear cub? Oh God. Why hadn't I thought of that before? "All of this—this entire experience…" I scrubbed a little harder at his gash, accidentally reopening the laceration. "It's definitely all coincidental."

"Damn, woman! Easy," he hissed. "Clearly I've struck a nerve."

I grabbed a towel, blotting his wound dry and staunching the newly surfacing blood. I paused, remembering the small vial in my pocket. Would sprite ash heal his brow? It was worth a try. It certainly wouldn't hurt. Even with his shitty dismissive attitude, I still felt compelled to help him. "I have some sprite ash," I said, presenting the vial. "It should heal you up quickly."

He jerked his head away from my hand as the blood welled again from the gash. "Sprite ash?" His lip curled like I'd offered him poison. "Of course you'd carry that filth around."

"It's not filth. It's medicine."

"Only cowards rely on sprite ash."

"Excuse me?"

"I don't need some drugged-up charity case playing nursemaid," he growled.

My jaw clenched. Without hesitation, I smeared the ash into his wound out of spite, giving no concern for how it would feel.

Jase rolled his eyes back, and for a second I wondered if it had been a mistake to apply it directly on his open flesh. He took a deep breath. His eyes closed and his jaw went slack. I watched the skin over his brow knit itself back together as a slow smile crept across his lips.

"Do you know what's in that 'medicine'?"

"The ground-up remains of sprites," I said it nonchalantly. I'd lost my patience with him and offered him the same respect he'd been giving me. "I think we're done here. Take as long as you need. I'm going back to the others."

He leaned back in the tub, taking a drag from the brimshade. "Things get too real for you?"

I paused staring daggers at him. Too real? Was he serious? He was the one denying the obvious magnetism between us.

"Let Nico know I'll be out in a few."

I left the washroom feeling conflicted. The others hadn't mentioned any of Jase's concerns. In fact, they seemed enthusiastic about our situation. What about the Book of Astrium? Could I really be the woman in the drawing? Were they intentionally keeping more secrets from me? I thought things were starting to align, but I now had more questions than answers.

THE WAR ROOM buzzed with heavy conversation. Jase's return had already begun to fade from the spotlight.

I couldn't keep my thoughts to myself any longer. "Have you all forgotten what it felt like to lose Gunner?" I shouted over the others, demanding their attention. "I can't believe that's how you chose to welcome your brother. Jase is home. That's what matters."

"Mic, I know it seems harsh, but we need more answers. His return doesn't make sense. We have to assume the worst until we're sure." Nico tried his best to defend their actions.

"What if Johan offered him immunity in exchange for selling us out?" Luca added.

"My Lady, with all due respect, your mates are right," Sawyer interjected, his tone calm but firm. "The situation seems suspicious."

"My situation is none of your concern," Jase interrupted, returning to the room.

"Jase, this is Sawyer," Nico offered, skipping formality. "He and his people are here to help."

"I stand by my statement," Jase muttered.

"Why don't you give him a chance to explain?" I asked the group. "Why are you all so quick to assume the worst?"

"Why are you suddenly best friends with him?" Lucius chided.

"Right? He was never exactly a fan of—"

"Let's not air personal grievances in front of our guests," Nico interrupted. "Jase, why don't you tell us how you escaped?"

He laughed. "And yet you want me to share mine in front of them? Nico, you make no sense."

"They're not leaving, so you might as well get used to them," Nico said. "Answer the question."

"I offered to buy my guard a week's worth of time at The Velvet Antler in exchange for holding a single dose of wolfsbane." Jase shook his head, laughing. "The promise of a few nights with a high-end whore had him practically begging to defy Johan. It was ridiculously easy. I sent my shadows to retrieve the key while the dumb ass was sleeping. Mathenholm was no match for my abilities."

"If it was that easy, why didn't you help Hunter and Finn?" Luca asked.

"Because we weren't being held in the same area. It was either save myself or risk us all reaping consequences of a failed escape attempt. If you couldn't tell by my appearance, Johan hasn't exactly been kind."

"That adds up," I said, drawing everyone's attention back to me. "I spoke with Hunter and Finn today." My cheeks warmed with the memory. "They mentioned Jase wasn't being held close by."

"That settles it. The boy's home. Congratulations," Amos blurted. "Can we shift the conversation back to something productive now?"

Everyone turned to Nico, as he stroked his beard in thoughtful silence. "I think that's a wise idea. We were just finishing up here." He paused. "Bruins, we'll continue this part of the conversation later."

"Jase, are you able to tell us anything about what's happening back in Aetherfall?" Sawyer asked.

With no safe way to gather intel from the city, we'd been forced to rely on rumors. But Jase—Jase had been there.

"I was locked up most of the time," he said. "But once I made it outside, I confirmed the horrors I'd been hearing among the guards were unfortunately true."

He swallowed hard. Whatever he'd seen had left its mark. I saw it in his eyes back in the king's chambers. He was carrying something exceptionally heavy.

The crowd awaited his next words with dread in their eyes. "Johan's been tormenting our people. Torturing anyone he thinks might know our whereabouts. Burning houses to the ground. Threatening to kidnap and even murder innocent children. I don't think there's anything he wouldn't do to find us. He's on a rampage. If it weren't for the atrocities he's raining down upon our city, I'd call his behavior comical. He's literally throwing a tantrum."

My stomach turned at the thought. I didn't want to believe what I was hearing. All these innocent people were suffering because we fled the night of the Crownspire. I couldn't help but think I was partly responsible for these poor souls.

"But Johan isn't the only reason for the despair in the streets," Jase continued. "Illness is spreading throughout the city. They've started burning the dead."

"The malediction will spread far and wide," Maxfield said darkly. "Nothing can stop it."

His words carried a heavy weight none of us were ready to accept.

"He wants Michaela," Jase said, his voice cutting through the silence.

"Wait, what?" My heart quickened. Why would Johan want me?

Lucius immediately pulled me close, his warm hands doing nothing to ease the growing anxiety.

"He has plans for her. I don't know specifics, but I can only assume they're sinister."

"Good luck getting through me first," Lucius growled under his breath.

"He wants to use her as bait," Nico said. "Do you have any more pertinent information?"

"What else is there to share?" Jase asked. "Under Johan's rule, Hiraeth will become a desolate shell of her former self. Our realm as we know it—will cease to exist."

DEEP within the dark hours before dawn, the cabin was finally quiet. Everyone was in their respective beds, sleeping. But not me. My mind was reeling. Every time I closed my eyes, flashes of Jase's macabre revelations haunted me. Things were changing rapidly. It seemed like every hour brought some new development crashing to light.

What if this was my fault? Well—maybe not all of it. But I definitely had a hand in it.

What if Jase was right? What if he was wrong?

Ugh. What if all of this was for naught?

There was no chance I'd fall asleep like this. It was

pointless. I got up and padded into the kitchen. Maybe some salmonberries would fill my belly and help me drift off.

I meandered silently around the cabin, munching on berries, lost in thought. The large floor-to-ceiling windows in the main living area offered a stunning moonlit view. I looked out, staring into the darkness. Thornwyn Forest was a stark contrast to the bustling energy back home. London never felt this still. Between streetlights and skyscrapers, you could barely see the stars. But here in Hiraeth, the sky stretched wide and endless—a glittering oasis of twinkling light. The beauty surrounding me was endless.

I had just finished my fistful of berries when the hair on the back of my neck rose.

One of them was in the room with me.

Before I could react, he was behind me, pulling my hair aside and over my shoulder. He traced his nose along my neck and drew in a deep breath.

"My beast can smell him on you," Jase whispered in my ear.

I froze instantly, my heart pounding. This wasn't the brother I expected. He'd never been this forward with me. In fact—he'd always been the complete opposite, rejecting me at every opportunity.

"Jase?"

"I've tried everything in my power to deny you," he said, biting my ear. "I won't fight it anymore. I know he's claimed your virtue. And now…" He dragged his tongue along my neck. "My bear wants what's his."

My insides melted. Wetness pooled between my thighs. I didn't know what to do. Hours ago, he'd all but denied our connection. Now his hands were on my waist, roaming my curves. Everything in my logical mind told me to shut it down. I shouldn't want him this way. He was cruel, heartless... and yet I wasn't exactly mad about it. Was this Divine fate at work? Would I ever have control over my emotions when it came to the Bruins?

"I know you want this. I can smell your arousal." His hands cupped my breasts, and I cursed the fabric keeping me from his touch. Nipping his way down my neck, across the top of my shoulder, he continued to explore my body with his mouth, pulling soft sighs from my lips.

He was right. I wanted this. In this moment, I wanted nothing more. My body was on fire.

A strange billowy sensation curled around my legs, drawing my attention downward. There—coiling around my calves, were smoky shadows gliding up my skin, lifting the hem of my nightgown along with them.

"Wait, Jase." I tried to hide the panic in my voice. What exactly was happening?

The others had told me he could manipulate shadows, but I'd never imagined this. It was...corporeal. A being all its own.

"Shh," he reassured me, whispering in my ear. "It's just my shadow." The fabric continued rising over my hips, while his hands freely roamed my body. "Say the words. Tell me to stop and I'll walk away."

"No…" The word slipped out, soft and unsteady. "Don't stop."

As soon as the words left my mouth, his shadow ripped the gauzy fabric from my body, leaving me naked. The moonlight streaming in through the window highlighted my curves, giving me an otherworldly appearance in the mirrored surface of the glass.

"Such perfection," he breathed. His voice dropped into something deep, primal. "Mine," he growled, his breath warm against my ear. Gliding his hands up my bare torso, Jase stopped to tease my pebbled nipples. My breath hitched, and I arched my back in a silent plea for more. He pressed his erection firmly against my ass—and I could tell he was just as endowed as his younger brother.

The shadow returned, this time spreading my legs apart while Jase continued to explore my body, trailing his tongue down my back and across my hips. He gripped my ass, biting my cheek. Then, without warning, his shadow dipped deeper—exploring more than just my legs.

Smoky tendrils slid into my core, igniting a sensation like nothing I'd ever experienced. I couldn't comprehend what was happening. All I could feel was pleasure—surging, unrelenting, all-consuming. Inside and out, the shadow caressed me until I moaned shamelessly, consumed with desire, completely oblivious to everything else.

"Shhh," he hushed me again. "I'm not ready to share you with the others."

I'd all but forgotten we were still in the middle of the cabin. "I can't," I whispered between gasps.

"You can," he said, covering my mouth, muffling my cries.

The shadow was relentless, leaving no part of my core untouched. Drawing out unyielding pleasure from me until it became too much and I crashed over the precipice. My legs wobbled beneath me and Jase wrapped his arm around my waist, holding me upright.

"That's my girl," he cooed, brushing his lips against my ear as the waves of rapture washed over me.

Before I could fully recover, the shadow coiled up my waist, split in two, and pinned my arms over my head. Jase pulled my hips back, using his foot to spread my legs farther apart.

The idea of getting caught like this—naked, arms pinned above my head, and my ass on full display had me reeling. Desire and anxious energy blurred together into something euphoric. I felt beautiful, like a moonlit goddess, and Jase—my Bruin—was worshipping at my feet. I wanted nothing more than to feel him inside me.

As though he could read my thoughts, he slid the head of his cock slowly along my slick entrance. Lining himself up, he hesitated for a moment before sliding in, completely sheathing himself inside my core. "Fuck," he hissed as I gasped at the sensation. "You're so fucking tight."

I tried to relax, but he was *huge*, and I was still sore from my time with Lucius. The stretch was intense—yet it only added to the pleasure building up again, deep in my core.

His thrusts were slow and deliberate. Each pull and push sent waves of sensation through me. Our muffled breaths and moans created a symphony of lustful sounds. I moved with him, pushing back, meeting him blow for blow as each moment drew us closer to the edge.

Jase's thrusts shifted into grinding as he molded himself against me. His mouth found that perfect spot—where your neck meets your shoulder—and bit me, hard.

I cried out before he could cover my mouth, the imminent orgasm tore through me—violent, undeniable. My muscles pulsed around his cock as he groaned, falling over the edge with me. His rhythm faltered as he came, pumping me full of his seed. His bear, claiming what was his to take.

He held me close, still inside me, our breathing gradually slowing to a synchronized rhythm, before he finally pulled out. "I'm sorry," he whispered.

"Sorry for what?" I reached for my shoulder, fingering the tender bite. "Biting me?"

"Go back to bed, Michaela."

His voice was different now. Distant. I grabbed the shredded remains of my nightgown and clutched it to my chest. "What did you say?"

He was already pulling his pants back on. "This was a mistake."

"It didn't feel like a mistake to me." My heart was

breaking. How could he deny our connection now? We were both there. I know he felt it too. "Why don't you ask your bear if it was a mistake?"

"That's the problem, Michaela. I let my bear take control tonight."

"But you acknowledge the connection? Jase—"

"Mic." His voice was cold. Final. "You're gonna wake the others. Go back to bed." He turned and walked away— leaving me naked and used in the dark silence.

I couldn't bring myself to move. I stood there, frozen in hurt and confusion, staring out the window once more. A moment ago, my face had been flush with pleasure. Now it was cloaked in sorrow.

A look I was all too familiar with.

PART
TWO

CHAPTER XVIII
BLOODMONEY
-MICHAELA-

I could barely see from the hiding spot Lucius had picked for me. Over a month had passed since our little rebellion started raiding Johan's shipments. I'd finally convinced Nico to bring me along, but thanks to Lucius, I was going to miss everything. I pulled aside the dense branches, but even without all the leaves in this thicket, visibility was poor. The last rays of sunlight had long since retreated, shrouding our raiding party in shadows. If it weren't for the bobbing torches, I'd be completely blind to the caravan rumbling down the pass.

Heavy cavalry led the way, followed by a seemingly ordinary ironclad wagon. A dozen foot soldiers flanked the shipment, along with a pack of shifted wolves patrolling up and down the lines. We'd been so successful, Johan had stopped sending his best carriages, opting for more armor and less opulence. The black and crimson banners of the royal standards had been stripped away to make them less conspicuous. But the sheer number of soldiers was a dead giveaway.

It had taken weeks of relentless training—and a fair share of begging—before they finally caved and agreed to let me join. I may have done some shameless flirting to get there, but I didn't regret it one bit. My blood was pumping with adrenaline. I'd been cooped up at Whisperhold for too long.

Now, the chill of the night air and the promise of battle had me feeling alive. I reached into my corseted leather bodice, pulling out the small vial of sprite ash hidden between my breasts. It shimmered in the moonlight. Innocent. Almost beautiful. Nothing like the "filth" Jase had likened it to. My fingers hovered at the stopper. "Only cowards use it," Jase's voice rang out in my memory, low and scathing.

Bastard. Always so quick to judge, like he was above ever taking a whisper of help. And yet, his words were a thorn I couldn't dislodge.

He didn't know what it was like to be in pain all the time —to have your own magic trying to kill you every day. I only needed a little. Just enough to get me through the raid. Through another night of him ignoring me. I had to be at my best. There was no room for my typical aches, pains, or wooziness. If that made me a coward, then so be it. One could never be too prepared during a rebellion. I tilted the vial with finality, rubbing the glittering ash into my décolletage, sighing as the rush hit me. A flood of warmth eased away all of my ailments mere moments before our unsuspecting guests arrived.

I held my breath as the caravan approached the choke point. A resonant owl's call carried over the creaking wagon and rhythmic footsteps—the cryptic signal I'd been waiting for. My heart raced in anticipation.

The whistle of arrows flying through the air was the last thing I heard before chaos erupted. The volley dropped several soldiers in their tracks. Our war cries were deafening, drowning out the bewildered screams of the enemy.

All at once, our forces converged on the foot soldiers. Bare-chested males painted in protective runes barreled down in wild abandon, cutting off any possibility of retreat. Johan's soldiers were pinned between our steel and the treasure they'd been paid to protect. The wagon had been halted at the perfect spot, preventing the mounted soldiers from turning to join the fray.

A line of bears emerged from the shadows, blocking the road ahead. At the center was Nico, his copper coat reflecting what little light there was. Sawyer stood at his right, his white fur almost luminous against the darkness, while Jase—his opposite in every way—was little more than a phantom. His ebony coat blended seamlessly into the night, as if he were one of the shadows he commanded so well. The wolves snarled in protest as they engaged, but their numbers were no match for the sheer size of the bears.

Luca leapt onto the back of the wagon, his blonde hair pulled into a topknot. Black paint and blood covered his body. He worked his way over the top of the wagon, eyes set on the three men at the front, a massive axe poised in his hand. One of the armed guards turned on him, pistol raised to defend the driver and the trembling dignitary who I assumed was the crown's emissary. He fired a shot and my heart jumped into my throat. If Luca was hit, he didn't show it. He closed the distance in two strides, drove a boot into the guard's head, and knocked him backward off the wagon. The gun flew from his hand.

The emissary slipped from his seat, disappearing into the forest as the driver made a panicked attempt to spur the horses forward, but there was nowhere to go. Luca was on him in seconds, his axe nearly decapitating him in one violent swing. The horses squealed, prancing about as hot blood splattered their flanks.

"Jase! The emissary went that way!" Luca called, pointing toward the black expanse of forest. Jase barreled into the dense woods, the snap and pop of branches following in his wake as he disappeared. I felt my shoulders slump in relief. Everything was going exactly as Nico had planned. The crown's guards were falling quickly, outnumbered and outmatched by our forces.

I took inventory, counting to be sure we hadn't lost anyone. That's when I saw him—our enemy crouched low beside the wheel well, cloaked in darkness. His eyes were trained on Luca, the discarded gun from the driver's guard in his hand. Fuck. Luca was completely unaware. I hesitated, knowing Lu would kill me, but I couldn't let anything happen to him.

With shaking hands, I pulled the eidris from my thigh, taking a cautious step from my hiding spot. Panic and fear were only diluted by my rising anger. I wouldn't stand by and watch him get murdered without doing anything to stop it.

The male was poised to strike. I couldn't wait any longer. I pinched the blade between my fingers and whispered a quick prayer. "Watch over me, Gunner. Make my blade fly true." It was a desperate plea. As soon as the words left my lips, I felt it—the warmth of his presence pressed against my back. The gentle blue glow of his spirit appeared as transparent fingers traced over my arm, adjusting my hold.

"Now," Gunner's disembodied voice echoed in my head, and I let the blade fly.

The male dropped the gun, reaching for the blade now protruding from his neck. I knew the moment his soul left his body. A tug—like a string pulled taut in my chest before snapping. I watched in awe as blue vapors rose from the fallen soldier and swirled like fine mist, disappearing into the night sky. I'd felt an echo of this before, the last time I'd taken a life, but this time the feeling was stronger.

Luca whirled at the sound, looking past the wilting male, his gaze locking on mine. An infectious smile lit his face, pulling me from my reverie. I shook it off, dismissing it as nothing more than a guilty conscience, and shot a smile back as he saluted me.

"You're welcome!" I shouted. "And thank you," I sighed, hoping Gunner could still hear—though I knew he was no longer with me.

Luca hopped down from the wagon, pulled my eidris from the male's neck, and kicked him aside. He ran the short distance to me, ignoring the remnants of the battle, which was being won handily by our rebels.

"I thought you were supposed to stay put?" he asked, pulling me into his blood-slicked arms. In other circumstances, it would've been appalling, but my body was buzzing with the high of battle and the lingering effects of sprite ash.

"Are you really going to reprimand me when I just saved your life?"

"That's beside the point. You completely disobeyed orders. What do you think your punishment should be?" he asked, mirth dancing in his eyes.

"I think saving your ass negates any punishment I would have otherwise deserved. And besides... there was a moment when I think I saw—"

"And I think seeing you with a weapon gives me a terrible cock stand," he interrupted. The story of my encounter with Gunner completely vanished from my mind with that lewd comment. "Maybe you'll indulge me and let me have a little bit of fun?" He picked me up, his hands cupping my ass, holding me against his hardness as he spun me around.

I giggled—an unconventional reaction with the scent of blood still in the air, but my life now was anything but conventional.

My feet hit the ground as his lips met mine. It was fierce —the two of us giving into primal instincts. He captured my lip, dragging it between his teeth before sweeping his tongue into my mouth, stealing a moan from my throat. His hand landed in my hair, wrapping my thick braid around his palm, holding me in place.

"Don't you have a raid to finish?" Nico said after clearing his throat.

I tried to pull away from Luca, but he kept me pinned to his chest. I looked over at Nico, my cheeks flushed from the kiss—and being caught. But they turned absolutely scarlet when I realized Nico hadn't bothered to dress after shifting back. Luca had awakened my need, and Nico was adding fuel to the fire. I drank in the sight of him, biting my lip as my gaze drifted over the v-cut at his hips, drawing my eyes directly to his cock.

"You're just jealous I got to her first," Luca said.

"Jealous?" Nico laughed, shaking his head. "Merely playing my cards right. Mic, are you alright? Or is this brute trying to take advantage of you in the woods?"

"I'm fine. Really," I rattled off, sinful thoughts running amok in my head.

His eyebrows raised when my gaze made it back to his

eyes. "Good. We'll share a drink later to celebrate. But right now, we need to collect the money and clear out."

Lu joined us, wiping a bloodstained blade on his pants. *"Are you good, Dove?"* His question echoed in my head.

"I'm perfectly fine," I said, trying to sound nonchalant and not think about the fact that I'd *killed* someone. Now wasn't the time to listen to Lu brooding over my safety.

"Are you hurt?"

"None of this is my blood," I assured him.

"Lucius, if you two are about done," Nico said, interrupting our silent conversation, "I assume everything has been taken care of?"

"Yes. Sawyer's collecting the goods. There's more than we expected. Carrying all of it home will be quite the feat. I think we're just waiting on Jase. He's taking his damn time collecting Johan's pawn."

"Don't let me hold you up, Lu," Jase snarked, stepping out from the bushes, the torchlight catching on his naked body. A pining ache resonated in my chest at the sight of him. He hadn't touched me since that first night. He'd barely even spoken to me. And that damn bond that tethered me to him felt like a vice around my heart, desperate to pull us together. I absently wondered if he felt it too.

"Where's the emissary?" Nico grumbled.

"My bear got a little too excited. But don't worry—I didn't kill him until after he spilled his guts," Jase said, rolling his shoulders and tilting his head until his neck cracked.

"Are you serious? You knew we wanted him alive and yet you killed him anyway? Why the fuck are we bringing you on missions if you can't follow orders?" Lucius barked. His patience with Jase was thin—bordering on nonexistent—and he took every opportunity to scrutinize his actions. I'd have to broach the subject with him at some point. I was getting tired of all this dick measuring between the two of them.

"That wasn't the plan," Nico huffed. "But at least fill us in on what you found out?"

"It was blood money. Johan was paying the House of Lycaon to get the nobles to increase conscription numbers."

"More conscripts? Damn, I think we've hit a nerve!" Luca laughed. "I bet Johan's squirming in that stolen throne as we speak. It's almost time, brothers."

"Does that mean we're close? To getting Finn and Hunter out?" I asked.

I hated the hesitant glances that passed between them. I wasn't sure how long I could handle Hunter's screams bleeding into my dreams. It was eating me alive.

"I need to get them back," I whispered, more to myself than anyone else. "Every second they're in that place feels like I'm failing them."

Nico's hand found my shoulder—warm and solid. "We're close. I swear it. Just a little longer. Lunavale is within the week. I'd like to have a feast, to honor the day.

We'll plan to hit the heart of Mathenholm after we've taken a moment to celebrate."

"We should move to strike on Lunavale," Jase challenged. "Everyone will be celebrating. They'll be at their weakest."

"And we should put our blind faith in you? The one who can't even follow a simple order?" Lu growled, stepping up to Jase, the two standing chest to chest.

"Perhaps I'm not the type to follow orders," Jase barked, shoving Lucius back.

"Enough!" Nico bellowed. "We are at war. We don't need to be fighting with each other. Jase, we're waiting until after we honor Lunavale. The people need this. And Lu… learn to choose your battles. Now, Michaela and I are late for drinks, and I much prefer her company over the lot of you."

"WHAT'S LUNAVALE?" I asked Maxfield, breaking the silence. Our lesson today consisted of sitting in a quiet spot and meditating. The calm of nature was supposed to help me connect with my magic—or some ridiculousness he'd come up with. I think he just wanted to take a nap in the woods and this was his way of accomplishing that without pissing off Lu.

A dull hazel eye popped open beneath a wildly bushy eyebrow. "I'm not here for a history lesson. I'm sure your princes are well versed in that."

"Oh, come on. I know it has something to do with magic, so technically that's your area," I said, trying to sound convincing. The celebration was in a few days and the camp was teeming with excitement. I'd overheard more than a few rumors, but there hadn't been a moment for me to ask Fallon. Nor did I want to bother the others with my curiosities while everyone was so busy.

"This is why you've learned nothing. You refuse to listen." He slammed his one eye shut again, rearranging his robes before setting his hands back on his knees.

"You're not teaching me anything. I'll never break the Tribulation if all we do is listen to the birds in the forest. I want to learn about magic."

"And I want to go home and be left alone. There! I guess neither of us gets what we want," he grumbled, pulling himself up from the ground and ambling back toward Whisperhold. "Lesson's over."

"I'll make you a deal. Tell me about Lunavale and I'll send Maeve to fetch you for our next meeting instead of Lucius."

That stopped him in his tracks. He turned around, scrutinizing me from under those bushy eyebrows.

"Ugh, fine. The only good thing about Lunavale is the serviceberry pie. But I'll grant you three questions. To the point, and don't be vague."

"Well, for starters, what exactly are we celebrating?"

"Lunavale is the day the Divine wove the bond that connected the people of Hiraeth with our beasts. The night the first four were born into existence. It is said that the spirit of the first shifters cross the veil to watch over their descendants."

"You mean the four houses, right? And what exactly are they watching?"

"Yes, the original four shifters make up the royal houses that exist in Hiraeth today. This isn't just a festival—it's a reckoning. A time to show strength and honor—the primal nature we were born to. It's very primitive. Those who prove their dominance in the eyes of the founding ancestors will be blessed in the coming year."

"So what about—"

"Ah, ah. That was three questions. We're done."

"It was not! I was confirming what I already knew. That's not a question."

"You are insufferable, child. One more blasted question and no amount of sweet talk will keep me from leaving."

"I heard there was a... chase?" I asked, my cheeks flushing as I thought of the females recounting the prior year's celebration. Nothing I wanted to verbalize to Maxfield, but I had to know if it was true.

"Ah yes, the Villrenna. The wild run. It is a mating chase. Males chase down their prospective female and, well... for those that manage to catch their prize, nature takes its course. But," he continued, his gaze flicking to me, "when it's a fated bond, it becomes something else. Something sacred. The land joins in the binding. Villrenna isn't just tradition—it's life. The magic in the soil, in the wind, in the very roots of the trees. When the fated run the wild together, the realm awakens to witness it. And when the bond is sealed..." He smiled like he'd seen it once and never forgotten. "You're not just tied to each other. You're bound to Hiraeth itself."

I may have been in a peaceful grove, but my heart was racing as if I was already being chased.

"Thank you, Maxfield. Maybe next time I can barter for some actual instruction on how to use my magic?"

The old shifter harrumphed as I wrapped my arm with his, my mind whirling with possibilities.

"You're buttering me up for something," he muttered, eyeing me from beneath his bushy grey brows. "I'm not blind, child. Or deaf."

"Can't I be nice?" I asked, giving him my best innocent smile. As much as Maxfield tried to hide behind that grumpy demeanor, I could tell he was softening toward me.

He grumbled again but didn't pull away as we walked back to Whisperhold.

"So," I said as casually as I could manage, "how long does sprite ash usually last? A full vial, I mean?"

I was pushing my luck asking another question, but I was burning through the ash quicker than I expected. With all the festivities and the possibility of rescuing Finn and

Hunter soon—I had to be prepared. My vial was getting uncomfortably low.

Maxfield stopped to glare at me. "The vial I gave you, if properly used, should last you a year. Maybe longer if you're not being wasteful. How much have you been using, child?"

I blinked as panic washed over me. "Me? Oh... only when I really need it. I have plenty left. I was only curious... you know, for the next time."

He eyed me for a long time, as if measuring the truth of my words. My hands began to fidget under the scrutiny.

"Good," he finally said, turning again toward the cabin. "Sprite ash contains potent magic. It's nothing to be trifled with. But a smart girl like you would already know that."

CHAPTER XIX
LUNAVALE
-MICHAELA-

I rubbed the back of my neck, trying to ease the ache in my shoulders after placing the final pallet of food into the underground oven. We'd been preparing the camp for tonight's festivities since dawn. The thick frost that blanketed the ground had finally thawed, but the season was shifting fast—snow would be here before we knew it.

My thoughts drifted to this morning, when Luca had made good on his promise to warm my bed, making it nearly impossible to get up and start the day.

The camp buzzed with excitement, and it was contagious. My hands were chapped from cleaning, nicked with more than a few cuts from peeling endless vegetables. Still, my heart was full and the anticipation was palpable.

The smell of food wafted in the air, turning my stomach.

I'd been pushing myself too hard again. The cancer—or curse—or whatever the Tribulation was, always seemed to be lurking below the surface. I needed to decide whether it was worth using the precious little sprite ash I had left. It was clearly something I'd need to ration now... unless I found another source besides Maxfield. The last thing I wanted was for the brothers to start worrying.

I was the last one to finish up. The other females had already gone to prepare for the celebration. I'd been avoiding it—mostly because I had little to work with. I'd acquired a few hand-me-down dresses since we'd left the castle, but nothing fancy. The one warm dress I had was clean, but the hem sagged with ragged holes I hadn't gotten around to stitching. It would have to do.

"Mic!" Fallon's voice rang from the cabin doorway. "Come here! I need to show you something."

Getting ready for tonight would have to wait a bit longer. Hopefully, my wit and charm would distract from my disheveled appearance.

Fallon, somehow, still managed to look every bit the royal she was, even in the middle of a rebellion. A sleek ebony dress hugged her corseted waist and flared at the floor, her short black hair slicked into a polished shine. She always added an edge to whatever fashions the others favored.

"You look amazing, as always," I said as she grabbed my hand and tugged me into the cabin.

"Yes, of course. Now let me work some of my magic on

you," she said, pulling me into the king's quarters—her permanent room since I'd refused it, preferring the bunkhouse with the princes. "I found some old dresses in Danya's chest." She gestured to a heap of satin fabrics piled across the bed.

"Who's Danya?" I asked, tracing my fingers over the red flowers embroidered on one of the garments.

"The queen. My brothers' mother."

"Don't you mean *your* mother?"

"No. We don't share a mother. Mine died a long time ago."

"I'm so sorry, Fallon," I said softly, squeezing her hand.

"Don't be. She died when I was very young for the unfortunate crime of not producing a male heir. Not that Danya fared much better."

"Seriously? I thought Artos was a good man. Everyone here talks like he was a great king."

"He was a great king. Maybe because he put the kingdom above everything else—including his family. When my mother died, he moved on to the next. I don't think he even shed a tear."

"Did he marry again? After Danya?"

"Oh gods, no. He wasn't interested in marriage. He only needed an heir. After that, females were only a means to an end. He'd sleep with anyone who struck his fancy or could advance his power. His favorite trick was bedding the wives of dignitaries who spoke out against him—or sending Lucius in his stead."

"Wait—what?" I asked, her words creating more questions than answers. What she was implying had my blood boiling.

"Well… shit." She muttered the last part under her breath. "Lucius hasn't told you much about his past, has he?"

"Not particularly, no," I admitted.

"Don't be upset with him. It's not exactly a story he's eager to share with you. But it's not my story to tell either. I'm sorry, Mic."

"Don't be. I'm sure he'll tell me when he's ready." I tried to sound understanding, but my mind raced, imagining what kind of torment Lu must have endured under his father.

"The dresses aren't extravagant," Fallon said, shifting the conversation without missing a beat, "but they're better than a woolen house dress with holes in it."

"I happen to like my plain house dress. I just didn't have time to mend it—I spent all day prepping for the feast that I sort of forgot about myself," I admitted.

"That's why you're the perfect choice," she said, rifling through the silks.

"Perfect choice? For what?"

"When my brothers inevitably retake Hiraeth, they'll need a strong female by their side. You're exactly the kind of queen this realm deserves."

"No, no, no. I'm not a queen. Nico has a betrothed. He

wouldn't give up a match that strengthens his claim to the throne. I'm just a sickly human—not queen material."

Fallon gave a dry, humorless laugh. "Nyla Taryn? You think he cares about that simpering leech?"

"Well, I assumed—"

"Please, Mic. That betrothal was arranged long before Nico ever got the balls to defy our father. Nyla was always in it for status, for proximity to the throne. Now that Nico's no longer the golden prince, I'd bet she's already licking Johan's boots."

"But it's not about what he wants. He has obligations. Making a human his queen could ruin everything. I won't force him to make that choice," I said, swallowing back the grief of a decision I knew would have to be made one day.

"I'm going to tell you a secret—but if you repeat it, I'll call you a liar and swear I never said it." Fallon leaned in, lowering her voice. "All of my brothers would rather see Hiraeth burn to the ground before they'd ever give you up."

"I respect your opinion, Loni, but you're wrong. After everything they've been through, that kind of sacrifice just seems... reckless," I said, trying to find gentler words for the truth none of us wanted to face. Beast princes, born to rule a kingdom, tied to a human girl who wasn't meant to survive long enough to see it? Surely Fallon, of all people, could see the futility in that match?

"I'm calling your bluff, Michaela Darling Carlisle. You're not the kind of female to lead them on if you saw no future in it. Queens aren't born with crowns. They rise when no one else can. You've already risen—even if you can't see it yet."

"I… well, I—"

"I think this one suits you." She held up a cream-colored gown, switching topics like turning a page.

"It's beautiful. I can't repay you for such a gift."

"It's not a gift. We're simply being resourceful," Fallon said. "Danya is dead. I doubt she'll need the dress anytime soon. But speaking of gifts, I have something for you."

She pulled out a parchment-wrapped package, neatly tied with a twill bow.

"It's for Villrenna. Custom says that females are gifted an outfit for their first chase by the elders in her family, and she'll wear it for every run thereafter until she's officially spoken for."

"Fallon, you shouldn't have. I don't have anything for you." I took the package from her, wishing I'd had the foresight to get her something, while silently cursing Maxfield for not having mentioned this particular custom.

"That's not how it works in Hiraeth. This is a gift. They're given with no expectation of return. It would be considered rude if you felt obligated to reciprocate. Now, open it."

I laid the package on the bed and pulled the tie. The parchment fell away to reveal a two-piece outfit made of velvety suede, decorated with tufts of fur and intricate beaded designs.

I lifted the top, realizing it would barely cover my breasts.

"Is this all there is?" I asked, heat blooming across my cheeks.

"It's a mating chase, Mic. It kind of ruins the moment if they have to do battle with corset stays and laces." She rolled her eyes, amusement flickering at the corners of her mouth.

"Are you running too?"

"Unfortunately, no. It's only for unwed females."

"I didn't know you had a husband."

"I don't—at least not anymore. He's dead and hopefully rotting in whatever afterlife exists. But don't worry about me. There's more than one way to get laid on Lunavale."

PEOPLE HAD FLOODED in from Dunharrow, joining us at Whisperhold alongside our allies in the Raven's Hand. Lunavale brought a new energy to our rebellion. There was something different in the air. The downtrodden faces I'd grown used to now shimmered with hope and anticipation.

Nico had given them something to believe in—and they were rising to meet it. The feeling was so contagious that even Maxfield wasn't immune. I'd managed to get a half-smile out of him when I presented him with the serviceberry pie I'd made.

The camp flickered with torchlight, centered around a

communal fire in the nearby clearing. The air was thick with the scent of woodsmoke, spiced cider, and roasting meat.

Amos's deep baritone rang out in lewd drinking songs between swigs from his flask. Fiddles sang, flutes trilled, and voices rose in raucous harmony as rebels linked arms and spun in wild, unbridled dancing.

Overhead, the full moon bathed the clearing in silver light, casting long shadows that danced with the glow of the bonfires.

Nico, Luca, and Lucius had all announced they would take part in tonight's Villrenna. Jase hadn't said either way. A part of me was afraid his answer might be no. The idea of the four of them chasing me down was as exhilarating as it was terrifying.

"Isn't it lovely?" Nico asked as he joined me, fresh from greeting the guests.

"Isn't what lovely?"

"Listen..." He leaned in. "No one's whispering about battle plans. No one's sharpening blades. Only the sound of our people enjoying what life has to offer."

"It's perfect," I agreed, unable to suppress the smile tugging at my lips. He'd said *our* people. That one word filled me with a sense of belonging, wrapping around the hollow spaces inside me.

Tonight was a reprieve. A sacred night of laughter, music, and revelry. A festival of defiance. A celebration of the simple fact that we still lived, still breathed, still fought.

"You didn't happen to have anything to do with the

unusually good mood everyone is in tonight, did you?" I teased.

"It's not from me. I promise. Completely natural. I haven't used my gift."

"Go talk to Lucius and you'll realize not everyone is in a good mood," Luca said, appearing behind me with a cup of mead. "You look absolutely stunning tonight. That dress... mmm." He growled softly, his eyes taking me in with a feral glint.

The dress was rather modest—a simple sweetheart neckline with capped sleeves—but the cream silk and the embroidered crimson petals cascading down made it truly breathtaking.

"Thank you for the drink, and the compliment," I said, pulling the fur mantle tighter around my shoulders. I felt self-conscious under their praise. "You'll have to thank your sister for the dress. Apparently, I'd look like a "filthy house gnome" if not for her intervention."

"Even on your worst day, you're the most beautiful creature I've ever seen," Lucius added as he joined us.

I gave him an exasperated look. "The three of you flatter me too much."

"The three of us have to make up for the one asshole who can't be bothered to show his face tonight," Lu scoffed.

"Where is Jase?" I asked, hesitating as I scanned the sea of unfamiliar faces.

A cold touch brushed my shoulder moments before a voice answered.

"This asshole is on guard duty tonight."

I spun and found Jase emerging from the shadows. His silhouette stretched in the firelight. He was clad in black leather armor and a sleek fur mantle draped over his broad shoulders. One hand rested on the pommel of a broadsword strapped to his hip.

He was dangerously handsome. My cheeks flushed at the sight of him, my body betraying me once again. He sauntered towards us, with his jaw tight and eyes narrowed —the only signs of the storm brewing beneath his calm exterior.

"You're the last person any of us want on guard duty," Lucius snarked, not even trying to hide the disdain.

Lucius didn't trust him. I didn't know if it had anything to do with the fact that Jase and I had... been intimate, or whatever you wanted to call what happened that night. I hadn't told anyone. Not even Fallon. But there was no hiding the fact that Jase had left his scent all over me.

"That was my call," Nico admitted.

"You can't be serious," Lucius snapped. "You've invited a slew of unvetted shifters into our camp, and now *he's* the one guarding our backs?"

"There are laws against battles on Lunavale."

"Because Johan's never broken our laws before," Lucius said, rolling his eyes. "This whole thing is reckless."

"I've set up sentries around the entire camp. But I needed one of us out there as a matter of principle. Since Jase isn't running the Villrenna tonight, and his shadows cover more ground than any of us. He was the best choice. Unless you'd like to trade places with him?" Nico raised an eyebrow.

Lucius clenched his jaw, but said nothing.

"That's what I thought," Nico said before turning to Jase, "If you're supposed to be on sentry duty, you're doing a piss-poor job of it."

"I need a word with Michaela."

Before I could respond, his shadows wrapped around my wrist. A cold caress that solidified into steel, yanking me forward. I stumbled to keep up, dragged in Jase's wake as he strode away from the others.

"What are you doing? You could have asked to talk to me, and I would've said yes!" I pulled against the dark form holding me in an iron grip. He didn't answer, just kept walking, only stopping to face me once we reached the edge of the encampment.

"Stay away from the river tonight. Head east on your run," he barked, his shadow slipping from my wrist.

"What? Why?"

"Don't ask questions. Just be a good girl and do what I say."

I stood there, wringing my hands. Was this it? Was this all our bond would ever be? A few curt words and the aching memory of how he'd taken my body in ways that now left me starving for his touch. His steely gaze softened slightly as I stayed silent, unmoving.

"There are males out there who wouldn't think twice

about snagging a little thing like you. Tonight, you're fair game. And I don't want to have to clean up after my brothers if they kill someone over it."

I clung to the seemingly small gesture, the *like* it meant more than it should. A small spark of hope flared in my chest. I knew it was foolish to pine after someone who didn't want you in return, at least not in the way I wanted him to. Not when I had three others openly vying for my affection. But I couldn't help it. And I cursed the damn fated bond that tethered me to him.

"I'll keep that in mind," I said quietly. "Why aren't you running in tonight's chase?"

"Trust me—you wouldn't want me out there," he grumbled, turning away from me and stalking off into the forest without another word.

FALLON WAS UNUSUALLY QUIET. She pulled me aside when it came time to prepare for the run, deftly securing the ties on the wrapped skirt that barely covered my ass without so much as a word or sass remark.

"What's wrong? Is it the outfit?" I asked, glancing down at the small swath of suede stretched across my breasts.

"No, the outfit's perfect," she said.

"I think if I run too fast, it might fall off. Is this really what everyone else is wearing?"

"It's not that. I just... have a bad feeling."

"Really? Have you told Nico?"

CHAPTER XIX

"No." She sighed. "I think I'm just getting more sensitive in my older years. We're in a fight for the realm, Mic. The idea that any of us are safe is merely a comforting fantasy to get us through another day." She gave me a half-hearted smile, her fingers adjusting the beaded straps over my shoulders. "This is just the beginning. The worst of it is yet to come. So enjoy the night. Who knows how many we have left before the fantasy ends?"

Fallon led me outside. The frigid night air hit my exposed skin, sending a violent shiver through my bones. The adrenaline in my veins was the only thing keeping me upright. The males stood blindfolded before the central fire, bare chests rising with slow, deliberate breaths. Runes were painted across their skin in bold strokes. They waited without a word, every muscle coiled in anticipation for the chase to start.

The soft percussion of drum beats began to rise. A slow, steady rhythm that buzzed through the ground beneath my feet. With Fallon's urging, I joined the line of females forming before the males.

"What exactly are we doing?" I whispered to the female behind me.

"So they can scent us," she whispered back, offering no further explanation.

Nico, Luca, and Lucius stood together at the end of the line. Their faces were stoic, arms crossed over their bare chests—unmoving—until I passed by. Their nostrils flared.

Luca grinned, elbowing Nico as he shifted from one foot to the next.

"Don't make it easy on us," Luca said. "You better run when the horn sounds."

Amos ambled into the clearing, staff in one hand and his usual flask in the other. He stretched his broad shoulders like a man preparing for a fight as everyone around him fell silent. Raising his drink in salute, he took a long swig, wiped his mouth with the back of his hand, and smiled like the deviant he was.

"Ah, my fine, wild creatures! Here we stand, ready to remind the realm that life is a chase, a feast, and a fine excuse to run half-naked through the woods!" he said with a hearty chuckle as he gestured toward the sky, his eyes gleaming with mischief.

"Some of you will run. Some of you will chase. Some of you will trip over a root and fall flat on your face, and let me tell you, the Divine is watching… nay, laughing. And it'd be a damn shame to disappoint."

The crowd erupted in laughter, myself included. He had a way of easing a bit of the tension that had settled in my spine.

"Let no chain hold you. Let no fear bind you. The Divine does not favor the meek nor the slow of foot! Run! And if you're caught, yield as all prey must—revel in the joy of the hunt. May we feast beneath the moon, drunk on victory and flesh!"

With that, he slammed his staff into the ground."Run, you mad bastards, RUN!"

I balked like a startled deer at the shrill horns. The females bolted, clumping together in a pack. I followed until I saw where they were headed—north. Toward the river.

The one place Jase had told me to avoid.

Against my better judgment, I broke off from the group, picking up speed as I barreled through the trees.

At first, all I could hear were my bare feet hitting the ground and the frantic beat of my heart. The moon bathed the forest in silver, casting shadows that played tricks on my mind. Was the darkness moving? I could've sworn I saw something curl around a tree trunk.

My legs ached, but the fear had taken over. Excitement was gone—only survival remained.

A branch snapped behind me and my steps faltered. I stumbled over a root—only to be caught. The darkness rising to meet me, steadying me before I could hit the ground. I froze, my breath ragged and curling into the cold night air in thick, ghostly plumes.

"Jase?" I called. "Is that you?"

No answer.

A fluttering of wings from the bushes broke the silence. I turned, backing away slowly. I was too exposed. How far should I go? What happened if someone other than my princes found me out here?

A strange grumbling chuckle rolled from behind the trees and terror crawled up my spine. Something wasn't right. I jolted back into motion, my tired legs finding new life as I ran. Someone was following me, but I didn't dare look back. The shadows at my feet writhed and seemed to push me forward. The sounds behind me grew louder—branches snapped, as if a giant was barreling through the trees. Panic threatened to swallow me whole.

Then suddenly, everything stopped. A low, guttural groan echoed through the woods, followed by complete silence.

I ducked behind a tree, desperate to catch my breath. My lungs burned, and my ears rang in the stillness. Damn Fallon. Damn this ridiculous outfit. I hadn't had a place to bring my eidris with me and I felt more vulnerable than ever.

I chanced a break, trying to retrace my steps—only to crash into something solid.

A rune-painted chest.

A scream tore from my lips as large hands encircled my arms. "I like it when you scream, little bird," Nico's deep, gravelly voice cut through my panic.

I threw my arms around him, letting the fear melt from my body. Every muscle turned to liquid, and I let the strength of him hold me up. Leaves rustled behind us, and my body went rigid in Nico's arms.

"Looks like you found our prey. She's faster than I thought," Luca said, an edge to his voice I hadn't heard before. "Our younger brothers may have gotten their way with her first, but it looks like we won the race."

"I'm beginning to think the lady prefers our baser instincts. She likes it when our beasts come out to play," Nico said, the two of them circling around me with hungry eyes.

"Now we get to enjoy our prize," Luca added.

Fear and excitement warred for dominance, but I couldn't stop the warmth blooming in my core as anticipation took hold.

"She's my prize. I got to her first," Nico asserted, the two of them locking eyes as they continued to circle.

"She's my fated, too!" Luca growled. I wasn't used to my happy-go-lucky beast being so aggressive.

"You can watch while you wait your turn. Or, by all means—challenge me." Nico beckoned him forward, and a part of me wondered if he was hoping for the fight. I stood frozen, watching the spectacle, feeling more like prey than ever before.

"You may be older. You may be bigger. But for her—I will take down anything standing in my way."

Nico growled in turn. "Are you going to watch, or are you ready to fight?"

Luca bowed slightly. "I'll wait. Someone has to finish her off when you leave her wanting."

Nico bared his teeth to his brother before grabbing my wrist and dragging me toward him. I slammed into his bare chest, and he growled in my ear, "To the victor goes the spoils."

Strong hands fisted in my hair, holding me still as his lips crashed onto mine, claiming my mouth. His tongue swept over my lips with urgent need, and I opened for him, letting him explore. He moved his hands from my hair, pushing up the tiny garment covering my breasts and cupping them. I found myself leaning into his warm caress, my desire rising to meet his.

In the flicker of a heartbeat, he was gone, pulling away and leaving me reeling. My skin chilled as the cold air rushed to fill the places he had just been. "Hold her steady and spread her legs," Nico commanded. "I want to taste her honey."

Luca's body pressed against my back, splaying a hand over my exposed belly and kicking my legs apart. The short skirt rode up my thighs, leaving me fully exposed.

My beast king kneeled before me, his hands running up the backs of my legs. He looked up at me briefly, lust flaring in his eyes before he buried his face in my sex. Pleasure coursed through my body.

"That's right, beautiful. Let us hear you sing," Luca whispered in my ear as a desperate moan slipped from my lips. He peered over my shoulder, reaching for Nico and grabbed a fistful of his hair, angling his head for a better view. "How does she taste?"

"Divine," he growled. "I'll crave her sweetness for the rest of my days," Nico groaned before continuing his ministrations, running his tongue over my clit in slow, rhythmic patterns.

I was lost, adrift in a pool of rapture when I reached my

hand down, twining my fingers with Luca's, digging my nails into his palm while his brother ravaged me. The cold night air on my skin, the primal charge surrounding us, and his relentless tongue working my tight bud drove me to new heights.

"Fuck, that's—so good." The words came out in panted mews as I tried to hold on to the sensation, riding the high before he inevitably pulled me over the edge.

I was thankful to have Luca behind me, holding me up. I shamelessly ground against his hardness, needing more friction.

"That's right, love. Keep doing that," Luca groaned in my ear. "Just one finger. That's all she needs."

Without missing a beat, Nico teased my opening.

"That's it. I know you're ready to cum. Let it go," Luca said, his hand pressing against my belly, increasing the pressure of Nico's finger inside me and sending me into sweet oblivion.

"Oh God!" The words spilled from my lips, and I writhed against his face, riding out my orgasm on his hand.

"Not a god—I am your king," Nico growled. "And watching my queen come undone for me is pure bliss."

Nico looked up at me with adoring eyes before sweeping me off my feet. My hand remained intertwined with Luca's. The two of them laid me down in a patch of moonlit moss. Luca leaned against a nearby tree, fisting his shaft and positioning himself for a show.

My king kneeled between my legs, pulling the ties on his

pants, releasing his massive cock from its confines. Everything about him was large, and that held true in every aspect. But I was too far gone to let it deter me. I wanted him inside me. Now.

His warm palm rested on my bent knee, while the other fisted his cock at the root, dragging his length through my wetness until he was slick with my excitement.

"Now, little bird, give me my bliss again," he growled as he slid inside, inch by slow inch until he was buried to the hilt. He paused, letting me adjust to the sinfully sweet burning stretch of him filling me.

Our eyes locked, sharing something I couldn't fully explain. That inexplicable moment when one soul fuses to another—when two become one. He began to move, his face drawing so close to mine that I could see the passion dancing in his eyes.

A warm, blue glow radiated between us as the pleasure grew. Lines of power seemed to come from the land, engulfing us in a luminescent cocoon. Everything fell away until there was nothing but us.

Each stroke brought me higher. Pleasure consumed me, blurring my vision into white points of light, as though the stars had collided.

"Cum for me, little bird," he said, his words melting me, falling over the edge and into the swell of an all-consuming climax.

"Turn her over," Luca commanded as I drifted back down to reality.

CHAPTER XIX

Nico pulled out, flipping me onto my hands and knees, pulling my hips back and sheathing himself inside me in one fluid movement, sending shockwaves over my sensitive flesh.

Luca left his spot against the tree, kneeling down beside me. He gripped my chin, tilting my head until I met his hungry gaze.

"That's it. Keep your eyes on me. I want to watch as he hits that spot that drives you crazy." He ran his thumb over my bottom lip before pressing it into my mouth, probing in and out, pushing further with each stroke until I gagged.

I was awash in sensation. The two of them working in conjunction to draw out every bit of pleasure from my body and I was on fire for both of them.

"Time to finish up, brother," Luca commanded. "I'm claiming her next one."

Nico's fervent pace picked up, his fingertips digging into my hips as he used me for his own pleasure.

"Don't you cum. Wait for me," Luca said, drawing my attention back to him. It was everything I could do to follow his orders, to hold myself back while his brother filled me so completely.

Nico stilled, fully sheathed inside me as a feral groan rumbled from his chest. The sound of him letting go was almost my undoing.

"My turn," Luca growled, grasping my arms and pulling me from his brother. The loss of Nico's length—the feel of his seed dripping down my thighs—was profound. I was on the brink of climax, and they'd left me desperate.

Luca pulled me over his body, drawing me into his lap. The warmth of him soothing the bite of the cold air as his hands caressed my back.

"I've been waiting my whole life for this," he whispered in my ear, pulling my hair to the side to bite my shoulder. His hands were on my ass, lifting me until the head of his cock found my opening. He eased me down, slowly impaling me on his thick shaft, my breasts pressing against his chiseled chest.

"You're perfect." Luca hissed. "You take me so well,"

His praise unleashed a need unlike anything I'd ever felt. I leaned my forehead against his, wrapping my arms around his neck, and began to grind. Shamelessly, rubbing against him to find the friction I was so desperate for. The lines of power were back, swirling up from the ground, circling around us in another blue vortex. The energy shifting between the two of us was heady—an otherworldly connection and I couldn't get enough of it.

"I can't—" I gasped, trying to hold back the dam that was about to break.

"Yes, you can. Wait for me," he groaned, holding onto me for dear life as he thrust into me with fervor.

It was almost painful, denying myself release. Each punishing stroke demanding deliverance, until no amount of willpower could keep me from tipping over the edge. A cry erupted from my lips as I lost all control. My climax seized my body, tensing around his length as I rode out the wave of pleasure.

Luca growled, his hips jerking as I drew him into his own rapture, the two of us sharing the high as we melted into one another. I stayed there in his arms while my body slowly returned to reality.

"You were made for me," Luca sighed, his face buried in my hair.

A second pair of warm hands were on my back, sliding under my arms, and pulling me from Luca's body. Nico cradled me to his chest placing a chaste kiss on my forehead before slinging me over his shoulder.

"You were amazing, little bird, Let's go home. We'll get you cleaned up and tucked into bed," he said, slapping my ass before stalking off into the darkness.

CHAPTER XX
THE EASY WAY OR THE HARD WAY
-MICHAELA-

I was on fire.

Luca and Nico lay on either side of me, the three of us tangled in a puddle of blankets we'd arranged on the floor of the bunk room. The two of them gave off so much heat, I felt like I couldn't breathe. I needed some air. Maybe that's what had woken me?

The room was still dark, but there was that subtle shift in the air that told me dawn wasn't far off. I untangled myself from the sleeping beasts, and when the cool air hit me, a shiver ran over my skin as though something, or someone, was watching me. I scanned the room. Everything was deathly silent. Even the beasts beside me slept soundly. My gaze caught on the doorway, shadowed and still. I couldn't be sure if my eyes were playing tricks on me, but it looked like a figure leaned against the frame.

"Jase? Is that you?" I whispered, trying to focus on the darkness, willing it to move.

Nothing.

The shape remained frozen in place. Lay back down and you'll fall back to sleep, I reasoned as I rubbed my eyes. Maybe it's a dream. Maybe I'm just exhausted.

When I opened my eyes again, the shadow was gone. A sliver of moonlight now highlighting the wooden frame. My heart pounded as I second-guessed what I'd seen. There had been a shadow. I'm sure of it. Right?

I padded across the room and inspected the doorway, but everything seemed normal—none of the icy foreboding Jase's shadows usually left behind. I slipped from the room, closing the door quietly behind me.

The cabin was packed. Every available inch of floor was filled with the lucky few who'd found a spot to crash after the night's festivities. A dull thud echoed through the silence, not quite loud enough to wake anyone. At first, I ignored it. Then it came again.

Something about it was off. Unsettling.

"Jase?" I whispered again, gingerly stepping between the sleeping bodies.

Still no answer.

When I reached the hall, I froze. The front door was open. It clanged softly against the frame in the breeze. A sliver of moonlight yawning between the gap. Where was

Jase? He was on sentry duty. He *never* would've left Whisperhold exposed like this. Not unless something was wrong.

Another gust shoved against the door, forcing it open wider with a groan. The house inhaled. Cold air slithered around my ankles like fingers. I reached for the door to pull it closed until a faint glow beyond the tree line stilled my hand. Lights flickered as if a processional approached the camp. A procession?

What in the bloody hell was going on? Was I dreaming?

I stepped out into the frozen night, blinking furiously. But the lights didn't disappear. They grew brighter until a nightmare took shape. A line of soldiers emerged from the woods—flaming arrows nocked and ready to fly.

A scream bubbled up from my lungs, but a firm hand slapped over my mouth, muffling the sound. A muscled arm wrenched me back. My feet left the ground as I twisted violently, kicking and clawing.

"I didn't believe them when they said you'd come right to us," a sinister voice whispered in my ear. I thrashed, trying in vain to break his grip, trying to raise the alarm for those sleeping mere feet away, but his hands tightened around me. "We can do this the easy way or the hard way. But in the end, you're coming with us. Johan eagerly awaits your arrival. And we don't want to disappoint the king now, do we?"

I fought him every inch of the way, but the moment we cleared the camp, a sickening whoosh echoed behind us.

Fire rained down. The dry wood caught like kindling. The cabin that had become my sanctuary erupted into an inferno.

The newly built shelters followed. Thatched roofs bursting into flame. I watched helplessly from the trees, my captor holding me still as we witnessed the destruction. The first screams came from outside the cabin. For many of them, it was too late, the flames had already consumed them before they'd even had a chance to fight.

"Time to watch your pathetic rebellion burn to the ground," my captor said gleefully.

It was a slaughter. The Crown's soldiers were prepared. Those who tried to run were met with blades. Others shifted into their beast forms, a last-ditch effort to defend themselves. Then—finally—Nico, Luca, and Lucius emerged from the fire, each carrying others to safety.

My heart lurched. They were alive.

Their eyes scanned the chaos, searching. Shouting my name. I tried to answer, but the fingers clamped tighter around my mouth.

"And that's our cue to leave, lovely," my captor snarled, dragging me deeper into the forest.

I bucked against him, desperate for some leverage, something to save me from whatever fate this was. I cursed the fact that I hadn't used any sprite ash. For not forcing Maxfield to actually teach me how to use my seemingly useless magic . I was helpless, and the feeling sent me spiraling into a rage that rose within me like a maelstrom.

My whole life, I'd felt helpless. At the whim of every evil thing that wanted its pound of flesh. And history was doomed to repeat itself.

The fighting behind us was a blur—beasts shifting mid-sprint, magic cracking through the trees. A small squad of Crown soldiers flanked my captor, and we slipped into the cloaking darkness of Thornwyn Forest.

I STUMBLED as they pulled me through the woods, each step further away from my beasts. It felt like we'd been walking for hours, but the sun was barely rising. I tried to drag my feet. At the very least, I'd give my beasts a path to follow when they came for me—because they *would* come for me.

"You think you're cute?" My captor snarled as he shoved me to the ground. "They won't make it through the night. Fight all you want. Come tomorrow, you're the king's property."

"Nico is the rightful king," I spat, back at him. "And he'll come for what's his," I scrambled to get to my feet. His heavy boot pushed me to the ground again, and they all laughed.

"That's the brilliance of it," he sneered. "We've given him an impossible choice. His fated or this rebellion. He chooses you—the rebels die. He chooses them—you're ours.Which choice do you think he'll make?" I remained silent. I couldn't answer. Nico's loyalty to his people was first and foremost. "Either way, Johan wins."

The soldier crouched beside me. He was the quintessential villain, basking in his monologue as I coward at his feet.

"Vairic, do you think the king will reward us once we deliver his pretty little prize?" one of the soldiers asked my captor.

"I think she's more valuable than we realized," Vairic replied. "I see why he wants her for Nocta Dominium."

"If he thinks the Bruins have left her untouched after all this time, then the Sigil has seriously addled his mind," another added.

"Seems like a good excuse. If she arrives well ridden, there's a perfectly reasonable story to tell."

The males talked excitedly among themselves as my mind whirled with the implications. What the hell was Nocta Dominium? I didn't know what the words meant, but I didn't need to. The look in their eyes told me enough and it made my blood run cold.

They closed in around me, fumbling with their belts, as wicked smirks cut across their faces.

Vairic pushed the others aside. "I outrank the lot of you. She's mine first. Zoryn—hold her down."

"No!" I scrambled back, feet slipping on the leaf litter. Even if I could escape, there was no way I'd outrun them. No way I'd overpower them. But my body geared up to fight anyway. A flood of adrenaline filled my veins, my heart racing into a frenzy. If they were going to sully my virtue, I would fight them every step of the way.

Zoryn grabbed my arms and I screamed. Without a hand covering my mouth, the sound echoed off the trees. But it didn't matter.

Vairic shoved up my shift, exposing my naked body as I kicked out, desperate to land a blow. Firm fingers dug into my thighs, pinning me to the ground while Vairic pulled out his cock. This was it. My body was no longer my own.

I tried to leave my body behind. To make it not real.

It's only flesh. It's not me.

The thought cycled over and over as he lined himself up. I closed my eyes, unable to watch.

I heard a sickening *thwack* and warm splatter covered my face. My eyes popped open to find Vairic swaying above me —an arrow protruding from his eye. He collapsed on top of me as chaos ensued. I squirmed under the corpse of my would-be rapist, desperate to be free of his dead weight.

Massive jaws snatched at the body, tearing it off me. Luca's bear nudged at me gently, his big tongue licking the offending blood from my cheek. I sobbed and pulled his head into my chest, burying my face in his thick fur.

I could hear a battle raging around me. Sickening sounds of males screaming and being instantly silenced. I clung to Luca, my fragile psyche couldn't handle anymore.

"Michaela!" Nico skidded to my side. "Little bird, are you hurt?"

I pulled myself away from Luca, dazed. Desecrated bodies surrounded us. He cupped my face, turning me away from the carnage to meet his eyes.

"You… you came for me?"

"Of course we came for you." he whispered. "We'll always come for you." He pulled me into his arms. I collapsed against him as a sob broke free.

Lucius' bear joined us, maw dripping red.

The three of them surrounded me as I shattered.

THEY TOOK TURNS CARRYING ME.

Shock hit so hard that I shut down. My sorry excuse for a body wasn't up for walking back to the ruins of the life we'd begun to build. Yet again, I'd cheated death—or whatever hell Johan had planned for me. The guilt of it ate away at me. How many had died back at the camp while my beasts were busy looking for me?

I was nothing more than a broken girl everyone was trying so desperately to save. And I couldn't come up with a single reason why their struggles had been worth it.

I could feel them life-binding with me again—always trying to fix me. But none of it was enough. Maybe they should've let nature take its course. I should've been long dead. Buried next to my parents back in London. What price were we willing to pay so I could go on living? Were the lives of all those innocent people the cost of extending my own?

The thought drew a visceral response. Pain rose like a tide, spilling out in the form of tears.

I smelled the acrid smoke before we arrived. A macabre welcome to what awaited us. The sun had fully risen by the time we reached what was left of Whisperhold.

"Put me down. I need to walk. I need to stand on my own feet while we face this," I said to Nico, his unwavering grip still locking me against him. He paused mid-stride, drew a deep breath, and then gently set me on the ground. The three of them looked me over cautiously, watching to see if I would simply collapse under the weight of everything. But I lifted my chin up. It was the least I could do. I had to see what had been sacrificed to save me.

Songbirds were drowned out by the moans of the injured. The only thing left standing was the skeletal frame of our cabin. Smoke lingered in the morning light, settling over the carnage and cloaking the few survivors that remained. A wave of shouts erupted as we approached. Fiona emerged from the haze, her face streaked with soot and blood. She pulled her bow from her back, knocking an arrow and pointing it straight at Nico.

"Traitor!" she shouted, fury and anguish twisting her features.

Lucius and Luca stepped in front of me as Nico raised his hands calmly. "I am not a traitor, Fiona. I'm on your side."

"Liar! You said you'd fight with us. That you'd fight *for* us. But now Levi is dead. *They're* all dead!" she cried. Tears tracked through the ash on her cheeks, her bowstring trembling.

"We *did* fight beside you. We should've done better—and I am truly sorry. But we couldn't let them take her. She's more important to Hiraeth than you realize."

"Being your fated doesn't put her life above all others," she spat back.

"She's not just my fated. She's fated to all seven of us. We don't yet understand the ways in which she's woven into our future. Please—give us a chance to explain," Nico pleaded. "We'll make this right. We'll avenge Levi and all those who've fallen today. But we can't do it if Johan divides us. We have to stand together."

Fiona's voice cracked. "Many were taken. Sawyer among them."

"And we'll get them back. Let us tend the wounded, regroup, and come up with a plan."

Fiona's bow clattered to the ground. A choked sound escaped her lips. Nico stepped forward and pulled her into an embrace as she broke down.

Shouts echoed from the other side of camp as more sentries returned. I felt the cold caress of his shadows curl around my ankles just before Jase emerged from the smoke. His black hair was a mess, and blood trickled from a gash on his cheek. The sword at his side still dripped with the blood of his enemies.

"You!" Lucius snarled, storming toward Jase. He

grabbed the front of his leathers, getting in his face. "You were supposed to be on watch! Where the fuck were you?"

"It was a diversion," Jase snapped. "They lured our sentries north. Engaged us there while a second wave hit the camp."

"Not good enough. Why didn't you send word?"

"I did. Obviously, he didn't make it back alive. What do you want from me, Lucius?"

"A reason to believe you're on our side."

"You better watch yourself before you say something you can't take back."

"I'm not hiding it. I. Don't. Trust. You."

"If that's the case, maybe you should've been out there risking your hide instead of chasing shadows."

"You bastard. You're the one who kept me from her! I should—"

"Enough!" Nico thundered. "We don't have time for your sibling rivalry." He turned to Jase. "How many losses did you suffer on the front lines?"

Jase shoved Lucius off and straightened his battered leathers. "More than half. Some tucked tail and ran. Fucking cowards."

"Damn," Nico muttered, pinching the bridge of his nose. "Jase, gather what's left of the sentries—anyone well enough to fight. Get them fed and armed. Luca, get Maxfield. Help him with the wounded. Lucius…" he paused, giving his brother a warning look, "aside from keeping your damn mouth shut, keep an eye on Mic. Johan clearly has a plan."

"Behold!" a thunderous voice bellowed across the ruined glade. We turned to find Amos striding into view, kicking a shackled male ahead of him. "The Divine has found me a traitor, and we are not pleased," Amos declared. "Ahh, you saw that, didn't you? That kick was for you," he added with a manic grin, addressing the sky.

"Amos, what've you got?" Nico asked as the sage shoved the bruised prisoner to the ground.

"This one begged to speak with you. Claimed he came to plead for forgiveness. But between you, me, and the Divine—I don't trust him. He reeks of Johan's stink."

"You've done well, Amos. Go get yourself a drink— you've earned it," Nico said, clapping a hand to his back.

"Aye. All's well that ends in a good drink. I'm sure there are a few sorry souls happy to join me before they meet the Divine." Amos ambled off, flask already to his lips.

"I have a message for you," the prisoner said, his hollow tone sending a chill up my spine.

"Is that so? Well, you have our attention. What's so important that you'd risk your life to deliver it?"

"The king grows tired of your games. The rebellion ends now. On the next full moon, all ringleaders from the Raven's Hand, and those conspiring in Dunharrow, will be added to the gallows—alongside your brothers. The king will spare the misguided... if you offer yourselves in trade."

His voice was cold. Deliberate. His dark eyes scanned us with hollow malice, as though savoring every word. "If you refuse to lay down your lives, we'll start the executions. The innocent will take your place. One every day… until you surrender."

"You're bluffing," Nico growled. "Johan wouldn't risk an all-out uprising."

"The people you claim to love will trip over themselves to deliver your heads to their rightful king," the male said, a slow smile curling his lips. "You're a foregone conclusion, Nico, son of Artos."

I felt the chill of Jase's shadows wrapping around my ankles, coaxing me backward. Something about this male— the vacant sound of his voice, the glint in his eyes—it all screamed danger.

"Let's see about that," Nico hissed. "You'll be happy to tell us everything you know… while we flay the skin from your body."

"Nico!" Fallon called through the haze, running toward us, arms waving frantically. I stumbled back instinctively, legs moving of their own volition.

The prisoner looked up with a sneer. "You have until the full moon," he snapped, "unless this is the end for us all."

His shackled hands reached into his shirt. Sunlight flashed off the golden solric as he pulled it from its hiding spot.

"Get down!" Lucius roared and then his body slammed into mine, shielding me just as the world exploded.

CHAPTER XXI
CATALYST
-MICHAELA-

A strange, icy blast filled the air around us. For a split second, time stood still. The memories of my short life flashed before my eyes. Deafening silence consumed me —a stark and ominous contrast to the absolute chaos erupting around us. Dirt and smoke fell like fog thick with hail, pelting me and clouding my vision, obscuring yet another one of my senses. I gasped, desperately choking for air that wouldn't come. The impact of Lu shielding me from the explosion had not only knocked the wind out of me—it had tossed us apart like we were nothing more than rag dolls. Panic. Fear. Terror. The onslaught of emotion was too much to process.

We'd all been nearby when the solric went off. What if —? No. I wouldn't jump to conclusions. I'd feel it, if one of them had... I couldn't even bring myself to finish the thought.

Catch your breath. Breathe.

The silence morphed into a high-pitched ringing. I rolled onto my back, wiping the grit from my face. Lucius appeared above me, horror in his amber eyes. He was alive! Thank all that is good—he was alive. Dust caked his face, and blood trailed down his forehead. His mouth was moving, but I couldn't hear anything over the immense squealing in my ears.

"Mic! Can you hear me?"

There he was. The sound of his beautiful voice filled my head and wrapped my fear in a warm, soothing embrace. *"Lucius! Yes, yes, I'm here. Are you okay? You're bleeding."* I reached for his brow, wanting to further investigate his wound.

"Never mind me. It's a nick. Are you hurt?"

"My ears are ringing, but I think I'm okay." I looked down at my limbs. Everything appeared to be intact. No blood. No sharp pain. Somehow, I'd made it through the blast without a scratch.

Gently, he pulled me to my feet. *"The ringing should subside quickly."*

"Where is everyone?"

"I'm not sure. I can't see much through the smoke."

"Mic!" Luca's muffled voice seemed miles away. It was barely audible, yet I could hear the sheer panic in his call.

"Lu, I think I just heard Luca calling for me. Go. Find Fallon."

"Luca!" I screamed, hoping he'd hear me.

"Are you sure you'll be okay if I leave?"

"I'm fine. Please, go!" I pleaded.

I prayed he'd find the others quickly. My mind wouldn't relax until we were all accounted for.

"Luca!" I screamed again.

Before I could respond, he was beside me, pulling me into a suffocating hug. "Mic, I was so worried. I couldn't see you." His hands trembled as he stroked my hair. "Thank the Divine. Are you okay?"

"I'm good. Are you injured?"

Luca frantically scanned me for injury. "Don't worry about me. Did you get hit with any shrapnel?"

"Luca," I said, catching his face in my hands and forcing his gaze back to my eyes. "I'm okay."

He pulled me into his arms again, holding tight. "I thought I lost you." His voice quavered. "Mic,"—He turned my face to his—"I love you. I've always loved you."

His confession was exactly what I needed to hear. Tears welled in my eyes. The night's events had more than overwhelmed me, and the sheer proximity in which I came to losing my life, terrified me more than it ever had. I wasn't ready to leave this fairytale. Not yet. I didn't need to almost lose them to know in my heart, I loved every one of them—but maybe this was the catalyst we needed to thrust those feelings to the forefront? To force us all to acknowledge the truth.

Maybe this was the light hidden in the darkness.

I reached up, wiping away the tears from his cheek and placed a chaste kiss on his lips. "Luca, I love you too."

"*I've found Fallon.*" Lu's voice pulled me from the moment, bringing me back to the situation at hand. "*She's a little bumped up, but overall she's fine.*"

"*Any sign of Nico or Jase?*"

"*Not yet. They can't be far.*"

"Lu found Fallon. She's okay," I shared the good news with Luca. "Where are Nico and Jase?"

"They were both standing in front of the prisoner when he… exploded."

"We need to find them immediately. They could be seriously injured." I couldn't hide the concern in my voice.

"They're going to be okay. I promise," Luca said, trying to reassure me as we picked our way through the wreckage.

"*Found them! It's not good. Hurry.*"

My heart dropped. The fear I'd been pushing down bloomed into full panic.

"Mic?" Luca caught my arm. "What is it?"

"Lucius found them. We have to go—now."

Debris littered the area. Chunks of bloody flesh and shattered trees were strewn about. The reality of what had happened continued to astonish me.

"There they are!" Luca pointed ahead, rushing toward a mound of shadowed figures. The explosion had thrown them several feet. Nico lay sprawled on the ground. Jase was sitting across from him, both of them covered in blood and gore. Fallon and Lu knelt beside Nico, trying to rouse his lifeless body, while Jase stared blankly, unmoving.

"Jase?" I called, hoping for any response.

He didn't react, just sat silently, his face completely stoic, watching his family crowd around his lifeless brother. His shadows erratically dancing in and out of his shoulders like dark bolts of lightning.

"Jase, are you okay?" He was dripping with viscera.

He ignored my question, continuing to stare at Nico. "Is he—? I tried," he said through panted breaths. "I tried to shield everyone. My shadows…"

Now it was making sense. We'd survived because of Jase. The icy blast I'd felt when the solric went off—it had been his shadows. I didn't want to think about what would've happened if he hadn't acted so quickly.

"Thank you," I said, reaching for his hand. "Are you hurt?"

"Forget about me!" he roared, pulling his hand from mine. "Help my brother."

Nico lay motionless on the forest floor. Fallon and Lu were trying desperately to rouse him.

"Nico, wake up. Michaela's here," Lucius said, glancing at me. "He's alive—unconscious, but he's still with us."

"How severe are his injuries?" I knelt beside him, trying not to panic. His left shoulder was definitely not where it was supposed to be. His shirt was torn exposing multiple lacerations. "There's an awful lot of blood. Fallon, what do I do? Should I life-bind with him?"

"Maybe he'll respond to your voice," she said, placing Nico's hand in mine.

"Nico," I said, brushing the hair from his face. "I need you to wake up. You can't leave me yet." I leaned in close to his ear and whispered, "I love you. Come back to me."

I felt his hand twitch. Then, faintly—"Michaela?"

"Nico!" Fallon gasped, tears spilling down her cheeks.

He tried to sit up, groaning in pain. Luca quickly placed a hand on his chest to stop him. "Stay down. There's been an explosion. You've been injured."

"Michaela," he called again.

"I'm right here." I squeezed his hand.

"Are you okay?" he asked, trying once more to sit up.

"You need to stay down." I gently pressed him back, careful to avoid his disfigured shoulder. "I'm okay—doing better than you," I quipped, trying to lighten the mood. "Everything's going to be alright. We'll get you straight to Maxfield."

"We're gonna need a place to recoup and treat our wounds. We can't stay here. Whisperhold is gone." Fallon was right—we needed somewhere safe.

"We'll take shelter with the Raven's Hand. Lucius, find help and fashion a stretcher for Nico," Luca stepped up, immediately taking charge.

"I can walk," Nico grunted.

"Just because you can doesn't mean you should. Your shoulder's a right mess. You'll rest while we sort out the details," Luca commanded. "Jase, unless you're injured, I need you to shake it off. We end this madness now—before we lose another brother. If Johan wants a war, we'll give him one."

MAXFIELD WAS ALREADY TENDING to the wounded when we arrived at the Raven's Hand's camp. Several innocents had been severely injured in the attack. Guilt twisted in my gut. We'd been the target, and thanks to Jase we walked away with nothing more than a few relatively minor injuries.

Maxfield made quick work of Nico's shoulder. The impact had dislocated it, and some large pieces of shrapnel had been lodged under his skin. A few yelps and a particularly pungent salve had him feeling almost back to normal.

Fiona helped settle us into a small but safe shelter. Four walls, a few chairs, and some bedrolls. A simple space for us to rest and lick our wounds. I was grateful we were all together. After everything we'd endured, the thought of being separated was unbearable.

Fallon sat alone in the far corner of the room, a brimshade cigarette pinched between her fingers. She looked detached, lost in thought, her face frighteningly stoic.

We all felt it—defeated. Like it or not, Johan had won

tonight. He'd taken prisoners, burned down our safe house, and stomped on our psyche.

"I know a way back into Mathenholm," Jase said suddenly, cutting through the heavy silence. "We should make our move now. Johan won't expect a swift retaliation."

"Oh, now you have information?" Lu snapped. "You've been back a month. Why didn't you mention this earlier? Now that we've been attacked and our home's a pile of ash, you conveniently know a way into the castle?"

"Lu," I said gently. "Let him speak."

"He's had plenty of time to share," Luca said bluntly. "Why now?"

"Jase," Nico remained stoic in the face of frustration. "Tell us what you know. And this time, try not to leave out useful information."

"I know for a fact, Johan has discovered the secret tunnels running underground. They're no longer a viable option, however he'd be expecting us to use them. There were guards posted at both ends when I'd escaped. I'd be willing to bet he has placed all of his fruit in that one basket."

"Good point," Fallon spoke up. "That fucking vulture isn't exactly intelligent."

"So if we can't use the tunnels, what's your big plan to get us in unseen?" Luca asked, dripping with skepticism.

"It's simple really," Jase said flatly. "We use the staff entrance."

Lucius burst into uncontrollable laughter. "Use the

service entry? Are you daft? The explosion must've knocked you out of your senses. I don't remember you being this stupid when I left the realm."

"You can't be serious," Luca scoffed. "You expect us to just stroll on in, like we belong there?"

"We do belong there," Fallon said, her voice dripping with vitriol.

"I'm dead serious," Jase stood up from his chair. "How do you think I escaped? The staff entrance is the farthest thing from Johan's mind. He's far too arrogant to ever step foot in the servant's quarters. He probably doesn't even know where the outer bailey is."

Fallon stood up, shaking her head. "This is hopeless," she mumbled under her breath as she walked out of the room.

"If it worked once, why wouldn't it work again?" I asked, trying to offer some glimmer of hope.

"Fallon had the right idea." Lucius stood up. "I'm done with this conversation. When you have something useful come find me. I'm going to have a large drink and devise a real plan. Luca, you with me?"

"That's the best idea we've had all night," Luca said, following him out.

"Jase," Nico shook his head. "I'd hoped you had some useful advice. It seems you may have suffered a temporary lapse in judgment. I pray the Divine clears your head quickly. We're running out of time. Finn, Hunter—now Sawyer—they're depending on us." He sighed, rising slower than usual. "I'm going to join the others. If you come up with a reasonable idea, come find us. You're a wise man Jase. Prove it."

The room was thick with tension. Jase stood and threw a punch at the wall. "Fuck!" he cursed, shaking his bruised knuckles as he paced.

"Why didn't you tell them you used your shadows to shield us?" I asked.

"I'm not interested in their approval. I did it for my own selfish reasons."

"For what it's worth, I think it's a brilliant plan. A little unusual,"—I shrugged my shoulders.—"but I think that's why it might work." I couldn't believe we were here again—me backing someone with a wild idea. Gwen and I had always had each other's backs, even when things sounded insane. My Bruins had a lot to learn when it came to trust. "Why does your family doubt you so often?"

"Because our father raised us to be that way," Jase hissed. "Strong rulers *must* question everything."

"Even family?"

"Family doesn't always mean safe, Mic. Power's a seductive mistress. She can taint even the purest of hearts."

His words struck me. After all the things Fallon had shared about their father, I was starting to understand the family dynamics.

"Your father sounds... charming."

Jase laughed bitterly. "He wasn't exactly 'fatherly.' He

was raising future kings. Sometimes he had to do things that others would consider cruel. It's just the way it was."

"I suppose there's... logic behind his methods."

"He certainly thought so." Jase scratched his head. "Go with me."

"I'm sorry—what? Go with you? Where?"

"Come with me. To Mathenholm. Tonight."

"Without the others?" Now he sounded a bit unhinged.

"They'll never be on board. They proved that tonight. We are running out of time. I can't sit back and wait for the perfect plan to arise while my best friend—my brothers, await their execution. I believe we can get in and get out before Johan even notices." He gripped his hair, becoming more animated as he paced faster, growing more agitated. "We'll be halfway back to camp before they even knew Hunter and Finn are gone. It'll work!"

"I don't know, Jase," I hesitated. "Do you really think the two of us can pull this off? My fighting skills are weak at best. The eidris is all I've got."

"That's the beauty of my plan. We won't need to fend off Johan's guard because they won't even know we're there. My shadows will do all the dirty work for us."

I didn't need a reminder of what his shadows were capable of—I'd experienced it firsthand. "So this would simply be a rescue mission?"

"Exactly. We get them out, regroup, and then take back what's rightfully ours."

"The throne?"

Jase nodded. "Mark my words, Mic—we *will* take back what's ours. Johan will pay for what he's done to Hiraeth and her people. So… are you in? Or are you going to wait around like my brothers?"

"Why didn't you suggest this earlier?"

"Because a few weeks ago, the guard was on high alert. It wouldn't have worked."

I pondered the idea. Jase had already escaped once. Growing up in Mathenholm had to give him some advantage, he knew the layout. We were cutting it close with Hunter and Finn. With less than a week before they would be publicly executed. It was now or never. Before I could convince myself otherwise, I made a choice. Maybe not the best choice, but a choice nonetheless.

"Okay. I'll do it. I'll go with you."

"That's my girl. You never shy away from danger, do you?" A playful smile slid across his lips as he celebrated his victory. "I like that about you."

"When your life's guaranteed to be cut short, you make peace with death." Dying never scared me—until now. That was the easy part. Living, on the other hand, terrified me. The last few hours of my life had given me a taste I didn't like, and the tides began to shift. I no longer wanted to take a passive role. I wasn't ready to leave this existence. I wanted more time. "How are we going to pull this off without them freaking out?"

"Easy. We leave once they're asleep. By the time they wake, we'll be too far gone for them to interfere."

CHAPTER XXII
INTO THE DRAGON'S LAIR
-MICHAELA-

"We really need to stop meeting like this," I teased as we quietly made our way out of camp.

"Why? Our best moments happen while everyone else is asleep." Jase playfully winked at me.

He wasn't wrong. That night in front of the window—even though it crushed my heart—was one of the few moments we'd really connected. He had given in to his baser instincts. Something I secretly wished he'd do more often. I think it was the only time I ever saw him in his true nature.

Thornwyn Forest under the blanket of darkness, offered a hauntingly beautiful backdrop. The night sky was alight with twinkling stars, and the nocturnal creatures were out making their evening rounds. A shiver ran through me, and

I wasn't sure if it was the cool night air or something more foreboding.

"If memory serves, we have a long walk ahead of us." I tried my best to distract my wandering mind with small talk.

"Mathenholm is a bit of a trek. We should go as far as we can before making camp. The others will be on our tail the moment they realize we're gone. And I'd be willing to bet they'll be pissed."

"Are we making a mistake?" I asked sheepishly. "Not telling them." In the hours before we left, I'd made the difficult decision not to leave a note behind. It was heartless, but not giving them a direction to search would buy us more time. I purposefully hadn't allowed myself to consider how they would feel about our hasty decision. I knew they would be angry. But honestly, Jase had made a strong argument. The next full moon was only seven days away. Surely, with time, they would understand.

"The only mistake being made was my siblings waiting for the 'perfect' opportunity. Johan has set the clock in motion. While they sat back and pondered the situation over a cup of ale, our brothers are being tortured while awaiting death."

That was all I needed to hear to relieve my concerns. "They'll forgive us once we have Hunter and Finn back, right?"

Jase huffed. "I don't think you're capable of doing something they wouldn't forgive. I'm not sure if you've noticed, but they are beyond obsessed with you."

I chuckled. "You really think they'll get over it?"

"Mic, I've never seen my brothers behave the way they do with you. I can all but guarantee you—in their eyes, you can do no wrong."

DAYBREAK WAS UPON US, and Hiraeth awarded our bravery with the most beautiful sunrise I'd ever seen. Rays of brilliant orange filtered through the towering trees, casting a warm, glowing light across the forest floor. The ferns sparkled with morning dew as they danced in the gentle breeze, giving an enchanted appearance to the shadowed ground. Wildlife all around us was waking up, and the ominous owl hoots of the evening hours were slowly shifting to the chatter of songbirds.

"Are we going to make camp soon? I could use a break and maybe something to eat." I considered using the sprite ash—not because my cancer was weakening me, but because it would give me a needed burst of energy.

"We need to get a bit further. Caldreim River should be just up ahead. We'll make camp there. The fish are plentiful. We'll eat well."

I remembered the cold, rocky waters of Caldreim well. We'd crossed them to ensure our scent couldn't be tracked while escaping Mathenholm. "Great... more fish." I scrunched up my nose.

"What's wrong with fish?"

"Nothing," I quickly retorted.

"Then why the face?"

"It's not my favorite. Why does it have to be so... fishy?"

He laughed. "I suppose we can keep an eye out for salmonberries. But you'll need some protein with all the energy we're expending."

"Fine, I'll eat the fish. Can we please hurry up and find the river? I'm exhausted."

"Typical female." He smirked, looking over his shoulder at me. "You all get cranky when you need a nap and a snack."

"Is that so?"

"Sorry to offend you with the truth. Deepest apologies, My Lady." He stopped and comically bowed before me. "Do you need me to carry you?"

I giggled at his mockery. "I'm fine, good sir."

"It's just a bit further. Promise."

It was more than an hour before we made it to Caldreim, and then at least another hour after crossing the rushing waters, searching along the riverbank for what Jase deemed a proper spot to make camp. We settled on a vacant den tucked into the side of an enormous boulder. A large evergreen grew at the base, its low-lying branches almost completely obscuring the entrance. The short walk from the forest's edge to the river made it an ideal location.

"Do you know how to start a fire?" Jase asked.

"Umm, without a lighter?" I already knew his answer.

"A lighter? What's that?"

I chuckled. "I can try."

"Don't worry about it. I'll take care of it. Gather some tinder while I get us some food."

Jase made his way over to the river's edge and began to strip. I tried in vain to keep my eyes to myself and focus on the task at hand, but my god, he was a delectable specimen. He waded about waist-deep into the water, stopping for a moment, looking down at the surface intently.

Was he going to catch breakfast with his bare hands?

Before I could ponder any further, he dove beneath the flowing current. A mere moment later, he popped back up —a fucking fish held tightly between his teeth.

"You'll find more firewood if you actually look for it," he snarked, making his way back to the river's edge. He dropped the fish on the rocky banks and headed back into the water.

"Touché. Can't blame a girl for enjoying the view." I blushed, embarrassed I'd been caught gawking. Sticks, Michaela. You're looking for sticks.

I foraged through the tree line, easily finding plenty of kindling. With my arms full, I made my way back to our den. I stopped and pulled out the vial of sprite ash.

A tiny dose won't hurt.

Jase was busy catching fish. He'd be none the wiser. I was exhausted. I just needed a little boost. Popping the top I collected the tiniest bit from the bottom of the cork and smeared it between my breasts, feeling that familiar buzz kick in instantly.

"How goes the hunt for firewood?" Jase startled me, regaining my attention. "I want to get this cooked quickly. The scent will be a huge tell. We need to keep our location hidden."

"Speaking of fish," I said, dropping the pile of sticks at the entrance to our hideaway. "Did I watch you catch that with your teeth?"

Jase looked at me blankly. "Have you ever tried to swim with a fish in your hands? No. I didn't catch it with my teeth." A smile crept across his face. "I could have, though."

I smiled at his playfulness. I'd never seen this side of him. His tough demeanor was slowly softening. He was in his element out in the wilderness—seemingly more at ease here than I'd ever seen him before.

I watched intently as he effortlessly started a fire. "Where did you learn to do that?" I asked as he tended the delicate spark, blowing at its base ever so softly, coaxing out a flame.

"Finn and I spent countless nights camping in the woods. It was a reprieve from our father's never-ending lessons."

"You and Finn? Are you two close?"

"Finn is more than just my brother," he paused, gutting the fish. "He's my best friend."

"I can relate to that." I nodded. "My sister has always

been my best friend. When our parents died, she became my everything. I owe my life to her." My heart winced at the thought of Gwen. We'd never been apart for this long. "I miss her."

"Here." Jase handed me a stick skewered with fish, motioning to the small fire. "Work on this one while I gut mine."

"Do you really think we're going to pull this off?"

"Did you make this journey with doubt in your mind?"

"Life's about taking chances— even risky ones. If I hadn't taken a chance with Gwen, I wouldn't be here in Hiraeth now." I paused, thinking back on all we had been through in such a short period of time. The entire trajectory of our lives had changed in a matter of weeks. "My life has been filled with difficult choices. Some downright scary, with no guarantee of a happy ending. The 'treatment' for what you call Tribulation in my realm is to blindly trust your 'healers' while they pump you full of poison, hoping it might kill off the cancer before it kills you." I reached up, feeling the lumpy port still embedded under the skin at my collarbone. "I guess I'm used to jumping into the unknown, hoping it works out."

"What were you just rubbing at?" he asked, pointing at my chest, his brow furrowed.

I placed his hand on my scar, allowing him to feel the device still implanted beneath.

His eyes widened. "What is that?"

"It's called a port, where the doctors—healers—would

administer my so-called 'medicine.' It was supposed to reduce the number of times they had to stick you with needles."

"Seems barbaric."

"To be honest, it was. But in my realm, it was the only option I had. Well, that or death."

"Sounds like we've both had to make a few questionable choices along our way." He offered a knowing smile and continued on. "I spent my childhood in Mathenholm. I know every hidden passageway, every dark shadowed nook and cranny. I could navigate her halls in complete and utter darkness. That has to offer us an advantage. Besides, Johan's guard is no match for my shadows. We'll succeed, Mic. Of this I'm certain."

"Your confidence is all I need."

"Good! Now eat your fish, and we'll get some rest. We have a long day before us."

Jase collected a few low-lying evergreen branches to pad the floor of the den. That, paired with the small blanket I'd tucked into my belt, would have to suffice.

"It doesn't look very comfortable, but it smells lovely," I said, trying to find something to take my mind off what loomed ahead.

"You brought a blanket?" Jase asked, his brow rising in question.

"What? I get cold." I hadn't grabbed much before we left, but it was getting cooler outside, and a blanket seemed like a necessity.

The den forced us to share a tight space. We could lie flat, side by side, but there was no getting away from each other. Jase laid beside me, resting on his elbow before pulling me back against his chest.

"I can think of much more effective ways to warm you." His words tickled the shell of my ear, instantly heating the part of me he'd ravished that night in front of the window.

Was this an invitation? My interest piqued. Feeling bold, I challenged his offer. I pushed my hips back, pressing my ass against him. A low, growling vibration emanated from his chest. Before I could react, his arm was turning me onto my back.

He had a way of making me fearful and excited all at once. My heart was pounding. Nervous energy coursed through my veins as he slid his hand up my body. He tilted my chin toward his own, and for a moment, I forgot how to breathe. His icy blue eyes held my gaze, dropping to my lips before he leaned down gently sealing his to mine. It was soft and sensual, as though he were testing the waters—seeking some form of nonverbal consent. The heat of his breath mixed with my own as I parted my lips, deepening the kiss. Jase had never shown me this kind of intimacy. The night at the window was something altogether different.

His hand was in my hair, gripping the back of my head to pull me in closer. We were lost in the moment. Consumed with lust. What had started out as a soft sweetness quickly devolved into fevered need, feeding that starved piece of our soul.

I pulled at his clothes. I wanted to touch him, to feel his skin. Breaking the kiss, I sat up, ripping at my dress, cursing the damned fabric keeping us apart

He reached for my hands, stilling me. "There's no need to rush. Let me." The familiar smoky wisps of his shadows crept over his shoulders and glided effortlessly up over my chest and behind me. One by one, the laces of my dress loosened.

Jase pulled his shirt over his head and, without skipping a beat, tilted my chin up, placing delicate kisses along my jaw trailing down my neck, while his gift made quick work of my dress. The shoulders slouched forward, and I slid my arms free, dropping it to my waist, leaving me bare.

Biting his lip, Jase watched intently while his shadows crept up my ribs, circling my breasts. Teasing me with their icy touch, they tugged at my taut nipples. Even though they were an extension of himself, he watched through jealous eyes.

"Fuck, Mic," he whispered under his breath. "Lift your hips so they can undress you. I want you the way nature intended."

The heat from his gaze made me feel like sin incarnate. I leaned back on my elbows, lifting the evergreen branches while the dark fingers slid off the rest of the material. Just like before, they leisurely wandered back up my legs.

"Surrender to them. Let them explore your perfection,"

Jase said with hunger in his eyes. "I want to watch you writhe."

Closing out the world, I focused on the cold, feather-like touch of the shadows gliding along my skin, sending shivers throughout my entire body. The torturous delight of the unknown had me in its clutches. Tendrils swirled up my legs, down my chest and arms. Every inch of flesh was alive with sensation.

And then, they closed in on my most sensitive parts.

I tried in vain to stay quiet. The last thing I wanted was to alert someone to our presence. But the feeling overpowered my sensibilities. A desperate moan escaped my lips as his shadows simultaneously tugged at my nipples and probed my throbbing wetness.

"Such beautiful sounds you make for us. Don't force me to silence you."

"Jase," I panted. "I can't. I—"Another cry slid from my lips as his wisps circled my swollen clit.

Darkness immediately climbed the column of my throat, invading my mouth. Panic washed over me as a strange smoky weight restricted my tongue, muffling my cries.

"That's my good girl. Breathe." I looked at Jase for reassurance and found him fisting his massive cock, the tip glistening with a bead of excitement. He was panting just as hard as I was. Enjoying the show his gift was offering up.

A cold fullness filled my opening, stretching me to the edge of gentle pain, forcing another muffled cry from my lips.

Jase climbed over me, settling in between my legs, pushing back my thighs, and spreading me wide. His tongue replaced the smoky fingers circling my clit. "Mmm." His sighs of content vibrated my sensitive nub, and my legs quivered. I couldn't hold on any longer. I lost control, every muscle in my body contracted as pleasure erupted from my core, throwing me into frenzied bliss.

I tried to call out his name, but the darkness still held my mouth hostage. My legs clamped around his head, my hips grinding out my orgasm on his masterful tongue.

"Your taste is bewitching." He looked at me as though I was prey, licking his lips and savoring the remnants of my release. It was clear he wasn't done toying with me. "I think it's best we leave you silenced."

The shadows bound my wrists, lifting them over my head, and twisting so that my body was forced to roll over. Lifting my hips, Jase exposed my sex to the cool air of the den.

"You have the most exquisite ass," he said, gripping my cheeks tightly and spreading them. "Tell me, have my brothers claimed this part of you yet?"

I shook my head no, and a wave of fear washed over me.

"No?" He questioned. "We'll have to go easy then."

My muscles clenched when he circled a finger over the uncharted area. Much to my surprise, the sensation brought forth a flood of wetness. A shameless moan escaped my muffled lips, delighting Jase, and emboldening him to explore some more.

"Breathe," he reminded me. "Relax"

I forced myself to take a deep breath and exhaled out my fear.

"Good girl," he purred. His praise stoked the fire burning in my core, and my compliance was handsomely rewarded. His cock was at my entrance, pressing against my slippery wetness, invading me inch by delectable inch until he was fully seated inside my core. And then his thumb, slick with my desire, was again circling at my back door. "Breathe, baby girl," he ordered again. But this time on my exhale, his shadows released my mouth as he pushed his thumb inside, driving my pleasure to new heights.

I tried in vain to keep my voice down, but the sensations were too strong. Once he started moving, it was hopeless. Animalistic groans fell from my lips as the tension inside me grew like a coiled snake ready to strike.

"Fuck, Mic," he growled, his pace quickening. "Your pretty little pussy takes me so well."

"Jase," I panted, "I can't...I'm going to cum," I warned as my insides clenched around his length.

"It's okay, baby. Cum for me. Cum on my hard cock." He wrapped his arm around my hips, stroking my clit till I hit the crescendo. My toes curled, body arching against him, and I fell off the edge into a sea of ecstasy.

With a groan, Jase collapsed over top of me, his deep

thrusting becoming jerky until he stilled, sheathed to the hilt. His shadows instantly recoiled, releasing my wrists from their grasp, as our breathing slowed, becoming synchronized.

Spooning naked with Jase, post coital, in a tiny rocky den was definitely not something I ever expected. Yet there we were. My stubborn Bruin lazily traced his fingers along my curves. The more time we spent alone, the softer his armor became. At least this time he wasn't running off dismissing what we had just shared. But one thing remained the same, and it was eating at me.

"Why do your shadows restrain my hands every time we..." Sex with Jase was something out of a spicy paranormal romance novel. His shadows added a layer of supernatural surrealness that I could never have with anyone else. But both times we'd been intimate, I had no choice but to play a passive role. And even though they scared me, his shadows were part of him and they excited me just as much.

"I like the way you look, helpless and bound by my will." I didn't know what to think of his answer. It was definitely giving psychopath energy. There was something about Jase that you didn't see in his brothers. Even his bear reflected the darkness inside with its obsidian coat. "Since we're asking questions: why did you use the sprite ash today? You didn't mention feeling ill."

"What?" I played dumb. How did he know?

"Mic," he said gently. "I have memorized every inch of

your beautiful skin. That pale blue shimmer between your breasts is not natural. Did I push you too hard?"

"I... I—" I panicked, stuttering my words. "I was tired, and I didn't want to slow us down."

"Did Maxfield say anything about using sprite ash when you don't need it?"

"No. I just thought, why not? It's harmless." At least I think it's harmless. Maxfield said it shouldn't be trifled with. But it never seemed to cause any trouble.

"Can I see the vial?"

I reached for my pack, retrieving the sprite ash and handed it to Jase.

"Mic, this vial is almost empty. How much have you been using?"

"I guess I wasn't really paying attention. I've spent my whole life feeling awful. Forgive me for wanting to maintain a level of comfort."

"I'm not reprimanding you. But I don't like the idea of you losing track of how often you reach for it."

"Jase, I need it."

"That's how it begins," he said sharply. "First it's just to help you get through the hard days. Then it's to get through all the others. One morning, you'll wake and need it just to exist. I don't like it. I'm going to hold on to this for you. When you need it, I'll give it back."

I stared at him in disbelief. My heart pounding with the thought of not having a safety net at my disposal.

He reached for my jaw, caressing my cheek. "I promise,

everything is going to be okay. I won't let anything happen to you. Come to me if you need to life-bind." Jase leaned in kissing my lips tenderly and pulled my body in tightly against his own. "You should try to get some rest."

I wasn't thrilled that he'd taken the ash from me, but I wasn't about to argue with him now. Instead, I closed my eyes, pulled in a deep breath, and tried to relax into the warmth of his body. Enveloped in the scent of the evergreen boughs beneath us, I fell into a deep sleep.

THE TREK to Mathenholm took several long and arduous days. The sight of the castle finally within reach brought on a level of anxiety I'd never experienced before. I hadn't been visited by Hunter or Finn since that day in the forest, and dread had begun to rot its way through me. Our greatest enemy was now less than a mile away. This—was what we had come for.

"Are you ready?" Jase asked as we crept toward the edge of the tree line.

"How close do we need to be to send in your shadows?"

"Once we're inside the outer bailey, we'll infiltrate the staff quarters. Thats where I'll release them."

"And how exactly are we getting into the outer bailey?"

"There's a section of loose stones on the southern wall.

We used it as children when sneaking out. Not once were we caught," he boasted proudly.

The first step out into the open field took every ounce of courage I had left. It was dark, yes—but without the cover of the forest. If someone were watching, they'd see us.

Nothing happened. It was exactly as Jase promised, we crossed without incident. Within moments, we were standing before the curtain wall.

One by one, Jase began pulling free the loose stones, revealing a narrow crawl space. "I'll go first. When it's clear, follow me." He kissed me quickly, then dropped to his knees and slipped through the gap. "It's all clear, Mic. Come on through."

I exhaled hard, trying to slow my racing pulse. I crouched, poking my head through the hole—and froze.

A cold, sharp point pressed against the back of my neck.

"Well, well. I gotta say, I didn't think you'd actually pull it off," an unknown male said above me. "Stand up!" he barked.

Slowly, I got to my feet. Jase stood in front of me. His expression was blank. Guarded. There weren't just one, but two guards waiting. They clearly knew exactly where we'd be. And worse—they were completely uninterested in Jase.

"It wasn't easy," he said quietly.

It wasn't easy? The world tilted. My thoughts reeled as the truth slammed into me with devastating force.

"Jase?" My voice was barely a whisper. I stared at him, searching his face—pleading silently for answers.

He simply looked away, refusing to make eye contact, dismissing me.

No. No, this couldn't be real. He wouldn't... he couldn't have. Not after everything. Not after what we'd shared. The long nights. The trust. The bond we'd started to build.

But the guards weren't guessing. They were waiting. And Jase hadn't been caught.

He'd delivered me.

The guards moved in, each one grabbing an arm with force. "Johan's waiting," one muttered. "He wants her in her old room."

There was no point in resisting. No one would defend me here. Not even the male I'd trusted. Jase had walked me straight into the dragon's lair and laid me at its feet.

And the worst part?

I'd walked in willingly

CHAPTER XXIII
DESPERATE TIMES
-NICO-

The sweet, intoxicating scent of her still clung to the walls of the shelter we'd been sharing.

But she was gone.

The hollowness in my chest confirmed it. I'd always felt the pieces of my soul that didn't belong to me, but now that we'd sealed our bond, now that we'd given ourselves to each other, I recognize the strands that wove us together. And I could feel her slipping away from me.

I pinched the bridge of my nose to dull the gnawing ache in my skull as I watched Lucius lose his head.

"He fucking took her against her will!" he shouted, tearing through the room.

"You don't know that for certain," Luca countered. Ever the optimist.

"You've seen the way he's been acting—his stories don't add up," Lucius barked.

"You said the two of you have some kind of mental connection. Can't you reach out to her?" Luca asked.

"I don't know how it works," Lucius snapped. "I've tried. Either she's too far, or he's done something to her."

"Or maybe she's just blocking you out. You are kind of a prick most of the time."

I held my breath, waiting for Lucius to start throwing fists. But he just glared, rage dancing in his eyes.

"She would have left a note. She would have told me!" He grabbed a chair, the only piece of furniture we had in the room, and slammed it to the floor. It shattered instantly, pieces of wood scattering across the shelter.

Lucius hadn't always had such a short fuse and a foul temper. Life had molded the sweet boy I once knew into a barely-contained fury. A blessing and a curse of being the youngest son. He was allowed to wear his emotions plainly while I had to keep mine always under wraps.

I stroked my beard, watching the spectacle as I carefully weighed my next words. I'd learned at a very early age that words held great power, and it was ill-advised to speak before knowing your heart. At the moment, mine was torn.

Lucius had been quick to pass judgment, grasping for any excuse to accuse Jase of the ultimate betrayal. It was true—his accounts never quite lined up, and odd occurrences seemed to trail in his wake. Now I had to decide if I'd been blind to them all along? Or had Lucius's paranoia clouded my judgment?

Being the eldest gave me a different perspective and a crushing sense of responsibility for them. I couldn't bring myself to believe Jase was capable of betraying us.

"She didn't even bring her pack," Lucius growled, chucking her still-full bag at me. "He took her by force. And I swear to the Divine, Nico, I will kill him when we find him."

"I've been tolerant of your behavior for Michaela's sake," I said, voice low and deadly. "But don't ever threaten one of your brothers again. If you ever try, I will put you down."

Silence settled over the room. All three of us glared at each other, tempers cooling just enough for logic to return.

"Let's look at this from all angles," I said, more composed now. "We laughed at Jase's ideas, while Mic embraced them. For all we know, she left with him. We need to keep our heads. Gather our forces. Establish a plan to rescue our brothers, and our girl. It's time to take back our kingdom."

I opened her pack. One last hope of proving Lucius wrong.

The contents were ordinary: clothes, a bedroll, rations. What I wasn't expecting was the leather-bound book nestled at the bottom.

I froze, staring down at the worn cover in stunned disbelief. There were dozens, maybe even hundreds of copies scattered across the realm. Each one a watered-down version of the original. But this was it. The true Book of Astrium. The original text that had been locked away in Mathenholm Castle. How had it ended up in Michaela's hands?

The supple leather warmed beneath my hands. I opened the ancient tome, flipping straight to the page that had haunted me for years: Michaela's likeness, drawn by some unknown prophet centuries before her birth. The vibrant blue lines of power connecting her to seven bears.

I traced the lines with my finger, feeling a deep keening need to tear through the woods until she was in my arms again. Had her hands run over the same images? Why hadn't she said anything?

"What do you got there, brother?" Luca asked, eyeing the book curiously.

"It's the Book of Astrium," I whispered.

Luca arched a brow. "The Book of Astrium? Are you sure that blast didn't addle your brain?"

"How in the Divine did she—"

"I gave it to her," Fallon said, entering the shelter.

"You what?" I turned to her, stunned.

"The night of the Crownspire," she clarified.

"That's impossible. It was locked away under magical bonds. Only Father—" I paused as the realization hit me. "He gave you the key."

She nodded. "Right before he died."

"That doesn't make sense. The king only passes the key to his successor."

"Maybe he knew more about his own demise than he let on. And besides, there was no king to pass it down to," she said, her voice edged with pain. "You weren't there."

"That still doesn't explain why you gave it to Michaela. If anyone had caught her with it—"

"She'd have been executed," Fallon finished. "I know. But we were already marked for death, Nico. I told you that before the ceremony. Michaela had the best chance at survival. I wasn't about to let the book fall into Johan's hands."

"Did you explain what it was?"

"No. I meant to. But when was the right time to tell her she's so deeply woven into the fate of Hiraeth that her face is in our most sacred text? I didn't want to dump that on her when we don't even know what it means."

"Fuck, Loni!" Lucius barked, his wrath swiftly moving over to Fallon. "Did you think she wouldn't open it? At least you could have warned her. No wonder she thinks we've been lying to her."

"Because you have been lying to her!" Fallon snapped, her gaze searing through us. "You should have told her the truth a long time ago."

"I'm done with this conversation. Every second we sit here arguing, Jase is taking her farther away from us." Lucius grumbled, rising with his arms crossed tight over his chest. His amber eyes burned with resolve. His bear stirred beneath his skin, restless and ready to act. "I'm going after her. With or without you."

I exhaled sharply. "Lu, listen—"

"No. I've listened to you for too long. Are you coming with me, or are you going to sit here and ponder every possible outcome while he drags her deeper into enemy territory?"

He stepped closer, daring me to stop him. I clenched my jaw, forcing myself to stay calm. He was running on instinct. I had to be the balance.

"Thinking is not wasting time," I said. "Mic isn't the only one at stake here. Our brothers are set to be executed in a weeks' time. The entire kingdom—"

"I don't care about the realm," Lucius said, his voice booming in the tight space, raw and unyielding. "I don't care about a dying throne or the alliances you think we can trust. I care about Mic."

"We have to think about this from every angle. We can't save her without sacrificing everyone else. She wouldn't want us to do that," I snapped.

Lu's jaw tightened. "All I can think about is what's happening to her out there while we waste time quibbling over semantics. You've known it all along. He's a traitor."

"You don't know that," I shot back, though doubt curled at the edges of my mind. "And even if he was, he would never... he *could* never hurt her. Not with the fated bond in place."

Lucius let out a sharp, humorless laugh. "No, but he can

deliver her to someone who would. He'd let them slit her throat if it meant getting into Johan's good graces."

I swallowed hard. I had to believe Jase had a reason. That there was more to the story. But Lu only saw the risk.

"And what about our brothers?" I asked, my voice quieter now. "You'll forsake them without a second thought?"

"You save them," he cut in. "I'll save Mic. Take her back to Neverland. I can protect her there. We could have a life."

"I want that too!" I snapped, sharper than I intended. Lu stilled. "You think I don't yearn for the same thing?" I shook my head, dragging a hand down my face. "But there's more at stake than just what we want. We have to be rational, not emotional."

His eyes narrowed. "Oh yeah? And how well has the rational path worked out for you?"

The words hit like a blow to the gut. He turned to me, the accusation heavy in his gaze. "Where did all your careful planning get us, Your Highness? What did following the rules earn us?" He gestured around, pointing out just how far we'd fallen. "We've been playing the long game for years, and we still ended up here."

I breathed through the sting. He wasn't wrong. But I refused to wallow in my own self-pity. "If we divide now," I started, willing the dire need in my words to come across, "we fail."

Lu's fingers twitched at his sides. His bear stirred under his skin. Ready to fight me for this.

"I'm begging you, Lu. Just one day. Let us meet with the Raven's Hand. With our allies in Dunharrow. We'll come up with a plan."

He didn't answer immediately. The tension between us was a taut rope, pulled to its breaking point.

"It's a trap," he said, stating the obvious.

"You think I don't know that?" I snapped. "We don't have a lot of choices. But running in blind is suicide." I didn't wait for him to argue. Instead, I flipped open the Book of Astrium and shoved it toward him. "Look."

His gaze dropped—reluctantly.

Michaela's face stared up at us, etched into the page, her presence immortalized in prophecy.

"She's meant for Hiraeth," I said. "You're not solely responsible for her protection. She belongs here."

His nostrils flared. "The picture shows seven bears, Nico. Gunner's already dead. The prophecy is broken."

I exhaled and flipped to another page—one he'd never seen. One Father had removed from the copies we'd studied. One that only existed in the original.

A rotting bear lay in the center, its corpse being torn apart by every animal of the forest. Above, vultures perched in the trees, waiting. Watching. I could visibly see Lu shudder.

"Father knew the House of Bruin would fall," I said softly. "And he chose to ignore it. I won't make that mistake. The prophecies always come true." I tapped the page. "Always."

For the first time, something uncertain flickered across Lu's face. Silence stretched between us, heavy and suffocating.

Finally, he exhaled and raked a hand through his hair. "Fine," he muttered. "One day. That's all you get."

I nodded, but my gut twisted. Because we both knew the truth. One day. Then he was going after Mic—with or without me.

WE MET in secret the following night. It had taken every ounce of self-restraint for Lucius to remain by my side while we arranged the meeting, but he stayed true to his word.

I'd let my magic run rampant, swaying the minds of the Raven's Hand and the rebel leaders of Dunharrow— manipulating them in ways I wasn't proud of. But after Johan's attack, many had begun to question their loyalty to the cause, and I couldn't allow those thoughts to take root.

I had envisioned myself as a better leader. But with Michaela missing and our brothers condemned, desperation had carved away my morals.

The waxing moon was high in the sky by the time we reached the ruins of the temple. One of the few places left that avoided the eye of the Crown's army. This fallen monument to the Divine had been all but forgotten. Stone columns loomed around us like broken sentinels, half-eaten by time. The air was thick with damp earth, forgotten prayers, and whispers of the Divine, who had long since turned their backs on Dunharrow.

I stood at the head of the gathering, arms crossed. A dull throb pulsed behind my eyes, making it hard to focus on the faces before of me. Luca and Lucius stood beside me. Fallon lounged on the shattered altar, annoyance stamped across her face. The temple was filled wall to wall with the resistance we'd managed to amass since our escape from Mathenholm.

Fiona had taken up the mantle that Sawyer had left behind, standing strong as the voice of the rebellion. She mirrored my stance, arms crossed and chin high. They had risked it all to stand by my side, and many of them lost everything, and still, she stood by me.

Luca glanced over, brow furrowed. "You alright?"

"Fine," I said, a little too quickly. "Too much magic spent getting us here, and not enough time to recover."

He didn't look convinced. But he didn't press. I couldn't afford weakness—not while she was still out there. I could rest when Johan was dead.

Amos wandered between the rows of warriors, the click of his staff echoing through the chamber. "Yes, yes, I'll tell them," he mumbled up at the dilapidated ceiling before taking a swig from his flask.

He cleared his throat. "Need I remind you this is sacred ground, and these are desperate times. The decisions made here tonight may very well seal our fates for good. We've been gathered here not by our own whims, but by Divine will. So don't fuck it up." He slammed the staff against the stone, then bowed to both parties and stepped aside.

"Thank you, Amos." My voice rang clear. "And thank you all for risking so much to be here. But time is not on our side."I paced before them, the weight of every life at stake settled in my chest. "The execution is set for the next full moon. That gives us seven days. If we wait, we'll be dragging their bodies from the gallows instead of saving them."

Lucius exhaled sharply. "We don't even know how many guards the bastard has inside. We walk in blind, we die. Isn't that what you said, Nico?"

The muscles in my jaw ticked as I ground my teeth. The last thing we needed was to show a divided front, but he was determined to fight me every step of the way.

"Then we don't walk in blind," Fallon countered, tucking her hair behind her ear. "Some servants are still loyal. They stayed behind when he took the throne, waiting for this moment. If we can get a message inside, they'll help us."

Fiona pulled a blade from her belt, twirling it in her hands as she assessed me with dark eyes. "And how do you plan to get it past the castle walls? Last I checked, Johan isn't in the habit of allowing traitors to slip messages through his own castle."

"It's not his castle!" I barked.

The room went still and wary gazes darted amongst them. A soft rustle of wings broke the tension. From the shadows, a small, willowy male stepped forward. "I'll take the message," he said, chin held high.

"This is Rook," Fallon explained, hopping down from the altar. "He's a finch shifter—and a page at Mathenholm. He delivers messages within the castle itself and abroad to the other noble houses."

Luca let out a low whistle. "Risky. If they catch you, I'm not sure—"

"They won't," Rook cut him off with a calm confidence. "I've been delivering execution announcements to the houses. I'm expected back to the castle. They'll never suspect me."

I nodded. "Then it's settled. Rook takes the message tonight. If we keep pace, we'll reach the city in five days. At Aetherfall, we split into two groups. The bulk of our forces will enter the castle walls with the supply carts. The bastard's throwing a feast to celebrate the executions. His gluttony will be the key to getting within the walls."

"And then what?" Lucius snarked. "You lead us into the perfect trap so we can be picked off one by one?"

I glared at him over my shoulder, a low growl rumbling in my chest. My patience with him was wearing precariously thin. If he ruined this for us, there would be no holding my beast back from taking it out on his hide. "We need a distraction. Something to draw attention away from those entering the courtyard."

I pulled a map of Mathenholm from my pocket and laid it on the altar. "On the morning of the execution, when the main courtyard is filling with onlookers, two smaller groups will hit the tunnels. One entrance is on the eastern wall, the other along the northern plains. Johan knows that's how we escaped last time, so they'll be guarded. Your job is to engage, allow them to raise the alarm. I'll send you with enough solrics to get the attention of every guard. Luca, I'm sending you to lead in on the eastern side and Fiona, you'll be in the north. Set fires in the tunnels then retreat, and make sure they see you do it. Circle back and wait in the shadows. We'll need cover when we make our retreat."

"Starting fires within the tunnels is one thing," Luca said, rubbing his beard. "But if the flames spread, there may be no stopping it. Then getting out will be a whole new problem."

"We won't be alone," Fallon reminded him. "The servants will open the secret passageways and hidden stairwells for us. Mathenholm was built with more than one escape route."

"And what of Johan?" Fiona asked. "Are we leaving him on his stolen throne? If we do, he'll only come back at us threefold."

"He believes he has the high ground. This was his plan all along. Draw me out to finish this once and for all. He won't run. But I won't risk the lives of my brothers—or my fated—or any of you who've stood with us. Once they're out, I'll go back for him. This needs to end."

The words tasted bitter, but I let them settle in my chest like an oath. This wasn't just about reclaiming a throne. This was for my brothers. For Michaela. For everyone who had bled for Hiraeth while a false king wore the crown. I would deliver vengeance and freedom, even if it cost me my life.

"So," Luca said, ticking the plan off on his fingers, "we sneak in as peasants, smuggle weapons under loaves of bread, set half the damn castle on fire, all while picking off guards in the chaos?"

Fiona flicked her dagger back into its sheath. "Now that," she said with a smirk, "sounds like my kind of rebellion. Levi's spirit isn't too far. I'll bring him sweet vengeance so he can rest in peace."

The wind howled through the ruins—a ghostly promise. I could feel the Divine's presence. I only wished I knew whether I was making the right choice.

In a week, Mathenholm would burn. And the usurper king would learn what it meant to fear the fallen.

I HUNG BACK as the last hope we had drifted into the night, readying themselves to put my plan into action. I'd won them over, but at what cost? My gift had flowed out of me, pushing minds toward choices they might not have made on their own. But I couldn't risk it. Not when Michaela's life hung in the balance.

The ruins fell quiet again. Only the three of us

remained. Luca and Lucius stood nearby, waiting to see if there was some other foolproof plan that I hadn't shared with the others. But these reckless decisions were all that I had to offer them.

Lucius broke the silence. "You know this plan—it's not going to—"

"Don't say it," I snapped, my nerves frayed. I dropped to my knees, hitting the stone floors with the weight of the realm on my shoulders.

I pulled the Book of Astrium from my satchel. The tome was heavy in a way that had nothing to do with the parchment within. "Please, Divine… do not forsake us," I whispered. "Why bind me to her if you only meant to tear us apart? I don't think my soul could survive it. Show me the right path."

I let the book fall open to the page that had ensnared my life. I traced Michaela's face, the lines worn smooth by repetition. "Do you ever wonder if we're living it right now?" I asked. "If we're already on the path written in these pages and don't even realize it?"

Luca sighed. "Nothing the Divine does is ever straightforward. You should know that by now. Even if we could translate every words, I doubt they would bring you any peace. It would only be more riddles to drive you mad."

Footsteps echoed through the ruins and my hand dropped to my knife. I let out a sigh when Amos emerged from the shadows. His eyes sharp beneath the weight of sleepless nights.

"They told me you'd still be here," he said, eyes drifting to the book in my hands. "You look like shit, my friend."

I let out a dry laugh. "I need answers, Amos. I have them right here, and still, it's like trying to read the stars through storm clouds. Has the Divine given up on Hiraeth?"

"May I?" he asked, motioning to the book.

I handed it to him. At this point, he could have the damn thing for all the good it had done me.

He fingered through the pages, a warm smile on his face as his aged hands swept across the parchment. "Used to be that knowing the language of the ancient ones was a death sentence. Too many thought they could bend the will of the Divine by silencing their messengers. Damn fools."

"And they've cursed the rest of us in their ignorance. That book's nothing more than good kindling now," Lucius muttered.

"Ah, but the Divine work in mysterious ways. Prophecies were never meant to hand you all the answers. Fate and destiny are a twisted, complicated mess—meant to maintain the delicate balance of life." Amos closed the book, clutching it to his chest, his gaze steady on mine. "Good begets evil. Evil begets good. Each of us has a role to play, and prophecy helps lead us down the right path. Sometimes that path isn't the easy one. Sometimes it's the one that breaks you. And that is why the weak cannot handle that kind of knowledge. What kind of leader are you, Nico, son of Artos?"

"I want to do right by my people. By my family... and by the woman I love." I held his gaze, hoping he could feel the conviction behind my words.

"Even if the cost is your life?" he asked. His typically animated features were stoic as he awaited my answer.

"Even then. If that's the price, I'd pay it gladly."

"Mmhmm." He nodded, a broad smile cracking his features as he looked up toward the ceiling. "I believe I'm the one that told you!" he called out.

"I'm sorry—what?"

"The Divine felt the need to confirm the truth of your words." He leaned in conspiratorially. "But I'm the one who told them you had a pure soul."

"I appreciate the vote of confidence, but that doesn't help me now." I sighed. "Silent prayers in ruined temples won't spill the blood of my enemies, and that's what I need now. Does the Divine care to explain how I'm supposed to defeat Johan when he has the Bloodstone Sigil? I've racked my brain and still haven't found the answer."

Amos reopened the Book of Astrium, flipping to the page I knew so well. "As it turns out, I know a thing or two about the ancient tongue. And what I can't manage, the Divine will whisper in my ear. But not until they've had their fun watching me struggle through it," he chuckled, his whole belly shaking as he slapped his knee.

I stared at him in disbelief. The old sage had just offered to translate a dead text, and he laughed as if he'd shared a tavern joke rather than offering the key to my entire fate.

"Are you serious? You've been able to read it the whole time and never said anything?" Luca asked, breaking through my stunned silence.

"Sometimes the right path comes exactly when you need it and not a moment before," Amos replied, waving away the accusation.

"Well, get to it. What does it say?" Lucius snapped, tone as sharp as ever.

"As I said, I only know so much. The Divine fills in the gaps when they're feeling generous." Amos squinted at the page, adjusting it this way and that, muttering under his breath as we watched in tense silence.

"I think he's had too much to drink," Lucius grumbled. "Maybe we shouldn't leave Mic's fate in his hands."

"Oh ye of little faith." Amos didn't look up. "Keep distrusting those who care about you, and you'll die a lonely death. Remember that. Now... this first part I can make out." He cleared his throat. "'Seven shall rise... when the— cap? No, that's not right. Crest, maybe?'" He turned the book sideways, then nodded. "Ah, thank you. *Crown*. That's it." He began again: "'Seven shall rise when the crown is undone... Beasts in the spirit... tethered to but one. A heart born frail... in shadow confined... Unbound blood cracks deep when the stars align.'"

He looked up with a wide grin, clearly pleased with himself.

"Like I told you," Luca growled, his voice like tempered steel. "All riddles and no answers. Prayers and prophecies won't bring you peace, and it sure as hell won't help Mic. We act now—or we lose everything."

He stalked out of the temple without looking back. Lucius sneered at me and followed after him.

"Keep the book, Amos," I said quietly. "Work on the rest... but I can't wait any longer. I'll have to make my own fate now."

CHAPTER XXIV
ALWAYS LISTENING
-MICHAELA-

The door slammed shut behind me. The unmistakable sound of a barricade sliding into place solidified my capture. Without a single word, the guards had locked me into my old room. Jase had made his exit back in the outer bailey, silently walking away. No apology. No explanation. He simply surrendered me to the enemy.

I stood in shock, trying to process what had just happened. Had he really played me—just to hand me over to Johan? My mind flashed through the last few days. We had really connected. Or so I thought. We'd definitely become more intimate. We couldn't keep our hands off each other. Was it all a charade? A calculated seduction to keep me marching toward my own demise?

The room blurred as tears threatened to spill down my

cheeks. Was I really that stupid? Everyone told me not to trust him—and boy did I. I clenched my teeth trying to stifle a frustrated scream. I don't think I'd ever felt so betrayed. I defended him, damn it!

No. There had to be more to the story. I refused to believe Jase simply handed me over. He'd shown me kindness these past few days. He'd helped me hone my skills with the eidris. In fact, he hadn't told the guards about the blade still strapped to my thigh. Though... he did take my sprite ash. Maybe I mistook his manipulation for care and concern. Maybe I only saw what I wanted to see. Either way, something didn't add up.

Now that everything had changed, I needed a plan—or at least a strategy. I never considered what I'd do if we'd been caught. Jase had been so confident in his plan. I wanted to believe in him. And now that I thought about it, the whole idea had seemed a little too easy.

My room looked exactly as it had the night we left. Nothing appeared to be out of place. In fact it seemed strangely untouched, almost as if time itself had stood still within its four walls. Had they even searched it?

I opened the vanity drawer—and there it was. Lu's gift, still tucked neatly into the corner. I turned the package over in my hands, the weight of it more emotional than physical. Whatever was inside had to be something truly special. I feared opening it would only further break my already crushed heart. Instead, I carried it to the wardrobe and wedged it up behind the doors, tucking it into the woodwork. No one would think to look for it there. Knowing it was waiting for me—my own little secret—gave me something to fight for.

The pillows! How could I forget? Too afraid to look, I slid my hand under the fabric, bracing for disappointment, but instead I felt the familiar edges of parchment. The Loquentes Cartis. It was still here! Maybe Gwen had written. God, I could use a bit of her reassurance about now. She had an uncanny ability to just go with the flow. Somehow things always worked out for her. I closed my eyes and whispered a silent prayer before unrolling the scroll.

Mic,

I pray this message finds you well. Considering the circumstances, I'll keep this letter vague. I've passed along the information you requested. I'm confident you'll be satisfied with the results.

It feels strange to share my happiness while you're facing hardship, but... things in Neverland are wonderful. Every day is a new adventure. I hope you'll be able to visit us soon. I miss you dearly.

We're here if you need anything. I know you. You'll try to do this all on your own. Please—I beg you, do not hesitate to reach out.

Love always,

Gwen

I couldn't keep the tears from falling. I missed her more than I'd realized. We'd always been so close. I wasn't entirely sure how to navigate life without her. And now I was staring down the very real possibility of being executed.

"My Lady?"

The familiar voice startled me. "Mirabelle!" I shoved the scroll beneath my pillow and rushed to her side, throwing my arms around her. "Thank goodness, you're still here."

"It's really you," she whispered, studying my face. Her beautiful smile quickly shifting back into a tight line. "I've been sent to prepare you for Johan."

"Prepare me? For what?" *Execution?* No... I was a valuable commodity. He wouldn't kill me—not right away.

"To be honest, I'm not entirely sure. He's been in a foul mood... until you arrived. I've sent for the hearth keeper and some hot water. You are to be bathed and put to bed."

"Bathed and put to bed?" What in the bloody hell was going on?

"My Lady, please don't argue this one. Johan has ordered it." Her eyes looked me up and down. "Besides you are positively filthy."

A WARM BATH next to the roaring fireplace was exactly what I needed to clear my head. My body ached from days of relentless travel. But I couldn't shake the feeling that my time here—my time *alive*—was nearly up. Johan would execute me along with the others. I was sure of it. I tried to enjoy the moment for what it was, but Mirabelle's gentle touch felt like the proverbial calm before the storm.

She'd informed me that Johan had ordered my door to remain locked, and posted two guards outside. He was obviously planning something. Why the sudden show of hospitality? There was no way he was gracious enough to treat prisoners—especially a lowly human—with any amount of respect. If I wanted any chance of surviving, I'd need to keep my wits about me. Play his game, and watch him like a hawk.

"Before I take my leave for the evening, My Lady, is there anything I can do for you?" Mirabelle asked, pulling a gauzy shift from the wardrobe. "Please try to get some rest. I've been ordered to return in the morning to ensure you're fit to receive Johan's company."

"What exactly is this all about?" I asked, desperate for some clue to his intentions.

"My Lady, I have no information." She reached for my hand. "But if you value your life, please, I beg you—submit to his commands. I have witnessed first hand, what happens to those who defy him."

The immense gravity of the situation was thrust back in my face. Johan had me in his grasp. The vulture wasn't circling anymore—it was salivating over our impending death. I could only hope he didn't enjoy toying with his prey.

"Mirabelle," I whispered, unsure how to ask what I needed to know. "Jase?" His name was all I had to say.

She froze, visibly afraid to respond. And suddenly, I didn't want her answer.

"Have you seen Hunter or Finn? Are they alive?"

"Shhh!" she hissed. "Do not speak their names aloud." She nodded toward the door, silently mouthing the words, "always listening." Mirabelle cleared her throat and whispered, "Johan keeps them isolated. Only he and his guards are permitted down into the dungeons."

"Are you... close with any of the guards?"

"My Lady, I'am but a simple servant to the house. I am not given freedom to speak to anyone outside of the staff."

"Forgive me. I understand." Clearly, I wasn't going to get much from Mirabelle. I couldn't fault her. She was as trapped in this castle as I was. It would be wrong to ask her to risk her safety simply to help me.

"I'll be back in the morning. Try to get some sleep." She turned down the bed and pulled me in for one last hug, whispering in my ear, "I'm so sorry you're here. I'll do my best to find news of your family. You have my undying loyalty."

Hearing those words gave me an unexpected sense of peace. I had a true friend here in Mathenholm. An ally I could count on.

"There is one thing you could do for me."

"What is it, My Lady?"

"The mirror. In the king's room within the House of Bruin."

"Yes. I know it."

"I need you to shatter it. Tonight. The sooner, the better." She looked at me puzzled. "It's a portal to Neverland. Please—I beg you—destroy it. I'll be forever indebted to you."

She hesitated… then nodded. "Consider it done. I'll head there now."

The door latched behind her, sealing me into silence. My mind was a mess of emotion. Now, with the portal gone, I had to write my sister, one last time.

My Dearest Sweetie,

I fear this message does not hold the cheerful outcome we had hoped for. As I write, I am being held prisoner in Mathenholm Castle by Johan Vellere—the usurper of the Hiraethian throne.

Sadly, we lost Gunner in battle. Finn and Hunter are to be executed the day after tomorrow. Things here have gotten out of control, and I don't see how we can successfully defeat our enemy.

Take a deep breath, for what I am about to tell you won't be easy to hear. It is very likely that I will be executed alongside the others. I know this is not what you expected me to say. I can only imagine what you are thinking as you read this letter. Maybe I'm wrong and we will prevail after all. But I couldn't risk not getting a final letter to you.

I love you. I need you to know that above all else. I couldn't have asked for a better sister to share this wild, chaotic life with. You always believed in me and my ability to overcome cancer. And Gwen, I almost did! I'd been working with a healer and learning how to harness the magic growing within me. Unfortunately, my skills are not nearly developed enough to get us out of this mess.

I have found real love here. The princes have shown me what it means to be cherished. I never would have experienced that type of intimacy had you not pushed me to seek a cure in Neverland. For that I cannot thank you enough.

I will think of you as I join our beloved parents in the afterlife. Live your life for me. Live it big and without regret. I'll be watching from above.

Love always,
Michaela

I wiped the tears from my face and placed a kiss on the parchment. Tucking it back under my pillow, I wished for my princes to end this nightmare once and for all. Not just for me—but for all of Hiraeth and her beautiful people.

"Michaela?"

Hunter's voice was soft and fleeting. I turned in every direction, but there was nothing—no shape, no light—just an endless void pressing in. Darkness surrounded me.

"Hunter?" I called out. "Where are you? I can't see you."

"I don't have enough energy to project imagery. I wanted to say goodbye. The full moon is…" His voice faded like a dying flame.

Panic surged through me. "Wait… Hunter, I can't hear you."

"I'm sorry. I'm having trouble maintaining the connection. I want you to know, I spent every day wishing we'd had more time together. The Divine took you from me before I got the chance to show you how much I could love you."

"Please don't give up, Hunter. There's still time."

"*I will* find you in our next life. Maybe then—"

I jolted awake. The bright morning sun accosted my eyes as Hunter's dream slipped from my memory.

Mirabelle returned moments later, exactly as she'd promised. This time with a hot breakfast in hand and a mauve-toned gown draped over her arm—leaving me no time to wallow in Hunter's final goodbye. I comforted myself with the notion that if I were to die alongside him, at least we'd have time in whatever afterlife awaited us.

The smell of eggs and fresh salmonberries had my belly grumbling with hunger pangs, but was I hungry enough to risk it?

Pushing the food around the plate, I contemplated whether or not it had been tampered with.

"My Lady, I assure you the food is safe. I gathered it from the cook myself. Please—eat."

I sighed and gave her a small smile. "Was I that obvious?" I took a bite, trying my best not to think the worst. "Forgive my misgivings. Thank you for the warm meal. Were you able to destroy the mirror?"

She nodded, a smile creeping across her face. "It is done."

Relief washed over me, knowing Gwen wouldn't be able to access the portal in an attempt to save me, and find herself tangled in Johans talons.

Mirabelle fussed over my hair while I ate, brushing it out before curling it into soft waves. Piece by piece, she worked tirelessly to pin it into an elaborate style atop my head.

"Why do I need to be dolled up if he's going to execute me?"

"My Lady, I wouldn't assume anything when it comes to Johan's motives." She pulled me from the vanity. "Come on —we need to get you into this dress before he arrives."

Fear thickened the air around me, suffocating me in anticipation. He was on his way. The food in my belly fought to stay down. The mere mention of his name had my skin crawling. It was time to play the game. I was about to face my nemesis.

"My Lady? Are you okay?"

"I'm sorry, I… I'm just nervous."

"Take a breath. You're a cunning young woman. All you have to do is play by his rules."

"It's his rules I'm afraid of."

The gown was simple, yet stunning. Embroidered along the hemline were delicate songbirds perched happily amongst barren branches. The thin, silky fabric clung to my curves, while the obscenely plunging neckline left me feeling dangerously exposed.

"This color—"

Johan burst through the door, stopping Mirabelle dead in her tracks. Every hair on my body stood on edge. The grimy smile on his face quickly morphed into a scowl.

"Why are you still here?" he barked at her.

"My Lord," she bowed, and I quickly followed suit. "Forgive me. I… I was making sure she looked perfect."

"Leave us!"

"Yes, my Lord." Mirabelle didn't argue. She scurried out of the room, leaving me alone with the vulture.

"Well, well, well. Miss Michaela Darling Carlisle. I do believe you have aligned yourself with the wrong house."

I stared at him blankly.

"Do you like the dress? I knew you'd look ravishing in silk. It clings to your curves in all the right ways."

He circled around, inspecting me like prey. I remained quiet, my chin held high, refusing to give him the satisfaction of a response.

"Thanks to Jase, you made it just in time for our special ceremony."

I swallowed hard at the sound of his name, forcing my breakfast to stay down. If I was going to get any information I'd have to engage in conversation. "My Lord, forgive my silence. What's this ceremony you speak of?"

"Tonight, after I honor Jase for his loyalty, we will partake in the Nocta Dominium."

Honor Jase for his loyalty, was all I heard. Loyalty? To Johan? No. It couldn't be true.

"I can tell by your dumbfounded expression you didn't know he was working for me. He's played a pivotal role in my plan. In fact, if it weren't for his help, you wouldn't be here now. He traded your life for Finn's."

Tears threatened to spill down my cheeks. I refused to believe everything Jase and I had shared was pure manipulation. Nothing but simple fodder to keep me on track. But even as the betrayal burned hot in my chest, I couldn't help but wonder: what would I have done to save my sister?

"Ohhh, I do love seeing tears in your eyes," Johan taunted. "Does it break your heart to know he used you?"

"Fuck you!" The words exploded from my mouth before I could consider the consequences—and I paid the price.

Johan slapped my face, nearly knocking me to the ground. "You will not speak to me like that. I am your Lord, and you will show me respect."

I bowed my head in defeat. "Forgive me, my Lord."

"I'll be expecting more from you this evening. You'd be wise to remember that you belong to me."

He closed the distance between us, lifting my chin to inspect the blooming handprint on my cheek. I froze, trying not to recoil at his touch.

"Seeing you so broken is getting my dick hard."

He trailed his fingers down my neck and thrust his calloused hand under the silk gown, squeezing my breast until I cried out in pain.

"Such a pretty cry. Holding out for tonight will be a challenge worth the prize."

He leaned in closer gripping my face, and dragged his tongue along my cheek, tasting my tears.

"I can't wait to taste the rest of you."

I refused to meet his gaze, forcing my mind to drift anywhere but here. Silently, I prayed for the moment to end.

"Your lady's maid will be back later to prepare you for the Nocta Dominium."

I'd heard that term before. The males who tried to rape me had said Johan wanted me for it—but I still had no idea what it meant.

"I'll be expecting your full participation." And just like

that, he turned and left the room. Leaving me frozen, holding my breath until I heard the lock slide into place.

I collapsed to the floor with a heavy exhale, finally allowing myself to fall apart.

I cried for my lack of intuition.

I cried for the betrayal I endured at the hands of Jase.

I cried for the violation of my body—no longer my own.

I cried for my heartache.

For my fated.

For my sister.

And I cried for our failure against Johan.

Everything we'd fought for was lost.

And it felt like it was all my fault.

CHAPTER XXV
NOCTA DOMINIUM
-MICHAELA-

"What is Nocta Dominium?" I asked Mirabelle the moment she arrived. It had been eating at me all day.

She stared at me, her brows furrowed and her mouth agape. "He didn't explain it to you?"

"All he said was he expects my full participation."

Mirabelle sighed. "Come sit down," she said, motioning to the edge of the bed. "Nocta Dominium is an old tradition that hasn't been enforced for centuries. It gives the ruling king the right to lay with any lady of the court, regardless of her will or marital status."

I felt the blood drain from my face. "No, no, no. That can't be what he wants. This isn't happening." I pressed a hand to my chest. My heart was pounding, adrenaline driving through my veins, begging my body to flee. "I will not have relations with that... that monster." My stomach lurched, and I swallowed hard to keep its contents down.

Mirabelle reached for my hand. "My Lady, you're trembling. Breathe," she spoke in a slow, measured pace. "In and out. There, that's it."

Things had gone from bad to worse. I pulled in another deep breath, trying to calm the growing panic. The room around me blurred with tears as I fought back the urge to cry.

"Michaela," she said, using my given name and breaking etiquette. "I understand your repulsion. But if you fight him on this, he'll only make it worse for you. It's merely your body he wishes to use. He cannot take your heart."

I stared at her, silently crying, tears spilling down my cheeks.

"Rumor has it he's quick between the sheets. Your beauty will have him spent before he even starts."

I knew she was trying to help, but her reassurances were useless bandages against a gaping, ever-bleeding wound. Johan would be coming for me in the next hour or so. I could hear the muffled celebrations in Jase's honor—the court gleefully rejoicing while I awaited the devil himself.

Did Jase know Johan planned to enforce Nocta Dominium on me? The thought of it had my heart in a vice. Would the betrayal ever end? I must have been seriously mistaken about what it means to be fated. He handed me over to be raped. Was this all just a way for him to save Finn? Or had he been on Johan's side the whole time, with saving Finn as a mere bonus?

"My Lady, forgive me. The hour is growing long, and I must prepare your body."

Before being dressed in a sheer gauzy shift, I was perfumed with a putrid oil. The scent could only be described as sickly sweet decaying flesh. I suppose it made sense, considering I was being made alluring for a fucking vulture. My hair was let down and brushed into pretty waves, and my cheeks were rouged with a soft pink glow. Aside from the disgusting smell, I looked every bit the reluctant virginal bride, frightfully awaiting her groom to steal her virtue.

I allowed Mirabelle to finish out her orders in silence, using the time to forge a plan. I wouldn't be able to hide the eidris on my person—the shift was too sheer. Tucking it away under the mattress would be my only option. My resources were slim. Whether I chose to fight or disassociate, I had to have something in place against the horrors I was about to endure.

Johan didn't knock. He burst through the door with such force, I thought it might fly off its hinges. He'd barely closed it behind him before he started peeling off his layers of finery.

"Ugh, this blasted ring!" he said, yanking a thick band from his red and blistered finger and looping it through his heavy gold necklace. A dark crimson stone glowed from within its silver setting. Was this the Bloodstone Sigil?

"Fortunately for you, the mead has me in a wanton mood." His words were slightly slurred and his movements unsteady. Perhaps I'd get lucky and his apparent inebriation would offer me an advantage. Or better yet, maybe his manhood wouldn't work.

I moved as far from the bed as I could, putting as much distance between us as possible.

"You can try to avoid me all you want. Believe me when I say I'll call for guards to hold you down." A shit-eating grin spread across his greasy face, and he chuckled. "I might do that anyway. Have them spread you... wide. I've been imagining what your pussy looks like all day."

Hearing his vulgar confession made me sick to my stomach. If I was going to be forced to participate, then it would be worth trying to bargain for a small consolation. "I'll cooperate," the words spilled out too eagerly. "If you allow me to see Finn and Hunter." I held my chin high, confident in my offer.

"Ha! You'll cooperate no matter what." He stumbled toward me. "How about this," he paused to hiccup, "you become my little whore... and I'll think about letting you see them before I stretch their necks."

"Let me see them first. I have no guarantee you'll honor your word."

Johan laughed darkly. "The lady thinks she can bargain. I'm growing tired of this game." He grabbed my arm, pulling me in tight. His breath was hot on my face. "You are mine... and I will do to you whatever I want." He gripped my chin tightly, digging his fingers into my jawline and slammed his mouth against mine.

I tried to pull away, but he only tightened his grip, deepening the assault on my mouth. It was wet, and his breath reeked of alcohol. His rough tongue forcefully thrust at my sealed lips until he broke through, flailing around clumsily, tasting me, while I fought the urge to gag.

I managed to pull away, backing into a corner, wiping at my mouth with the sleeve of my shift. I wanted the foul taste of him gone. In my efforts to keep space between us, I had completely trapped myself. There was no way out. My limbs began to tremble, knees threatening to buckle under the weight of my fear.

Johan ripped off his shirt. His gluttonous belly was covered in black hair and damp with sweat. Though he was a few feet away, I could smell his filthy body. His grey, lifeless eyes locked onto my now heaving breasts. The sheer fabric of the shift offered me no modesty. I could feel his gaze violating me. "Please, I beg of you, don't do this."

"Like a fawn caught in the jaws of a coyote, your pathetic cries for help only turn me on more. Beg," he growled.

"Please," I whimpered as he inched closer, stalking me like helpless prey. I wasn't going to win this battle. It was hopeless. If my begging pleased him, then I refused to indulge him any longer.

"I'm ready to see what toys my new plaything has to offer." He reached out and tugged the simple tie holding up the flimsy nightgown, stripping me in one quick tug. I turned my head away, closed my eyes, trying desperately to shift my mind to a better place.

His hands were on me. Groping. Roaming. Touching me like I was his possession. Then I felt it. The assault against my most private place. His fingers forcing their way into my delicate folds, painfully probing at my entrance.

I watched in horror as he lasciviously licked his fingers. "Mmm, I see now why the Bruins wanted to keep you."

I spit on his vile, disgusting face. And it earned me a slap across the cheek.

"Such a shame, Michaela. I could have made this good for you. But you leave me no choice. You want it rough. That works for me." He picked me up and threw me over his shoulder. Kicking. Screaming. He slapped my ass with a resounding crack.

The sound of him wrestling with his pants, freeing himself before he threw me down on the bed, had my mind blaring with alarm. Adrenaline coursed through me like lightning, causing my limbs to tremble uncontrollably while I struggled to get out from beneath him. His little red cock stood at attention, bobbing with his desperate attempts to align himself.

I fought for what felt like hours before finally succumbing to his weight. Exhausted and out of breath, he had me pinned down, my legs caught between his belly and my own. My knees pressed so tightly against my ribs. I could barely breathe. He had the perfect angle to take what he wanted. There was nothing I could do to stop him.

"Once my scent is infused with yours, your precious bears will want nothing to do with you."

I couldn't hold back anymore. His words hit me with a force unlike anything I had ever experienced. Never in all my years—not even my diagnosis had ever broken me like this. Uncontrollable sobs poured from my body.

His penis was at my entrance. Poised and ready to take what wasn't given. "Look at me while I defile you," he demanded. "I want you to remember it was Jase—"

His eyes suddenly grew wide, and the smile on his face morphed into confusion before a loud gasp escaped his lips. And then—he was pulled off me.

Jase stood over him, a bloodied blade gripped firmly in his hand.

"Mic! Are you—" He turned his gaze to Johan, who had scrambled away, blood oozing from a stab wound in his shoulder blade. "You fucking bastard!"

"You stabbed me?" Johan stared, stunned. "Guards!"

"No point in calling for help. I've already disposed of them." Jase stalked after him, closing in. "You never said anything about invoking Nocta Dominium," he growled.

"Since when do you care about the human? She's nothing more than a wet piece of ass."

Jase's eyes went dark. His lips pulled back, teeth bared.

Rage tore through him, erupting in a deafening roar. He lunged forward in an attempt to make contact.

Johan stumbled back, nearly losing his footing, and Jase took full advantage—advancing on him once again, slashing at his groin. But he slipped sending them both to the floor in a thud. The two wrestled in a chaotic flurry of shadows and flailing limbs.

It was over before I could react.

Johan rose, blood soaking his torn pants from a deep gash along his inner thigh. Jase lay on the floor gasping for air, clutching his gut. Blood was everywhere. I couldn't tell who or what wound it came from. I remained silently frozen on the bed, clutching the linens to my chest, terrified to move or draw attention to myself in any way.

"You traitorous coward!" Johan hissed, spitting on Jase. "You've been weighed and measured. May you rot in the afterlife knowing your betrayal is the reason Finn will hang tomorrow." Then his eyes landed on me. "Lucky for you, I'm in need of a healer. Mark my words, human—this isn't over. I'll have my way with you, and you *will* pay the price for his insolence."

He hobbled towards the door, leaving behind a macabre scene in his wake. "Enjoy the company of his corpse. It'll be the only courtesy I show you."

"Jase!" I gasped once Johan was gone. Ripping the sheet from the bed, I rushed to his side. "Jase, what have you done?"

I moved his hands to assess the wound. The moment I

lifted pressure, blood gushed. "No, no, no." I shoved the linen into the laceration, ignoring his pain-laden wail, and pressed his hands back over it in a desperate attempt to staunch the bleeding. It wasn't good, and we both knew it.

"Mic… we haven't got much time," he fought to get the words out.

"No, it's going to be okay."

"It's not." He gulped, choking back his tears. "I have… to tell you…" He paused between labored breaths. "I'm sorry."

"Jase—"

"No… let me." He groaned, trying to lift his head. "I tried to stop him sooner. I didn't… I was a fool. I've made so many…wrong choices. I… I denied… my fate. Denied my beast. And now… I'm paying the ultimate price." He swallowed hard. "Michaela… I love you."

I couldn't believe what I was hearing. Tears spilled freely down my cheeks. Consumed with emotion a silent scream erupted from my chest. "Why?" The word broke out in a sob. Why, if he loved me, had he betrayed me so violently?

"I was… afraid." He coughed, blood seeping from the corners of his mouth. "I've never… never felt… such overwhelming desire. Mic…" He reached for my face, brushing away my tears. "It's too late." His eyes closed. His brow furrowed and he let out a groan of agony. "Forgive…"

"Jase," I called, trying to rouse him. He was on death's doorstep, and fading quickly. "Jase? Don't leave me. Not yet. I…"

"Forgive... me," he whispered.

"I forgive you," I cried. "Please, don't leave me."

I was drowning in fear. Lost in a rising tide of heartbreak. I had to tell him before he was gone. He couldn't die not knowing.

"I love you, Jase."

He stared back at me blankly. His body limp in my arms.

"Jase? No, no, no."

He was gone.

"Please," I sobbed, pulling him into my arms, rocking him back and forth. "I love you. I love you," I repeated, praying he would somehow be able to hear me in death.

CHAPTER XXVI
HARBINGER OF DEATH
-MICHAELA-

The morning had finally arrived, bathing the two of us in a puddle of light, giving a false warmth to skin that had long since grown cold. I knew my arms should ache from holding him all night, from pressing on a wound that had stopped bleeding hours ago. But I was numb. My face felt tight, a reminder of the countless tears I'd shed. They'd finally subsided when my body had nothing left to give. But I knew they'd return.

I fixated on the back of my hand, entranced by the blood that had dried there, memorizing the pattern of cracks. Wondering if my soul looked the same. I was in shock, and somehow that was easier than the thoughts that took turns tormenting me. At this point, I welcomed the madness.

My emotions swung wildly. One moment, I was sure that if I just held him for a little while longer, he'd stop staring at the wall, past what my eyes could see, and tell me everything was alright. The next, I was back in the nightmare where Jase was dead, and it was my fault. If I had never come to Hiraeth, none of this would've happened. Gunner would still be alive. So would Jase.

I had become the one thing I hated most. A harbinger of death. A curse on the House of Bruin. Had I unwittingly made a bargain with the reaper? Every time I denied him my soul, was it another notch in his belt against me? Another life to be claimed in my stead?

His dagger still lay beside him. I picked it up with shaking fingers, wiping Johan's blood from the silver blade. He hadn't even bothered to take it. A testament to his assessment of me —I was no threat. A fragile human girl posed no challenge to him, and my perceived vulnerability made anger well inside me. Not because he'd underestimated me, but because he was right. I had done nothing to save Jase. Or Gunner. I was a liability to everyone I loved, and the knowledge made me sick.

I gripped the blade in my hand, the cold steel of the hilt biting into my palm. I hadn't been able to save Jase or anyone else with this knife, but maybe I could spare the lives of those who loved me. If I ended my life here and now, no one else would suffer for me. No more lives lost because of me. No more pieces of my soul stripped away.

The more I allowed myself to go down that dark path,

the more it felt like mercy. I lifted the blade to my wrist, laying it across my pulse. It would be so easy. A single cut. With Jase still in my arms, I could go with him. "I'm sorry, Gwen," I whispered to my sister, my emotions caught thick in my throat. The tears breaking loose again.

But before I could move, shadows poured from my palms, curling around the dagger. The darkness snapped me out of my spiraling thoughts. The blade dropped from my hand and hit the floor with a dull thud.

"Jase?" I breathed, hope leaching into my mind. I scurried out from under him, his body lying limp on the floor. I had seen his shadows. They had stopped me from doing the unthinkable. That meant something—didn't it?

I dropped my head to his chest, listening. Desperate for a heartbeat. But there was only silence.

The door burst open. "Oh my Divine, My Lady! Are you alright?" Mirabelle's voice filled the room as she rushed in, eyes wide at the macabre scene before her.

"Mirabelle," I said her name like a plea. "Help me. Please! I think he's still alive."

She dropped beside me as I leaned over him. I saw the moment her panic faded into resignation.

"Michaela... look at me." She grabbed my shoulders, gently pulling me upright. I met her eyes, already knowing what she was going to say. I could see it written all over her face.

"Don't say it," I whispered. "Don't. I can't take it." I

raked my fingers through my hair, my voice rising. "You haven't even listened. You don't know for sure."

"I don't need to," she said softly. "He's gone, Michaela." She let the finality of her words sit heavy between us as I shook my head, refusing to believe it. "You know it's true. You can feel it."

She was right. It felt as though the same wound punctured my gut and a part of me had died with him. A sob escaped my lips and Mirabelle wrapped her arms around me, rubbing my back like a child while I fell apart in her lap.

When my sobs had quieted, she held me at arm's length. "We have to go, My Lady. I need to get you out of here. There's another guest room down the hall and—"

"No," I said, retreating from her touch. "I can't leave him. Not like this." I recoiled from her, throwing myself over Jase protectively.

"This"—she motioned gently to his still body—"isn't him anymore. And I need to prepare you for... Well, that doesn't matter. I have news."

"You're right, it doesn't matter. Nothing matters. Just leave me here to die."

"Don't say that." Her voice sharpened. "Your princes are coming for you. We got word last night—they're planning to infiltrate the castle. I need to get you ready. You can't stay here."

"I don't want them to come," I whispered. "I only bring death."

A pinched look crossed her face a moment before her hand connected with my cheek. The slap wasn't hard, but it was enough to cut through my hysteria.

"I'm sorry. But I had to do that. And I'm truly sorry about Jase. You need to pull yourself together. They're coming for you whether you want them to or not. Staying here only puts them at risk. Is that what you want?"

"No," I whispered.

"Good. Then kiss your prince one final farewell and let's go."

I turned to Jase one last time, drinking in the details of him—his face, his hair, the dagger beside him, still whispering the possibilities of sweet oblivion. I reached for it, clutching it to my chest. I had Gunner's blade. Now Jase's. My morbid mind wondered if I would have a collection of seven before this ended.

I shoved the thought away. This wasn't a curse. It was a promise. I would never let this happen again. I brushed the hair from Jase's brow and pressed a final kiss to his forehead. "Come find me in my dreams," I whispered before getting to my feet and leaving him forever.

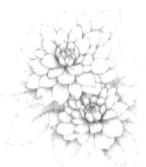

"I'm not wearing that," I said when Mirabelle laid the dress on the bed. The dark mauve color reminded me of old blood, and I knew Johan had everything to do with the selection. My stomach turned at the thought of wearing it for him. "I'll wear black."

Mirabelle sighed. "I'd love nothing more than to place you in a dress of mourning, but this is the only option we have. You have to play nice for a little while longer."

I ground my teeth, knowing I had no say in the matter, but neither did Mirabelle, so I couldn't take it out on her.

I stood stoic, allowing her to dress me in the ridiculous ballgown, with its puffed shoulders and embroidered sleeves that hung all the way to the floor.

"Lift your arms," she murmured, adjusting the corset with practiced fingers.

"Before you finish," I said quietly, reaching into the folds of my cloak, "I need you to help me with this." I reached for Jase's dagger on the vanity.

Her hands stilled. Her gaze met mine, uncertainty clouding her eyes. We both knew grief had made me reckless.

"My Lady—"

"Please," I said, my tone harsher than I intended. "Just help me secure it. If anyone sees, they'll take it from me."

A tense moment passed, but then she nodded, reaching for the blade with careful hands. She tucked it between the boning under my breasts, adjusting the folds of silk to hide the outline. I winced as the cold steel kissed my skin. The laces tightened uncomfortably, but I didn't complain when the stays dug into my sides. I welcomed the physical pain. It kept my focus away from the emotions that threatened to drag me down.

Once she finished, I walked back to the vanity. I wasn't sure I recognized the woman staring back at me. Even with all the makeup Mirabelle had painted on my face, the dark circles under my eyes still showed. Nothing could hide the fact that my cheekbones were too prominent, that you could count every rib with this revealing neckline. I hadn't had access to sprite ash, and death was growing impatient. I was fading quickly, and the sight actually made me smile. Maybe nature would simply take its proper course and I'd be dead in a week.

I spotted an inkwell on the vanity. I picked it up, toying with the cool glass bottle. Its dark depths seemed like a perfect metaphor for my soul. Without a second thought, I tipped it over, pouring the black ink down the front of the dress. I'd wear the costume he picked, but I'd make my own statement.

"Johan wanted this body, but he has to know I'm already dead inside," I said, feeling a flicker of strength return as I voiced the truth aloud.

Mirabelle gasped. "My Lady!" she chided. "You may want to keep that bit of truth to yourself right now. Johan can hurt you in more ways than physical. I don't want to see that happen to you."

Her words were punctuated by a rumbling blast that shook the doorframe, sending dust trickling from the ceiling.

Both of us jumped at the noise, scanning the room for any sign of danger.

"What was that?" I asked.

"I don't know. Maybe part of the plan?" Another blast rattled the stone walls, and my heart raced with a potent cocktail of anticipation and fear. Was it my beasts? Had they truly come for me?

The loud rumbles continued on in quick succession, sending Mirabelle and I scrambling toward the walls as a commotion sounded in the hallway. Muffled orders grew louder as they approached. Mirabelle and I clung to each other, her tiny frame shaking in my arms as we waited to see if whomever was in the hallway would simply pass us by.

Mirabelle shrieked when the door was kicked in. Guards poured into the room—sun glinting off their drawn blades and polished armor. Mirabelle stepped in front of me, steeling herself for whatever came next.

"How dare you enter the ladies' chambers while she is preparing herself! Have you no decency?" she snapped.

"There's been a change of plans," a male grumbled as he stepped forward. A badge marked him as captain. "The king's moved up the execution ceremony now that all the prisoners have arrived. He's called for the girl. So ready or not, she's coming with us."

What did he mean, all the prisoners have arrived? Another blast shook the room, and I shuddered.

"This is no way to treat a lady," Mirabelle spat. "If the king wants her, he should escort her himself."

"The king is preoccupied, and I'm growing tired of your insolence. Stand aside, or I will pull you aside. Your choice."

"It's okay, Mirabelle. Now is as good a time as any," I said, placing a reassuring hand on her shoulder and gently eased her aside.

The captain inspected me, lingering at the low neckline where my breast threatened to spill over. His smirk soured into a scowl when he noticed my ruined dress.

"I'll see that you're assigned a more... thorough lady's maid in the future. But you'll have to do. Earlic!" he shouted over his shoulder. "I need your seed. The king wants it to look real."

The guard in question bowed curtly, his cheeks flushing crimson before he dropped his pants. He began jerking off while the others waited. What in the bloody hell was going on?

"We haven't got all day, Earlic!" the captain barked. The male picked up his pace, flogging himself in wild abandon. I only looked away when his hungry gaze settled on me and my stomach turned. He let out a groan, and the sick sound of slapping finally ceased.

"About time," the captain said, striding toward me. He grabbed my skirts, yanking them up.

"What are you doing? Don't fucking touch me!" I protested as I tried to pull away. His free hand captured my wrist and squeezed until I cried out.

"Easy now. Earlic just needs to add the finishing touches. Be a good girl and stop fighting."

Panic clawed at my throat.

Earlic knelt before my nakedness. One large hand forced my thighs apart, while the other wiped his cum between my thighs and over my sex. I wanted to vomit. I could feel my stomach turn on me as the warmth of it dripped down my thighs—all I could do was wretch as my body trembled.

"Those bastards will smell him on her from a mile away. The king will be pleased," he said as he stepped back.

The captain dropped my skirts as a sob crept up my throat. I'd been defiled. Even though he hadn't forced himself on me, I felt violated. I swallowed down the tears with every ounce of courage I could muster. I refused to give them the satisfaction of seeing me break.

The captain took one last appraising look as though he were assessing livestock for slaughter, before turning on his heels and heading for the door. "We're late. Seize her and let's be off."

Two guards came at me, grabbed me around my middle and hoisted me off the ground. "Put me down! Now!" I kicked and flailed, but it was useless. I was no match for them. My own vulnerability and the sticky mess between my legs gutted me to my core.

CHAPTER XXVII
SOMETHING I NEED TO FINISH
-MICHAELA-

The Crown's guard delivered me to an enormous vestibule. Beams of light poured in from impossibly high skylights. A set of large wooden doors were the only thing that stood between me and my beasts. I could hear the din of the crowd, and a shiver ran down my spine. What was happening out there? The blasts had finally stopped— or perhaps we'd reached a part of the castle where we could no longer hear them. I'd stopped fighting, choosing to conserve what little strength I had left for whatever might come next.

Johan stood at the center of his entourage. A gangly valet preened over him, adjusting a gaudy golden crown that was far too large for his head.

"Simply marvelous, Your Highness. The way the new

crown sits upon your head is absolutely splendid. No one will notice your limp. The healers have done a masterful job. Once you place the Bloodstone Sigil on your finger, no one will be able to deny your status," the valet gushed.

"Yes, yes, that'll do, Hysserion," Johan said, waving him off as he pulled a necklace from under his doublet. A thick ring hung at the end of the chain. He eyed the band—the infamous ring of power—rubbing at the red blisters encircling his finger. With a deep breath, he slipped it over the angry skin. A muscle ticked in his jaw, and sweat beaded on his brow. The ring was affecting him. And not in a good way. But what did it mean?

"Your Highness," the captain called. "I've brought the human, sir."

He dragged me forward until I stumbled. His bruising grip was the only thing keeping me from falling on my face. Everyone in the vestibule fell silent as I straightened, making a show of smoothing the ink stains on my dress.

The sneer on Johan's face when he saw me was worth whatever punishment he had in mind. "What's the meaning of this?" His eyes flicked from one guard to the next.

"This is how we found her, Your Highness. And due to the urgency of your request, we didn't want to keep you waiting. The lady's maid has been relieved of duty. Everything else has been done to your specifications."

"Those damn peasants are completely useless." Johan strode toward me, a thick velvet cape trailing behind him. "Lift her dress."

I stood stoic, closing my eyes as they exposed me yet again—this time for his inspection. He sucked in a breath through clenched teeth, then licked his lips like he was tasting the air.

"A bit more crude than I would have preferred, but it's enough to plant the illusion."

"This was your doing?" I hissed, allowing my anger to take over for the broken girl beneath the surface.

"As you well know, I'd planned to do it myself. But our little run-in last night derailed my surprise for the sons of Artos. Speaking of—how is Jase this morning?" A cruel smirk twisted his lips, and I cracked.

"You bastard! I'll kill you!"

I lunged for him before I could think better of it, my hands going for his throat. Even the light in the room seemed to darken with my wrath, but it was short-lived. Strong arms held me in place as I seethed, desperate to wrap my hands around his throat and watch the life fade from his eyes.

"Humans," Johan tsked. "Rather emotional creatures, don't you think?" His entourage laughed at my expense. "Chain her ankles. I don't want her getting any bright ideas in front of the court. If she cannot uphold decorum, I may need to find that lady's maid she's so fond of and hang her along with the others. A little incentive to mind your manners."

"Go to hell," I growled as the guards locked the iron

shackles around my ankles. My skirts hid them completely as they fell back into place.

"So ungrateful. Here I am, about to give her this beautiful gift, and yet she speaks to me as if I'm not her king." He stepped in close, waiting to see how far I'd push him.

"I don't want your gift. Let them go. Then I'll be thankful."

"Ha! Let them go? I'm doing you a great service by severing your fated bonds. Then you'll be free. Free to bear my offspring. Children immune to this terrible plague that's culling the lesser of our kind. We'll usher in a new era for Hiraeth. Eventually, you'll learn to respect me."

"Nico will kill you before he lets that happen. They all will," I shot back, allowing myself that small fraction of hope.

"I've already apprehended the imposter," he said coolly.

I studied his face. The deep furrow in his brow, the slight tick in his jaw—he was bluffing. "I don't believe you."

"Nico's capture is a foregone conclusion. You, my lovely, are the bait he cannot resist. Fitting, don't you think? My consort, single-handedly responsible for the fall of the House of Bruin. The news will spread far and wide. Hiraeth will thank you for cleansing the realm of their bloodline."

"No matter what you do to this body, I'll never be yours," I choked out. It was weak, but it was true. My beasts might die today... because of me.

"Shall we? Let's not keep our guests waiting." He

reached for my hand and tucked it into his arm, leading me toward the grand wooden doors. My destiny waited just beyond this threshold.

The sunlight was blinding. It took a moment for my eyes to adjust, the muted tones of the courtyard slowly coming into focus. Johan led me onto a raised stone dais, waving to the crowd as we reached the railing.

The sea of people stretched beyond the gates. Peasants in drab clothing stretched out before us. It was sickening, how many had come to watch the execution of innocents. I scanned the crowd for familiar faces, but there were too many.

A wall of guards stood between us and the masses. More were scattered throughout, on high alert, as if they knew danger was already among them. The crudely constructed gallows rose from the center of the courtyard. Six wolfsbane nooses swayed gently in the breeze. Smoke rose from the northern and eastern wings of the castle, but the crowd remained. If anything, the air crackled with a grim anticipation—as if the realm was preparing for destinies to be made or lost this day.

Johan lifted his arms, and the crowd fell silent. He let the moment stretch, milking the tension before finally shouting, "Bring them out!"

An ominous drumbeat echoed through the courtyard and the crowd erupted. A smug smile curled Johan's lips as they came into view.

A line of battered servants stumbled onto the gallows,

their tunics torn, faces bloodied, hands bound with wolfsbane ties.

Rook.

My breath caught. The young page who had helped Mirabelle dress me the night of the Crownspire. His solemn gaze found mine as they pushed him into place, fitting the noose around his neck. Despite it all, defiance burned in his eyes. The sight gave me strength, even as my tears fell.

An old sage stepped onto the platform, pushing up his sleeves before addressing the accused. "We commit your souls to the Divine, to cast their ultimate judgment. Let your spirits find peace beyond the veil, carried upon your sacred breath. In life, they stood against the crown. In death, may they stand before you. So it is spoken. So it shall be."

"Let this be a lesson to all who would conspire against my reign," Johan bellowed. He raised a gloved hand.

A black-masked executioner yanked the lever. All six dropped.

I flinched as Rook's body jerked, his strangled gasp lost beneath the crowd's collective exhale. The ropes creaked. Their feet twitched. One by one, the fight left them, until they hung limp, swaying like broken marionettes.

Bile burned in my throat. I wanted to scream. To fight. But I was frozen. Useless. Shackled and forced to watch the slow unraveling of everything I held dear.

They wasted no time discarding the bodies and marching out the next prisoners. My heart squeezed when I saw Sawyer's massive frame leading the way. Blood matted his silver hair and wolfsbane bindings dug into his wrist as they dragged him forward.

Johan stood. "This one gave us more trouble than all the rest. But like the others, he is nothing before the crown. His death will cripple that pitiful rebellion. No one will rise against me again."

I squeezed my eyes shut, trying to ignore him and come up with something that resembled a plan. I couldn't let this happen.

I felt them before I even opened my eyes. The air shifted —the energy pulling taut as Finn and Hunter were marched into the square. Iron chains hung heavy over the wolfsbane binding their hands. I gasped at the sight of them. Their faces were gaunt and bruises in varying stages of healing covered their skin. And still—they walked with their heads high.

The crowd pelted them with rotten food, but they didn't flinch. Hunter's piercing eyes burned with restrained fury, but he kept his focus on the gallows. Finn's gaze locked onto mine.

"Do not look away." His voice echoed in my head, barely a whisper at the edge of thought. The wolfsbane dulled his magic, but he was still there, pressing against my thoughts.

"Stay with me, Finn. They're coming. We'll get you both out of this." Tears blurred the scene, but I didn't look away.

The drums began again. Slow. Steady. A death knell ringing over the courtyard. Johan accepted a scroll from his valet and unrolled it with practiced formality. His voice was deep and measured, as though he'd recited this speech a thousand times.

"Finn and Hunter, sons of the fallen House of Bruin. I hereby declare you guilty of treason, conspiracy, and rebellion against the rightful crown."

The crowd roared as guards tightened the ropes around their necks. I should've been searching the crowd for help. I should've had a plan. But I couldn't tear my gaze away from them.

"We'll have time to love each other in the next life," Finn whispered.

"Don't say that," I breathed. *"I'm not letting you die today!"* I needed him to believe it. To *fight.* But his eyes held the calm, distant look of someone who'd already said goodbye.

Once the crowd settled, Johan raised his arm, and the moments seemed to slow into an eternity. Each agonizing tick of the clock could be the last before my world shattered. I reached into my bodice, my fingers finding Jase's dagger. If I could sink the blade into Johan's neck, maybe taking out the head of the snake would end all of this? It would likely cost me my life, but it would be worth it.

All eyes were on Johan, waiting for his signal. This was my moment, and I steeled myself for whatever the consequences might be. Before I could make my move, the whistle of an arrow filled the silence. It breezed past my face, landing with a sickening thunk. Johan's valet dropped at his feet with an arrow in his chest. I turned back to the crowd, all of them parting to reveal a cloaked male with a bow in hand. He pulled his hood back and my heart leapt —Lucius.

"You!" Johan seethed.

An explosion rocked the courtyard. The ground trembled as rebels surged into the square. I lost sight of Lucius as the crowd dissolved into chaos, panic-stricken faces scattering in all directions. Johan was instantly surrounded by his personal guard. Urgent fingers dug into my flesh as a guard seized me. This time, I was ready. I plunged the dagger into his thigh with a scream. He dropped me with a cry of his own, and I didn't waste the moment. I twisted the blade and ripped it free. I threw all my weight into him. Before he hit the ground, I was in motion, throwing myself over the railing and into the crowd. I headed straight for the gallows, running as fast as the iron shackles allowed.

"Executioner! Finish it now!" Johan boomed from behind me.

The executioner pulled the lever. A deafening *crack* echoed through the square as the trapdoors dropped open. My heart seized in my chest as I watched Hunter, Finn, and Sawyer plunge downward, each falling until the ropes snapped taut around their necks.

"No!" My scream ricocheted off the courtyard walls. I wasn't close enough. The crowd was too thick. I couldn't get to them.

Dark shadows curled from every corner.

"The dagger, Michaela. Throw the dagger." Gunner's voice

echoed in my mind and I froze, momentarily blindsided by the sound of my lost Bruin.

"There's no way I can make the shot." I was too far, and the ropes were too small of a target.

"You can do it. Do it now." His voice was calm, a pillar of strength in my frantic mind. I felt the warmth of him at my back and I allowed it to wash over me.

I pulled in a centering breath, gripping the dagger firmly in my hand. Blue lines of power swirled around my wrist. I took a heartbeat to aim before I let the dagger fly. The rope snapped, and Hunter fell to the ground. Relief surged through me, but Finn and Sawyer still hung, their faces turning purple as they struggled against the ropes.

"Michaela!" Nico's voice cut through the chaos. I turned to his voice, his eyes meeting mine. He was only a few feet away from me, but there were still so many bodies between us. "Get down!"

He pointed skyward. A volley of arrows swarmed above. I dropped a second before they struck. Screams erupted from the crowd and bodies fell all around me. I felt the impact before the pain raced up my thigh, and my own scream joined the rest.

My name rang out from every direction, as if all of my fated could feel my pain. A crack of thunder shuddered the air, and the sky opened up, pouring down on us. The thunder ebbed, replaced by the guttural roars of my beasts. The gallows splintered and collapsed. Finn had shifted despite the wolfsbane—his bear lay atop the rubble. Sawyer curled in on himself, barely conscious.

Nico reached me, kneeling by my side. "Little bird, are you… your leg."

"How did he do it? How did he shift?"

"They all did—for you. The need to protect you was stronger than the wolfsbane," he said as he pulled off his belt and cinched it around my thigh. "We have to get you out of here. Take a deep breath. I have to remove the arrow."

He held my gaze as I gave a nervous nod. I clenched my teeth, swallowing back the scream as he tore the arrow from my thigh.

Lucius barreled through the crowd in his bear form. He sniffed the air, catching the sharp tang of my blood. A growl rumbled deep in his chest, dangerous and possessive. His eyes locked onto mine for the briefest moment, a silent vow that nothing would touch me again.

"Focus, Lucius. She'll live. We'll take our retribution after she's safe. Right now, you have to get her out of here. Mic, hold still."

Nico paused, long enough to raise a pole axe over his head and cleaved my ankle chains. He hoisted me onto Lucius' back.

From there, I saw the battle raging all around us. My beasts fought side by side with the Raven's Hand, pushing the guards back.

"Time to go, little bird," Nico said, a pained look on his face.

"Aren't you coming with us?"

"I have something I need to finish. I'll be right behind you."

He didn't believe what he was saying, I could see it in his eyes.

"Get her out of here now!" He slapped Lu's whither, and we were in motion. I grabbed a fistful of his coat to remain seated. He moved through the crowd with surprising speed. Finn, Hunter, and Luca flanked us. Every rock, every jolt of his gait jarred my wound. But the pain was a distant notion. My thoughts were only on Nico.

We stopped when we reached the tree line, the dense forest giving us enough protection to pause and catch our breath. Lucius shifted and pulled me into a crushing embrace.

"Did they touch you?" His voice broke, trembling with barely restrained violence as he scanned me for injuries. "Their scent… it's all over you."

"He didn't—I'll be fine."

"They got too close to what's mine. Tell me what they did?" he growled, fear and anger warring in his eyes.

"I can't. Not now, Lucius. Give me some time."

He pulled me back into his arms. "I thought I'd lost you," he mumbled into my hair, not pressing for answers.

"Lucius, we have to go back for him." My voice trembled, but my resolve was steel.

The wind howled through the thicket of trees where we'd taken refuge, carrying the scent of blood and fire from the battle. Finn paced like a caged beast, his eyes flicking toward the castle where his brother remained. He shook his coat as if trying to shed the horror of going back to the nightmare he'd just escaped from. Lucius knelt beside me, still catching his breath, his broad chest heaving. Hunter and Luca remained in their bear forms, scanning the horizon like they expected Nico to appear at any second.

"You saw the way he looked at us," I said, hands clenched at my sides. "He stayed because he didn't think he'd survive. He was trying to save us. I won't let him die alone."

Lucius clenched his jaw. I knew I was asking too much.

"Michaela, if we go back in there—"

"If we don't, we lose him," I cut in, stepping closer. "I won't lose another mate. Jase—" His name stuck in my throat. Tears threatened to spill down my cheeks. "I tried to save him, but I…"

"Shh, it's alright, Dove," he said, brushing away a wayward tear. "None of this is your fault."

"If we leave him behind, he'll die. And I can't live with that. I'm not asking any of you to come with me—but I have to go. He needs me."

They all stared at me in silence, their beasts eyeing me up and down. Luca shifted, a sharp grin tugging at his mouth.

"You didn't think we'd let Nico have all the fun, did you?

I think we all deserve to spill Johan's blood. But you can't go into battle with that leg."

I felt his power surge into me—blue lines racing across my skin, healing every ache, stitching my skin together. I sighed as his power renewed me.

"Now that's better," Luca said. "Lu, where'd you stash those clothes? Or are we charging in with nothing but our tattoos to cover us?"

THE CASTLE LOOKED DESERTED. Smoke billowed from shattered towers, casting an ominous haze over Mathenholm. The crowd was gone. Only a trail of destruction and dead bodies remained.

The few guards left behind, once fanatically loyal to Johan, faltered at our approach. Whispers of the true king echoed through the halls. Some dropped their weapons and fell to their knees. Others fought—half-heartedly. The tide had turned.

Lucius and Luca met steel with steel, while Hunter and Finn, still in bear form, tore through what resistance remained. I fought beside them, my strength restored, a borrowed blade singing in my hands. My heart was fixed on Nico.

"Where are they?" Lucius snarled, his sword at the throat of a young guard who had surrendered.

"I… I think I saw them go that way." The guard tripped over his words, waving down the grand hall. "The king—"

"He's not the king!" Lu barked.

"Yes, yes, of course. Johan lured him to the throne room. Said his powers are stronger there."

I didn't wait for more. I bolted down the hall, my name echoing behind me as the others called out—but something deeper pulled me forward. The world tunneled. My breath ragged in my throat as my skirts tangled around my legs. My heart hammered—not just from the sprint but from the bone-deep fear that I was too late. That I'd reach the throne room just in time to watch Nico fall.

A trail of chaos marked their path—chipped stone, overturned furniture, splashes of blood and dead guards told a story that had my blood running cold. What would I find when I finally reached him? Had he already been mortally wounded? There was so much blood.

Boots thundered ahead of me. A detachment of guards rounded the corner, swords already drawn. I skidded to a halt—too late to turn back. There was no way I could avoid them and one sickly human was nothing against these battle-hardened guards. I stood my ground, bracing for the inevitable.

But it never came.

They charged past, eyes wild. One brushed my shoulder with a hissed curse, like he'd passed through a cold draft.

They hadn't seen me.

I looked down. Shadow clung to my limbs like a second skin, curling like smoke across my bodice and around my hands. Moving when I moved. Shielding me in plain sight.

I didn't understand how it was possible. A sob clawed at my throat, but I forced it down. I didn't have time to wonder how Jase's shadows were protecting me even from the grave. I was a ghost in the enemy's halls.

I glanced back once, a silent prayer for my beasts to hold the line—and surged forward. Each step lighter, shadows parting before me and stitching themselves around me again.

The grand doors to the throne room lay shattered across the floor. The room still bore the scars of the solric that had taken Gunner from me. Only Johan and Nico remained standing. Steel clashed, echoing off the walls.

Nico was larger by far, but his body was battered. Bloodstains soaked his clothes. He heavily favored his right side, his arm tucked in close. While Johan looked fresh, untouched. His guards had done the hard work.

Jase's shadows evaporated—snuffed by the wards within the throne room.

I hugged the wall, slipping through what natural shadow remained, slowly circling behind them. A distraction now could mean certain death for Nico.

"You can't win. The Bloodstone Sigil ensures I overpower you ten to one," Johan said, chuckling as he defended Nico's blows with ease as they made their way up the dais.

"The Sigil's just a tool. It doesn't make a king. Only the Divine can do that," Nico growled, eyes flicking to the throne that should have been his.

"And yet here I stand, the Sigil would have struck me down otherwise and yet it still sits on my finger. Proof enough."

"Then take it off and we'll see who's the better male. Beast against beast."

"The Divine favor minds, not muscles. That's why they let your father die when I killed him with my bare hands. Seems I was the chosen one after all."

Nico faltered, taking a step down the dais, his eyes wide as the realization hit him. "How could you? He was like a father to you. He was your friend."

"He betrayed us all," Johan said, standing before the throne. "You can ask him of his crimes when I send you to meet him."

I broke from the shadows, angling toward Johan's back. One well-placed thrust of my sword, and it would all be over. He wouldn't even see it coming.

I raised my blade—but Johan spun with unnatural speed, seizing my wrist in a crushing grip.

"No!" Nico lunged, but Johan dragged me between them, arm locking around my waist as he wrenched the blade from my grasp.

"Well, well," he sneered, breath hot against my ear. "Look what the Divine dragged in."

"Michaela," Nico breathed, horror in his eyes. "Let her go. She has nothing to do with this."

"On the contrary," Johan purred. "She has everything to do with this. You see, I've learned a thing or two now that the Sigil has passed down every secret the kings of old kept from us. Have you ever heard of the blood rite? Our ancestors knew how dangerous a true fated pair could be and in their infinite wisdom, they found a way to break them."

He turned me in his grip, pressing his palm flat to my stomach "It's quite the ceremony. Vows. Blood. A binding of souls across eternity. And in her case,"—he stroked my arm in mock tenderness—"a cleansing of all those inconvenient bonds. Every Bruin claim to this pivotal human, shattered. All it takes is a vow and her blood mingled with mine."

"You wouldn't," Nico snarled. "You can't bind someone against their will."

"Oh, but she'll agree," Johan said softly. "Because if she doesn't, I'll use the power of the Bloodstone Sigil to gut every last one of your brothers in front of you, one by one. If she agrees, I'll let them live. Banished, yes—but alive. Isn't that what you want, my dear?"

My breath caught in my throat. I looked to Nico, whose eyes were wild with helpless rage.

"He's lying," I said. "The Sigil has rejected him. He cannot wear it for long. I saw his hand." I seethed.

"A minor detail my sages are working on. Much has happened since the founding houses forged the stone. It's about time for an upgrade. Once they're done, you'll reign beside the most powerful king in the history of Hiraeth. Now, my dear, what is your answer? Life…or death?"

I bit down until I tasted blood behind my teeth. I had a choice to make, but there was no choice in it at all.

"I'll do it," I whispered. "I'll say the vows."

"No," Nico said. "Michaela, don't—"

"I have to." My voice cracked. "I won't let him kill you."

Johan grinned. "Excellent."

He began reciting the old vows, ancient words I couldn't understand. I simply repeated them through clenched teeth, each word a blade to my soul. I may have been sealing my fate with Johan, but in my heart, the words were meant for Nico. My gaze never left his.

When the last vow left my lips, Johan grabbed my wrist, holding it high. With a swift motion, he drew a small dagger across my palm. My blood poured hot down my hand, running over his fingers before spilling onto the Sigil. The moment it touched the stone it began to hiss.

He dropped my hand like a hot coal, a scream bellowing up from his gut as his ringed hand trembled. I stumbled backward and watched in horror as the skin around the Sigil began to melt from his hand.

Crack!

The sound cut through Johan's screaming. A jagged split tore through the ring. Light burst from within like a star collapsing. Johan fell to his knees, staring at his ruined hand.

"No! It's not possible. What have you done?" He turned toward me, accusations burning in his feral eyes.

With a roar, Nico lunged forward, his blade drove into Johan's ribs. "This is for my father," he growled. Johan's eyes widened, his hands clutching the hilt as blood spilled from his lips. Nico drove the blade up through his chest. "And that is for thinking you could claim her for yourself."

Johan choked on his own blood, reaching for the shattered ring as the color drained from his face. He slumped forward, his body collapsing against Nico. With his last breath, the remnants of the ring shattered completely, fragments of the Sigil scattered across the marble.

The others crashed through the door, sliding to a stop as they took in the scene. Johan's eyes had gone vacant. For a moment, there was silence—stunned, aching silence. The sons of Artos absorbing the vengeance they so justly deserved. My eyes caught shadows looming behind the throne, a flicker of soft, blue light. I swore I saw Gunner and Jase watching over the scene. An eye for an eye had finally been settled. The balance had been restored. Before I could make sense of it, the light ghosted away, leaving nothing but shadows.

Nico turned, his storm-dark eyes softening. We had won. The kingdom was his again.

"I knew you could do it on your own," Luca boomed, breaking the somber mood in the room, a wide grin cutting across his face.

I rushed into Nico's arms, holding him, feeling his solid weight against me. He was alive. His arms wrapped around me, strong and sure.

"You came back," he whispered.

"Of course I did." My fingers curled into his hair, my voice breaking. "I'm never leaving you."

He cupped my cheek, his thumb brushing away a tear. His gaze was fierce, full of something I had no name for, something vast and unbreakable.

Then he staggered backward, breaking away from me.

"Nico?" I caught him as his body wavered, his face paling as his strength gave out. His breath came in ragged gasps, and his skin burned under my touch.

He sank to his knees, taking me with him, his grip tightening as if he could hold on to me through sheer will alone.

"I have it, Mic," he rasped. "The malediction."

Panic surged through me. "No. No, that's not possible," I said, gripping his face. "You're not dying. We just got to the good part. I won't lose you now."

The others gathered around us, the joy of victory evaporating into something far colder. I refused to believe it. There was some mistake. It was a sick trick. The Divine wouldn't let him win, only to strike him down like this.

This couldn't be happening.

He'd fought for this kingdom and won. He'd done everything to save us. For *me*.

Now, it was my turn to fight for him.

To Be Continued...

WHAT'S NEXT?

A PLAGUE
ON THE
HOUSE OF BRUIN

MICHAELA'S STORY
CONTINUES IN PART II OF THE
HIRAETH CHRONICLES

78KinleyBooks.com

More From T.S. Kinley

The Neverland Chronicles

-Prequel-

-Volume I-

-Volume II-

-Volume III-

THE NEVERLAND CHRONICLES
HOOK'S SAGA

PART ONE

PART TWO

TSKINLEYBOOKS.COM

Also Available

The Smut Diaries

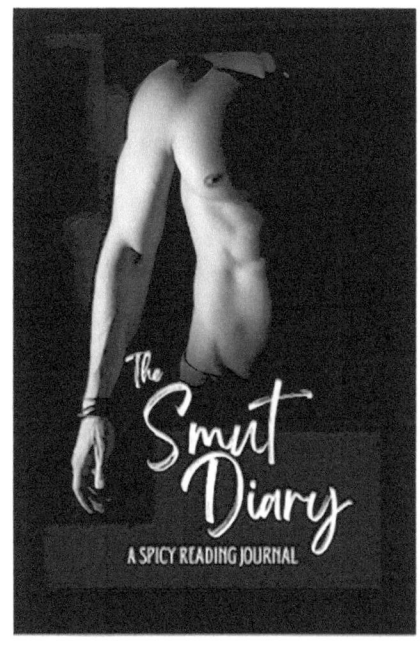

ABOUT THE AUTHOR

T. S. Kinley is a passion project created by two sisters with a shared obsession and vision. We came together with the dream of creating something beautiful, imaginative, and yes... SEXY. *Once Upon a Time...* it all began with sisterly gossip about erotica and romance novels. Our conversations quickly became fantasies about our own desires to author such work. We would muse how some day in a utopian future, our fantasy would become reality. Ultimately we decided rather than wait for the future to find us, we would create utopia ourselves. Using our love of books, natural gift of creativity, and some savvy study on publishing itself, the concept for our very first book was born. We started off as a Cosmetologist and an RN, and quickly developed into a dynamic writing team with a style that lends a unique perspective to our books.

If you haven't signed up already, please subscribe to the T.S. Kinley newsletter.

Receive exclusive sneak peeks on new releases, contests and other spicy content.

Visit www.TSKinleyBooks.com and sign up today!

Follow T.S. Kinley on social media. Let's be friends! Check out our Instagram, Facebook, Pinterest, and Tic Tok pages and get insights into the beautifully, complicated mind of not one, but two authors! You have questions, something you are dying to know about the amazing characters we've created? Join us online, we love to engage with our readers!

LIKE WHAT YOU READ?

Did you enjoy your journey into The Hiraeth Chronicles? Be a love and leave a review on Goodreads. While you are there give us a follow.